"CUT ME DOWN W!
Do it or I'll kill you, I s

"Your chance for that

"Is it?" Köthen cock   t
wide. It missed Hal's bel,   s
sword from his hand. Erde breathed a split-second's prayer.
He would kill or be killed. She must do it now, or it would
be too late.

She sprang forward, ducking the long blade as it whistled past.

"No! You mustn't!"

She lunged and grabbed the scythe handle. Köthen
hauled on the handle, sending Erde tumbling toward him.
He caught her deftly with his free arm, twisted her around,
and pinned her to his chest with the scythe blade at her
throat.

"What are you . . . no!" Hal lowered the dagger he'd
drawn. "Let the girl go."

"No. Stay where you are if you wish her alive
tomorrow."

Erde caught Hal's worried look, shook her head once,
and smiled. "It's all right. We're taking him with us."

Hal's eyes widened. "Now?"

She nodded as best she could, with a blade at her neck.
She reached for her companions in her mind, and found
each waiting. Then she said, "My lord of Köthen, prepare
yourself for a journey."

Kothen said, "What?"

And the dragons took them both. . . .

Be sure to read the first three novels
in MARJORIE B. KELLOGG's
powerful DAW fantasy series—

The Dragon Quartet:

THE BOOK OF EARTH (Volume One)
THE BOOK OF WATER (Volume Two)
THE BOOK OF FIRE (Volume Three)

MARJORIE B. KELLOGG

THE BOOK OF

FIRE

——— Volume Three of ———
The Dragon Quartet

DAW BOOKS, INC.

DONALD A. WOLLHEIM, FOUNDER

375 Hudson Street, New York, NY 10014

ELIZABETH R. WOLLHEIM
SHEILA E. GILBERT
PUBLISHERS

First Printing, July 2000

1 2 3 4 5 6 7 8 9

DAW TRADEMARK REGISTERED
U.S. PAT. OFF. AND FOREIGN COUNTRIES
—MARCA REGISTRADA
HECHO EN U.S.A.

PRINTED IN THE U.S.A.

To Lynne Kemen and Bill Rossow

Who have found so much time in their busy, busy lives to give tirelessly of their expertise and help an anxious writer see what she's written.
Who appreciate the necessity of a dry white wine and fresh coffee from Zabar's.

Endless thanks.

In addition: much praise and gratitude to my tireless editor and publisher, Sheila Gilbert.

Thanks also to my agent Joshua Bilmes, to Allen and Annie Rozelle, and to Antje Ellerman.

PROLOGUE

The Creation

In the Beginning,
and a little after . . .

In the Beginning, four mighty dragons raised of elemental energies were put to work creating the World. They were called Earth, Water, Fire, and Air. No one of them had power greater than another, and no one of them was mighty alone.

When the work was completed and the World set in motion, the four went to ground, expecting to sleep out this World's particular history and not rise again until World's End.

The first to awaken was Earth.

He woke in darkness, as innocent as a babe, with only the fleeting shadows of dreams to hint at his former magnificence. But one bright flame of knowledge drove him forth: he was Called to Work again, if only he could remember what the Work was.

He found the World grown damp and chill, overrun by the puniest of creatures, Creation's afterthought, the ones called Men. Earth soon learned that Men, too, had forgotten their Origin. They had abandoned their own intended Work in the World and thrived instead on superstition, violence, and self-righteous oppression of their fellows. They had forgotten as well their primordial relationship with dragons—all, that is, but a few.

One in particular awaited Earth's coming, a young girl

who knew nothing of the secret duty carried down through the countless generations of her blood. Her name was Erde, and she knew her Destiny when she faced a living dragon and was not afraid.

Thereafter, Earth's Quest became her own, and together they searched her World for answers to his questions. Some they found and slowly, along with his memory, Earth's powers reawakened. But the girl's World was dark and dangerous and ignorant, and the mysterious Caller who summoned Earth could not be found within it. One day, blindly following the Call, Earth took them Somewhere Else.

In that Somewhere Else, they found Earth's sister Water and her Companion N'Doch. N'Doch's World was hot and crowded and full of noise, and mysterious to Erde until she understood that she had traveled to Sometime, as well as to Somewhere. It became her task to teach N'Doch about the dragons and their Quest, for he did not know his Destiny and did not join them willingly at first.

Water, too, had heard the Caller. She could answer some of Earth's questions about the Work, but added many of her own. Soon, the dragons were convinced that an unknown Power not only blocked their Search, but threatened their safety. Evidence pointed to the dragon Fire, but why would their own brother conspire against them?

When the dangers of N'Doch's world, both human and inhuman, closed in around them, the four in desperation returned to Erde's time, with nothing but N'Doch's recurring dream of a Burning Land to tell them where to go to continue the Search.

And in Erde's time, conditions were deteriorating. . . .

PART ONE

The Summoning
of the Hero

Chapter One

It's the wind, she tells herself. Only the wind. Making a little adjustment, minute but perceptible, like a singer sliding off-key. But she stills her breath anyway, to listen around the hard dry corners of the wind's howl for whatever might have waked her.

"Only the wind." Paia whispers it aloud. An incantation of hope: the wind, and not some herdsman famished into an ill-advised grudge. Not the murderously disillusioned acolyte that she's always fearing will hack a path through the several layers of her bodyguard and gain her inner sanctum. Perhaps a timid servant, then, one of the newer ones, stumbling upstairs in haste to inform her of the God's return.

But the door does not burst open. There is no warning clatter down the hall. Just the wind. It has to be.

Paia eases one hand beneath her pillows. The move is slow and noiseless, through folds as silky as feathers, glimmering in the dull red night. Whoever it is might already be in the room. Her hand is a wave under sand. It's only the wind, but with the little gun cradled in her palm, almost cool against her heated skin, she feels much better.

Paia resettles herself. If she can make herself stop listening, she can will sleep to come. She has learned to sleep with the gun. She's trained her right hand to rest on it lightly, immobile, relaxed but ready. The God insisted, when he presented it to her: she must keep it close by at all times. At *all* times. Especially at night. At first, it was like carrying a live scorpion around. She hated it. She did

everything she could think of to convince the God to re-
scind this command. She accused him of being paranoid
and overprotective. He assured her he had good reason.
She implied he was afraid someone would steal it—such a
rare relic, priceless, really, a functioning firearm. The God
waved a gold-ringed claw and snorted. She threatened to
sell it. Another snort, and a reminder that while the little
weapon might be *her* most valuable possession, he—the
God—was magic and could simply conjure another. And
by the way, he noted, it would only take the one time she
needed it and didn't have it on her for all her protests to
be moot.

So that was the end of it. The God would trust no one
to instruct her, which was awkward, as the only training
he himself could supply was verbal. Paia taught herself by
experiment how to care for the thing, and how to shoot it.
She had a soft leather harness crafted, part garment, part
holster—and learned to live with it.

And now she feels half-naked without it.

She's stopped listening, she realizes, except in the usual
reflex way. There's nothing to hear, nothing but the inces-
sant wind, swirling past the upper terraces, moaning among
the steel balustrades. But Paia is wide awake, and her body
is taut with an odd, restless energy that cannot be ac-
counted for as mere adrenaline rush. She rolls over and
runs an inventory: not thirsty, no hotter than usual, no need
to visit the privy. She rarely has trouble sleeping, except in
the early hours before a major festival, when her brain
won't cease rehearsing every step and detail of the coming
ritual. But tomorrow isn't even a minor holy day. In fact,
tomorrow her temple calendar is practically empty. So what
is this? She feels like she's downed a big swallow from the
Sacred Well. It's the same sort of liquid invasion, power
and pure sensation coursing toward the very ends of her
extremities, pooling in her toes and fingertips: alien, sweet,
and chill. She wonders what it means.

She flips aside the pale sheet and sits up. An unlit lantern
waits on her bedside table. When the lectric first went off,
she kept a flame burning through the night. Then the God
pointed out that the light left her just as visible to any
potential assailant. So, as she learned to live with the gun,
she learned to sleep in darkness. It's never total darkness

anyway, not in any room with a window. Paia squints into the deeper shadows at the corners of the room. She considers waking the God, to solicit his opinion of this peculiar sleeplessness. The God has an answer for everything. Paia can't recall him ever saying, "I don't know." Then she remembers he's not at home. Off on one of his mysterious week-long expeditions. He'd be irritable as a viper anyway, having his sleep broken without (what he would consider) due cause, like if the Fortress was under attack, or if it began to rain.

Sitting alone in the hot red gloom, Paia allows herself a moment of self-pity. If only she had someone to talk to. Not just servants and acolytes, or her subordinate priests, always jockeying for position. A friend. The God, of course, would insist that he's all the friend she needs. When he's around, he encourages all manner of intimacy. But Paia knows he doesn't really listen unless she's talking about something that directly concerns him, such as the accounts of the monthly tithing, or his own participation in the next Sacred Festival. He does show a keen appetite for news of her meetings with the various Official Suitors. He demands the finest details, yet leaves her with the distinct impression that he considers this pretty tame stuff—as if, each time, he's hoping for something racier. When he instituted the requirement that all Suitors disrobe, Paia assumed this to be another of his endless security measures, or a (typically) crass way of allowing her to fully inspect the goods on offer. But she recalls him chiding her sternly for exempting Suitors she knows she will reject the moment they enter the Hall of Audiences. She wonders now if what the God *really* enjoys is the full spectacle of each poor man's vulnerability and abject humiliation.

She gets up abruptly and lights the lamp, as if its pale spot of flame could dispel the shadows left in her heart by the last such encounter. She might have favored that one a little, if not for the dull gleam of hatred he could not keep from his eyes as he dropped his robe and stood before her. She wanted to say she would not ask it if the God did not insist, but that would be questioning the God's word in public, a dire offense. As the God has told her many times: he is the God. His word is law.

Paia turns up the lamp flame. The light throws the coffered ceiling into high relief and deepens the folds of the velvet draperies into columns of mystery. She quells her rush of resentment with a sour, quiet chuckle. One day soon, she vows, I will begin to embroider my reports. Catch the God by surprise. Describe in painstaking detail all the clothing *I* took off, and then what happened after. She wonders: would the God be jealous?

She leaves the lamp burning on the table, her emphatic stride muffled by the layers of antique and threadbare carpets strewn across the slate floor. In her cavernous dressing room, her hand finds the dead light switch by instinct, pressing it before she can stop herself. Paia grimaces. She prefers not to be reminded that the lectric is now a precious commodity, reserved for an hour or two of pre-curfew darkness, or for any and all Temple ceremonies. Better to pretend that it's always been this way. She grabs the nearest robe and throws it on. When she was a child, the House Monitor ran twenty-four hours a day . . . well, at least when it wasn't broken. Climate control, music and light, intercom and sonic cleanser, ice water, hot water—all this in every one of the hundred or so rooms in the House. That's what they still called it then, a house, even though it was already becoming a fortress. When the God came, he deactivated the Monitor and gave all of its functions to people. But people, Paia is just old enough to remember, are not nearly as reliable as machines. And it's hot all the time now, whatever season, whatever time of day, though cooler in the Citadel than outside, due to the interior temperature of the bedrock, and the giant circulation fans turned by the windmill array at the top of the scarp.

She wraps the robe around her, and then her arms as well, hugging the thin fabric against her ribs as if its embroidered sheen could smooth away her unexplained restlessness. Halfway to her favorite window alcove, she stops, turns on her heel, and paces back to the dressing room, shedding the robe as she goes. Rooting in drawers, she tosses out fistfuls of clothing behind her—sheer, clinging silks and brocaded robes, cloth-of-gold vests and gowns studded with seed pearls, strewn all across the floor in her search for the garb she can wear only when the God is not around: her old sweatpants, worn soft with use and laundering, and a tunic-length T-shirt. Her chambermaid disapproves of these garments as much as the God does, and tries to hide them from her. But Paia uncovers them with a quiet whoop of victory and slides into them, grateful for the rare opportunity to be unaware of the shape of her body.

Now the odd surging inside her feels good. Strong and positive. Purposeful. She's awake and comfortable; so far, she's roused no one with all her moving about, and suddenly she knows what to do. The restlessness has left her extremities and withdrawn its force tidelike into her interior. Images are washing up on the shores of her mind in waves of white and green and blue. Nothing specific yet— that will come only when the right language is available, when she has a brush and colors in her hand.

Her fingers are on the doorknob when she remembers the gun. She races back to the bed to snatch it from under the silken pile of pillows and shove it into a pocket. Across the room again, Paia twists the knob soundlessly and hauls on the door. Chances are good that the sentries outside in the hall will be asleep, due to the God's absence and to an archaic and inefficient system of seniority that, for his own private reasons, the God has chosen not to overturn. It makes a certain kind of dull sense, Paia admits, to station the youngest and most vigorous downstairs at the points of entry into the Citadel. But she doubts that the God is aware that higher rank also means high priority for the booze ration. She would complain, except that this tends to work in her favor, granting her an extra measure of freedom now and then, as long as she's quiet about it.

Another thing she's learned since the God came: to move about the endless stairs and corridors in near total silence. And because she's positive that her guards try to cultivate a convenient layer of rust on the hinges, she foils them by oiling them regularly. Twice as tall as she and two arms' lengths wide, the heavy slab of paneled oak drifts toward her without so much as a murmur.

"Ha," Paia grins.

A soft chorus of snores floats through the narrow opening. A discord of drunken slumber. Paia pokes her head around the edge of the door. There are four of them, two men and two women—the God thrives on symmetry. There's not a booze jug in sight, but the sweet-sour aroma hangs heavy in the still air. They've all loosened their braided formal collars and drawn up the most comfortable of the stiff, half-upholstered chairs that inhabit the corridor. Their single lantern is burning low. Paia marvels at their bravery. If the God were to materialize here suddenly, their lives would be ended. But the God is not home, and besides, he'd be forced to appear in man-form in order to fit in this human-sized space. For reasons that Paia does not comprehend, most people find the God less frightening in man-form. Perhaps these four have told themselves that as a group, they could take him if they had to. They would be wrong.

It's the implied presumption, even more than their lack of proper discipline, that rouses Paia's ire. Who do they think they are, sleeping on the job? Is this how the Honor Guard of the Temple protects its High Priestess? When her father was alive, she would have reported such insubordination without a qualm. Their sodden snores abruptly disgust her. She thinks she might report them after all. She draws herself up in the doorway, ready to end their careers, if not their lives. Then she remembers her sweats and T-shirt. How can she appear before these men and women, her servants, her Faithful, dressed no better than they would be in their own homes? Her hair isn't even done. What would they think? Even worse, what would the God say if he found out? Paia is well aware that this issue of reporting infractions goes both ways.

Her shoulders sag. Her chambermaid is right. The High Priestess of the Temple of the Apocalypse needs to be protected from her own impulses.

However . . .

She just cannot imagine going back to bed. There is still this swarm of images inside her head, demanding to be dealt with. Even if she could resist, this opportunity is too precious to waste. She peers at the snorers more carefully, then eases around the edge of the door and ghosts it shut behind her.

Scattered about the hall, tilted this way and that in their straight-backed chairs, the sleeping guards look like a child's tin army abandoned after play. Paia negotiates a slalom course through red-clad legs and spit-polished black boots, careful to create no draft that might alert their soldier's instincts. She's counting on the booze to keep them oblivious.

To her left yawns the wide, dark well of the stairs, leading down to Level Five and further, younger contingents of the Honor Guard. To her right, several shadowed doorways, more chairs and windowless corridor: true darkness. But this is the most "secure" part of the house, and Paia's feet know the way by heart. Now she welcomes the darkness as an ally, abetting her escape. She pads along with her arms stretched low to either side, in case some forgetful cleaner has moved a chair. Sensing a turn, she slows but continues straight ahead until her fingers touch the cut-velvet wall fabric and the hard edge of a deactivated picture box. She does a silent right-face, gliding one hand along the wall—no furniture left along this corridor to avoid. She moves down one long hall, a left turn, down another, until her fingertips find and trace out the intricate profile of the molding that frames the entrance to the tower. Just inside the arch is a little niche for a lantern and matches.

This rising stair is narrower than the formal staircases leading down, which are sized like the corridors to allow a regiment to march through in formation. The tower's steep steps, barely one person wide, coil up serpentlike around a central stone shaft. Paia's hands are shaking with eagerness to be at the top. As if her head might shatter like a dropped melon if she can't let loose the raucous crowd inside. She strikes a match. Once upon a time, the House Monitor's sensors would have provided light, and then betrayed her presence to an on-duty House security guard. But all those banks of screens are dark now. Raising the lamp, Paia begins her climb.

It's a long climb, but Paia claimed this part of the house as her own precisely because of the tower, knowing that its claustrophobic dimensions and its exhausting, dizzying spiral would discourage any but the most determined visitors. She's counted the steps: there are sixty-six of them, carved from the rock of the cliff itself. The front edge of each bears a shallow depression, worn smooth during the two and a half centuries since her family's retreat to this stronghold. There is a faint stain of handprints at waist level along the outside curve of the wall.

She gains the top and steps into a large vaulted chamber

lit by the dim red murk pressing in from outside through
a far wall of armored glass. A polished stone floor gleams
ruddily. Paia's lantern illuminates a chair and a few simple
tables, and then the unfinished rear and side walls, still as
coarse-textured as if blasted out of the rock only yesterday.
Leaning against the walls, rows and rows of stacked canvases. In front of the vast glass wall, a tall wooden easel,
empty now, but not for long.

The thrumming in her body intensifies. Paia sets the lantern down on a table, afraid she'll drop it. Then she hurries
around the room, gathering up every available lamp and
candle, sets them near the easel, and lights them all. She's
only adding to the heat in the room, but she doesn't care.
Her hands move almost without her knowledge. The image
waves are breaking harder and faster now. Her brain is a
tornado, a storm at sea. She doesn't want to have to grind
and mash and mix and measure, the patient, painstaking
process of paint-making that she normally enjoys. She
needs to get right to work. She gathers in a hopeful breath,
uncovers her palette, lets out the breath in a rush. The
paint is still workable. She finds brushes, oil, and an unused
canvas. She sets the pale, blank oblong up on the easel and
stares at it for half a millisecond. Then she dips her brush
and begins to paint.

When the red murk lightens to pink, then to dusty orange, Paia stands back to look at what she's done. Hours
have passed unnoticed. Her palette is scraped dry. She has
used every last daub of paint available, often not caring
what color it was; at least she would lay down form and
texture on the canvas while the inspiration burned in her.
Even as her candles and lanterns guttered and went out,
she kept at it, in the end painting as much by feel as by
sight. Not until she lays her brush aside does she realize
how tired she is. "Spent" is a better word, she decides.
Tapped out. Like she feels after the ten-hour Harvest Festival. As if the whole complex engine of her body has sud-

denly run out of fuel. Only now does it occur to her how unusual this is.

And what has this frenzy produced?

Impulsively, she'd chosen a large canvas, two meters wide by a meter high, and she has covered every inch of it. The brushwork is taut and kinetic, even for her, and it turns out, the painting is mostly about color, or the sense of light and life that color can convey. Vibrant purple, magenta, and blue shadows stretching beneath sunlit golds and viridian and mauves. Colors she hardly ever uses, which is why they were left over on her palette. She can see this even in the too-amber light of early dawn, before the sun outside has broken the horizon, and she finds it mildly uncanny, since color was the thing she'd given up all control of, sure that she lacked the right pigments.

But her definition of "right" is being challenged by the canvas in front of her. It's a landscape, or rather, a fantasy landscape, because it's like no landscape she's seen or could have seen within her own lifetime. For one thing, it's full of greens, or the colors that green can become when suffused with sunlight. She'd hardly any true greens on her palette, so she made do with what she had. Another thing— it's full of trees. Hardwood trees. She recognizes their shape and texture from the trees left in the little Sacred Grove within the Temple walls. But in this painting, there are entire hillsides of them, a whole valley, in fact, lined with oak and birch and maple as if with the richest velvet. Nestled within the velvet, like the finest satin, a vast and rolling meadow. And the shining jewel caught in its luscious green folds: a silver ribbon of water . . . a river.

A river! Paia is transfixed. How has she done this? She guesses she must be recalling images from her recreational research forays into the family archives—old photographs, prints and paintings, and even video, when the God allows her use of the machines. She frowns, looking around at the other canvases stacked against the walls. Painting after painting of barren hills, dry streambeds, and rocky crags, of air swirled with dust and soot, of sun-parched villages huddled among dying scrub pine. All dry browns and reds and bleached-out yellows. She had thought them beautiful, perhaps because the God always admired them. Now she is not so sure. Since she first picked up a brush, Paia has painted only what she saw in life: what she saw from the upper terraces of the Temple, what she saw from her bedroom balconies or from this luxurious stretch of glass, her giant eye upon the world, perched high in a tower embedded in the sheer rock face of a cliff.

All of a sudden, as if her eyes have turned inside her head, she has painted a landscape she could only hope to dream about.

Chapter Two

That first night back at Deep Moor, Erde was so weak with joy, and so wrung out by all she'd been through, that she forgot to worry about the dreams.

Besides, she felt safe at Deep Moor, even in the snow and wind and unnatural cold. The women there *knew* things. Surely the dreams would not dare to follow her there.

And it began innocently enough, of course, with a calm and silent landscape, sunk in winter. Gentle mounds of snow scattered here and there across a frozen white plain. A rasping of ravens above. A gleam of river ice in the distance, and mountains.

But then she saw, or rather, understood—in the way of dreams—that the mounds were bodies, soldiers dead on the field and covered with snow. Even in her drifting dream state, Erde was shocked. What kind of army would not make time to bury its dead?

Suddenly, a far-off echo, a drumming of hooves. She wanted to turn toward the sound but could not. Her dream gaze was fixed: on the bodies, on the frozen river, on the mountains beyond. The hard rhythm approached, like metal on stone, and with it, an aura of terrible urgency. As the lead horse pounded past, the urgency snatched her up, as if an arm had been hooked around her throat. She was dragged in the horse's wake, and still she could not look behind, could only hear the hoarse cries of the men and the struggle of their horses to catch up.

The lead horse was a tall and powerful gray, well lathered but not yet winded. His rider was oddly unhelmeted, despite the cold and the peril of his horse's mad race. He was hunched forward over the gray's outstretched neck, and Erde could not see his face. But she knew this rider anyway. She knew him from the bold blue and yellow of his worn battle tabard, from the stubborn set of his ice-flecked shoulders, from the wind-whipped gold of his hair. And because it was always his life that the dreams drew her into.

Her enemy. Adolphus, Baron Köthen. A man she had met only once. Allied with her traitorous father against the King. Or had been. Now his loyalties were unclear. But enemy or no, in the way of dreams, she had no choice but to ride with him. She found this both terrifying and exhilarating.

Behind, the men cried out again, incoherent with distance. It seemed that she recognized one of the voices. But her gaze was still fixed, as Baron Köthen's was, and he did not look back. She would not have expected him to. He was too intent on urging the utmost out of the speeding gray. As usual, he was unaware of her presence, as she flew along at his ear like a gnat. Only once had he seemed aware, had he seemed to listen when she spoke to him. That time, she had saved his life. Or she thought she had, and it confused her that she'd done so. The man had been her *enemy*, perhaps still was. Of course, dreams were just dreams, mere illusions, with no connection to real events. Erde told herself this, but in her heart, she did not believe it. Her sense of being there with him was too . . . complete.

The gray swerved suddenly, then launched himself over a snow mound too massive to be avoided. The corpses were strewn more thickly as horse and rider neared the river. The harsh valley winds had scoured the concealing snow, exposing terrible amputations and dark faces frozen in pain and horror. Köthen glanced up now, and Erde saw that there were horses and soldiers between him and the ice-bound shore. Many of them. Ten, twenty knights at least, plus a squad of infantrymen, all of them armed and ready, and watching Baron Köthen's full-tilt approach. But Köthen did not slow the gray horse or turn him aside. Instead, he reached across his thighs for the sword tucked into its saddle sheath, and aimed the gray straight into the middle

of them. Soon they were close enough for Erde to recognize the hell-priest's colors on some of the infantrymen. Just like Brother Guillemo, Erde thought grimly, to put uniforms even on his foot soldiers. The thought of Guillemo made her shiver. Could Köthen and the hell-priest have made up their differences after all, and was he racing back to rejoin the usurping army? If so, he was her enemy again. Erde's beloved grandmother the baroness, may she rest in peace, had brought Erde up to be a loyal subject of the King.

Or perhaps the soldiers ahead were some of Baron Köthen's own men, gone renegade from the priest's army out of loyalty to their lord. But that hope died in the flash of steel across the closing distance, as the knights converged into defense formation. Erde understood that Baron Köthen's charge was an attack. What was the man doing? He would be cut to pieces, without a doubt. And still Köthen drove the gray toward them.

Enemy or no, Erde did not wish him dead. In fact, the idea filled her with a surprising dread. She imagined again that, through the dream, she could speak to him, and she begged him to turn aside. She knew he was a brave man, but she had not thought him reckless. Why would he charge willingly into such overwhelming odds? Had he been driven into this trap by the men behind him?

But then those riders' desperate shouts came to her more clearly, particularly the one voice that had seemed so familiar. They'd been calling him back, and now gave up their shouting to ride as hard as they could. Erde heard their horses coming, faster than before, or was it only that she hoped so for them to catch up? Surely they were too far behind to be able to save him. She pleaded with Köthen to be sensible, to slow down at least, to wait for the others. Dream-wraith that she was, she still could feel the anger in him, heating him like a fever. He was too full of blood-rage to hear her or to listen to reason. Or perhaps he did hear, for once she saw his head jerk when she spoke, as if shaking off a fly. But he neither stopped nor slowed. And glancing ahead, Erde saw why. In their shifting protective dance, the mounted knights drew briefly aside, revealing the man at the center of their formation: the hell-priest himself.

Guillemo. Her nemesis. Stocky and dark, and with his
once wild beard now trimmed to obsessiveness, he looked
almost ordinary. His white monk's hood was thrown back
from his mailed head as he barked orders to his men and
raised his short, southern sword as if it were a processional
cross. His big horse gleamed as pure and white as the snow
around him, or the frozen river beyond. But, oh, what a
danger, to think Guillemo either pure or ordinary! Erde's
blood ran as cold as that ice-bound river. The snake-eyed
priest was staring straight at her, his full red mouth curled
in a sly smile of welcome.

So, witch. We meet again.

His voice, right there in her head as she slept. Deep, rich,
insinuating. Erde was horrified by how surely he homed in
on her. No casting about this time, no sniffing the air. He
saw her, as surely as if she were a visible presence in his
world. He could speak in her mind.

She recoiled from the fierce beam of his stare as if from
a blow and pulled herself inward as if she could become
infinitesimal and so escape him. Or conceal herself behind
Baron Köthen's head, safe in the warmth beside his ear.
But Köthen was barreling full-tilt toward his own destruction, his mind empty of everything but rage and revenge.

The horses behind did seem to be nearing. Erde thought
to distract him in some way, if only to slow him down until
his allies could catch up, before the big gray burst into the
midst of twenty well-armed knights. Forgetting the disem-
bodiment of her dream state, Erde wrapped both invisible
hands around Köthen's bridle arm and hauled back hard.
His head jerked up. He tossed a sidelong glance behind
him and shook his elbow as if to free it from a thorn
branch. But there was no branch. Encouraged, Erde hauled
back on him again, with all the strength she could imagine.
Köthen's eyes rolled sideways, widening in confusion and
a touch of fear. The gray horse sensed his fear and missed
a step, slowing, nearly stumbling. Erde counted the seconds gained.

But ahead of them, she saw the hell-priest grin.

*He fears you, witch girl! Remember, he is only a man,
without understanding. Whereas . . .*

NO!

She screamed it with all her dream-strength, drowning

out his poisonous murmur. As much as Baron Köthen drew her, the hell-priest repulsed and terrified her. At first, she'd assumed he was only after her to burn her at the stake. Now it was clear that he wanted something else. His ability to find her in the dream world was frightening enough. If he ever found her again in the real world . . . Erde's only thoughts were of escape. Her entire being contracted in denial, a vast implosion toward the infinitely small. As her consciousness faded, it occurred to her that anything, even death, would be preferable.

And then someone was shaking her gently awake.

A woman's voice said, low and calm, "Erde? Come back to us. Come back to us, sweeting."

"I've been trying that for ten minutes!" said another, not nearly as collected as the first. "Ever since I heard her cry out! Look! She's not even breathing!"

"Shhh. She's breathing. Help me raise her up a little."

From the verge of the infinite, Erde heard the women's voices like a faraway whisper, carried on the wind. The priest was after her, searching, but she knew these voices. These voices meant safety. Moments from the edge, she veered away and sped homeward toward them.

The snow began falling on their way across the meadows, even before the storm clouds closed in. Big crystalline flakes floating down like autumn leaves. Erde tilted her chin to let their weightless ice melt on her tongue. Even the snow of Deep Moor tasted sweet. She'd never thought snow could be so welcome.

But welcome only because familiar, she reminded herself. Welcome to her as proof that she was *home*. Not so welcome to the two women walking beside her or to anyone in Deep Moor, or even to the laden pony that trudged along behind. Erde wished she could race about kicking up drifts and making snow angels as she might have done months ago when she was still a child in her father's castle.

Snow angels were a proper way to celebrate. She thought she restrained herself out of respect for Raven and Doritt, but in truth, after the events of the early morning, her heart wasn't in it. Gratitude and relief were the best she could manage. But even that offended the taller woman's gloom.

"It's all right for you," Doritt grumped, winding her knitted scarf one more turn around her long neck. Erde would swear Doritt was taller than she remembered. But surely she was too old to be still growing? Perhaps it was her chin-to-ankle-length coat, snugged around her sturdy frame like a woolen shroud. Or perhaps, her man-sized leather-and-canvas boots.

"Why just for me?" With Erde's every step, the white layers exploded upward in powdery gusts, reminding her of baking day in the castle kitchens. At that thought, she felt a surge of guilty joy.

"Snows all the time where you come from."

"At Tor Alte? It does not. At least, it didn't used to." Erde wasn't sure what things were like at Tor Alte lately, and she wouldn't ever want to be caught in a falsehood.

"Bet it's snowing right now." Doritt glanced behind to check on the pony's progress. His load of hay and grain and dried fruit was rather precariously balanced on his shaggy, narrow back.

"In the winter, it snowed a lot."

"But it isn't winter yet," Doritt noted grimly.

Erde fell silent. She knew Doritt's concern was not so much the snow itself, but the fact that it was snowing now, only three weeks into September. But she was more worried about the dragons, gone back on an errand of mercy to that hot land she'd so recently returned from, that alien place that made her grateful for snow in September. However bad it was here, it was worse there, and she wished they'd hurry up and come home. She wanted so to talk to them about her dream.

"Doritt doesn't think snow was meant to be enjoyed," said Raven.

"Not true! Everything in its place is just fine with me."

But Raven's eyes were merry. Erde felt her spirits rise again just looking at her, in her usual feathery blue, layered against the cold, and her dark unfettered hair netted with snowflakes like some kind of woodland queen. Erde always marveled, looking at Raven. If she could choose to look like anyone in the world, it would be Raven, no doubt of it.

"Now," said Raven, "you promised to tell us what it was like where the dragon took you."

"It was hot!" Erde allowed herself a little dance step between them, of joy and relief and affection. "Truly! Hot as a smithy's forge! And smelly. The sun beat down on us all day! And you couldn't drink any of the water."

"Why not?"

"N'Doch said it would make us sick. And to make matters worse, he insisted on boiling whatever we drank! Can you believe it?"

"That's what my mother taught me to do with bad water," said Doritt.

"Really? Why?"

Raven laughed. "Because her own mother did it, I'll bet, and her mother's mother before her. Women's wisdom."

Erde made a face. "Well, I hate drinking hot water. I was thirsty the whole time! Couldn't even wear clothes!"

Doritt's eyebrows peaked. "No clothes?"

"Well, you know . . . not proper ones."

"No wonder you turned up so suddenly in your shift!"

Raven's laugh was so warm and musical that Erde was sure she heard it echo around the entire valley, bouncing off the pine-studded hillsides, tangling in the bare branches of the maples and birches, skating along the winding course of the ice-choked river. But the river reminded her of the dream again. To banish its shadow, she grabbed Raven's hands and whirled her around, arms outstretched, to make her laugh some more. Together they sketched a circuit of merry pirouettes around tall Doritt as she forged doggedly ahead, refusing to crack a smile.

Erde flung her arms wide in a whirling embrace of sky, moor, and mountains. "I'm so glad to be home!"

And saying it somehow made it so. This was home now, Deep Moor, this magical, hidden valley. Not Tor Alte, the castle of her birth, home of Baron Josef von Alte, her father. Poor deluded man. Interesting that she could finally think of him without a wince, that she could even imagine meeting him face-to-face. Perhaps this was because she finally understood that home didn't have to be where you came from. It could be where you felt you belonged. Or perhaps it was because, after all she'd seen, in this her fifteenth year, she'd begun to learn how to forgive. She twirled Raven around again, head thrown back in joy. "Hoooommmme!"

"Well, you've certainly come out of yourself since we've known you," remarked Doritt, not unkindly.

Erde slowed, relaxed her hold on Raven's hands. "Have I?"

Doritt rolled her eyes.

"Oh, yes." Raven reached to tousle Erde's thick, short-cropped hair. "Such a sober young thing when you first came to us."

"I had a lot to be sober about."

"You still do," replied Doritt. "We all do."

"Oh, again! Mistress Grim!"

But Raven's retort was halfhearted, and Doritt's reminder hung in the air like smoke, bringing a momentary silence. Erde's thoughts strayed back to the dream these women had shaken her out of just hours before. It occurred to her that she didn't yet know if Adolphus of Köthen was dead or alive.

"Isn't it time to talk about the war?" she asked. "I wish you'd tell me the news and how things have been going!"

Raven squeezed her shoulder. "Linden insists you're to be rested and smiling again before we start loading you down with all our problems. Look at how hard you were sleeping this morning!"

"I'm smiling. I'm fine." She hadn't told them what they'd woken her from.

Dorritt clucked. "You slept for two days straight before that."

"Please? I know Linden means well, but I'm not a child anymore. Just some little bit of news?" She couldn't bring herself to actually ask about Baron Köthen. If he were dead, she knew she'd burst into tears like a child, when she more properly ought to be celebrating. "What about Hal?"

"Hal is well, at last report," offered Raven. "We'll all tell all at dinner. There's a lot of your news we haven't heard either."

Erde sighed. She'd hoped for news as a distraction as much as anything else. She didn't feel so giddy anymore, and probably she should tell them why. She glanced over her shoulder at the sky. Billowy gray clouds were massing over the valley's northern end, above the sprawling farmstead that nestled there. She could almost see a material darkness sifting down like ash to smother all cheer, all life within.

"Sometimes . . ." she began finally. In the quiet, even her murmur sounded like a shout. "Sometimes I can hear him, you know . . . Brother Guillemo . . . in my dreams. Like he's speaking to me."

Raven's glance was sharp. "Really? Have you told Rose?"

"I've hardly seen Rose! I've been sleeping so much! I was so tired! I've been . . . !" She was shaken by the sudden anxiety that gripped her, but she couldn't make herself admit to them that she'd dreamed the hell-priest right there in Deep Moor. If he could find her so easily in her dreams, could he locate her in life?

"Well, then," Raven advised, "you can tell her soon as we get back to the house."

"I will. I promise."

In unspoken agreement, the three women quickened their pace. With memories of mad—or maybe not so mad—Brother Guillemo dogging Erde's thoughts, the pristine snow and crisp chill were not so inviting anymore. Instead, a longing gripped her for the sweet tall grasses and wildflowers of the summer meadows, of the Deep Moor she'd known not even a month ago. She'd felt safer then, even though she'd been in the greatest possible peril. And now, Deep Moor was threatened, too. Not just by the weather, but by the homing eye of the hell-priest. She'd promised herself to act like an adult, even more than they expected her to, but she must have shuddered or made some small sound of distress, for Raven curled an arm about her shoulders and gave her a gentle hug.

"Never fear, sweeting. A lot of good minds and hearts are working on this problem. We'll think of something."

Erde nodded dutifully. Before this morning, she had believed that the women of Deep Moor could stand against the hell-priest, against anything. Now she was not so sure.

The Grove loomed ahead like a ruined cathedral. The bare branches of its encircling oaks reached up like burned timbers grabbing at the sky. The thick, dark trunks curved in even ranks like the charred piers of a fallen apse. Erde scolded herself for the childish thinking that had let her hope to find this stand of sacred oaks still green and heavy with summer, with the warm sighing of leaves and birdsong. But the leaves lay buried beneath the snow and the birds were stilled. She moved among the huge, knotted trunks in a daze, as if she'd lost something precious. She wished the dragon were there. His very existence was a comfort. Erde knew she could never completely lose hope, as long as there were dragons in the world.

In the center of the Grove lay a pond no bigger than a cottage and as smoothly circular as the face of the full moon. Erde had suspected there was Power in this pond the first time she laid eyes on it. Now she was sure. The shallow crystalline water glimmered softly, without a trace of ice. All around its perfect silver arc, the snow pulled back, as if out of respect, revealing a brief but cheering fringe of green.

Raven and Doritt led the pony to the bank and began to unpack the load. Doritt untied the two big sheaves of hay and spread them out beside the water. Raven cleared patches of snow, then handed out sacks of fruit and grain to scatter on the ground.

"Hope this'll hold 'em," Doritt muttered.

"Oh, tut," Raven reproved cheerfully. "There's plenty more for a while."

"As long as it's the *usual* while."

"We've lived through long winters before."

"Not winters that started in early September."

"We have stores for a year. *You* always insist on it." Raven emptied her last sack with a flourish, then whistled up into the barren branches. A sudden flutter of wings broke the silence, and small flocks of birds whirled in to settle among the seed. Off among the trees, Erde saw the deer waiting. And then something else caught her eye.

"Raven, Doritt, look . . . on the other side of the pond. See that odd bunch of sticks?" The sticks formed a tall but neatly rounded pile, very like something she'd seen before. "Doesn't it look like . . . ?"

"Windfall," said Doritt. "No, too neat. Someone's brush pile."

"No one would be cutting wood in the Grove," Raven countered.

Then Erde remembered. "I know! It's . . ."

"Like a beaver lodge," Raven murmured. "Hmmm."

"Oh, my," said Doritt. "Could it be . . . do you suppose . . . ?"

"Got to be."

The two women dropped their empty sacks and hurried around the pond. Erde followed close behind. The pile was larger than it had seemed from across the water, but much smaller and more hastily thrown-together than the one she'd seen before, on the quiet shore of a lake. No soft moss climbed these walls and no comforting smoke coiled up from the center of the roof. Raven circled around to the far side.

"Aha!" she exclaimed, and stepped forward briskly to knock on a crude wood-plank door set among the twigs.

"He won't answer, you know," offered Erde faintly, drawing on her own brief experience, now intensely recalled.

Raven smiled and knocked again. "He will for me."

Erde thought this rather overconfident, even for Raven. "Hal practically had to beat the door down."

Raven grinned. "That's always been Hal's problem."

"What's he doing here is the real question." Doritt leaned in worriedly to peer at the door.

"Exactly what we're going to find out." Raven knocked a third time, no louder than the first. "Are you there, Gerrasch? Open up, dear soul—you have visitors!"

A wild rustling and grunting erupted inside, making the stick pile shudder. Erde took a long step backward. The plank door cracked open. In the narrow darkness, she saw a familiar pair of beady eyes above a shiny damp nose.

"About time!" the darkness growled.

Raven trilled her musical laugh. "Well, now, sweet, if you neglect to announce your arrival, you can't expect your welcome to be spectacular and timely!"

Doritt leaned farther into the doorway. "Hallo, Gerrasch, old thing. What brings you all this way?"

"Cold. Cold cold cold cold."

"Is it warmer here, then, than out there?" Raven raised an eyebrow at her companions.

"Yes. No. No food, no food. Hungry. A big snow coming."

"You came to the right place—we've food enough to share."

"Big *big* snow. Scared."

"What? You? In your cozy lakeside burrow?" Raven crouched to bring her nose level with the beady eyes. "Scared of a little snow?"

"No! No, no. Listen! Men. Horses. Burned my house. No home. All gone."

"Men burned your house?" The women traded glances. Erde recalled that dark and smoky hovel, hidden in the curl of a brush-choked cove, crammed to its twiggy rafters with jars and bottles and herbs and . . . well, *stuff.* How awful for him to lose all those years of collecting.

"What men?" asked Doritt.

But Erde shuddered, remembering a terrified woman tied to a stake in a far-off market town. She didn't need to ask what men. Who else was going around burning everything in sight?

"Guillemo," muttered Raven darkly.

"Want to burn *me*!" The planks creaked and swung inward. A furry, long-nailed hand gripped the doorframe, then Gerrasch's shaggy, rag-draped bulk filled the opening and Erde recalled why she'd first thought he was some kind of gigantic beaver. "Want to burn me!"

"Poor creature!" murmured Raven.

"Burn us all if he could," Doritt remarked. "How'd you get away?"

Gerrasch's bright eyes, until now fixed entirely on Raven, shifted to the older woman with a crafty squint. "Run run. Scurry. Around, around, cover trail, around around more, cover trail, around around . . . come here."

Raven laughed and patted his hand. "Clever thing! Brave old soul! Well, you're safe here."

"No!" Gerrasch shook his mane until the whole stick pile trembled. "Not safe! No one safe!"

"For a while at least."

The creature took a breath, sighed. "Yes."

But Doritt's mouth tightened. "How long, do you think?"

Erde shivered. What Doritt was really asking, no one

could answer: how long could they keep Deep Moor hidden from outside eyes, now that the priest's forces ranged the land so widely? One misplaced confidence, one single soldier of the wrong stripe stumbling upon their secret path— that was all it would take to bring the hell-priest's armies down on top of them. And then there was her dream. What if the hell-priest could follow her here? Gerrasch's glance slid away again. He let it round an entire circuit of the Grove before returning to settle it for the first time squarely on Erde.

She smiled at him wanly. "Hello, Gerrasch. Remember me?"

He gasped. "It speaks!" Then he cracked a huge grin.

Erde grinned with him. It was impossible not to. "Yes, my voice is back. You were right—there was a word stuck in my throat. It was somebody's name, a friend I thought had died horribly."

Gerrasch blinked at her, sobering, then leaned forward to lay one stubby finger gently across her throat. "Yes. Ludolph."

Raven sucked in a breath. "Ha."

"No . . ." replied Erde carefully. "That was not his name."

"Yes."

"No, Gerrasch, it was . . ."

"Ludolph!" Gerrasch insisted, then he smiled again, dazzlingly. "Will be."

"Ludolph?" murmured Doritt. "The dead prince?"

"The not-dead prince." Raven chuckled.

"He's saying Rainer is Ludolph?"

"He wouldn't be the first person."

Doritt clucked. "Oh, how would he know about such things!"

"You have your ways, don't you, Gerrasch? And won't our Hal be delighted to hear you agreeing with him for once!"

Erde pondered her own ambivalent response to this news. Did she even care anymore if Rainer was the King's lost heir? He was lost to her already. Besides, she had more important responsibilities now. And as if this thought was some kind of signal, Gerrasch stepped forward suddenly, his nose lifted in the direction of the farmstead. At the same moment came the familiar soft explosion in Erde's head that heralded the dragon's return. Her heart reached out joyously to welcome him.

"They're back!" she exulted. "They're back!"

Gerrasch's nose worked furiously. "Two! Oh, two. Two two two!"

Raven nodded. "Yes, clever thing. Our Earth has found himself a sister. A beautiful blue sister!"

Doritt's eyes narrowed. "How did he know?"

Erde didn't care. The dragons were back! Now she could celebrate in earnest. "Yes, a sister! Her name is Water. You'll like her, Gerrasch! You can go swimming together!" She tugged at Raven's sleeve. "Come, let's go back!"

Raven chortled. "Gerrasch hates swimming. Absolutely has to live by water, but never goes in."

"Come on! Hurry! Let's all go!"

"Right," said Doritt. "Come on, Gerrasch. Gather up anything you need, and we'll load it on the pony."

Gerrasch raised both hands, exposing his soft pink palms. "No. No no. Big storm."

"Yes, so you don't want to stay out here alone, do you? You'd be much safer at the farm."

"No no no." He backed into the shadow of his doorway. "New house. I like it."

"It'll blow apart in the first gust, Gerrasch!"

"Will not!"

Doritt took a step after him. "Of course it will! You could have a nice warm spot in the barn . . ."

In the barn with the dragon, Erde realized. Probably Gerrasch did, too.

"No!" He withdrew his head entirely and slammed the door.

"You are so rude!" Doritt yelled after him.

Raven touched her arm. "You've made him anxious, dear. You can't pressure him. You know how he is. Let him do as he likes."

"But . . ."

"He'll be as safe in the Grove as anywhere. He knows that. That's why he came here."

"It could be the dragons," said Erde. "He didn't want to meet Earth before either. But he knew, didn't he . . . he sensed their return almost before I did."

"He's connected with them in some way," guessed Raven. "As he is to many things."

Indeed, Erde noted. Connected in some way she didn't understand. She must be sure to ask the dragon about it. Certainly it was no mystery to her why the hell-priest wanted to burn this odd creature. She herself was unsure if Gerrasch was man or animal, or some uncanny combination of the two, and Brother Guillemo feared anything that smacked of a power he couldn't control or comprehend. She put aside her impatience to be with the dragon long enough to lean close to cracks in the plank door. "Maybe later, if the weather holds, I'll bring them out to visit you. Would that be all right?"

No reply from inside the stick pile. Erde glanced back at Raven and Doritt, then shrugged and let her dragon's return fill her mind entirely.

Chapter Three

Halted on the narrow stairs, N'Doch steadies himself and lets the dragon's return blast through him like a drug rush. It's okay. He knows how to handle it now. He's given up any serious resistance. But he tells himself he'll never really get used to it, maybe never even like it much, this simultaneous elation and submission, the ecstatic release of self that the dragons inspire. The girl is into it bigtime, but it makes N'Doch feel invisible.

Maybe he *should* get into it. Might be the only way to face what's waiting for him at the bottom of these creaky old wooden stairs. Strange faces, different customs, a language he doesn't speak, a whole new world to step into, with this magic, dragon-mended body of his which fits him stiff and tight, like a new suit.

The image of himself in an actual suit makes N'Doch laugh, and his ribs ache. The pain isn't much, just enough to remind him that those ribs were lately in a million pieces. Barely twenty and already he's died and been resurrected. Or so they tell him, these witchy women who've been overseeing his recovery. N'Doch has no memory of the event. Only this floaty sense of not quite understanding how the world works anymore. Kind of like standing out on the ledge of a high-rise in the middle of a hurricane.

He does recall, in searing detail, the dream he had while he was coming out of it. Not a dream, really, more like a vision: of red heat and dust and ruined buildings, and himself running. And an awareness, even in his woozy state, that he must store away every detail he can of that blasted landscape, because someday soon he's gonna need to get back to it.

He tests his legs, still wobbly beneath him. Long time 'fore he'll trust these legs to run again. He knows he should get on downstairs and find out if they brought the old man back with them, see if he's all right, or if he would even come. *Hell, I could ask them from here, right from this step.* Then he wouldn't have to move and show how awkward he is in his body since they revived him. He could just open up the old mind channel and give the blue dragon a call. But he won't. Bad enough doing it when he really has to.

He looks slowly around, like the practice at taking in detail is a good enough excuse to postpone the inevitable. He sees walls of wood and plaster, low dark ceilings crossed with thick beams, a fat candle burning behind the sooted glass of a sconce at the turning of the stair. He could be in one of those Ye Olde theme parks, one of the v.r. ones. He moves quietly down to the landing, where a small square window offers a view of snow-covered fields and enclosing mountains, stuff he's only seen in vids. He lays a palm to the rippled glass, feels the cold seeping through the panes to meet the warm draft rising from the rooms below. He shivers. For some weird reason, he's wondering how his mama's doing.

He hears footsteps, and one of the witchy women appears at the bottom of the stairs, not the healer but the shorter, older one with the earth-colored dress and the really intense voice. He thinks her name is Rose. She's smiling up at him like she knows everything he's going through, so like, there's no point in even bringing it up.

N'Doch can't help but smile back. A grin, really. Kind of weak and sheepish. "Here I am," he says.

"Indeed you are," replies Rose in her accented, faintly formal French. "And are you coming down, or spending the afternoon on the stairs?"

N'Doch likes her already, though he's damned if he's gonna let her know it. "Thought I might just hang, y'know? 'S nice here." He nods at the intricately carved beams above his head. "All this old-timey wood and stuff. You folks really know how to build back here in 913."

"Actually, this part of the house was built at least two

hundred years ago." Rose's mouth quirks. "Even before my time . . ."

"Hey, not as much as before mine." N'Doch likes that he doesn't have to explain himself to her. Probably the girl has done that already. He wonders what kind of stuff she's said about him. Mostly bad, he suspects. He knows how she doesn't approve of him. He studies Rose's face, to see if she looks old-timey, too. Certainly her clothes do. Even her shoes look handmade. But aside from her funny accent, she walks and talks like a regular person. N'Doch is so relieved, he doesn't even bother to be surprised.

Rose sets one foot on the bottom stair and leans amiably against the railing. "How does it feel to be on your feet again?"

He readies his usual smart-mouth answer, then swallows it in a puff of breath and feels it settle like gas into the pit of his stomach. Her compassion is ready and genuine, and her eyes go straight to his gut. Already he's tired of listening to himself. "A little shaky," he says instead.

Rose nods. "Well, when you're up to it . . . there's a certain dragon outside eager to see you alive and well."

"Yeah. I know." N'Doch notices how the word "dragon" comes out of her mouth without a hitch, like it's nothing new, she's known of such things all her life. He wishes he could say it so easily. He squints at the wall beside him, strokes a finger across the fine stippling of bumps. His own dark hand is like negative space moving against the plaster's whiteness. Downstairs, all the faces he sees will be white. "Did they bring the old man?"

"No."

N'Doch glances back at her. "No? Hey, why not?"

Rose holds his gaze steadily. "Why don't you ask her?"

He remembers the old man asking him that, in the very same tone. *She's witchy*, he reminds himself. Just like Papa Dja. They talk to you like they know everything about you. "Why don't you?" he blurts, and then he's sorry for it.

Especially when she says, "Because I cannot talk to dragons. That is, not without a lot of trouble I'd rather not go to just now. Talking to dragons is your gift. That's why you're here."

And that's about the only reason, N'Doch tells himself. For sure that's why they brought me back to life. He knows he's carrying this stubborn thing far beyond sense, but he can't quite let it go. Maybe it's his last chance. He's been waiting for the dragon's siren music to come up here after him, into his brain like she usually does. But so far, she's left him alone. Announced herself, then let him be. She must be busy. Too busy to bother with him. "What about the girl? She talks to 'em better'n I do."

"Erde went with Raven and Doritt to feed the animals in the Grove."

Since none of this information means anything to N'Doch except the girl's name—which he never uses anyway—he lets it pass. "Okay, just give me a sec. I'm coming."

"Are you?"

"Do I got a choice?"

Rose's smile warps gently. "Do any of us?"

N'Doch can't think of a smart answer to that one. He's not sure there is one. "I'll be there."

Rose nods, then turns away and disappears from his line of sight, N'Doch lets his gaze drift back to the little window, where huge white flakes are drifting down from a lead-gray sky. He sees himself running, through flames, through a city in flames, trying to . . . desperate to . . . he can't remember. Only the place itself. That he sees, outlined against the milk-white snow, with gut-wrenching clarity.

"I'll be there," he says again, without moving.

Chapter Four

Paia is still staring at the painting when the squat red sun clears the scrawl of mountains. Her tower studio burns with dusty light as the first traces of the daytime heat bleed through half a centimeter of armored glass. She can hear the morning gongs now, faint and rhythmic. If she lays her palms against the window wall, she'll feel the heat and the dull reverberations from below, a metallic conscience calling to remind her that the day has once again begun and with it, her solemn duties in the Temple.

Of course, she'd much prefer to stay where she is, floating guilty and free among trees and rivers in this blue-green world of her imagination. But they'll come looking for her eventually, her guards and chaperones. An alarm will be raised if her bed is found empty, and a crisis of such vast proportions will ensue until she's found, that Paia hasn't the heart or nerve to set it in motion.

She takes a step back from the painting, hoping this one brave move will break its spell. But the distance only sharpens her longing to be there, not beside it but *in* it. This is worrisome. She repeats to herself a few of the God's stern admonitions about the danger of nostalgia, what he calls "the Green Heresy." His catchphrase is *Survive the day.* He's even worked it into the Temple litany. The God, in his own hedonistic way, is a pragmatist, and Paia sees the sense in it. So she steels herself and turns away, searching for a square of oilcloth to cover the still-moist paint, to hide the siren landscape from her susceptible gaze, or from

anyone who might venture up here. For it is perilously subversive, this painting she's made. It makes one yearn too
piercingly to have what one cannot, and be where one can
never go.

She roots out an antique plastic tarp, crackling with age.
She had been saving it, as a relic of her childhood when
plastic things were everywhere and still relatively functional. But opening it now seems the right thing to do—to
risk a little shredding along the fold lines for the sake of
her sanity, to properly blot out the demon image. She
should paint it over, is what she should really do. But she
can't bring herself to do that. Already she's planning how
she can set time aside during the day to sneak back upstairs, to draw aside the faded blue tarp, and gaze once
more on this forbidden landscape. Paia wonders if she's
having a crisis of faith.

She remembers a word from her studies, an ideal from a
long time ago when an image of wilderness could embody
paradise and perfection. It's a name, a concept, really. She
decides to title the painting "Arcadia."

And once the concealing tarp is in place, it's easier to
pack up her paints, drop her brushes in oil, and head down
the winding staircase, snatching a trailing silk robe off a
handy hook to hide her undignified T-shirt and sweats.
Traipsing along the empty corridor, like she's just been for
a walk, she surprises the dawn contingent of the Honor
Guard as they're settling into their watch. They snap to
startled attention as she sails past them with an august
wave, too fast for them to even consider her unkempt appearance, and shuts the door firmly in their faces. Oh, later
they'll remark on it, and there will be questions asked down
below, about how she came to be outside her quarters when
the retiring duty guards each have sworn—in the God's
name—that the High Priestess slept through the night,
peaceful and undisturbed. No doubt there will be new faces
outside her door tonight. Paia doesn't care. Only that if a
general alarm is avoided, the commandant is unlikely to
inform the God of a few minor changes in personnel. She's
never tried keeping a secret from the God before, but lately
he's been railing harder against what he calls "sybaritic
visions" of the lost green past, a subversive mythology encouraged by a few stubborn pockets of hereticism who, in

order to sow unrest among the Faithful of the Temple, raise false hopes of a new "Greening." There are even rumors, overheard only in whispers, of a Green messiah. So Paia knows if the God sees this painting, he'll have it destroyed. And she's not sure she could bear that.

Seconds after she's shed her sweats and mashed them guiltily into a bottom drawer, her chambermaid is knocking discreetly at the door with the morning water ration and the breakfast tray, ready to draw her bath and lay out the appropriate Temple garments for the dressers when they arrive. One of the privileges of rank that Paia treasures most is her access, however intermittent and undrinkable, to hot and cold running water. The lower floors of the Citadel are without hot water these days: the God won't allow them the energy to heat it. When he threatened to turn her own hot water off, Paia argued that she'd inherited the right to it. After all, it was her ancestors who'd chosen the site of their final retreat with enough prescience to build on top of a deep and integral aquifer, not to mention their subsequent protection of it with all the force and technology their considerable fortune could buy. Two hundred and fifty years later, the water still flows, though not with the purity or volume that it used to. Now the water is filtered and boiled for human consumption. and lately, the God has talked of it running out, perhaps within Paia's lifetime. This could be his usual apocalyptic rhetoric, or it could be true. With the sensors deactivated, she has no way of knowing for sure. She does know that raising the water up to the surface has become consistently more difficult as conditions worsen. But for now, the God has let himself be convinced. So Paia has water to bathe in, though she's not allowed to squander so much as a drop. From the drain in her tiny bathtub, the water falls directly into a cistern that feeds the Citadel's water-starved kitchen gardens.

The only mystery in this neat system is the Sacred Well in the Temple yard, which remains filled to the brim even in the deepest drought and without encouragement from the aging pumps or the windmills that line the top of the Citadel's ridge. The sacred water needs no purifying. It even tastes different, always icy cold, clear, and sharp as a gust from off the pole. This inexplicable wonder and the God himself are the twin foundations of Paia's faith.

The chambermaid knocks again while Paia is searching for her discarded nightgown. She finds it, throws it on, and flops down in her favorite window alcove to calm her breathing before calling permission to the girl to enter.

The breakfast tray is laid before her on a cloth of gold embroidered with images of the God Rampant. Paia thinks he looks very handsome that way. She also thinks that the breakfast looks more than usually appetizing—one of the much pampered melon vines must finally be bearing. She's grateful that today's duties in the Temple are not ones that require fasting. Her long night's exertions have left her famished. It would be a shame if the chambermaid does, as Paia suspects, subsist entirely on her mistress' leftovers, because this morning, the High Priestess intends to devour everything put in front of her.

Paia lets her voice rise in the call to prayer, in the precise tone and pitch that the God has taught her. The intense heat in the Sanctuary rimes her body with sweat, and the metal band of her jeweled headdress itches intolerably. But the ritual is nearly over. This is the final prayer, where the Faithful are to echo the formal pleadings of the High Priestess for the God to lead them safely through the Last Days of the World. After that, there's only the processional, a short march out past the Sacred Well to the Temple Plaza for the purification and sacrifice. Already the huge bronze doors have swung open as if by magic, and the lethal sun has laid a bright path between the paired columns of the inner court, straight down the center aisle between the shadowed ranks of kneeling Sons and Daughters of the God.

Yet this is the part that always frightens Paia the most: the moment when she must come down the seven holy steps from the raised and gated safety of the dais, and walk among the Faithful with only the God's little gun for protection. To be sure, the side and rear walls of the Sanctuary are lined with well-armed members of her Honor Guard. But always at this moment, they seem a very long way away, certainly longer than the easy arm's length she is from potential death with each row of celebrants she passes. But the God insists that she do this at least once in every ceremony. These are fearful and violent times, he agrees, and there is fear and violence in their hearts. But it's a sign of her favor with him, he explains, that she dares to walk so freely among them. Besides, those lost in fear and violence have the greater need for her compassion. *Her* compassion, Paia notes, not his. Finally, he says, the Faithful need the actual contact with her "reality." So, while Paia wishes that the God's idea of priestly vestments allowed for a little more coverage, she's grown used to them touching her, men and women alike, to the drawing of their worshipful palms and fingers across the bare skin of her arms and legs and back. It is, she reflects in her more profane moods, the only touching she gets, or will get, until the "right" Suitor comes along and is approved by the God.

Speared by the hot shaft of sunlight, Paia slow-steps down the aisle with her head held high and her eyes on the freedom of the open doorway. A low-ranking Daughter is leaning out into the aisle ahead, out of eagerness, not disrespect. An older woman, missing one hand. Not a likely threat. Paia glides by, feels the woman's stub brush her back reverently. She must never rush, never show an inkling of fear. But she will feel safer when she reaches the shaded Inner Court, near the Sacred Well, or even outside in the sun-drenched but open Temple Plaza. Her favorite ceremonies end in the Inner Court. The Temple Sanctuary is the God's domain, as is the Plaza. Her own holiest of holies is the Well.

She clears the mammoth doors with a private sigh of relief, pauses at the Well's smooth dark oval to scoop icy water with her own sanctified hands into a golden bowl offered by one of her priestesses, then moves out onto the pale marble paving of the Plaza. She is trailed by the rest of her retinue, twelve thin First Daughters in red robes and red veils with whom she is not allowed to socialize. She's never even seen them without their veils—would not know them if she ran into one of them in the hallways. The God says the High Priestess must declare her august stature and superior dignity by not mingling. For this reason, she is not a Son or a Daughter, but a Mother to them. Mother Paia. It makes her laugh. In truth, she is nobody's mother, and she is not sure her dignity is best preserved by being always alone.

A contingent of the Honor Guard falls in behind the

Twelve, and then come the Faithful, shuffling, eyes down-cast, crowding up against each other like herd animals, even in the stifling heat. Now there's the sacrifice to be got through.

Paia turns left toward the huge Altar of the Winged God, an oblong ton of raw granite stained with the blood of countless prayers to the Deity. The usual complement of the lower priesthood awaits her there, ranged formally behind the tall and impressive figure of First Son Luco, Paia's immediate subordinate. Of all the colorless functionaries the God has surrounded her with, this is her favorite. Paia almost likes Luco. He is kind in his own odd way and more often amusing than irritating. He's uninterested in her sexually and ambitious for the Temple, which is no doubt why the God permits her a limited association with him. Perhaps he hopes the good examples set by Luco's unswerving faith and devotion to duty will rub off on her. It is Luco who actually manages the day-to-day affairs of the Temple, so his avid claim on the giant sacrificial Knife is a favor Paia is only too willing to grant. He holds it crosswise in front of him now, its heavy golden hilt tucked to his hip like a favorite child. In front of him on the altar, a sturdy Third Son, stripped to the waist, restrains a young goat.

Paia suppresses the frown that would betray her surprise at seeing a sacrifice as major as a well-formed goat kid being offered at so inconsequential a ceremony. The God has explained the need for the sacrificial rite rather patiently, given how many times Paia has been bold enough to suggest that it's a waste of valuable livestock. She falls back on this practical argument, knowing that notions of mercy will be lost on him. His reply is always the same: "For the true believers, only the spilling of blood is a proper recognition of the nobility of their sacrifices for the Faith."

In other words, only blood will keep them quiet. Paia wonders if this goat has come from the Temple flocks, or if some merchant's wife is finally pregnant and hoping for a healthy child. And Luco, she notes, is decked out in full makeup and all his best finery—his billowing and dazzlingly white Temple pants, clasped at the ankles with bands of gold and sapphire, his tallest headdress, his sandals with the heels. A crimson velvet vest—his favorite, sewn with winged images of the God in glittering gold—frames the shaved and oiled muscles of his chest. Sometimes Paia suspects that Luco dresses to look like the God in man-form, though this has to be unconscious. It would be, officially, a sacrilege. But First Son Luco is wily enough to know that imitation is the sincerest form of flattery, to which the God is famously susceptible.

Approaching, Paia nods to Luco in ritual welcome. She accepts the golden bowl from her priestess and takes her place to Luco's right at the head of the altar to begin the Invocation of the Winged God.

She's halfway into it, the vessel of sacred water raised above her head, when she feels the God return. Elation and terror churn in the pit of her stomach. She stumbles over a word, holds firmly to the bowl but leaves out an entire line of the prayer. She is waiting for that high, vast, swooping shadow to darken the sun over the courtyard. He is here. Her awareness of him is like the Temple gong sounding inside her. But he does not show himself. Paia blinks and steadies her voice. Her own belief in the God of the Apocalypse has less to do with his messianic promises than with her uncanny sense of connection to him. She fears him, often hates him, but she loves him, too. Until his arrival in the Citadel, she had never felt entirely whole. Even now, his return completes her, in a way no human ever could.

Paia finishes the Invocation, aware of the First Son surreptitiously readying the Knife as the sacred water blesses the altar with its precious moisture. Luco hates to be caught unprepared. He takes great—some might say, unholy—pride in finishing off each sacrifice with a single graceful stroke.

The young Third Son steps back, leaving the goat alone on the altar. Luco's giant shining blade arcs skyward. All eyes follow but Paia's. She has seen one too many small creatures bleed their innocence away on the rough, stained stone. For this reason, and for this reason only, she spots the brief flash among the crowd of priests and acolytes to the other side of her. She is already ducking away from the smaller knife when it slashes across the empty space where her throat has just been. The throng presses around her. She cannot see her attacker, only a robed arm and a moving blade, thin and deadly. Beside her, Luco swings his gilded curve of steel, down, down, and completes a perfect stroke. Blood sprays outward. Paia, fumbling for her hidden gun, falls against a First Daughter behind her. She thinks for a moment that the blood is her own, particularly when the young priestess screams and snatches at Paia's stained limbs in horror. The formation at the altar breaks rank and erupts with shouting and outrage. Luco is jolted out of his post-sacrificial trance. He leaps to Paia's side with the holy blade at the ready. Paia points. The attacker is spotted forcing a desperate path through the worshipers crowding the Plaza. He gets nowhere. The Faithful grab him, bring him down, sucking him into their maw with cheers and wild eyes and raised fists.

And then, a vast shadow sweeps across the hot sky, across and back, fleeter than any cloud, nearing, descending. The throng stills as the shadow circles and drops with a flare of scales and sun and golden wings onto the paving stones in front of the altar.

The throng of the Faithful draws back with a gasp of reverence, then spits out the attacker, sprawling and face-down. The terrified man mewls and grovels at the feet of the God, who pins him to the stones with a single golden claw at his neck, then lifts his great horned head and roars to the heavens until the air itself vibrates. The Faithful moan as one and fall to their knees. When silence has settled again, the God returns his attention to his groveling victim. He snarls and unleashes a sudden blue-white gout of flame that sears the man to a spasming cinder.

The crowd sighs. Their God has returned.

Paia's knees buckle. Son Luco catches her.

"Look sharp, now," he murmurs in her ear. "Everybody's watching."

Chapter Five

A woman laughs and calls out a name. A last set of footsteps fades. A door shuts softly. N'Doch feels the house empty out below him. He inhales the silence in long slow breaths. They're all out there now, in the snow, probably crowding around the dragons, petting and cooing like women do. Something in him disapproves of that. Like, the fact of dragons is amazing enough . . . why make a big thing of it, let it go to their heads? What he'd never admit is that he might be a little jealous. She's *his* dragon, after all.

N'Doch shifts his weight and stares resolutely out at the falling snowflakes. He sees they're starting to blow around a little, and for a moment he thinks how he'd really prefer to be one of them, floating free in the crystalline air. He hates this feeling of being caught, of being seduced and repulsed simultaneously. But he knows he can't spend the rest of the day halfway down the stairs, like the clever, witchy Rose woman ribbed him about. That would be even more ridiculous. Ought to take a look around. Ought to get this patched-up body moving.

Right.

This gets him down the stairs and partway across the dim, low-ceilinged room at the bottom, where he's stopped dead by the undeniable reality of everything he sees. How could he have thought that VR was an equal substitute for the real McCoy? For these heavy wooden chairs with woven seats, those long tables, or that stone fireplace half the width of the wall. Or this neat stack of wood, that bucket of twigs for kindling. That one lantern burning on a stool at the far end.

Of course it's real, he tells himself. The girl came from here, and she's real enough. But now he sees that, ever since he woke up in that tiny, strange room upstairs, he's been reserving the possibility that it all might be some kind of illusion, dragon-induced, a dream. And that possibility has kept him sane and balanced . . . until now.

He drags one hand along the planks of a table by the fireplace. The wood is silky with age and wear. And suddenly his heart is pounding and his hands are in fists. He's taking in air in great heaving gulps. He wants to run, run, escape, like he's trapped, buried alive beneath the very *real* weight of this alien century. But there's nowhere he can run to, he knows that now, at least not outside these particular walls. Nowhere he can go that will be anything like home.

N'Doch flattens both palms on the tabletop and presses downward until his skin molds itself to the cracks and the worn grain of the wood. The pain lets him focus. He forces himself to relax. His life's never been easy so far, and he hasn't survived this long by letting panic rule him. He lets out a shaky but controlled sigh, straightens, and looks around.

The room is long and low, lit mostly by bright flames from the hearth and cold gray light from the many windows along one side. On the table beside him are baskets of shelled nuts, and wooden platters piled with dried podlike stuff that N'Doch doesn't recognize. In front of the window nearest the fireplace sits a tall wooden wheel with a little seat attached and a spike wound with fuzzy looking string. There's something familiar about it, but N'Doch can't quite place the device, or what it's for. There are garments and bits of fabric scattered here and there, and a clay pitcher and cups on one of the smaller tables. The room looks well broken-in, like it gets a lot of use but also, a lot of care.

He steps toward the windows, feeling the chunky hand-cut beams skim past just above his head. Must be he's a lot taller than the folks who built this place. There's a door between the windows, but he doesn't go there just yet. He stoops for a look through the glass.

Outside the windows, a roofed stone terrace runs the

length of the house. Opposite the door, a few steps and a stone path lead off through a screen of leafless bushes. Past the bushes, a big open space is rapidly filling up with snow. And there she is.

Ah.

No matter how resentful or resistant he's been to her, the dragon's beauty has never failed to take his breath away. And against this cold white landscape, her colors shine like sapphires and emeralds, or at least this is how N'Doch imagines such fabulous jewels would look. The other one, the big guy Earth, he's there, too: all dark and bronzy like agate and smoky quartz, the cheap stuff you could find in the markets at home. Earth's only claim to beauty is his curving ivory horns. His stout and gleaming claws are made less threatening by being softly blunted at their tips. N'Doch thinks you'd have to go some to find the big guy threatening, but he admits he didn't always feel that way. And he decides that Earth looks handsomer than he remembers him. Maybe a bit bigger, too, and not so downtrodden-looking. There's even a hint of glimmer to his plated sides.

The dragons are sitting side by side in the clearing, and the snow is melting right out from underneath them as the women crowd around to pet and admire them. N'Doch's mouth twists. His heart wants to be out there, or a part of it does, stroking Water's silky hide, letting her warmth drive out the bone-deep chill he's felt since he woke up from his vision of running. He doesn't see the girl anywhere yet, so probably he should be out there translating. But his feet won't take him. Not just yet.

He turns back into the room, away from the dragon-tinted light. He spots a big, stringed instrument, kind of like an acoustic guitar, propped against a chair. It's like a searchlight in fog-shrouded darkness, an anchor in stormy seas. He makes a beeline for it, picks it up reverently, and smooths his fingertips across its strings—a parched man reaching for water. There are more strings than he's used to, and the body is bulbous and pear-shaped like one of those little bush mandolins made out of a gourd. But this sucker is big and built out of smoothly joined pieces of wood. There's a lot of it to hang on to. N'Doch cradles it in his arms.

The long neck is fretted in a more-or-less familiar way, but the head with its many wooden pegs is set at a sharp angle to the neck, so at first it looks to N'Doch as if it's broken. He hauls a chair back and sits. The tone is sweet and resonant. It sends shivers of desire across his back. He hasn't played an acoustic anything for a long time, but the thing comes up into his embrace like a lover and he's sure he can get the hang of it.

The moment he curls his fingers onto the frets, he feels the dragon inside his head, waiting. He knows what she wants, so he ignores her, fiddling with the strings, learning the spaces between, the shape of the chords. He's amazed how easily it comes to him, and he suspects that she's helping. N'Doch doesn't mind. Not this. This is the thing that works best between them, after all, the making of music.

He works the strings, light and fast, his ear bent close to catch their whispered thrum. There's a tune been bothering him a while, one he couldn't make come out right, so he stuck it away in the back of his head. But here it is now, coming right out through his fingers. It's been there all along, only waiting for the proper instrument to play it. N'Doch stops, slaps the flat face of the box lightly with his palm and stands. He's ready. He can do it now. This'll be one way of thanking them. A soft woven strap is attached to the neck and the base of the box. N'Doch slips it over his head and moves toward the door.

The cold hits him like a wall as he steps out onto the terrace. But he knows if he doesn't freeze solid before he gets to her, he won't be cold for long. He shuts the door quietly and eases across the stones, down the steps and into the snow. He'd like to give the snow some time—it's his first, after all. And the cold, too, as well as the dark, spiky pines—he recognizes those. He's seen 'em lots of times in vids. But all that'll have to wait. Right now, he's intent. On a mission.

He pulls up behind the circle of women. He counts at least a dozen of them, all in their old-timey clothes and their braided hair, murmuring the alien syllables of their native German. Their laughter is not like the laughter of the women N'Doch knows. It's full-out and boisterous, like they don't care if there's a man listening. And, he notices, he's the only guy in sight—unless you count one big brown dragon.

So he guesses it's time. He settles the instrument more comfortably, so familiar, so strange, then gives her the briefest of warnings.

Hey, girl . . .

She's way ahead of him. No big soppy greeting. No oh-thank-god-you're-alive. She rolls her big eyes toward him and arches her silvery neck.

Yo, bro. You all warmed up? I need a voice to talk to these people.

N'Doch grins. One day he'll catch her out. Maybe.

So do I. Think these ladies are ready for this?

My brother, this here's your ideal audience.

He runs off a short riff, and the women turn and notice him. Something about him, his thin, muscled height or the darkness of his skin, makes them fall back a step. But he sees no fear in them, only respect and readiness. Maybe it's that he was all but dead last time they saw him. Or maybe the dragon called it right: they're the ideal audience and they're only waiting for him to perform. Will they care that he's singing in French? No one but the dragon needs to understand the words.

He's nervous now that the moment's at hand. The new song is there ready to go, but the accompaniment will be real thin until he gets a better hang on all these strings. It's another song about his dead brother Sedou, but it's a strong and happy song, not like the last one he sang her, which gave her the shape she needed but nearly broke his heart. He hopes this one'll work just as well, but the only way to find out is to play it. So he does.

His resurrected voice starts off as shaky as his legs. The dragon listens through the first verse, while the big guy's ivory horned head leans in toward her. He watches his sister steadily with huge golden eyes. N'Doch can feel her in his head, anticipating, humming a little harmony, and his voice steadies to match her. A line into the second verse, the dragon begins her change. The women sigh with wonder and admiration—no faint hearts in this valley . . . except his own. N'Doch looks away. He hates watching her shape-shift. It makes him queasy, even though it's him singing her destination. He bends his head over his fingering and keeps on singing. Soon enough, he's at the end and the women are offering a round of applause. Then he looks up and into his brother's eyes, and his heart nearly stops all over again.

"Damn!" he says aloud. "I ain't never gonna get used to this."

"Sure you will," says Sedou's voice. A strong dark fist pounds him on the shoulder, and N'Doch knows he's done it. He's sung her a younger Sedou this time, a happier Sedou, a Sedou who doesn't yet know how short his life will be.

And a Sedou who speaks German, apparently. Must have learned it from the big guy. N'Doch watches the dragon-as-Sedou move among the women with greetings and introductions, a handsome dark man, laughing and at ease. More at ease than N'Doch, who reaches out in confusion and shakes his brother's hand.

Inside his head, the dragon is still singing.

Chapter Six

After she thinks about it for a while, Paia understands that she's been had.

She goes to Son Luco first, charging full tilt down the polished steps from the vestry with her hair half-braided and her temple bracelets jangling like a box of glass tumbling down a hillside. Luco is lounging in the priests' private cloister in nothing but a loincloth, oiling his skin.

"You worked it out with him, didn't you!" she accuses. "I could've been killed! Was it his idea or yours?"

He leaps to his feet in alarm and reaches for a towel. Paia's amazed how he willingly exposes himself to more uv-drenched sunlight than his job requires. Though his natural color is as deeply golden as the God's, he's convinced that a darker tan will help him look younger.

"His, of course!" Luco seems disturbed by the suggestion that he might have had a thought of his own, or worse still, acted upon it. He watches Paia pace back and forth, then lowers himself back onto his chaise. "I hope you've not been running around the Temple looking like that, *Mother* Paia."

Paia glares at him. He knows the title irritates her. "Like what?"

He makes a peace offering, water from the jug beside his chair. "It's cool. Just up from the cellars." Paia continues to glare. Luco shrugs, patting oil on the taut skin under his chin. "Revenues are down, you know. He says he can feel—and I quote—'a definite sag in the intensity of the worship.' He thought we should . . ."

". . . murder the High Priestess just to liven things up a little!"

Luco lifts himself up indignantly. "He'd never let that happen! You were safe at every moment! I was right there and I was, as you may recall, quite adequately armed!"

"Ha!" Paia moves into the shade of the surrounding portico to pace and sulk at the same time. "You could have warned me at least!"

"He wouldn't let me! He knows you—he said you'd never agree to it." Luco swings his muscular legs over the chaise and sits with his elbows on his knees, regarding her as if she's a lighted fuse he can do nothing to dampen. "You have a hard enough time with the use of *animals* for sacrifice."

"You don't mean . . . not the poor sucker who . . ."

He nods. "One of the kamikaze squad."

Paia clamps her eyes shut, mid-pace.

"You see? He was right." Luco shrugs, shakes his head. "They will do these things for him, you know. Sometimes their truer devotion shames me. Often, in fact. Of course I stood up for you and said you'd do anything the God deemed necessary."

"Of course you did."

"Well, I did."

"Maybe he should just stay around more, instead of going off on all these jaunts of his." It always rouses Luco when she speaks of the God as if he were some sort of temperamental employer.

"He is busy converting the Infidel. It's important work."

"And vital to the Temple revenues, I know." Paia continues pacing. "But do you know that's what he's doing?"

"Of course, if that's what he says he is."

Paia stops. She props herself against one of the slim marble columns. "Do you want my job, Luco?"

The priest's forehead tightens. He leans forward as if in pain. "NEVER! I mean, no, I . . ."

" 'Cause if you do, you can have it." She knows he doesn't—he's too scared of the God, no matter how willing he is to plot with him. But she's not ready to let him off the hook quite yet. "Maybe there doesn't have to be a

High Priestess. Maybe a High Priest. Or maybe they still do sex-change operations somewhere in what's left of the world."

She's so delighted by how badly she's shocked him that her anger drains away like she's pulled the plug.

"They used to, you know," she continues gleefully. "I read up on it in the Library."

His bright blue eyes grow round at this sacrilege, and instantly she regrets admitting that she's used her most sacred and solemn privilege—access to the House Comp database, occasional and only when the God allows—for no higher purpose than her own amusement. Merely hoping that he is will not make Luco someone she can talk to this freely.

But he doesn't scold or lecture. He gasps and says, "Really? Did it work?"

Paia can't help laughing. It isn't the sacrilege that's bothered him after all. "I guess." She smiles, then goes back out into the sun to lean over and kiss his cheek lightly and smooth back his long hair. "Poor Luco. Just when you thought you had everything you could possibly want . . ."

She's glad she's run off most of her rage before confronting the God. He'll have sensed her turmoil anyway, the way he always does, but by the time she faces him, it'll have lost its grip on her. And she knows it's unwise to be too emotional in his presence. The God will take advantage of any vulnerability.

She's in her rooms, dressing carefully for her scheduled evening audience with him, exposing the correct amount of skin, redoing her makeup with all the art she can muster, when he surprises her by coming whistling down her corridor in man-form. She feels him approaching, like dogs sense lightning—in the days when there were dogs—and she hears the guard detachment outside her door snap to attention with horrified alacrity. Paia sucks in a breath. At least he has the grace not to simply materialize in her bedroom. She wonders why. Probably he enjoys terrifying the guards.

One curt warning, her name barked like an order, and he's through the door, all aglimmer in the cloth-of-gold business suit he favors for his most casual moments. It's the same cut Paia's father used to wear, before there was no more business to transact. But her father preferred sedate browns and blues. The God wouldn't be caught dead in brown or blue. She's heard him say as much. He halts grandly in the doorway, claps his hands sharply, then steps into the room to let two acolytes whirl in past him carrying a low gilt table and a silver tray glittering with antique glass and a bottle of Paia's father's best champagne. They set it all down together with a hunted glance at their priestess, then at their God. The God waves them out of the room. They cower and hesitate, then scurry away when he glares at them, one of them turning back hastily to shut the door.

Paia bows low. "My lord Fire. What a pleasant surprise."

The God snorts, jerks his head at the champagne. "You'll have to pour it yourself, of course."

Paia raises her eyes. No wonder the servants cower. Everything about the God's chosen man-shape is calculatedly reminiscent of his true and terrifying reality. He is tall, broad and beautiful, and supremely arrogant of bearing. His finely chiseled lip seems always poised for a snarl. His skin has a human grain and tawniness, but its surface is luminous with a faint metallic sheen. His hair is longer than her own, and the rich flame-gold that Son Luco labors so hard to emulate. Sometimes the God wears it loose, in shimmering waves across his shoulders. Tonight he has it in a neat queue down the middle of his back. Assuming his most civilized aspect, Paia notes uneasily. Unlike most of her faithful, she prefers dealing with the more obvious terrors of God's natural shape. In man-form, he is always at his most devious.

"The Temple has missed you, my lord. Was your journey a successful one?"

Perhaps, if she can keep him in his present good mood, he will tell her something of what he does in his travels. She has asked before. Usually he tells of his tours among the farther-flung villages of the Faithful. Once he came home particularly sullen and flicked a finger in response. "Old business," was all he would say. Once, he even made a joke: "Visiting a relative." And Paia had laughed. How could a God have relatives?

She moves obediently to the table and picks up the bottle. The heavy old glass is deliciously cold. He's even made them chill it, probably in the Sacred Well itself. She'd like to hear what Son Luco thought about that. She pours a little into her great-grandmother's crystal and raises it to the God in salute. He returns a mocking, courtly nod, and she drinks, savoring the trail of icy, sweet liquid down her throat, but not the shiver she feels trying to guess what the God has up his gilded sleeve this time. She sips her priceless champagne and eyes him, waiting.

"The Temple has missed me? What about you? Have you missed me?"

He stares her down, golden-eyed, until she must avert her glance. Then he saunters over to her bed. With a nod he shapes her pillows more to his liking and reclines among them as gracefully as a lizard. He puts his feet up and clasps his manicured hands behind his head. His illusion of substance is flawless, and his eyes offer their usual frank invitation. Again, Paia asks herself why he bothers. Perhaps to keep her off balance, which it surely does. Perhaps because he can't help himself. Perhaps even a little wishful thinking. She's often wondered how different their fractious relationship would be if the God in his man-form possessed the actual material reality to carry out what his eyes always promise. It would certainly solve the Suitor problem, but would she have more power over him, or less?

Watching her watch him, the God grins his snarkiest grin. "Well, I know. But it *was* a pretty good show, you've got to admit."

Paia sips, trying for even a fraction of his self-possession. "Do I?"

The God throws his head back in the pillows and laughs.

"A man gave his life for your 'show' . . ."

"Oh, yes. And was convinced that such an end was worth more than all the sorry rest of it put together."

"You bullied him! You threatened him!" Only when he is in man-form can she say these things to him. "He did it out of fear, not faith!"

He cocks an elegant eyebrow. "Is there a difference?"

Paia looks away. She used to think there was. Lately, she's not so sure.

"These people have so little to look forward to in this life. The life after is their only hope, as we race hell-bent toward Armageddon. A hope only I can offer them." He rises up on one elbow. "Are you having another crisis of faith, my priestess? Over the life of one peon?"

A crisis of faith? Paia stills. Could he have read her mind, as he often claims? Desperately, she blocks all thought of the heretical painting, distracting herself with how much she hates it when he mocks her for what he calls her 'womanly compassion.' "I see we are not to agree tonight, my lord."

"I hope that will not be the case . . . my love."

Paia's throat tightens as the banter ends. "You wish something of me, then? What is it?"

A smile. "You."

With effort, she controls a tremble. "How about something you can actually have?"

His smile clicks off, like a light. He does not appreciate being reminded. "All right. A child."

Not wanting to shatter her ancestral crystal, Paia sets her glass carefully on the table. "You . . . a what?"

"A child. You heard me." He rises, quick as a snake strike, and crosses the room. He looms over her, traces the line of her jaw and lip with a long nailed finger. Paia feels nothing but heat, a faint current of air and electricity. Still, it requires every ounce of will she possesses to remain calm.

"Your child, my love," he murmurs. "As soon as you can possibly manage it."

". . . uh . . . how can we . . . ?"

"Oh, not mine. Unfortunately." He turns away, flicks a gilded fingernail. "One of those Suitors, pick one, I don't care. It's time." He levels his bedroom eyes on her again. "I'm sure I don't have to tell you *how*, do I?"

"What do you mean, pick one? Any one?"

"A healthy one, naturally."

"Up till now, you've been rejecting them as often as I have. Now suddenly any one will do?"

"I could choose for you, if you prefer."

"I don't think I'm . . ."

"You are. Ready, that is. Or I am, which is the same thing."

"Wait. This is . . . I won't do this."

The God laughs lightly. "Of course you will."

"I won't."

"But I am your God, my priestess. It is your duty to serve me."

"Not this way."

"In all ways."

"NO!"

He shrugs. "Must we descend to melodrama? There are ways, you know . . ."

"You wouldn't dare!"

He gives her a thin, chill smile. "Choose someone you'll tire of quickly."

Meaning that once he's served his purpose, this Suitor won't be around for long. "Are you doing this just to punish me? What could you want with a child?"

His golden eyes blink slowly, in a time frame not her own. "You wouldn't understand."

"Try me."

"It's time, that's all."

"Time for what? What's different? What's changed?"

Without seeming to have moved, he is at the door. "You have," he says, and vanishes.

Chapter Seven

N'Doch can feel the girl's eyes on him, once the song is ended and the dragon-as-Sedou is busy chatting up the women. She understands a little about him now, must be, since she's waited until he's done singing before bobbing up at his side to hang on him like she's his kid sister or something. Which, he guesses, after all they've been through together, she sort of is. He's surprised she seems so glad to see him, and besides, he's grateful for a familiar face, so he can't resist slinging an arm across her thin shoulders and giving her a hug. To his surprise, she lets him, though he knows her well enough to do it quick and back right off again.

"N'Doch!" she beams. "We were so worried about you!"

Her understatement makes him laugh. "Me, too. Not every day a guy gets blown to bits and wakes up to tell about it!"

Her little nose puckers. "Not to bits, really. But it was bad. Blood everywhere! Those gun-things are a dreadful weapon, N'Doch."

She's speaking French, he notices. Not Rose's antique Frankish, but real French. *His* French. No more need for dragon intermediaries, then. No more excuses for silence or miscommunication between them now. There's so much he wants to ask about what happened after, that is, after he stopped remembering. About Lealé, and Baraga—in all the confusion, did the slimy bastard get away? And how was it seeing him dead and all? But the moment's not right, or maybe he's not ready. Instead he says, "Been keeping up with the language lessons, huh?"

She nods, hunching her thick woolly layers farther up around her neck like some kind of Eskimo. She has tall fur-and-leather boots on now, and the whole outfit looks as weird to him as it did back home, except he reminds himself that this is what people wear here in 913, and probably if he doesn't get something like it pretty quick, he's gonna freeze to death. He shivers, remembering that he's standing barefoot in half a meter of snow, and this long shirty thing they've given him just isn't cutting it.

"Lady Water is just the best teacher of all!" the girl exclaims, with the same precise and literal manner in French that she had speaking German all the while the dragon was translating in his head.

"Nah. You're just a good learner." He kicks at the snow experimentally and grins when it flies weightlessly up into the air. "I guess you're glad to be home."

"Yes, yes, I am, but . . . it won't be for long, you know."

"No. Probably not." The dragons would see to that. N'Doch wonders again how this young girl, with her whole life before her, could so willingly give it up to serve this infernal "Purpose" that the dragons are so obsessed with. He's about to ask her that, when she answers one of the other questions he's been trying to make himself ask. "They went back for Master Djawara as soon as they could, you know. He wouldn't come with them."

N'Doch feels at least one of the tensions deep inside him relax a little. "But he's okay?"

"Yes, he's fine."

"Why wouldn't he come?" But N'Doch is not really surprised. He can't imagine the old man willingly forsaking his beloved hidey-hole out in the bush, or his pack of mangy dogs.

"Said he had too much important business to tend to," says his brother's voice, coming up beside him.

N'Doch starts, then blows out a breath and shakes his head. "Never. Never gonna get used to this."

The dragon-as-Sedou laughs, a rich and youthful baritone. "Gotta say, though—it's more convenient than four legs and a tail."

"Freaks me out," N'Doch admits, for the first time in the girl's hearing. "You're dead, and I oughta be."

"Look at me, bro."

Reluctantly, N'Doch meets his brother's eyes. It's like staring straight into the sun. Meanwhile, the dragon is speaking inside his head.

I am your memory of Sedou. Nothing more, but . . . nothing less.

N'Doch looks away, swallows. "Right."

"Okay. So Papa Dja says he'll be watching out. He sees signs of more activity back by us, he'll let us know somehow. Says to tell you to keep your head down."

"Too late."

"Never too late. Let's get on in, huh? I'm freezing my ass off!"

The girl giggles. Sedou grins at her, reaches out, and tousles her black curls. "Hey there, kiddo."

N'Doch sees he's got some catching up to do. "By the way, remind me to tell you 'bout this vision I had."

When he sits down at the long wooden tables laid out for dinner in the big room with the fireplace, N'Doch realizes that he's still the only guy in the place—not counting Sedou, who's really a she-dragon anyway. He looks around, counts fifteen women of various ages, including the girl. Maybe the men are all out fighting this war she's told him about. He's got a well-used platter in front of him, like a big fired-clay plate, and a tall tapering mug of the same material grasped in one hand, already filled with some foamy dark brew. He's floating on that cushion of unreality again, with the girl seated on one side and Sedou across from him, both ready to translate. The seat on his left is empty until the most beautiful white woman he's ever laid eyes on plunks a big steaming dish down in the center of the table and settles in next to him. She smiles and says something he doesn't get, then holds out her hand.

"This is Raven," supplies the girl from his right.

"Oh. Hello, Raven." N'Doch can feel Sedou's eyes laughing already. He takes the proffered, lovely hand and raises it, just like he's seen in vids, gallantly to his lips.

Later, when Raven gets up to refill the jug of ale she's just emptied into his tankard, N'Doch no longer cares what century he's in. These women's homemade hooch tastes pretty damn good to him and the company couldn't be improved upon. Now that he's got the chance, he leans over to the girl and whispers, "So where's all the men at? They out fighting or something?"

She blinks at him, then wags her head in understanding. "I forgot—you wouldn't know. There are no men at Deep Moor."

"None?" He glances around, sees two or three young girls who've got to have had a father at some point.

The girl follows his gaze. "Oh, well, just the occasional visitor."

He grins. Wow. She's actually making a joke.

"No, really. Like Hal. I told you about him. He helped me escape from the hell-priest after I ran away from my father." She leans in closer. "Hal is Rose's . . . well, um, you know."

"Her husband?"

"Oh, no. He's her, um . . . ." She gestures uselessly with one hand.

"Her brother?"

'No!"

"Her lover?"

The girl blushes and nods.

At first, N'Doch thought she was uptight. He's come to accept that it's actual innocence, so he tries real hard now not to let her prissiness irritate him. But he can't help pushing her just a little. Somebody's got to teach her the ways of the world. "Go on, say it. He's her *lover*."

She's even touchier than usual. She glares at him from under her lashes, then bolts up and scurries away. N'Doch hasn't expected quite this reaction. He's left with empty seats on both sides of him and Sedou all the way across the room, in deep with the pale-haired healer woman, probably swapping secrets of the trade. But he decides that things are looking up. He'd had a moment of panic at the thought that no men at Deep Moor meant that these women didn't like men. Now he feels free to entertain his fantasies of luring the spectacular and vivacious Raven into bed with him. Maybe he's not going to mind it so much after all, being back here in 913. At least, for as long as the dragons will let him. He figures he's gotta work fast.

Erde escaped the embarrassing conversation with N'Doch and fled to a shadowed corner of the kitchen to wait for her blush to subside. Nervously tracing the stained grout lines between the stove tiles, she wondered why— after all she'd seen of life in the ungentle world of 2013— a certain subject was still so hard for her to talk about, especially with N'Doch. For, though he was like a brother to her, he was still very much a male. In fact, here in her world, he might even be labeled lecherous. But she'd seen how it was where he came from. People just said what they felt, right out, and looked where they wanted to look. There, she'd been the odd one out.

But to be honest with herself, something she was trying harder to be lately, Erde had come to resent the extreme modesty of her upbringing. She envied N'Doch his worldly ease. She was sure he could answer just about any question she might ask about what really went on between men and women, and he'd have not the slightest qualm about filling in all the details. But she could not bring herself to have those conversations with him, no matter how curious she was, conversations she would have had with her mother, had that dear lady not died in Erde's early childhood. Conversations her grandmother the baroness had been too busy to have. Conversations she could never have had with her father because of the way he'd begun to look at her and touch her in the months before she fled Tor Alte to escape the clutches of the hell-priest.

Ever since she'd begun to grow, men had grabbed at her in one way or another, as if it was their right to lay hands on her without her permission. And this man-right seemed to demolish all class and duty lines, even religious vows. To Erde, it was more than just disconcerting or dangerous. It overturned a very basic principle of her childhood: men were meant to protect the women in their charge. Like Hal. Having tracked her down in the deepest wilderness, he could easily have taken advantage of her. But Hal Engle was a King's Knight, and true to the oath he'd sworn. And a decent man, besides.

N'Doch, too, had kept his hands to himself from the very beginning, though Erde could hardly call him a *gentleman*, the way he looked at every other woman who crossed his path. Erde ceased tracing the grout lines and began to pick at a particularly offensive clot of soot. And then there was . . . *him*. The man who kept invading her dreams, as if she had no choice.

It wasn't just the dreaming about her enemy that disturbed her, or even that she worried about his well-being. It was that she was so . . . attracted to him.

The very notion brought up her blush again. Erde was not too innocent to notice how consistently any thoughts of what men and women did together brought Baron Köthen's bright image to her mind, to disturb and confuse her.

"Erde, dear? Are you all right?"

Raven, returning from the beer cellar with a fresh pitcher. Erde hoped the shadows would hide the evidence of her unseemly thoughts. Although, she reflected wryly, Raven would not think them unseemly. She smiled and shrugged. "Just tired. Still so tired."

Raven circled her free arm around Erde's waist. "Sweeting, it's only been three days. Remember what you've been through."

Erde could not think of how to reply. Raven set the pitcher down on a nearby joint-stool and wrapped her in a hug. This helped Erde banish the image of Baron Köthen and find her tongue again. "And think of what's still ahead, when the Quest resumes."

"Ah, yes," Raven agreed, "but you mustn't worry about that for now . . ."

"No. Not for now."

Raven let her go and took up her pitcher again. "The young man seems very nice."

"Who, N'Doch? Nice?" Erde couldn't imagine such a thing.

"Well, then . . . charming. A little overeager, perhaps. But very lovely to look at, don't you think? So tall and . . . exotic."

Erde stared. Was she kidding?

"No wonder his dragon enjoys taking man-form," Raven went on merrily. "I think she might be just the slightest bit vain, don't you?" Then she caught Erde's expression.

"Hmm. I see. Well, you and the boy *seem* fond enough of each other. Comrades-in-arms and all that."

"He's not a boy."

Raven chuckled. "No, and I expect he wouldn't want to hear me calling him that either. Come, tell—have you not been getting along?"

Erde felt no urge to detail every disagreement she'd had with her fellow dragon guide. After all, he had improved noticeably since she first met him. "He doesn't know very much about dragons," she offered instead, realizing only then that of all N'Doch's irritating qualities, this was the one that bothered her most. "Or the duties of a dragon guide. People don't even believe in dragons where he comes from!"

Raven smiled. "Ah, but he has a dragon who knows a great deal about men. And from what I observe, she seems to be managing him very well."

"She does?"

"Certainly. There are other ways of turning a man to your purpose besides ordering him to follow. Lady Water discovered who in his life her destined guide was most likely to listen to seriously. Since it wasn't her at the moment, she simply . . . became that person."

"Oh, well . . ."

"No 'oh, well.' Think about it. It's brilliant, and it works."

"Then what does he do for her?"

"He sings her a human shape. He gives a dragon a way to work in the world of men, as you do for Earth. You just have different ideas of how to go about it. Are Earth and Water the same dragon?"

"Of course not!"

"Then why should they require the same dragon guide?" Heading for the door, Raven glanced back. "Do you think, sweeting, that it might be time to have that little chat with Rose?"

Erde thought about dragons and methodologies for a while. It was true she'd been stubborn about her own assumptions. And it was true that N'Doch had surprised her. He'd come through in the end. Perhaps she was going to have to accept the possibility that there would always be people in the world doing things that she just could not understand. Armed with that disturbing notion, she gathered up her courage and returned to the Great Hall, where N'Doch was taking another refill from Raven's pitcher, the redheaded twins were clearing platters and tableware, and Doritt was tossing a huge log into the fireplace. Erde prayed that the dragon was warm enough out in the big hay barn, finally getting the rest he deserved. She went to claim the empty seat beside Rose.

She listened quietly while Rose finished up a discussion with Linden, Deep Moor's healer, about how long her supplies of herbs and physicks would hold out if the snow continued unabated into the true months of winter. Linden's jaw-length flaxen hair draped like separate strands of spider silk around her white cheeks, hiding her worried glance in the softened shadows of lanternlight. Her long-fingered hands moved restlessly in her lap. Erde found this more worrisome than all the facts and figures of their conversation. She'd come to rely on Linden being a very calm, still person.

"Well," Rose concluded finally, "we shall do what we must."

Linden nodded, then offered Erde a small, silent smile and padded away, gathering up a stray armload of dirty dishes as she went.

Rose watched after her soberly. "She fears our medical supplies won't last past January. Her final harvest is usually in early November, and here it is, just September. Even if we do get a thaw, who knows what will be left alive under all this snow."

Erde thought of the parched peanut fields around Master Djawara's home in what N'Doch called "the bush." "Where I just came from, there's not enough water. Not anywhere, except the salty oceans. And here there's too much. And there, they kept saying how it was so much hotter than usual."

"And here, too cold. It's all gone out of balance, hasn't it? I blame this priest and the evil he's stirred up." Rose let a pensive moment fall between one thought and the next. "Which reminds me, Raven tells me you've had some dreams I should hear about."

"I guess." Erde loved Rose, but often found her directness and air of authority intimidating. Even her beloved grandmother, a powerful baroness required to work in the world of men, had been somewhat more . . . feminine in her approach.

"What kind of dreams?"

"Um . . ." Erde found a sudden reason to fuss with the hem of her sleeve. "Do you really think Brother Guillemo has brought all this wrong weather upon us? Is he truly a sorcerer?"

"You know his power as well as I do, child, perhaps better. But we were speaking of dreams. Come on, now, out with it."

Erde brushed invisible crumbs across the worn planks of the table. "Well, they're . . . umm . . ."

"If you told Raven, you can certainly tell me."

"I didn't tell Raven . . . not really. Well, I told her I'd seen the hell-priest in my dreams, which is true, but . . ."

"But? There's something more important than Fra Guill?"

Spoken aloud, the priest's nickname made her shiver. "I don't know. It's all mixed up together." There was a larger significance to these dreams than her own confused feelings, and it was her duty to reveal them. "Fra Guill is part of it, but . . . well, um . . . what would you say if you had dreams, I mean, really *real* dreams, as if you'd actually traveled there, about someone you knew was your enemy, and he's there in your dream and you're almost talking to him and he doesn't seem like he could really be your enemy, and then suddenly he isn't, because the real enemy is someone else?"

"Goodness. Breathe, child!"

Erde realized she hadn't been.

Rose waited a moment before asking, "Does this no-longer-an-enemy have a name?"

Erde nodded. The hardest part of all was going to be speaking it out loud. Her lips moved uselessly.

"Haven't we been through this before?"

"No, this is different. It's not Rainer." Whose name had lodged in her throat the night she'd thought him murdered by her father's order, and rendered her mute for months until she had discovered him alive again. "I mean, I can say the name. I just . . ."

"Then just say it and get it over with."

"Adolphus of Köthen."

Rose sat back a little. "Dolph? You've been dreaming about Dolph?"

Rose was surprised, but Erde was even more so, to hear Baron Köthen spoken of so familiarly by someone without estates or title. Or perhaps Deep Moor was Rose's estate. Erde had never thought to ask. Now she nodded and braced herself for ridicule. But Rose pursed her lips thoughtfully. Raven glided past behind them, trailing a fond hand across their shoulders. Rose caught the hand and held it. "You might want to hear this."

Raven leaned over. "Is that all right, sweeting? Do you mind?"

Erde shrugged. Her humiliation might as well be total.

Raven sat, reaching for Erde's hand to press it lightly between her own.

"Our Erde has been dreaming about Adolphus of Köthen," Rose announced.

"Really?" Raven laughed deep in her throat. "Can't say as I blame her."

Erde looked down, heat and confusion flooding her cheeks already.

"Raven, please . . ."

"Can't I compliment her on her good taste?"

"Just listen," said Rose irritably.

"I don't understand . . ." Erde began.

Raven squeezed her hand. "Don't feel badly, sweeting. It's all rather . . . complicated. Isn't it, Rose?"

"I think we'll leave your past out of this for now," said Rose. "Now, child, when you left for, well, this other place you've been, Baron Köthen was in revolt with your father and Fra Guill to usurp the King. So you must have had news of the war since you returned, yes? I mean, about Dolph's, shall we say, conversion?"

"Conversion?" She needed to hear it again. She needed it confirmed. Beyond all misunderstanding.

"You heard he switched sides."

The smile bloomed on Erde's face before she could take control of it. Her dreams had been true. "And is he now leading the King's armies to victory?"

Rose and Raven exchanged glances.

"No," said Raven. "Not exactly . . ."

Erde's heart contracted. They were telling her he was dead. And since her dreams had been true, she knew how it had occurred.

Rose laid a hand on her wrist. "If you've not had news, why did you say he was no longer your enemy?"

Now that Baron Köthen's name was on the table, the rest of the tale came out in a rush. "Because I dreamed it. That's what I'm telling you. I saw the enemy camp. I saw my father in it. I saw everything that happened: the hell-priest murdering poor Prince Carl and making it look like suicide, then trying to blame it on Baron Köthen, and when that didn't work, accusing him of witchcraft and heretical practices, so that the only thing left for the baron to do was to flee to the other side! He meant to bring Prince Carl's body home to the King." She glanced from one to the other, awaiting their painful revelation. "Did he?"

"Don't you know?" asked Rose.

"That dream stopped there, and no one has said if . . ."

Raven leaned forward. "He brought the prince's body to Hal, who he knew would receive him. But few people know this. The official word is that Carl survived to go into hiding, and that Fra Guill is faking the reports of his death to suit himself. No one knows the truth besides His Majesty, Hal, and a few trusted allies, plus Dolph and the men who stayed loyal to him."

"And you." Rose tapped a fingernail rhythmically on the tabletop. "You have had a true dream, Erde von Alte."

"More than one," Erde murmered. There was still the truth of the last one to be gotten over with. "They frightened me. Sometimes it was like being a bird on his shoulder. So close. I even spoke to him, and once, I think . . . no, I am sure he heard me."

"In the dream he heard you?" Raven rested her chin in her hands. "What did you say to him?"

"It was in the clearing where he found Prince Carl's body. The priest had him outnumbered. I told him to run, save himself. I could see how he hated Fra Guill, how he despised my father."

"His own fault for taking them as allies," remarked Rose.

"He regretted that." But here Erde was on shaky ground. She didn't know that for sure. "So I told him that a true prince might still live, not a weakling like poor Carl, but a rightful heir that he could feel proud to pledge fealty to. But then, worst of all, the priest heard me, too! And unlike Baron Köthen, he knew it was me! 'The witch-girl,' he called me. 'She's here! The witch-girl!' And then I couldn't wake up . . . !" Erde buried her face in her hands with a shudder. The mere memory of her subsequent journey to and from limbo terrified her all over again. She wouldn't tell that part of the tale just now.

"It looks like poor Dolph has been telling the truth," Raven observed quietly. "At least, his version of it."

"The part he's willing to let himself understand," agreed Rose.

Poor Dolph? But at least they were speaking of him in present tense.

"Then . . . he's alive?"

"So far," said Raven, "No thanks to his own efforts."

"Information has been scanty," Rose added, "what with the weather and our needing Lily and Margit close to home for our own protection. Hal's sent a bird now and then when he remembers."

She hardly dared to ask it. "When was the last one?"

"Not long ago. A few weeks."

Not long, no, but long enough for a man to lie dead and frozen on the field like the others she had seen in her dream. Erde pushed the thought away and let the rugged, able image of a *living* Baron Köthen fill her mind's eye. The very image of a leader. " 'Poor Dolph,' you said? Did anyone doubt him?"

Raven spread her hands. "Inevitably."

"But they mustn't! It's all true! I saw it with my own eyes. I was there!"

"Well, no. You weren't," said Rose.

"But it was *like* I was there!"

"Apparently. And that is the interesting thing." Rose sat back, rubbing her palms together. "Truth is, I wouldn't mind hearing what Dolph has to say. We'll not stop Fra Guill until we fully understand the nature of his power. Another version of this story might just shed some light on that mystery."

"Dolph is a boy's name," murmured Erde, unaware until Raven laughed that she had spoken this thought out loud.

"He was a boy, or very nearly, when I knew him. A beautiful boy."

"No longer," said Rose heavily.

Raven nodded. "Bright ambition in the youth can darken to obsession in the man . . . especially if that ambition is thwarted."

Erde felt she'd lost the thread of their conversation. "But if he's alive and on our side now, what can the problem be?"

Rose eyed her sympathetically. "I don't know what he has done to so earn your good opinion of him, but you must realize, dear child, that in one fateful moment, Adolphus Michael von Hoffman, Baron Kothen, went from being the most powerful and respected younger lord in the kingdom, with his hand poised for the throne, to being a fugitive of dubious integrity, under suspicion of sorcery and without lands or forces to call his own. We're told it's been hard on him."

"But what about Hal?" Didn't he . . . couldn't he . . . sorcery? She had imagined the two of them, man and mentor, joining forces to win great victories together.

"Hal's kept him alive and out of the hands of the witch hunters."

"Whom he's had so much practice eluding himself," noted Raven.

"But Hal Engle, as you know, serves His Majesty first and foremost, and even he can't be sure of where Dolph's true loyalties lie."

Erde's mouth took on a stubborn tilt. "King Otto is old and weak! My father always said so. Baron Köthen only wanted the throne so he could keep the kingdom together. I heard him say so to Hal. You'll see—when the true prince is recognized, Adolphus of Köthen will pledge to him and help him make the kingdom great again!" If indeed, she added silently, he is still alive to do it. She wouldn't know, until the next bird arrived.

"Well," said Rose, raising a doubtful brow.

But Raven smiled. "I guess there's no doubt where your loyalties lie."

It isn't until the three men turn up out of the blizzard that N'Doch comes to and realizes what a fool's paradise he's been living in. They ride in out of the storm and bring the cold light of reality with them. He only needs one look at their grim and weary faces.

This Deep Moor place, he reflects, is like one of those fancy damn R&R resorts, where the army sends the battle-crazed recruits to pump 'em up with enough hooch and tail and m.j. so they can send 'em back out to the front again. But then he can't help but grin. *So far all I've gotten is the hooch.*

The dragons have gone down the valley for exercise, as if the storm was nothing to them. But they come flickering in out of nowhere, bringing the first sighting of the intruders' approach. The girl bursts out of the house to greet them. N'Doch is out in the yard, now that they've found him some serious clothing to wear, learning how to shovel snow. There's plenty of it to shovel, and he keeps at it while the girl confers with the dragons.

"Visitors!" she exclaims, then hightails it back into the house.

The dogs report in next. N'Doch loves how they bound along, just like the herd of antelopes he saw in a vid once, silent and eager, sailing through snowdrifts as high as veldt grass. They race straight to the tall woman Doritt, who seems to have the same sort of way with them that Papa Dja has with his mangy pack of strays. Some things, he thinks, never change. Like how she squats her odd angular body down among them in the wind-driven snow, patting and murmuring, then gets up and marches into the Big House like she's got their actual words to convey.

N'Doch likes how the farmstead is always busy, even now, in the midst of a storm. Paths snake through the snow between all the outbuildings. It snowed yesterday and the day before, and now the snow is falling again, a soft swirling mist that whitens the air and fills in the path behind him. He has to work hard to keep up with it. Storm or no storm, there are cows to be milked and chickens to be fed and eggs to be collected. When he really thinks about where he is, timewise, he's not so surprised that these women have to do everything by hand. He's learned there's a bake house, a laundry, an old-time forge, and a potter's kiln among the many smaller wood-and-stone buildings that circle the big central farm house. And even a man who was blown to bits less than a week ago gets a shovel stuck in his hand or a load of wood to carry.

N'Doch doesn't mind the work. It keeps him warm and gives him something to focus on, which is good, 'cause he's still feeling pretty damn floaty. He likes being part of the bustle. It's like the village he grew up in where everybody had a function, before things got real bad and his family had to move to the city. Besides, he figures he owes these women something for all they're doing for him. He can't remember how long it's been since he had three safe squares a day and a real bed to sleep in every night, the same bed even, warm and rat-free, where he can sleep without fear of being robbed or murdered for maybe the first time in his life.

But then the men arrive, and it's like being jolted out of a pleasant daydream. Suddenly N'Doch is wondering how long it'll be before this war the women all gossip and debate about comes spilling over the valley walls like the proverbial tsunami. He's sorry about this. He's just left his own sort of war behind, and he doesn't wish it on them for a moment.

He leans on his shovel when Doritt comes back out on the terrace with Raven and the girl in tow. Raven squints up at the sky, hugs a heavy shawl around her. Doritt, in tall leather boots, heads for the horse barn. "I'll get Margit and Lily saddled up."

"You can't send them out in this," Raven calls after her. Margit and Lily are the trackers, N'Doch knows. Margit is also the blacksmith. He likes those two women. They remind him of the girls in his old gang. Lily has promised him a ride out to the Grove if the weather ever clears. N'Doch has never been on a horse, at least not a real one, never touched one in his life, and just this morning, Doritt had him mucking out stalls. Talk about total immersion. He shakes his head in amazement.

"Somebody's got to see who's coming in." Doritt disappears around the corner of the barn.

"I told you, it's Hal," insists the girl.

Raven shook her head. "Hal's got a war to worry about

now. He can't just take off whenever the fancy strikes him."

"Earth knows Hal and he's sure it's him."

"How close did he get?"

"Not too close, just in case. But . . ."

"It can't be Hal. There's three of them. Hal'd never brought a stranger into Deep Moor in his life until he brought you."

"And there goes the neighborhood," says N'Doch from the yard.

Both women look at him, but nobody laughs. He shrugs and goes back to his shoveling. But out of the corner of his eye, he watches Raven as she stands, hands on hips, staring across the farmyard toward the snow-shrouded valley as if there was already something to see out there.

Doritt comes back from the barn. "They say they'll go out as far as the Grove—they've been wanting to check on Gerrasch anyway—and escort whoever it is back in, whether they're welcome or not. Margit says to have the troops ready."

"We've got time. It'll take them at least an hour from where the dragons spotted them, maybe longer in this weather." Raven touches the girl's arm. "Go tell Rose—she's working in the library."

The girl jumps like she's been daydreaming, then races off inside. N'Doch can see she's worried about something. Doritt does an about-face and strides back to the barn, leaving Raven alone on the snow-swept porch, the white flakes catching in the dark cloud of her hair. N'Doch would like to say something to her. Not a come-on or anything. She looks too sad and worried all of a sudden. Well, maybe a *little* come-on, just to cheer her up. Raven understands how to play the game. But he speaks no German. She speaks no French. All he can do is smile encouragingly.

Uh-huh, he tells himself. Time to start learning another language.

The storm has blown up into a real howler by the time the three men struggle in. The dragon-as-Sedou stands next to him in the lee-side shelter of the spring house, where Doritt has stationed them.

"Just in case," she says, shoving stout poles into their hands.

N'Doch uses the pole to brace himself against the wind. He'd prefer his trusty old fish blade that's gotten him in and out of many a tight scrape. But nothing came back with him through the veil of centuries, nothing but his flesh and bones, in several pieces. Even his clothes were in tatters. He hefts his pole. It's about two meters long and maybe three centimeters thick. He turns to Sedou. "What d'ya think?"

Sedou's grin is veiled with snow. "We can take 'em. Whoever they are."

N'Doch levels the staff at him endwise and feints. Sedou counters with the stick held across his chest in both hands. Instantly, N'Doch sees that's the right way to use it, like, to ward off a blade. Particularly a real long one. It occurs to him that these guys are probably gonna be carrying swords. His anticipation quickens.

Sedou's still wearing the same old dashiki and jeans that N'Doch's song had conjured him in. N'Doch shivers. He can't remember ever being so cold. Suddenly he feels like it's him who's the older brother. "You ought to get some clothes on."

"Cold doesn't affect me."

"Well, it looks weird. People might think you're showing off."

"Since when did that bother you?" Sedou raises his staff and takes a stance. "Wanta do something about it?"

They joust a little among the drifts until N'Doch's feeling warmed up and breathing hard. He pulls back with a laugh. "Do we have to go to all this trouble? Couldn't you just, y'know, spit fire at them or something? Instant barbecue?"

Sedou sobers. "Not me. That's my brother."

For an instant, N'Doch is confused. Then he says, "Oh, that brother. The big guy can do that? No kidding."

"I meant the other one."

Right. The *other* one. N'Doch recalls it well enough, pounding hell-bent down that long tunnel in Lealé's mystical house, pursued by a roaring gout of flame, breathing in the searing heat, sure he was about to be incinerated by a dragon he'd never even met. Come to think of it, his vision of running was a lot like that. His two dragons had gotten all excited when he described his vision to them. Earth made him repeat every detail of the burned-out, ruined landscape.

Water had asked: *Is it a fix?*

Earth had replied: I THINK IT IS.

"The other one," N'Doch says now. "I remember. The one we gotta go after."

Sedou nods. "And soon. But only when you're ready. When your body is healed."

N'Doch flexes his shoulders, wrinkles his nose to the snow and wind. "Feels pretty good right now." In fact, too good. The suspicion is growing that he feels not only different but better than he ever did before. "Say, listen, did you guys . . . did you, like, put in any improvements when you worked me over?"

But the dark man opposite him just smiles back at him blandly, a distinctly un-Sedou smile. N'Doch can see the dragon in his brother's eyes and knows this question won't get a straight answer.

That's me, all right. Just a poor dumb soldier on R&R, kickin' back, enjoying myself, while a coupla dragons shape me up for the next big battle.

Later, he hears the sharp halloo of the dogs escorting the intruders in. But the snow is flying so thick in the gathering dark that the riders are halfway into the farmstead before N'Doch can pick them out. The snow muffles the sounds of their approach, but the alert has already been downgraded. Lily has ridden in ahead to give the okay to light the lanterns and call the watchers in from their posts. One of the riders, at least, is known to her. N'Doch figures it must be this Hal they all talk about. The women have gathered in the yard. Doritt and the twins warm their hands at the flame of a tall torch they've uprighted in the snow. N'Doch thinks it looks festive, but he can feel the tension beneath the women's cheerful chat and banter. It's not normal for visitors to show up unannounced in the middle of a blizzard. There might be something wrong. Rose waits on the stone terrace, bundled up in a bright woolen shawl, all reds and rusts and oranges, as if she could banish, with bold wielding of the spectrum, the approaching gloom of night. Her often stern face is lit with a womanly anticipation, and N'Doch recalls that according to the girl, this Hal, if it's him at all, is Rose's lover. The girl is there next to her, front and center to greet him, but she's still looking worried. Even more so than usual.

He hears a soft rhythmic chink, metal against metal. The riders fade into view at last, darker shadows rising up through a field of darkening gray. They are hooded, and wearing epaulets of snow. N'Doch realizes he's gripping his stick as if his life depended on it. He relaxes his fingers inside his gloves, but not his stare. Margit rides ahead, then two men abreast and one behind. Reflexively, N'Doch susses out the power structure: Margit, of course, the guide. Then the Chief Honcho, the tall guy on the left, alert but relaxed. To the right, the challenger. He decides this due to the tense, forward jut of the guy's chin and the angled slope of his shoulders. And then behind, erect and on edge, the Bodyguard. N'Doch thinks this one looks less sure of himself than the others, but all three of these guys look as tough as any gang leader he's ever known. For that matter, so does Margit. He can almost smell the aura of blood and gunpowder they bring with them. Well, no, probably not gunpowder. Not yet. He looks for weapons, sees none. Now he wishes he'd taken Papa Dja up on some of those history books he was always offering. He'd like to know what to expect.

They pull up in the center of the yard. Margit vaults off her horse and the dogs fall silent, like this is some sort of signal. The women crowd around immediately, reaching for bridles and reins, calling out greetings. The horses are steaming. Ice stiffens their manes and tails, mounding up in the straps and buckles of the tack. A laden packhorse straggles in out of the gloom and is led aside.

The tall man on the left swings stiffly out of his saddle. He shrugs back his hood, brushing snow from the folds of his cloak. In the glow of lantern light, N'Doch catches a metallic glint in the wide cuffs of the man's gloves, and in the close-fitting headgear worn under his hood. Curious, N'Doch steps in a little closer, until he can make out the fine steel links meshed together, and understands that the man has on body armor. *Chain mail.* The term floats up from some memory of an ancient history vid. Wow, N'Doch marvels. I'm seeing knights in armor.

The Honcho wears a tired, apologetic air. But he calls over his shoulder to the Bodyguard in the low kind of voice that carries, casual with command. "You may uncover, Wender."

"Yes, my lord."

My lord. N'Doch's never heard anyone say that for real before, and it might strike him funny if this wasn't clearly such serious biz. The musician in him relishes the addition of a few bass notes to the symphony of women's voices he's listened to for so many days. And he notes approvingly that Margit has been sensible about security. Before shoving off his hood, the Bodyguard yanks down the blindfold he's worn for the inward journey and lets it hang knotted at his throat. He blinks and looks around.

The Honcho hauls off a glove and combs back his mesh headpiece, revealing cropped gray hair, a damp, weathered face worn thin with travel, and a flash of red within the darkness of his cloak. N'Doch studies him. An older man, not old. Still strong and vital, but with a lifetime's hard messages revising his features. Raven has come forward to meet him and is holding his horse's bridle. His smile speaks mostly of relief as he bends to plant a quick kiss on her cheek. "Can't fight worth a damn in this weather. Thought we'd come visit."

N'Doch wonders if the Honcho's easy informality is an artifact of dragon simultaneous translation, or if he's got a few more expectations to dump. In the vids, knights in armor always spoke real stiff. He'll never know for sure till he can speak the language for himself.

"Strange company you're keeping," Raven murmurs.

"Isn't it?" The Honcho straightens, his eyes scanning the little crowd until they settle on Rose, standing still as a statue on the terrace, smiling.

"Rosie," he murmurs. "Forgive the unannounced intrusion." He strides across the hard-packed snow to take Rose in his arms.

Rose says, before her rich voice is completely smothered in his cloak, "It's just as well you've come. The dragons have returned."

He lays a finger to her lips, tossing back a quick nod at the men in the yard. But his face lights with boyish wonder. "Dragons? There are more than one now?"

With the Honcho for sure identified, N'Doch turns his attention to the Challenger, who's remained slumped and silent on his horse. The women seem awkward with him. They haven't gathered around to greet him like they did the Honcho, like he's a stranger, or maybe it's something else. It's too dark to tell, but N'Doch senses a glare smoldering under the shadow of the guy's hood, and a tight-sprung readiness to him, even in his current posture of total disregard which N'Doch reads as a sullen fiction. The Body-guard dismounts, giving his horse up to one of the red-headed twins with a grateful nod. He comes around beside the Challenger's horse. He's big, this Bodyguard, almost as tall as the Honcho but younger and broader, the very defi-nition of muscle. N'Doch would not like to meet him alone in an alley. But his manner is clearly deferential as he shoots a quick glance up at the hooded rider.

"My lord, if you will allow me . . ."

The Challenger lets his horse dance a little, and looks away. N'Doch decides this guy is gonna be the trouble.

Pulling off his own gloves, the Bodyguard, who the Hon-cho has called Wender, clamps them between his teeth, then reaches up to the front of the guy's saddle to untie a long piece of red cloth. N'Doch is interested to see that they've bound the Challenger's wrists. Wender pulls the cloth free, then grabs the horse's reins at the bit to steady it so the rider can dismount. The man does not move. Wender looks like he'd rather not plead. "My lord baron?"

"Let me," says Raven, easing up beside him. The big man looks down at her, then bows a little and stands back. Raven lays a familiar hand on the rider's calf, still neatly stowed in his stirrup. Again, N'Doch spots the dull gleam of mail. "Hello, Dolph," said Raven. "Aren't you coming in?"

The man raises his hands, shakes his wrists out. Slowly, as if making a big ceremony out of it, he reaches to loosen the blindfold that had been invisible under his hood. Then he turns to stare down at the woman beside his knee. He lets out a little snort of disbelief. "Christ Almighty! Raven?"

"Yes, it's me, Dolph."

"I thought you were . . ."

"Dead? Well, that was the general idea."

"Where am I? Why are you here?"

"I live here. Finally found my proper calling in life. My, haven't we both grown up a lot since I saw you last . . . ?" Raven smiles up at the guy, and N'Doch feels just the faintest stirrings of jealousy.

The guy studies her. He looks like he's gonna say something, then thinks better of it. Instead, he flicks his boot out of his stirrup, swings the opposite leg up and over his horse's neck and is out of his saddle, upright and ready on the ground before N'Doch can take a second breath.

Now that he's down, N'Doch sizes him up: not tall—both N'Doch and the bodyguard are taller, and the Bodyguard is broader. But the Challenger is solid enough, and *fast*. He'll be the one to worry about in a knife fight. His hood has fallen back, and N'Doch sees he's also a handsome dude, if you like the blond, rugged type. He wears a neatly trimmed beard, probably to make him look older than his men, since he can't be a day over thirty. His eyes are dark for a blond, though. He has that sort of intense gaze N'Doch has seen on hungry fish hawks. Even without looking in his eyes, N'Doch can feel the reined-in anger radiating from him like heat. He's surprised the snow doesn't just melt right off the guy.

Raven seems to expect some further greeting, but she doesn't get it. The guy throws a quick glance at her, an even swifter punishing glare at the bodyguard, then lets his eyes sweep the darkening farmstead, the yard, the outbuildings, the Big House itself, and the little crowd of women who are now watching him, awaiting his next move. He takes his time—N'Doch admires his control—before he locks eyes with the tall man up on the terrace and growls, "Heinrich, where in hell have you brought me?"

Chapter Eight

The God's dais is empty when the High Priestess makes her entrance with her retinue into the Hall of Audiences. Paia is relieved, though the thick air bears that dry tang of heated metal that the God brings with him, and she suspects he's just been there, then left on another of his jaunts. She has not seen the God since he delivered his ultimatum, which she has begun to think of with a capital "U," but given its general subject matter, she did expect he'd show up to supervise this month's Presentation, if only to make sure that she didn't reject any even half-likely candidate.

Paia mounts the three wide marble steps. As usual, the Hall is hot and stuffy. Orange afternoon light slants through the clerestory to fall artfully on her ceremonial chair. Without seeming to, she tries to adjust the thin cut-velvet cushion to a more comfortable position. Its gold-wire tassels are as big as her fist and always in the way. The chair itself is high and wide and brilliantly gilded. Its tall, square back is deeply carved with geometric detail framing a huge central icon in the brightest gilt of all: the Winged God Rampant. The sharp edges of his thousand intricately wrought scales poke Paia in the back if she leans against it. She bites off a groan. "Survive the day," indeed. If only she can survive *this* day.

Before, she hasn't thought much about the physical discomfort involved in almost all of the god's ceremonies. Often, she's been ironically grateful to have a reason to stay awake during the more tedious of his endless rituals. For twelve years, she has accepted without question whatever the God demanded of her. She was practically a child, recently orphaned, when the God came to the Citadel. She has fitted herself to his needs ever since because the payback has been her survival. By becoming his Priestess, Paia was allowed to continue living in her family's fortress, fed and protected from the terrible world outside, as her father and sister had fed and protected her until they died.

But in the Library this morning, the House Comp informed her that today is her birthday, as it has on every other birthday—an event that would otherwise go unremarked, for the God does not believe in giving notice to the passage of earthly time. But this birthday is her twenty-eighth, and for no reason that she can articulate, Paia finds this significant. The same way she finds the God's Ultimatum significant. She has recovered from her initial shock about it, but of all the duties the God has ever pressed on her, this seems the most thoughtless and tyrannical. Well, not thoughtless. Paia knows he's up to something. But it actually makes her angry with him, in a way she's never dared to be.

Meanwhile, she's also aware that she's beautiful, twenty-eight years old (now), and still a virgin. She knows what sex is. The House Comp has told her all about it, and she thinks she deserves a little. But her access to men is strictly controlled by the God. If she so much as looks at a servant or soldier, the man in question is never seen in the Citadel again. So part of her is ready to give the God's plan some serious thought. She cannot see that she has any other choice. She's spent too much of her youth alone on a dais or up in her studio in front of an easel.

She settles herself as comfortably as she can on the impossible throne. At least, being within the Citadel, she has been able to leave the God's gun behind and doesn't have to find an invisible place for that hard little lump. Three of the nameless First Daughters flit about, arranging the filmy, glittering yards of her train so that the folds fall seductively around her long, bared legs and nearly naked torso. The fabric sticks to her clammy skin in long damp wrinkles. She can't imagine this to be alluring, but how can she know for sure? Despite the God's empty dais, the Honor Guard stationed in the shadows along the four walls of the Hall all stare stonily away from her.

Paia knows she's beautiful. She can see it in the hastily averted eyes of the soldiers, even in some of the women's. She can see it in the hungry glances of the Suitors. These men submit to the humiliation of a Presentation for the same reasons that she does the God's bidding without question: fear, and a desire for the safety and comfort that becoming Consort to the High Priestess of the Temple would allow them. But part of that comfort—she can see it in their eyes—would be possessing her exquisite body, with its firm full breasts and unblemished skin. She is a rare and precious commodity in the world: an unmutated, undamaged, perfect physical specimen, an Ideal. The God has told her so himself. It's why he chose her as his Priestess. His own terrible beauty and power is another such Ideal, he says. It is their duty, then, to the Faithful of the Temple, to exhibit themselves openly, so that their despairing flock can be uplifted by the sight of their perfection. The God's perfection is of course unobtainable. But hers, he has decreed, is not . . . at least, for the right man.

Paia's thoughts drift to the painting up in the tower, shrouded on its easel. Another ideal, one not about power or possession. But also, an ideal that no longer exists. At least, Paia muses, I am still around to be possessed. And controlled. She has long understood that all the elaborate trappings and solemnity surrounding the Presentation of the Suitors are a masquerade for the God's own personal breeding program. Crossing her perfection with another's should produce an even more perfect child. And Paia does not object. Why not improve the chances that her children, should she prove able to produce any, will be healthy and able? If the Sons and Daughters of the God of the Apocalypse are to take up the reins of the world in its Last Days, as the God has promised, the more superior they are, the better. The greater their chance to pull the world back from the brink. But there's time for that, surely. Why is the God suddenly so impatient?

Paia senses that she is wandering into uncharted territory. She leans back to press her bare shoulder blade against the spiky carving of the chair. A sharp dose of the here-and-now always serves to bring her back from the edge. Too much speculation is dangerous. When she has her balance again, she nods at Son Luco, who has taken up his station at the bottom of the steps leading up to her chair. Luco loves the Presentations. The closest thing to real intimacy that Paia ever shares with him is their private meeting afterward, during which they are supposed to review the virtues and drawbacks of the various rejected Suitors, but which invariably descends into dish and gossip.

Now he stands, imposing and erect in all his shining regalia, one step into the shaft of hot sun from the windows above. His gilt-sandaled feet toe the edge of the narrow strip of carpet that cuts the Hall in half, from the Priestess' throne, straight down the center to the main doors at the far end. Another strip crosses at right angles midway, leading to the Left and Right Disrobing Chambers. Luco raises the heavy gilt staff held in the crook of his arm, and two acolytes pull open the doors of the Right Chamber.

The first Suitor enters. He is robed in white, as he is allowed to be, until the High Priestess requests a Viewing. Paia wonders if word ever gets around that she's been making this request less and less often. Could this account for some of the God's impatience? She has developed an Ideal of her own, during the three years since the Presentations began, which she has not discussed with the God. Perhaps she should. She wouldn't wish to be compelled to accept a Suitor who does not fit it.

She knows this particular Suitor will not do the moment he turns the corner in mid-hall and comes toward her at the slow, ritual pace. He is good-looking enough, his bronzy features are more or less regular, with only the slightest list to his nicely broad shoulders. But she sees terror and piety in his eyes, and not much else. She lets him approach and kneel. He does not even try to meet her gaze. He's very young, she sees. His hands, holding the robe closed across his chest, are trembling. Perhaps his parents have put him up to this. They as well would stand to gain from his new-won riches. She offers her most gracious Nod of Rejection, and dismisses him without a Viewing.

The next candidate is older than usual. He turns the corner briskly, the long folds of his robe neatly composed and invisibly held in place. He kneels, presenting himself in a respectful but businesslike manner, as if hoping to impress her with his maturity and his understanding that this is, after all, just another kind of trade-and-barter. A merchant? She's told there are one or two left. Paia is intrigued. Takes a certain strength of mind to carry on with commerce during the Last Days, after all. And this man would probably be kind to her. He might even be interesting to talk to. But the skin on his cheeks is patchy and much too pale. Although each candidate is required under Temple oath to swear themselves free of disease, Paia doesn't trust that formality. Again, she is gracious but sends the man off without a Viewing.

The third is darkly handsome, but she hears in his voice the same dullness she's seen in the eyes of the first young man. The fourth is thin and suppressing a cough. Paia thinks what a desperate act of delusion it has been for this one to subject himself to the cost and time and procedures required for becoming a Suitor. More than once, she has wondered what happens to all these failed candidates. Do they return home to disgrace or is it seen as just another chance gone wrong in a life made up of such things?

And so the afternoon wears on, through a fifth, sixth, and seventh. Paia is getting bored, and she can see Luco shifting his weight as if his tall, bright sandals are pinching his feet. So she calls for a Viewing just to placate him, to stir him up a little so he won't disgrace himself or the Temple by falling asleep where he's standing. The eighth Suitor drops his robe to his shoulders and spreads it hesitantly. Paia spares him merely a glance, but signals him to turn so that Luco can receive the full effect. When the poor man has been kindly dismissed, Luco rolls his eyes. The irony is not lost on Paia, and surely not on Luco either, that he himself is the closest thing to a perfect physical specimen that's walked into this hall in a long, long time. Perhaps the God would be satisfied if she had Luco's child. Paia eyes him speculatively, wondering if he could manage it. At least there would be no complications about romance.

A ninth Suitor enters. Paia's attention is caught by the unusual grace and confidence of his bearing. His well-shaped head is held high, allowing his long chestnut hair to ripple across his muscular shoulders. When he rounds the corner, Paia hides a reflexive little gasp. Something new at last. The man's robe is already open, artfully and partly revealing a sculpted chest, neat hips and strong, trim legs. He has high cheekbones and a fine, chiseled mouth, now relaxed into a sultry smile. His dark gaze fixes Paia with the same intense kind of invitation that the God lures her with when he wants something from her. But this man is material. No doubt he can deliver what his eyes are promising.

Paia is momentarily stunned, not just by his boldness but by the sharp thrill that rises in her, by her undeniable urge to peer into the shadows of his open robe. She has seen a lot of naked men during the course of the Presentations. But this one is different. She retreats behind her sternest mask of authority, but her show of chill scrutiny does not fluster him. He stands patiently while she studies him, then shakes his hair back a little and shifts his weight imperceptibly so that his robe falls farther open. His eyes do not stray from hers for an instant. He is beautiful. He is a perfect specimen. Suddenly Paia wishes the God were here, to help her choose. What if it is . . . is this the one? Already she wants to touch this man, wants him to touch her, everywhere. But she can't see his hands. A man's hands are important, but this one has left his hidden in the folds of his robe while all the rest of his assets are fully offered to her view. Perhaps there is something wrong with them, some injury or deformity. She ought to request a full Viewing, except now she's feeling oddly possessive of him, resentful that she must publicly display this beauty that could be meant for her alone, for his eyes say he sees nothing in the room but her. She asks him his name to hear him speak, and his voice is throaty and low, as if he, too, is overcome by this encounter. She hears the name he offers but can't recall it a moment later. She beckons him nearer, then realizes that he has not yet knelt to her. But she cannot help but notice that her nearness is causing his sex to swell and rise within the caressing shadows of his robe. She knows, and he knows, that only she can see this, and he lets it happen. She cannot make herself look away. He smiles at her over half-lidded eyes. His lips part to show the very tip of a roving tongue. He lets his hips loll forward lazily, offering himself to her, and Paia is seized by an erotic madness, though somewhere at the back of her lust-fogged brain, an alarm is going off. She forgets that there are several dozen other people in the room. She leans forward and presents her hand, thinking only of how much she needs him to feel the sudden warmth between her thighs.

His left hand appears from beneath his robe, unmarked and whole. He reaches, grasps her hand. With one firm tug, he pulls her into his arms. Paia does not struggle. She feels him hot and taut against her and her body is already molding itself to his nakedness when the alarm goes double-time in her head. A cool kiss of steel slides past her hip as his right arm curls around her back to press her tightly to his groin. He is stronger than she ever imagined. She tries to cry out, but he smothers her cry with his mouth and tongue. One hand, warm and longing, slips down around her thigh to invade the softness between her legs. The other, cold and hard, rises between her breasts. His blade is at her neck but in the instant that he hesitates, betrayed by the heat of his own very real desire, Luco is on him from behind, hauling him off, hurling him away from her, kicking him viciously and pinning him to the floor with the gilded staff of office. By then, the Honor Guard has bolted across the room to take over.

Before Paia can collapse into a heap of shock and humiliation, Son Luco scoops her up as he might a child and hustles her from the hall.

He is not so gentle when he gets her up to her chambers, trailed by the panicked captain of the Honor Guard and a few of his more alert men.

"He'll burn you to goddamn cinders, the whole sorry lot of you!" he bellows at them as he shoulders the door shut in their faces. He dumps Paia unceremoniously onto her bed and looms over her, his big hands waving. "What were you *thinking*?"

Paia huddles, shuddering. She can't really believe it herself. "I wasn't. I wasn't. I just wasn't!"

"I'll say!"

"I'll never . . . I couldn't . . . help myself."

She weeps a bit, while Luco paces back and forth, from

bed to window. "Never seen such a spectacle in all my life! You spoiled brat!" He throws up his hands and paces away again.

"I'll thank you to remember who you're talking to," she sniffs.

He stops, folds his arms. "I'm talking to a spoiled brat! You could have been killed! Did you even think about what he'll do to the rest of us if we let anything happen to you?"

This brings her upright to look at him. He's wan and shaken himself, and angry enough to have lost all his decorum. She's never had Luco in her rooms. He looks bigger here, and rougher-edged. Like he's somehow taking up more space than usual, perhaps because she's never, ever seen him so furious. Rage is not one of Luco's public moods. She decides to let the name-calling go by. "So I guess this wasn't another of your revenue-producing plots . . . ?"

Luco rounds on her. "How could you even think such a thing?"

Paia buries her head in her arms. "He can't hear of this, Luco. He can't! He's not very happy with me right now."

"Of course he'll hear of it! How are we going to keep it from him, when you insist on displaying your lust in front of the entire world!"

"I don't have lust, I . . . well, maybe I did a little."

"A *little*? My dear girl . . ."

"It's the God's own fault! He's the one pushing me to pick a Suitor all of a sudden!"

"He is? Really?"

"Really. Like it was an order."

"Huh. Well, you can bet he didn't mean a trained assassin got up as a street prostitute."

Paia stares at him. "Assassin? Prostitute? Was it so clear to everyone but me? Oh, no!" Somehow this is worse than practically losing her virginity right there in the Hall of Audiences. She throws herself back on the bed, sobbing.

Luco slows his pacing, then sits down beside her. "Well, not everyone. Most of them were half-asleep by then. And, I admit, he was beautiful."

This makes her sob all the harder. "Why, Luco? Why do

they do it? What have I ever done but serve them as the God requires?"

"It's simple: they go after you because they can't get at him. And this was a novel strategy, using your own worst impulses against you. The guy planned it very well, I must say."

His pragmatism soothes her, despite a certain undertone of relish. She rolls over to look up at him. "All by himself? A heresy of one?"

"Most likely the Greens again. He was only the weapon."

"Was? Surely, the God would want him kept alive for questioning?"

"I thought you'd rather the God didn't hear about all this."

"No . . . yes, he must know. I mean, how could someone get a knife through all his security procedures?"

Luco crosses his legs. He roughs his long hair back and lets his top leg—still wrapped in its gilded sandal—swing restlessly. "Stupidity or betrayal. It's always one or the other. And I suppose I'll have to bear part of the blame. Our only hope is that he'll be too distracted by this business over the hill to care."

"What business?"

He waves a dismissive hand. "Oh, some minor disagreement with one of the villages. He's down there dealing with it."

Paia has never been to the villages. But for the God's frequent evangelical forays, she might even forget they're there, supplying the Temple with food and service personnel in return for the God's protection. "Well, anyway, you won't take the blame. It was my fault. Besides, you saved me!" She realizes she hasn't even thanked him yet. Maybe she is just a spoiled brat. She gets up on her knees and puts her arms around him from behind to kiss his cheek. She's never been that familiar with him before, and is not sure why she's doing it now, except that the . . . incident has left her feeling unusually vulnerable. She needs to assure herself of Luco's loyalty and support. He accepts her embrace but does not particularly warm to it. "I'll tell him everything, I promise!"

"You better."

It occurs to her how much the God will enjoy hearing her tell this particular story. "Oh, Luco, I wish you could just be my Suitor. Everything would be so much easier."

Luco barks a dry laugh, pats her arm. "I don't think so, dear girl. I don't think so."

Then Paia remembers what the God had said: *choose someone you'll tire of quickly.* Sometimes she thinks Luco understands the God better than she does.

When he's pulled himself together and straightened all his priestly regalia to his satisfaction in front of Paia's full-length mirror, Luco delivers a stern warning to think twice the next time she's about to do something foolish, then puts on his Temple face and leaves her alone.

Paia immediately strips off her ceremonial garb and digs out her beloved T-shirt and sweats. It's not the right time for hot water, so she douses herself with cold, regardless of the waste. She feels exposed, rubbed raw by this near-fatal encounter and the madness that precipitated it. Her madness. Luco is right. What could she have been thinking? The shapeless soft garments enclose her. They comfort her with concealment. She braids up her damp hair, pulling it back tightly from her face. She hopes she looks awful. She stows the God's little gun in a hip pocket. She won't let herself be without it ever again. Now she feels sleek and efficient, and calm enough to confront the guards outside her door who will, no doubt, be shocked by her undecorated appearance, and will try to dissuade her from leaving her rooms.

A doubled contingent of chastened faces slew around to stare at her when she opens the door. The duty captain is an older woman whose eyes are already exhausted by the vision of her own anticipated incineration at the hand of an angry god. Right now, she couldn't care less what the High Priestess is wearing.

Paia nods. "I'll be working in my studio until dinner, Captain."

"Yes, Mother." The woman looks faintly relieved to see her alive and apparently unharmed. And no doubt she has feared some further madness to be dealt with, some scheme or reckless journey by their unruly High Priestess that the Guard will be duty-bound to keep up with. But these win-

dowless, dead-end corridors, even half-lit, are easy to defend. The captain bows, and when Paia turns down the hall,
she signals four of her squad to follow at a discreet
distance.

Paia gains the tower entrance. Light sifts down from an
invisible skylight high at the top of the shaft. She starts her
climb without a backward glance. She knows the guards
will not follow. The deal is, when she's up in the studio,
they guard the bottom of the stairs. She takes the steep
stone steps as briskly as she can manage, driving herself up
without a rest even after she's gasping for breath. A dose
of self-punishment, Paia reflects, and minor enough, given
the severity of her offense.

In truth, she cannot believe how stupid she was, letting
appetite win out like that over good sense and training and
the God's constant reminders that his High Priestess is always a target. *Mere appetite? Ha.* The blinding force of the
need she'd felt in the Hall still lingers in her body like a
drug, evaporating her calm with its little aftershocks. It was
almost as if the urge had come upon her from outside. Like
the evil eye, or a spell, she muses. But Paia does not believe
in such things, so the blame must be turned inward, on
herself.

On the top step, she stands panting. The big room is
bright with hot afternoon glare. The shadows are long and
as sharp-edged as knives. She's not even sure why she's
come, except that she felt compelled to. Not by the familiar
eager stirrings of an idea brimming in her head. Paia hesitates. Her eyes are drawn to the shrouded easel, and she
can no longer deny it. She's come to see the painting. To
take comfort from its lush and restful tones. Usually, when
she finishes a painting, she sets it aside. None of her stark
portraits of the neighboring slopes and crags decorate the
walls of her bedchamber, or any other walls in the Citadel.

But this painting calls out to her. The mysterious circumstance of its creation hints at some pernicious heresy rising
in Paia's soul. But perhaps it can offer her some corrective
insight or message of truth, if only she can decipher it.

She moves quickly to the easel and throws back the concealing tarp. Once again, the rich, moist life of the landscape leaps out to envelope her. The tree-softened curve

of its hills and the lost peaceful sweetness of its silvery river bring a start of tears to her eyes.

Then Paia notices two things.

The sky overhanging her pristine imaginary valley is not as clear as she remembers. Clouds are massing behind the smoothly rolling horizon, a dark crenellation as architectural as the ruined skylines of the cities she secretly reads about in the House Comp's library. She can't imagine how she missed noticing them before. But she'd been spent and bleary-eyed after the long night's work, and one of the miraculous qualities of a painting is how it often reveals itself over time. If you bother to go back and look at it again, which Paia rarely does.

The thing she is sure was not in the painting when she left it is a small, folded scrap of paper. It's pinned to the tray of the easel with the sturdy blade she uses for cutting canvas.

Her first reaction is to grab at her hip pocket for the God's gun, and take a swift look around. Someone has been here, and might be still. After the treachery in the Hall of Audiences, Paia is no longer confident about either the skill or the loyalty of her guards. But this room has few corners that could hide an assailant. A quick search confirms that it's empty.

Her next thought is almost as unnerving. Someone has seen this painting. Some other person has shared this revelation of her inner longings. Longings more secret and forbidden even than sex. Someone who might report her to the God.

Paia's hand trembles as she jerks the heavy blade free and unfolds the paper. The note is brief, neatly handwritten in a reddish-brown substance that Paia fears is blood.

It reads: *"What price survival?"*

Paia folds the note away in her pocket and walks quickly toward the stairs.

The God does not come visiting that evening, as she has feared he would. When her chambermaid has arrived with the evening ration, helped her undress, turned down the bed, and bowed her way from the room, Paia takes a cup of water to her window alcove and draws the heavy drapes aside. She unwraps the note in the light of an oil lamp, and reads it again.

What price survival What could it mean?

To the south, the ruddy sky is brighter than usual. In the ragged notches between the crags, she sees a distant glow and flicker. Somewhere out there, something big is burning.

Chapter Nine

He looked exactly as she remembered him, not as she would have wished to remember him, as the golden lord in that fateful barn in Erfurt. He was as she remembered from her dreams, which had revealed to her so clearly the sad progression of Baron Köthen's disillusionment. She should not have been surprised by Rose's unflattering description. But she had not wanted to accept the truth of her dreams quite so literally.

From a shadowed corner of the great room, Erde watched Köthen move into the lantern light as if into a dungeon. She saw his eyes sweep the borders of the room the way he'd swept the night air with his sword in the clearing where he'd found the murdered prince, arc after glittering arc of shamed outrage. He wore civility like an ill-fitting garment. He stopped in the middle of the room, and as he stood there uncertainly, his face for an instant was as raw and open as a child's, exposing to any who observed him his impatience at being kept from the battle, his horror at being suddenly powerless to command his own surroundings. Erde had seen that he'd arrived with his hands bound. She could not imagine what could have induced Hal—who should have understood him better than anyone—to submit his former foster son and squire to such humiliation. Rose said events had been hard on Baron Köthen, but this was clearly an understatement. All the ease in him was gone. Now he moved like man whose skin was filled with broken glass.

A moment later, his face closed again, as he let habits of breeding and pragmatism master his outrage. As a guest of the house, he would be expected to behave. Yet Erde saw how close he was to the limit of his own good sense, how his dry humor had turned bitter, how rage was eroding his optimism as well as his grace. And how, when she stepped bravely out of the shadow to greet him, his eyes swept past her as something unrecognized, unfamiliar, unimportant, in his single-minded search for answers to his predicament.

She saw all that, and also saw how Hal eyed him with covert concern. How the third man's attention never left him. The two of them, watching Baron Köthen sidelong, as one might a drunk or a madman, to keep him from hurting himself, or someone else. Soon, she couldn't bear to see it any longer. She slipped out of the room into a back hall and fled to the consoling company of the dragon in the barn.

"Under the protection of *women*, Heinrich? You think less of my skills than ever I thought." The Challenger grins in a death's-head sort of way and tosses his wet cloak down on a stool.

Coming in behind him with the others, N'Doch notices how this guy walks into a room like he owns it, or if he doesn't yet, he will soon enough. Idly, N'Doch wonders if he could learn how to do that.

Deliberately, Rose picks up the cloak and hands it off to one of the twins. "Do you intend to leave him, then, Heinrich?"

The Honcho spreads his hands. Now N'Doch understands his air of apology. "If you'll take him, Rosie. Don't know how else to keep him alive."

"Or even if you should," remarks Rose.

The Honcho sighs. N'Doch reads pain in him, and not a little ambivalence. "His last escapade cost me three of my best men."

"How I love being talked about in the third person!" The Challenger turns neatly on his heel. "My lady Rose.

Forgive my ill manners. I haven't yet greeted you." He bows to her, low and crisp. "The years have not diminished your beauty nor your fabled wisdom. But I was unaware that you had gone into the business of arrest and detainment."

Rose returns his satirical stare. "Don't be sullen, Adolphus Michael. It doesn't become you. Don't worry. We'll keep you employed and busy. You'll see it's all for the best."

"I fail to see how."

Rose moves past him like he's some misbehaving son she's ignoring. She catches the tall guy's cloak as he shrugs it off, and passes that one, too, into waiting hands. The issue of why the Challenger is here seems clear to everyone but N'Doch. "Come, warm up by the fire. You must be cold and hungry."

"An understatement," mutters the Challenger.

"Rosie," says the Honcho, "This is Dolph's captain, Kurt Wender. The best of men. If you're willing and up to this, he'll be keeping our good baron company."

The Bodyguard steps forward with a bow, much more polite than the Challenger's. "My lady."

Rose smiles at him. "I'm nobody's lady, Captain Wender, except perhaps Heinrich's. Call me Rose. Please, come by the fire. You are welcome."

Wender nods gratefully. He finds a bench by the fire and drops onto it with a sigh. He accepts a mug of heated wine from the other of the twins. N'Doch's glad to see he's too much the man's man to carry all this bowing and scraping any further.

Raven fills another mug from the big crock warming just inside the fireplace. She offers it to the Challenger, who looks her over. N'Doch sees speculation but little interest. Still, he can't help eavesdropping.

"Where have you been, Raven?"

"Oh, here and there. Mostly here."

"Ever since?"

She nods. "I was sorry to hear about your father."

"It's seven years since I assumed the title, Raven."

"Still. He was always kind to me."

The Challenger frowns, as if he resents any pleasant memory. "A good man."

'Yes. And you? You look thin, Dolph. Slim pickings along the road?"

"Is it any different here? Out there, people are killing each other for food now. Blizzards in September! The countryside is starving."

"Can't something be done to help?" Raven asks mildly.

The Challenger flicks her a disbelieving glance, then shakes his head. "That, dear Raven, is what I was *trying* to do."

Raven just smiles at him and again holds up the steaming mug. He takes it, then looks at it as if he's forgotten what it's for, and sets it aside. He's already moving about, measuring the walls of his prison. "The hell with war and politics. By the way, where is here?"

"Welcome to Deep Moor."

"Many thanks. What's Deep Moor?"

"A place apart. Away from the ills of the world. Or so we thought."

The Challenger snorts. "Until I arrived to spoil your idyll." He paces back to her, stops, brushes her chin gently with the back of his hand. "You've grown no less beautiful, Raven."

"Nor you, Dolph "

"Are you the bait, then?"

"Pardon?"

"To keep the prisoner docile and pacified during his incarceration?"

Raven tilts her head. "Such bitter thoughts, Dolph."

"I have cause," he growls, and turns away.

Raven shrugs. She joins Rose as she draws the Honcho into the warmth of the big stone hearth. "We were just making dinner when you arrived."

"Dinner!" The tall guy's booming laugh is over the top, N'Doch thinks. Like the poor man's hoping the black mood he's brought into the room can be denied by applying the proper amount of cheer. "Wender! When d'you figure our last meal was?"

"Two days past, my lord, at least."

"My count also. And a poor meal it was at that." He reaches eagerly for the mug Raven has put on the table beside him. "I'm any day glad to ride into Deep Moor, but this time gladder than ever. It's bad out there, Rosie. It'd be bad even if we weren't trying to fight a war. Stores are running low everywhere, and when the hell-priest provisions his armies, he leaves nothing behind for the villages. Not a scrap, not a bean! So they're angry at any soldier who rides their way, no matter whose side he's on!" He pauses, looks at the floor, his cheer deflating into frustration and despair. "Truth is, we could use a good feeding."

"And you shall have it."

The prospect seems to buck him up a bit, and he grins. "You might even get Dolph to eat something. He's not been fond of my cooking."

Over his shoulder, the Challenger retorts, "If you can refer to hacking at a hunk of frozen bread with your sword as 'cooking.' "

"Picky, picky," mutters the Honcho, but N'Doch can see he's pleased to have raised even a sprout of humor from such stony ground. He sips from his mug, shaking his head with grim appreciation, and sips again, drawing Rose aside. "But what news? If the travelers have returned, where is Milady Erde?"

"She's . . ." Rose looks around. "Oh. Well, she was here . . ."

From her seat by the fire, Raven says, "I think she went out to the barn."

"Not here to greet me?"

"Well, *he's* in the barn, no doubt expecting a visit."

"Ah. Yes, that's it." Again, he looks pleased, "Then we must comply immediately. Did all go well with their journey?"

"News over dinner," says Rose, "and a visit after. First, there are other introductions to be made."

She looks N'Doch's way. Suddenly he realizes that the group he came in with has evaporated quietly to the other parts of the house. In the kitchen, the clatter of food preparation starts up like background music. He and the dragon-as-Sedou are left stranded by the door, with the girl nowhere to be seen. Rose beckons them forward out of the shadows. All three men turn at the creak of their footsteps across the old wooden floor.

It's weird, but N'Doch wishes he had a guitar in his hands. He feels at a distinct disadvantage. Not that one song, even the right one, could explain or justify his presence here completely. But it could sure help.

With the shedding of the long, concealing cloaks, he sees that the men are dirty and wet through, that their faces are bruised, that their layers of silk and leather and mail are muddied, bloodstained, and torn. What's more, weapons have come into view. Not on the Challenger, of course, but the Bodyguard Wender and the tall guy both wear sleek, leather-sheathed knives at their waists and swords on their hips. Swords. Real ones. Fine steel, glinting with firelight. To N'Doch, these big blades seem impossibly long. He can't see how you wouldn't trip on them. The tall guy is just unbuckling his to lay it aside when Rose brings N'Doch and Sedou to his attention. Having done so, she looks momentarily at a loss.

N'Doch grins. Rose speechless? He hasn't seen this in the whole week he's known her. *"Mais, par où commencer?"* he says to her. *Where do you start?*

"Eh bien, mon petit. J'en sais rien."

He sees the men eyeing him, over Rose's shoulder. Taking in his youth, his height, how his head nearly grazes the ceiling's lowest beams. Noting Sedou's athletic build, and the shared alien ebony of their skin, the *difference* in their faces. These men have seen most of what their world has to offer, N'Doch can tell, but probably their world doesn't include Africa yet. They don't know what they're looking at, and they're not used to that. He recalls how the girl stared at him so much at first, mostly when she thought he wasn't looking. These guys are not so polite. They start staring and keep right on at it.

The dragon stirs in his mind.

We could be men to them, or demons.

It gets real quiet for a moment in that darkening room, and N'Doch wonders if he's in any danger. The windows have gone all iron gray, blank with night and snow. Nowhere to run. He's got his eye on the Honcho, whose bright, curious gaze shifts from himself to Sedou and back a few times, questing, reading for information and understanding. This guy knows something important's afoot, when strangers—male, alien strangers—have preceded him into this women's haven at Deep Moor.

But Rose reels off the names with the ease of a talk

show hostess, like there's no one but us humans in the room. She introduces the Honcho as Heinrich von Engle, late of Weisstrasse. He throws a smile their way and, real quickly, adds, "Just Hal Engle."

The Challenger apparently answers to the name Adolphus Michael von Hoffman, Baron Köthen, a name longer even than Engle's sword, but he volunteers no short-cut of any kind. N'Doch remembers the girl saying her father was a baron and that she grew up in a castle. Must mean this Köthen dude is somebody important.

Rose keeps up the talk show chat as she explains the language problem, that one of these "foreign" visitors speaks German, the other doesn't. N'Doch notices there is no mention of the always ongoing simultaneous translation by dragon power. He decides he's just regained several points of lost advantage. Then the tall guy Engle surprises him by saying quietly to Rose, "I have read of dark men such as these. Have they come from the south below the sea? Is one the mage his lordship sought?"

"No, but N'Doch and Sedou have traveled back with Lady Erde from the place that she went with him."

"Ah." Engle holds up a finger, shakes his head once. His eyes flick toward the Challenger, who's moved off restlessly to stare out a window.

Rose gives this some thought. Then she says aloud, "He doesn't know?"

"Rosie . . ." Engle murmurs.

"If you've brought him to stay, Heinrich, there's no way we can keep it from him."

Engle looks flustered. Oddly, he glances at Sedou, like the "dark man" has said something to him, or might be about to. "I don't think it's . . . well, I hadn't expected them back so soon."

"Really, I'm such an inconvenience to you, Heinrich. Why don't you just get rid of me?" The Challenger turns from his study of gray on gray outside the window. "What don't I know?"

Engle stares down at the floor, then up again at Sedou. His eyes narrow, then refocus suddenly in a kind of veiled wonder, as if he's been asked an unexpected and remarkable question. N'Doch doesn't want to look. He's afraid the dragon's chosen a really stupid moment to shape-shift.

"He wouldn't have believed me if I did tell him, Rose. Never has. He'll require the proof of his senses."

"This is interesting," murmurs Sedou.

"Well," says Rose. "No time like the present."

"I don't . . ." Engle begins. "Wait. Wait." He chews his lip, overgrown with a shaggy mustache, then regards Rose from under lowered brows, like a child planning mischief. "But you said, Rosie, more than one . . . ?"

"Two."

"Is the . . . other . . . ?" He tilts his head toward the barn.

"Not exactly."

"Ahhh. I wish the girl were here to guide me."

"No, you don't."

N'Doch realizes there's some old sort of game playing itself out here between Rose and her lover, like if she just came right out and told him everything he wants to know, he'd be disappointed. Even though it's clear he wants to know it desperately. His gaze drifts back to Sedou.

"Ah. That's it," he says again, more softly. His eyes flutter closed, as if in utter gratitude. N'Doch hears in his voice the same veiled wonder that had been in his look. "Shape-shifter."

Beside him, Sedou stands a little taller.

At the window, the Challenger clears his throat. "Am I to die, my knight, before being offered enlightenment?"

"Wait. Wait. A moment, please. You cannot know how . . ." Engle gropes behind him for the sword he's laid on the table. He takes it in both hands and pulls it slowly from its sheath. N'Doch suppresses the primal shiver that seizes him at the cool rasp of that much steel being drawn. The blade grabs his attention like a shout. It flashes bright shards of firelight into his eyes. Both its faces are honed to an invisible edge, but he can see scarring up and down the length. This blade has been well used. He had a machete once that looked almost as murderous, a weapon he loved, so he is both horrified and mesmerized, like the snake before the mongoose, as Engle sets the empty sheath aside and comes toward him. The man moves easily still, not like an old man but a fighter. N'Doch holds his ground. But it doesn't matter. Engle's wondering gaze is not fixed on him.

The dragon is a whisper in his head.

He knows.

"What? How?" murmurs N'Doch out loud. "Like Baraga?"

The last guy who twigged to what Sedou was had blown N'Doch to bits.

No. Just knows. I'd say, good instincts and a lifetime of study.

Engle approaches, his eyes on Sedou. Five paces away, he stops. "Rosie," he says hoarsely, over his shoulder. "Am I right about this?"

Her reply is loving, and so quiet that N'Doch can barely hear it. "Yes, Heinrich. You are the finest dragon-hunter of them all."

Hunter? N'Doch readies himself, his mind tossing up all the ways he might wrestle that mean-looking gorgeous blade out of the tall guy's hands. Except that Engle is not raising the sword to strike. He's turned it hilt-upward, set its point gingerly to the floor, and gone done on one knee, head bowed, at Sedou's feet. When he speaks, it's in Frankish, more fluent than Rose's, and N'Doch gets an inkling who she learned it from.

"My lord," says Engle. "My sword is ever at your service."

Rose smiles. "Actually, Heinrich, it's 'my lady.' "

"Is it so? An excellent symmetry! My lady, then." Engle is unfazed. "I thought my life's whole purpose satisfied when I pledged myself to one of your kind, my lady. I never dreamed of the good fortune that will allow me to serve two."

The hair stands up on the back of N'Doch's neck. There's something so pure, so absolute in Engle's tone. Without any proof, the guy just *believes.* And Sedou shows no embarrassment at having this old soldier down in front of him. N'Doch watches as his brother grasps the offered sword like he's handled one all his life. The hilt is carved, with the winged figure of a dragon coiled around a tree. Sedou lifts the blade and holds it upright in front of him. He brings it close, lining it up with his nose until his breath fogs the polished metal. Then he sets it back a bit, regarding its gleaming ferocity with solemn bemusement. Like he's moved by thoughts he can't possibly begin to express or explain. Like the sword itself is a whole story to him. The reflection that N'Doch sees in the steel is the dragon's eye, not his brother Sedou's. The voice is Sedou's, but the words come from another time and place as he answers Engle in perfect old German.

"I am glad, Sir Knight, that we meet first at a moment when I possess the hands to take up this blade in gratitude, and return it to you with my acceptance of your pledge of service." Sedou reverses the hilt and extends it forward. N'Doch lets go a breath, amazed. The Challenger, he sees, is staring at them in disbelief.

"What service may I perform?" Engle intones, his eyes shining.

"We will speak of that."

Engle rises, takes the sword, and drops the blade by his side. Then he stands back with a final bow. It all goes so smoothly, it's like they've rehearsed it. Or like they both just instinctively knew what to do. N'Doch feels he's in the presence of something ancient beyond understanding. Beyond *his* understanding, at least. One of the things he likes about life, he decides, is that it's still always catching him by surprise. He thinks of the girl, always going on about dragon lore and dragon purposes, all the stuff he's supposed to know for some reason, and doesn't. *A lifetime of study,* the dragon had said. This must be some of what they're both talking about.

And as quickly as it began, the ritual is over. Engle relaxes, and the dragon-as-Sedou is just Sedou again, a big dark man with a smile that could eat you alive. Engle turns to N'Doch with a little bow.

"And you are her guide? Welcome."

N'Doch starts to stick out his hand, then holds back and returns the bow as best he can. This whole event is feeling like one big performance anyway. But he can tell it's real enough to Engle. And maybe to the others. Across the room by the fire, the Bodyguard Wender is looking pretty weirded out. He's on his feet, easing his half-drawn weapon back into its scabbard as if he's not sure he should.

But the Challenger has set his bearded jaw. "Keep me in the dark, Heinrich, if you must, but explain at least why a King's Knight kneels so readily to this . . . stranger!"

"Ah, an ancient and venerable stranger!"

"I repeat, kneels to a *stranger,* but would not to the best pick among us for healing the kingdom?"

"Not the best until you learn a little control," Engle tosses back with half his attention. He's still grinning and elated.

"What?"

"Or even the best, yes, but not the most legitimate."

"Legitimate?" The Challenger jabs a finger in Sedou's direction. "Is *this* legitimate?" N'Doch notes how quickly the hard rage in him breaks into the open. "What, have you found us some new pretender? One that Otto himself doesn't even know he's sired?"

"No need to be offensive," Raven murmurs from the fireplace.

Engle flashes Sedou a complicit glance, then turns back to the room looking flushed and victorious. "Dolph, Dolph, you misunderstand. This is another thing entirely. You'll be on your knees yourself when you're faced with the truth of it."

"Never!"

"Don't doubt it, lad."

"Don't call me that!" the younger man snarls.

Engle spreads his hands. "Dolph . . ."

"No! Never again! This is ended, Heinrich!" He spins away, then back again immediately, his wrists pressed together in Engle's face. "You bound me! Me! In Erfurt, I showed you greater honor!"

At last Engle focuses on him. "Yes! You did! I freely admit it! But, Dolph, here . . . here in Deep Moor, I could not indulge your current death wish, for the sake of others. You cannot know how precious the thing is that's being guarded here."

"A kingdom is precious, Heinrich! What could be more?" The Challenger moves up on him again, circling. Wender's hand returns to his sword hilt.

"I've tried to tell you, Dolph, how many times over the years! Before I knew myself for sure! I even tried to tell you in Erfurt, but you were so interested in a crown, you wouldn't listen! Now even you will be unable to deny it!"

The Challenger halts his advance. His shoulders go slack like he's had a sudden realization. "What in hell are you talking about?"

"I'm talking about the truth!"

"The truth of what?"

The two men glare at each other until Rose says. "Really, Dolph, the best way to explain it is simply to show you." Rose takes Engle's arm, and then the Challenger's. "Come, gentlemen. This won't take long."

Earth had already been anxious when she fled to him: worried about her, about the war and the safety of Deep Moor, and increasingly impatient to resume his Quest. But it was the big dragon's way to be anxious, just as it was his way to soothe and comfort those in need. Especially his dragon guide, though Erde knew he did not understand why she wept so disconsolately as she curled up against his plated chest.

ARE YOU ILL? YOU SEEM HEALTHY. HAVE YOU NOT EATEN?

I'M NOT HUNGRY.

YOU KNOW YOU SHOULD ALWAYS EAT WHEN YOU HAVE THE CHANCE.

DEAR DRAGON, I FEEL FINE.

YOU DO NOT SOUND FINE. PERHAPS YOU HAVE NOT RESTED ENOUGH?

She had thought her mind completely open to him. Now Erde wondered if certain subtleties of human emotion were simply incomprehensible to a dragon. She found them mysterious enough herself, and she was the one experiencing them. Why should she be so stricken by the plight of a man she barely knew? And how could this sadness also feel so sweet?

The dragon would be no help here, though he'd continue to try until she worried about worrying him, about distracting him from the truly important considerations, like the Quest. For the dragon's sake, then, she must dry her tears and seem to take comfort as he bent his great head over her, rumbling his concern into her mind.

She'd nearly dozed off when she heard the big door slide open. Lanterns glowed at the distant front of the barn. She heard Rose's voice and Hal's, then Köthen's muttered reply. She and the dragon had watched the meeting in the great room through Sedou/Water's eyes. She knew Hal would be obscenely cheerful, as he was now able to raise his life-count of dragons from one to two. And Baron Köthen would be . . . well, perhaps the dragons could help him feel better about his situation, if she could get him to talk with them. She knew from her own experience that the dragons could heal the mind as well as they had healed N'Doch's broken body.

As voices and lanterns approached, Erde scrambled up from her warm nest beside the dragon's foreleg and hid behind the hayrick. Beside the dragon's left claw, her own lantern flickered in the draft from the open door.

"I've a mind just to send you in first and let him eat you," she heard Hal say. "But come on. This way."

She'd chosen a good vantage, a full field of view once they rounded the corner of the big open stall where the dragon lay sleeping. He looked beautiful, she thought, huge and glimmering in the lamplight, fading into darkness behind, so that his true size was exaggerated by the dancing shadows. She saw Hal's eyes light with the fire of a devoted lover. He forgot Baron Köthen for a moment and strode straight to the dragon, to touch two reverent fingers to a huge ivory horn. "My lord Earth," he whispered. "Are you well?"

Köthen followed more slowly, caught a glimpse of what lay massed before him in the dim lamplight, and—midstride—went utterly still.

He looked away, looked back, then for a long time, only his dark eyes moved, absorbing, measuring each detail, assuring himself of the reality of an existence that, all his life, he had denied the possibility of. He shook his head twice in a wordless negative. Finally, he let out a long, long breath and swore softly to himself.

Hal stirred and noticed him standing there. Without a trace of the triumph he must surely be feeling, he stepped aside to gesture Köthen forward. Slowly, Köthen, moved up beside him, his eyes fixed on the dragon as if it might vanish the moment he looked away. His hand strayed to the older man's shoulder, as if nothing awkward had ever passed between them. Whether he was giving or taking support, Erde couldn't be sure. Together, the two men stared up at the dragon's bronzy head and scimitar horns.

"Impressive, my knight," Köthen said, as if speaking was no longer the easiest thing. "Is it alive?"

"Oh, yes."

"Really? Am I dreaming?"

Hal laughed softly. "No, lad, you're not dreaming."

Oddly, Köthen seemed to accept this. "Sweet Jesus. A dragon. Does it . . . breathe fire?"

"No."

"No? How disappointing for you. Does it turn lead into gold?"

"That's alchemy. Have you forgotten all I taught you?"

"Only the stuff I never thought I'd need," Köthen replied ruefully. "Well, does it *hoard* gold, then? Are you rich again?"

"Hah. If he was a hoarder, he'd be unlikely to give me so much as a coin of it." Hal regarded the dragon fondly. "No, there are many things he isn't or doesn't do that one might have expected a dragon to be or do. He doesn't fly either, that is, not as you might define flying."

"As I might?" Köthen turned his gaze from the sleeping dragon to study Hal's face. "And how might you define it?"

Hal grinned at him. "It was he who snatched me from your grasp at Erfurt."

Köthen's chin lifted. "Ah. The first nail in my coffin."

"No, the first was raising your sword against your King."

Köthen frowned, dropped his hand from Hal's shoulder, then let the remark go by. Erde decided his curiosity had got the better of him. "It is true that your sudden disappearance was never adequately explained to me. I blamed all the confusion on the earthquake."

Hal cocked his head, increasingly unable to restrain his immense satisfaction that this conversation was finally taking place. He drew in the air with a finger, outlining a pair of shining ivory horns and a vast swell of plated hide. "He was the earthquake."

"He what?"

"His name," Hal offered, "is Earth."

"It . . . he . . . made the earthquake?"

"Is that so hard to believe, now that you see him before you?"

Köthen frowned again. "I'm afraid it's all rather hard to believe, my knight." He gripped Hal's shoulder again, briefly, then turned away. "A dragon. Congratulations. It's all you ever wanted."

"Not all. I wanted my estates once more in hand, the King secure on his throne, and you fighting beside me."

Köthen growled in his throat. "Leave it, Heinrich!" He paced away, out of the lantern light, saw Rose waiting silently in the shadows, and swerved aside like an animal evading capture.

"But," Hal continued lightly, "he's a fine consolation prize."

Köthen's path became circular and brought him around to be startled again into stillness as the sleeping dragon loomed once more before him. "Jesus Christ Almighty," he muttered. And then he grew thoughtful. "Will it help fight the hell-priest?"

"Perhaps. Although he has a great Mission of his own that he must pursue. A dragon has his own mind, you know." Hal gave up his struggle for restraint and turned his joy on Köthen like a beacon. "I told you there was magic in the world, Dolph!"

Köthen stared back at him, then looked down with a small laugh and a shrug. "So you did, my knight. So you did."

His words were agreeable, but his tone was bitter. Erde guessed that the past weeks together had been a horror of mutual recriminations for these two men, honing this argument and others to a lethal edge. At any moment, they could come to blows. She decided to intervene. She sent the dragon a mental nudge.

SHOW HIM ALL YOU ARE, DEAR DRAGON. HELP HIM TO UNDERSTAND.

The dragon woke and opened one golden eye, as tall as a man. In the darkness of the barn, his gaze glowed with inner fire.

Köthen recoiled. His hand jerked reflexively for the sword that was no longer at his hip, then dropped uselessly to his side. Next to him, Hal Engle bowed, then knelt to bask in the unearthly light. Erde saw Köthen's fingers tremble as the actuality of a living dragon finally overtook him. Before, it could have been a fake, a statue cleverly lit. But now, that one great eye, alight with ancient life—and now the other, as Earth stirred and lifted his big head. Like a man in a raging cyclone, Köthen fought the urge to kneel as Hal had told him he would—and won that skirmish. *This man thinks he should kneel to no one,* Erde noted. But the battle of belief was over, it seemed. Baron Köthen saw no reason to suspect the evidence of his own eyes.

"A dragon," he murmured again, to no one in particular.

Hal rose, complaining of stiff joints. With his formal greeting and obeisance accomplished, Erde knew he would now feel free to treat the dragon as he usually did, with a good deal less reverence. Which meant he'd be wanting to talk to him, and would need her to translate. Erde grinned from her hiding place as he leaned closer to scratch Earth familiarly on his horny snout, in just the spot she'd once revealed as the dragon's favorite. She was so relieved to see him alive and well, after her terrible nightmares of the war. Greetings were long overdue, and she knew it was time to face Köthen in a normal way. She'd been down this road only too recently, this foolishness of thinking that a man had noticed her when really, he hadn't, at least not in that way. And how much more presumptuous of her to think this of Adolphus, Baron Köthen, a powerful lord and nearly a stranger to her, than of a childhood companion like Rainer. Never mind the fact that he was nearly twice her age. Besides, if Köthen hadn't recognized her back in the farmhouse, there wasn't even going to be that awkward moment she'd anticipated.

Erde slipped around behind the manger and came up beside Rose.

"Ah," said Rose, moving forward as she did. "Here she is."

"Milady! At last!" Hal honored her with a deep and courtly bow, then grasped her hands warmly. "Ah, look at you! A gown and everything! My little squire-boy is more grown-up every day. I wish I could say the same of myself."

"But we are both alive and that's what matters." Boldly, Erde went up on tiptoe to kiss his cheek. "I worried about you all the time I was away!"

Hal laughed. "You know you're getting old when the young ladies feel free to kiss you without consequence!" Then he said to Rose, "I can't get used to having her talk."

"Get used to it," Rose warned. "She has a lot to say."

She took Erde's elbow to turn her gently toward Köthen. "Dolph, I think you've met Lady Erde von Alte?"

Köthen nodded politely, his mind still on the dragon. "Yes, I do believe . . ." Then he turned his head slightly, as if memory had failed him, or was just then returning.

"Erfurt . . . ?" Hal supplied helpfully.

Erde raised her head to glance sidelong past Köthen's frown. She could not look him full in the face. She felt more than saw him focus on her, felt the steel come into his gaze.

"The witch-girl," he muttered.

"So Fra Guill would have it," Hal agreed jovially, "but of course it isn't true."

"Isn't it?"

Köthen's tone chilled Erde to the bone. Was he recalling Erfurt only, or her dream-presence as well? That night in the clearing, or his suicidal charge? Erde let her glance drift back toward him. She hoped he'd be looking at Hal, so she could observe him unawares. But he was staring straight at her. Their eyes met and held, and she saw how angry he was.

"My lady, a pleasure." He stepped close to lift her hand politely to his lips, then murmured for her hearing alone, "Better to have stayed that night and died with honor."

So he'd been aware of and remembered everything. Worse, he blamed her for what had befallen him since, when he'd heard her dream-warning, heeded it, and fled.

"Oh, no, my lord baron," she protested faintly. "Surely not."

"Surely yes." And then he stepped back with a curt bow. To say more would bring inquiries from the others she was sure he did not wish to answer.

He might as well have struck her. Drowning, Erde let her courtly training take over. She returned a gracious curtsy. "My lord baron. How charming to see you again."

Oblivious, Hal chuckled and rolled his eyes at Rose. "Look at the graceful thing she's getting to be. Is this your doing, Rosie?"

"None of mine. This child is dragon-raised."

"We should all have so excellent a parent." He drew Erde toward the dragon. "Come, nearly-grown. Your skills are needed. What can my lord Earth tell us of where he's been and where he'll be off to next? How stands the Quest?"

Thinking each moment that she might fall to the floor, Erde struggled to give to the elder knight all the cheer and enthusiasm she knew he deserved. But she could not fool Rose, Rose who saw everything, Rose who took up her elbow again with a firm sisterly grasp.

"Let him rest, Heinrich. You can talk to him tomorrow. He's been working hard, and sorely tired of late. Besides, you know how long-winded a dragon can be, once you get him started. We've plenty of our own news to exchange and it's much too cold in here to be standing about. Let's all go in to dinner, shall we?"

Chapter Ten

At dinner, after the men had slaked the first rush of their hunger, they talked about the war, or mostly, Hal did, now and then referring to Captain Wender for reinforcement or a clarification of fact. He spoke quietly because the news was bad.

"We've been beaten up at every turn. An army without training or proper weapons facing the barons' mercenary knights and infantry . . ."

"These farmers' hearts are gallant," put in Wender. "But most would do better by the plough than by the sword."

Hal nodded. "Still, if mere numbers would win the day, we'd have a fighting chance. And all's not lost. We had split the army even before we heard of the Prince's death. Rainer's taken part of our force west to raise men and provisioning among the estates not corrupted by Fra Guill on his first tour through the countryside." Hal made maps on the tabletop, with spoons and platters and lines of bread crumbs. "I sought to draw the rebels southward. When it became clear that this mad priest would go on fighting no matter what the weather, I sent His Majesty west to Köln, where hopefully, he will last the winter. He is not well, and Carl's death has grieved him sorely. The truth is, we'd be in full retreat but for these recent heavy snows, which have forced even Fra Guill to call a halt."

"A mercy," Rose murmured.

"If it was an honest winter, there'd be a mercy in it. But this weather's as unnatural as the priest himself. It'll clear and we'll have a bit of a thaw, just enough to sink every cartwheel hub-deep in mud. Then as soon as we're good and stuck, it'll freeze and the hell-priest'll be on us again. It's uncanny. There's some saying he has the weather in his thrall."

Rose nodded. "Those rumors have reached even this far."

"How could such a thing be?" muttered Doritt.

Hal blew out a long sigh. "Well, I'd hate to credit it, but somehow he's always prepared and we're always surprised. We could use a few month's rest, not a few days. Aye, Wender?"

"Aye indeed, milord." The captain lifted his mug of ale in salute. "Were there food like this to rest with."

"Or any place left to rest in." Hal gathered the bread crumbs into a pile as if saving them for later. "Guillemo's ordered his men to burn any village or farmstead that refuses to pledge to his cause."

"And join his march," added Wender. "The roads are filled with refugees, even in this weather. The devil's own spawn, he is."

Captain Wender was just as Erde's dreams had presented him: Köthen's most favored and loyal man, a tough battle veteran who had followed him unquestioningly into exile. But she thought Wender seemed a bit more at home on the King's side, which might explain Hal's easy way with him, and his willingness to trust this former enemy, while not his superior lord.

That lord sat silently now, a bit apart, as if news of the war no longer interested him. He had eaten little—just enough, Erde thought, to keep from making a show of refusing his hostess' hospitality. Nowhere near enough to sustain him, and certainly not enough to soak up the quantities of drink he was consuming. Raven had at first taken up station across from him, laughing and sipping from his cup in a flirty, familiar way designed to keep it out of his own hands as much as possible. He'd replied briefly, politely to her queries about people and events in the past, the youth they'd obviously shared, but he would not speak of the present, the war, or his situation. Eventually, Raven gave up and left him alone.

Erde wished he wouldn't drink so much. He reminded

her too much of her father. But surely it was more than rage and shame twisting in him. He was like one grief-stricken, like a woman who's lost an only child, or like Josef her father, who'd lost a beloved wife. Erde wondered how a mere throne could mean as much, but nonetheless, she thought she understood Baron Köthen better than anyone in the room, and she felt heartsick for him. She did not even ask why. She herself could hardly eat, even though Sir Hal, in his courtly way, had reverted to the habit developed during their travels together, of transferring the tenderest morsels to her own platter.

"And how has the King received young Rainer?" Rose inquired.

Hal shrugged. "In public, merely politely. In private, he has expressed some possibility. Wisely, Rainer has not pressed his claim officially. We let the rumors circulate, but there yet remains the problem of proof. Our best hope is popular acclaim."

Down the long table, Baron Köthen stirred. "Fine conspirators you are, so beset by moral standards. Can't you discover a convenient birthmark? Isn't that the usual ploy?"

Hal eyed him with impatience. "Dolph refuses to believe that Prince Ludolph could have survived the baron's plotting. After all, a *true* heir—one who actually wants the throne—would be very inconvenient to his purposes."

Raven propped her chin on her fists. "What if Rainer of Duchen is the lost prince?"

"He isn't," Köthen growled.

"But what if he is? Speculate. What would you do?"

Köthen looked cornered. He sipped his wine and seemed to find great interest in the decoration of the cup.

"He's young, strong, intelligent, probably very able," Raven pursued. "It seems he's even charismatic. What if he is, Dolph?"

Köthen refused to meet her bright, insistent stare. He laughed lightly, gestured bravely with his goblet. "Then there would be no further use for me."

"A strong king needs strong advisers," Rose countered.

"I can think of several uses for you," Raven smiled.

And Erde wondered if it was only she who heard, not a

fallen lord's drunken plea for sympathy, but a man's sober, bitter conviction. That his life was over.

Finally the empty bowls and trenchers were stacked and cleared. Doritt threw more wood on the fire. The women refilled their cups with heated cider or wine, and everyone—except Köthen—drew nearer. Erde understood that it was finally time to tell her own story. She reached out to the dragon in the barn, for his support and commentary, then gathered N'Doch and Water-as-Sedou beside her.

"Well . . . after Lord Earth rescued Hal and Rainer and myself from Erfurt and brought us back to Deep Moor, he heard the voice of the Summoner ever more strongly, calling him back to the Quest. So we left to follow it."

"Without even warning us," Hal complained.

She tipped her head apologetically. "You were so distracted with the war and the idea that Rainer was . . ."

"I know, I know, but the Quest . . ."

"Would you have gone?" asked Rose. "Would you have left the war behind? Would you have deserted your King?"

Hal pursed his lips. "A difficult choice."

"So, you see? The wise beast saved you that choice."

"Let the child continue," demanded Doritt from the fireplace.

Now Erde felt self-conscious, with the entire household watching. She cleared her throat. "Anyway, the Voice did not lead us to the mage we sought, or even to itself. It led us to N'Doch and Lady Water." She was shamed by the awkward formality that tied her tongue in knots. But soon the tale took hold, telling itself of its own accord. "We were in a place called Africa, so fantastical and strange that I grew at last to believe N'Doch's assertions that the dragon had transported us not only in location, but in time."

"2013, no doubt of it," N'Doch put in. "Eleven hundred years from now. When I laid eyes on these two, I was sure they were some kind of special effect. Took me a real long time to figure it otherwise."

2013. Amazed by the thought yet again, Erde translated for him, stumbling over the equivalent of "special effect." Murmurs and headshakes ran around the table like a ritual response. "And then immediately, we were being pursued . . ."

"There's always someone after my ass, y'see," explained N'Doch.

". . . but N'Doch took us to his grandfather Master Djawara, a great mage himself, though not the one we searched for."

"Papa Dja's no mage, whatever that is, but he's witchy, all right." N'Doch beamed his dark smile at Rose. "Like you ladies."

"Master Djawara sent us to the city and Mistress Lealé, a dreamer and prophetess . . ."

"A scam artist, you mean."

Erde bit back a pout. Perhaps she should just let N'Doch tell the story. The listeners around the table seemed to enjoy his posturing, his willingness to try for a laugh even with his own dignity at stake. Then she could sit back and translate his exaggerations and embellishments, at least as directly as she could bear to without blushing, or worrying that his boasting was reflecting poorly on her. But the dragon in the barn had an opinion about that.

ALL SIDES OF THIS TALE MUST BE TOLD. IT IS MORE THAN JUST AN ADVENTURE STORY.

Erde agreed. She saw Hal warming to N'Doch's colorful description of the escape into the bush, questioning him directly in Frankish and eagerly sharing out his replies. She cleared her throat once more and gently interrupted. "And, remember, there at Mistress Lealé's, we uncovered the first hints that the Summoner might be the dragons' elder sister Air, and that the Summons might be a call for help."

Water-as-Sedou had listened quietly from the start, but now he caught Erde's eye. Relieved, she let him take over. With Sedou, there was no need to translate or worry that the proper telling of the tale would get sidetracked. And when he spoke, the entire room quietened.

"There is much," he began in a voice like the tolling of bass bells, "that the dragons did not remember when they were waked from their long sleep, my brother Earth from under the mountain, myself from beneath the sea. So suddenly awake, so engendered by urgency and purpose, yet ignorant of how or why to put it to use. But memory returns." Sedou wet his lips and surveyed his listeners gravely. "You have heard our sister Air mentioned. But there is yet another: our brother Fire."

"Four!" Hal exclaimed softly. "Of course there would be."

"Indeed, Sir Knight. You perceive the symmetry. But the symmetry is incomplete. Our sister Air is nowhere to be found. Were all in balance, there would be no need for dragon to be seeking dragon. We'd be four and already about the task we were awakened to accomplish."

"You've discovered the Task, then?" Hal asked hopefully.

Sedou shook his head. "This knowledge requires a four-way understanding. No one of us is sufficient unto herself."

"And what of Lord Fire? Do you know his where-abouts?"

Sedou paused, and Erde strained to pick up the brief dragon-to-dragon conference, too fast for her human senses. "We have hints. Worst of all, we . . . that is, some of us suspect him of working against us."

Hal frowned, made a small sound of protest.

"Hear me out, Sir Knight."

At this point, the tale caught even Baron Köthen's attention. His bowed head, bronzed with firelight, lifted and turned ever so slightly in their direction. Erde watched his listening profile and thought she'd never seen anything more beautiful. Except, of course, the dragon Earth. She had not included her dreams in the telling, though the dragon encouraged her to. She could not bear to put the baron through that, to make him relive his humiliation in front of all these eager listeners. So she sat silently and let Sedou unwind the story of their time in Lealé's mansion, of the fighting in the city outside, and Kenzo Baraga's treachery. There was little she could add. The dragons knew better how those final bloody minutes had fallen out. N'Doch listened silently as well, curling and uncurling his fists as if amazed to find them on his wrists and still working.

A long silence followed Sedou's finish, broken only by the snap of flames in the grate.

Then Hal said to Rose, "He was dead when he came to you? Truly?"

Rose tilted her chin at Linden, several places down the table. Linden nodded. All eyes turned to N'Doch, who grinned uncomfortably, though he usually loved an audience.

"Wonderful," murmured Hal. "Wonderful."

Captain Wender shook his head. He poured himself a half-mug of ale, then only sipped at it gingerly, as if working to keep himself from draining it in a single gulp. "You could find yourself an honored place at any hearth in the land with a tale like that."

"Those that are left standing," added Hal with a hollow chuckle. "But now, what of the task ahead?"

Sedou sat back. "Our journey has just begun, Sir Knight. Now that our company is rested and recovered, we must be on our way to find our brother Fire, and quickly, for it seems that only he can lead us to our sister Air."

"Told ya," N'Doch murmured.

Erde looked at him sidelong. Earth had also said as much when she'd gone to him for comfort in the barn. The urge that drove these dragons was their sole reason for existence. It could be put aside no longer. Their time of peace and safety was at an end.

"We are correct to understand that the dragon Fire is implicated in this treachery?"

Erde had to glance down the table to assure herself that it was indeed Baron Köthen who had spoken. He was toying with his empty wine cup and meeting no one's eyes. It was as if he'd spoken to himself. Then he looked up at Hal. "He sounds like the sort of dragon you always swore, was a slanderous myth invented by fearful churchmen, my knight."

"I'm sure we've misunderstood about Lord Fire," Hal began.

"Not at all." Sedou turned to Köthen, a long look down the table, as if noticing him for the first time. "You are right, my lord baron, though there is some difference of opinion about this within our ranks. My brother Earth wishes me to note that he is not yet convinced of Fire's betrayal."

"Betrayal? Impossible!" cried Hal. "A misunderstanding, surely! Dragons are all that is good and noble in God's creation!"

Erde recalled her own shock and disbelief when Lady Water first suggested that Fire might be out to destroy them. N'Doch murmured something filthy and cynical that she refused to translate, and Sedou laughed, a bass rumble felt in the back of the throat, a laugh no true human could have produced. "Would that were true, Sir Knight."

Köthen filled his wine cup and drained it. "You do persist, Heinrich, in believing in what other men have given up on long ago."

"Oh, really?" Hal retorted. "I believed in dragons, and lo . . ." Sedou restrained him with a big hand on his arm.

In the pause, Köthen looked up, found the dark man watching him, and looked away. The wine cup made several revolutions in his restless hands. Finally, he asked, "And how do you expect to locate this paragon of evil?"

"There is a way we travel, a kind of translation through time and space that is enabled by the identity of place. And so, with my brother Fire: we have an image in mind of where he is, or in N'Doch's mind actually, as it's he who received it. We won't know where it really is until we get there. But he will be there. I am sure of it."

Köthen stared at him. Erde could see he had not expected so direct and technical an answer. "You can go anywhere you like?"

"If we can see it clearly, we can go there."

"How long will it take?"

"No time at all, my lord baron. The travel is instantaneous."

"Magic," Wender muttered, and crossed himself covertly.

Köthen's eyes flicked to Hal. "You've traveled like this?"

"I have, yes."

"Let me guess: from Erfurt."

"And to Erfurt. How did you think I got in without you knowing in the first place? You had that town guarded like the king's own storehouse."

Köthen looked back to Sedou. Some part of this had snagged his interest. "And so, you'll just go?"

Sedou nodded. Köthen let out a breath. Erde saw a bright, quick moment pass between them, man and dragon, an exchange: the envy in Köthen's eyes for the challenge in Sedou's.

But Köthen turned away and refilled his wine cup to the brim. "Well, Heinrich, as usual you're right. I've been a fool all these years. A fool to believe in the nobility and strivings of mere men. What's the point? Let's stop this war right now. We'll just let these dragons rule the kingdom. How do you think Fra Guill would feel about that?" He drained the cup and reached again for the jug.

"Dragons do not meddle in the affairs of men, my lord baron," Sedou said quietly.

Köthen laughed bitterly. "They seem to have meddled in mine fairly thoroughly."

Oddly, Sedou smiled. 'That is your fault for being at the center of things."

The baron eyed him suspiciously.

"When there is something larger at stake, we will do what we must."

"Since men live in the world, Dolph," said Rose, as if waking from a deep reverie, "they will be threatened when it is threatened."

"The world?" Köthen scoffed. "My lady Rose, I'd never have suspected you of apocalyptic thinking."

Sedou said, "Were it not the case, I'd still be peacefully sleeping in the ocean depths, and my brother Earth beneath the mountains of Tor Alte. Do you think, my lord baron, that dragons are awakened for no purpose?"

Köthen merely stared at him.

You're asking too much, Erde thought. Too much for him to absorb in the turn of one day. Too much to believe. For this man understands the consequences of belief. Good Captain Wender, in the corner, can just shake his head in wonder and then accept that there are indeed dragons in the world, just as his grandmama always said there were. But this man cannot just accept. He has an inkling of how profoundly all his definitions of the world will change, and he's not ready for that. *No more than I was,* she mused, *when N'Doch tried to explain his world to me.*

And indeed, Köthen poured himself more wine yet again, then stood and shoved back his chair. He swayed, steadied himself with a brace of fingers to the tabletop. "We're fools to listen to all this." He shoved back from the table and strode across the room to stare out of the window into snow and darkness.

"He'll come around," Hal murmured.

No, he won't, Erde thought, though she loved Sir Hal for his steadfast belief in this man whom he'd raised and trained and who had eventually betrayed him. But Adolphus of Köthen wouldn't simply "come around." It would take something drastic. But, oh, she thought rapturously, if that thing should happen, what a boon to have his skills and intelligence turned to our problem.

With Köthen gone from the table, Hal turned his attention back to Seldou, with the next in his scholar's lifetime list of questions he'd always wanted to ask a dragon. Erde could see he was overjoyed to have one he could speak to directly, and since this one was likely to leave soon, Hal wasn't going to waste any more precious time on his wayward ex-squire than was absolutely necessary. Erde hoped Sedou would be patient with him.

The women of the household began to drift off to bed. Beside her, N'Doch stirred. He'd been very quiet for a long time, she'd noticed. How very unlike him.

"So. Looks like we're outa here."

She nodded. The rising tide of dragon urgency was growing irresistible, as if the telling of the tale had completed some necessary ritual, and there was no reason left to linger. Time to be about their business. "When, do you think?"

"Soon."

"Are you ready? I mean, are you truly healed, N'Doch?"

He smiled at her, one of the things Erde had to admit he did best. Like Sedou, and even their grandfather, Master Djawara. This family had a smile that could light up the darkest corners of a room. But she thought that this particular smile was rather overstretched with bravado.

"Does it matter?" he asked.

"Of course it does."

"Not to them."

She knew he meant the dragons. "Oh, N'Doch, not true, not true."

He shrugged. "Well, anyway, I'm fine. I'm better than ever, and as ready as I'll ever be. How 'bout you?"

She felt very close to him right then. Her own rush of fellowship surprised her. For all his ignorance of the lore, there was so much that only he knew, only he understood—with her—about this business of belonging to dragons.

"You had all those brothers, N'Doch. Did . . . do you have any sisters?"

"Nah."

"Well, you have one now." She laid her pale hand beside his dark one. "We are like night and day, you see? Each one a half. Together we form the whole."

This time, his smile was genuine.

She woke in her upstairs room in the darkened farmhouse from a dream she could not remember, and for that, she was grateful. She listened, first inside her head, in case it was the dragon sending a dream-image to wake her for some emergency. But the part of her consciousness that the dragon normally occupied was empty and still. He must be out hunting, a final meal before their impending departure. Then she heard a noise down below. Her little room was near the staircase, and sound floated freely upward. Someone was moving around in the lower room.

Erde got up quietly, more curious than afraid. The women of Deep Moor did not roam their halls at night unless something was the matter. The room was freezing. The fire in the tiny grate had burned out long ago. She pulled her prentice boy's linen shirt over her shift and hauled on her woolen leggings. For silence, she kept her feet bare. In the other narrow bed, the twins remained wrapped in the quiet sleep of the guiltless.

She slipped into the corridor and down the stair, stopping at each landing to listen. Whoever it was did not care if he or she was detected. She turned onto the final run of stairs. From there, she had a view of the front part of the great room and the fireplace.

Captain Wender had stretched himself out in front of the dying coals, smothered in the thick quilts that the women had brought him. The unaccustomed warmth and wine and good company had clearly been too much for this valiant man-at-arms. He was fast asleep. A glimmer drew Erde's attention away from him.

At the far end of the table, away from the fire, sat Adolphus of Köthen. Several wine cups and more than one stout jug were stationed beside his elbow, but he was not drinking now. He was staring at the gleaming blade of a dagger, turning it restlessly in his hands as he had done with his empty cup earlier. Wender's dagger, no doubt surreptitiously lifted. He studied it as if it might speak to him, and then he did something that sent Erde's heart pounding into her throat.

He set the dagger to the inside of his left wrist, made a fist, then pensively traced the raised blue lines of his veins with the blade's keen point. Erde was down the stairs and confronting him across the table before she'd even thought about what she was doing.

"Oh, no, my lord, never!"

His eyes flicked up at her, startled. Erde drew back. She hadn't recalled there being so much darkness in them.

"Why the hell not?"

He said it so bleakly, she could not immediately reply. There was little trace of the rage he'd first greeted her with in the barn. He was drunk for sure, but in that state beyond mere loss of sobriety, where clarity returns with a focus as sharp as a lance. Erde saw the signs. She knew them all from dealing with her father, who drank hoping to forget but only ended up remembering more than he ever did when he was sober.

"Please, my lord . . . you've had too much," she said inanely, because she had to say something.

"Clever girl."

"I mean, one should never heed a decision made under the drink's influence."

Köthen laughed softly. "You mean, I might *live* to regret it? No, my lady Erde, my hand is steady, drunk or sober." He dragged the dagger back along his wrist, then shifted his grip and pulled, letting the edge bite. Blood flowed along the path of the slice.

"NO!" Erde threw herself against the table, flinging her arms across to snatch at the blade and pull it away from his skin. Köthen jerked the blade from her grasp, then swore and tossed it aside to grab her hands and peel them open. Blood welled up in her own palms. The rush of it frightened her.

"Make fists and hold them," he ordered tartly. Suddenly, he sounded cold sober. In the next instant, he was on his feet and rummaging through one of the satchels the twins had brought in from the packhorse. All he could find was the same length of soft red cloth that had bound his wrists on the way into the farmstead. "A better use for it anyway," he muttered, tearing it cleanly in half with his teeth.

He came back to the table and wound a strip tightly around each of her bleeding palms. "Surface wounds. They won't scar."

As if she cared. Already, he'd forgotten his own wound, a thin red line become mostly an ugly smear on his wrist, drying up already. Hardly a wound at all. He had been playing with her. When he was done wrapping, he slumped back against his chair and fixed her with that too-dark stare.

"You seem, my lady, to have a compulsion to keep me alive, even when it is not in my own best interests. Do I dare ask why?"

Her heart was too full to even speak.

He tilted his head speculatively. "Perhaps you have some witchy purpose for me? There's been a great deal of talk about purpose this evening, and as I seem to have lost mine . . ."

"My lord baron, I am not a witch."

"Then what are you?"

"A girl. I'm just a girl."

"Who talks to dragons and travels to times that haven't happened yet and whispers in a man's ear at night when he's about to make a fateful decision. *Just* a girl?"

To Erde's surprise, he let her reach for the dragger and draw it away from him into her own hands. She folded her wrapped palms over the blade. "Very well, then. I am a dragon guide."

He settled back a bit more. "Go on."

"That is no witchery. It is a silent, holy duty passed down through countless generations of blood from the earliest times, so that one would always be ready, should the need arise."

"The need?"

"The waking of the dragons, which is the dire sign. The actual need we have yet to determine." She dared to look up at him, to meet his steady, noncommittal gaze. "May I show you something?" He merely shrugged, but she reached beneath her mismatched layers of linen for the treasure she always kept pinned next to her skin. She undid the clasp and laid the brooch before him on her red-wrapped palm. "See? My grandmother's, and hers before that."

Köthen leaned forward, squinting in the dim firelight, then reached for it. "If I may . . . ?"

She held it out. He took it and rose, carrying it to the hearth to peer at the ancient blood-red jewel with its delicate incised carving of a dragon rampant. "It has wings," he murmured.

"Yes, I know. I think it doesn't stand for my dragon, but rather for the essence of dragon."

"Or for what men *think* of dragons. It's old, but not that old. Probably it was made as a reminder, a key to ancient memories."

She smiled at him, though he wasn't looking at her. This was the closest thing they'd yet had to a conversation. "My lord baron, I do believe that some of Sir Hal's dragon study has rubbed off on you after all." And then she could not believe she'd spoken to him so boldly.

But he only snorted, turning the jewel in his hands with the same intensity as he had the dagger. "He fed it to me with my morning porridge. How could I help it?"

"And yet you chose not to believe?"

"I chose not to, yes."

"And now . . . ?"

"Well, clearly I was wrong, as I have been about so many things of late."

"No, my lord . . ."

"Yes." He came back to the table and placed the dragon brooch deliberately in the center of her cushioned palm, then sat down and faced her directly. "How is it that you could speak to me in that clearing? That the priest could sense your presence? If not witchery, by some dragon magic, is it?"

"I don't know, my lord. I had . . . dreams . . . several dreams, in which I saw you as clearly as I do now, in your camp on the battlefield, with my father, with Captain Wender and then with the . . ."

Köthen hissed, rose, and paced away. "Curse the day I made that unholy alliance. Greedy, too greedy, Adolphus!"

"Fra Guill has deep powers of his own, my lord. See how easily he cozened my father . . ."

"Your father is a drunken sot!" At the edge of the shadows, he stared up into the darkness of the stairwell. "Have you any notion what your witchery cost me, girl?"

"My lord, I am a baron's daughter, and the granddaugter of a baroness. I think I know something of the ambitions of the courtier. And I never intended . . ."

"Courtier?" Köthen was appalled. He whirled on her, his fist raised and clenched. "I had a kingdom within my grasp!"

Erde stared at the red jewel in her hands so that her eyes would not stray to the litter of wine cups and empty jugs between them on the table. She did not see how she alone could be responsible for his loss. At some point he must have realized that the hell-priest would never have crowned him king. He was far too strong and able, not the hell-priest's creature like her father. In truth, she understood little of courts and the lust for power. She had merely tried on some of N'Doch's bravado. It did not fit very well, she decided.

Köthen took a breath, planted both palms on the table, and loomed over her. "Well, isn't he? A drunken sot?"

Silently, she nodded. But her meek agreement seemed only to enrage him further. He snatched up all the wine cups on the table and hurled them into the fireplace. "I am not a drunk!"

The smash of crockery so close to his ear brought Captain Wender bolt upright out of his deep sleep. "What? My lord? Are we under attack?"

Köthen waved him back irritably. "No, Wender. Merely an accident. Go back to sleep. You're better off."

Wender shook the drowse from his head to survey the unfamiliar, darkened room. His eyes found Erde, and he cocked a scarred brow in inquiry. She nodded reassurance, then made the little hand sign that her father's house guards always used to warn each other when the baron had been drinking. Which was, of course, most of the time. Wender's lips twitched: a faint, complicit, admiring grin was born and died before it could give both of them away. He nodded and lay back in his nest of blankets and seemed to be instantly asleep again. But Erde was sure he would not be so caught by surprise again that night.

Köthen observed the end of this exchange, and it was not lost on him. But he also saw that she did not betray him to his man-at-arms by revealing the purloined dagger. He threw himself back into his chair, dropped his face into his hands, then dragged them roughly across his cheeks and beard with a ragged sigh. "Henrich says I am past all reason. Do you agree?"

After a moment of consideration, she replied recklessly, "Yes, my lord."

Köthen laughed, a short, bitter sound, more of a bark than an expression of mirth. Then he folded his arms to lean forward on them and stare at her closely. "You are an earnest and well-brought-up child, I can see that much, despite your fool of a father . . ."

"I beg you, my lord . . ."

"A thousand pardons, my lady, for my intemperance. I meant . . . your honored parent, Josef von Alte."

"I am grateful, my lord." Let him be as ironical as he pleased. She had his attention at last and perhaps, as her father often did, he would talk himself to sleep, and then there would be no more threats of a blade to the wrists, at least, not this night.

"And for these virtues I credit your noble grandmother, may she rest in peace."

To hear him speak of her beloved grandmother nearly broke her resolve to remain tearless. "Did you know her, my lord?"

"Aye. As loyal a subject of the King as ever there was." He paused, then grinned sourly. "Plotted against her many times."

Erde glanced up at him, alarmed. For a moment, his dark eyes softened inexplicably. So sad, she thought, almost tender. *But not for me.* For his gentled gaze was directed somewhere inside his own head, at some memory, perhaps, some personal musing. Yet he seemed to be looking at her when he said quietly, "I believe that you did mean me well, for I see that you are incapable of meaning ill. How enviable."

She sensed the direction of his thoughts, turned against himself as keenly as the dagger's blade. It would do no good to protest that she had mean thoughts every day, about her fellow dragon guide, for instance, and certainly about the evil priest.

"And therefore," Köthen continued, one hand fitfully massaging his brow. "You will think it most immodest of me, most unbecoming in a good Christian man, when you hear me say that the kingdom has need of me." He regarded her speculatively, as if trying to decide if he could talk to her as an aware adult. "My lady Erde. Ours is a land in crisis. The peerage is slothful and corrupt. Their people have lost all faith in the structures meant to protect them. Why else do you think the priest has won so many converts? He has nothing real to offer them. But this is a time of fear, not of faith. A strong, enlightened leader is needed, and I am the man for it. I could heal this sickness, if they'd let me. I know it, and Henrich knows it, but he lets his infernal principles get in the way. Like you do, my lady. No wonder you're such great friends."

"A rightful monarchy is ordained by God, my lord."

"Wrong!" Köthen slammed a fist against the table, causing Wender to mutter and turn over in his quilts. "That is a convenient fiction invented not too many generations ago to legitimize the current reigning family . . . Otto's grandfather, who took the throne by force from some other sorry 'rightful' sot! As I hoped to do! When the weak rule, the strong must offer remedy! It's traditional! Did the baroness not teach you *history,* child?"

"I am not a child, my lord." But in her heart, she marveled at his magnificence, chin up, back straight, his eyes bright with the fire of conviction and righteous wrath. Here was the man she remembered from the barn in Erfurt. But it was a fleeting image.

"Not a witch, not a child . . . what are you, then? Oh, yes, I remember . . . a girl. You did tell me that, forgive me."

Erde took two deep breaths and forced her shoulders away from their stranglehold about her neck. "I believe you wish me to think ill of you, my lord."

"That'll do for a start. Then maybe you'll stop trying to save my life!"

"But it hasn't been by choice, don't you see?" Carefully, to hide her desperation, she balanced Wender's knife between her bandaged hands. Only the absolute truth would do. "Except for just now, of course. After all, I hardly know you. My dreams were . . . I was called into them. I had no say in the matter."

"Were you aware in the dreams?"

"Of course, but . . ."

"Then you could have dreamed some other outcome?"

"My lord, I don't think so." Even now, a plan was forming itself in her head. Erde felt she owed him at least a hint. "I suspect some larger purpose to all of this, my lord, in which we must both take part."

The tension ran out of him like water. "Purpose? You've been listening to those dragons again. I have no purpose, remember?"

"Not so, my lord."

"Ever so, my lady." He reached for the wine jug nearest him, which turned out to be not yet empty. He upended it in a long, thirsty tavern swallow. Then he set it down, cradled between his palms, and eyed Erde with owlish challenge. "I am not a drunk, but I do wish to be drunk. Unless you have some better idea of what a useless man should do with his time."

In fact, she did. And her plan was clearer now. Oh, it was reckless, so reckless. She couldn't believe she was thinking of such a thing. But because she loved him—for whatever inexplicable reason, and now that she understood this—she had to try to help him. She had helped the dragon, after all, so lost and ignorant when she first found him. A dragon now magnificent with purpose, even if he was not always sure exactly what it was. As this man had been magnificent, and would be again.

But she said nothing of this to Köthen. She lowered her eyes and said, "Not I, my lord baron."

Köthen shrugged, theatrical in his regret. "Then I guess it's the jug for me. It's a longer way to do one's self in, but in the end, just as effective."

Erde slid the dagger to the edge of the table and swept it into the folds of her shirt. She judged that the crisis had passed for the night, for this night at least. "In that case, my lord, I will leave you to your own devices."

When she rose from the table, he seemed surprised that she did not intend to stay and joust with him for what remained of the night. She could see that, despite himself, and witch-girl or no, he found her interesting. Perhaps he'd even enjoyed her company. And that, to Erde, was one very large step forward.

One that left her trembling inwardly, as if she'd charged blindly out onto a precipice with no thought for how she might ever make her way back to solid ground. Walking back to the stairs and up them with composure and grace may have been the hardest thing she'd ever done.

Chapter Eleven

Nor did she tell Hal or the women of Deep Moor about her plan, not even Rose. She claimed she had broken a bowl, and cut her palms on the shards. She avoided Baron Köthen, which was not difficult, as he mostly stayed in the room Rose had given him and sulked, while Captain Wender lounged patiently outside his door. Hal labored in the winter farmstead alongside the others, insisting he must do the work of three.

But, with trepidation, Erde did tell the dragons. To her surprise, they approved, as Earth worked his healing magic with her hands. The next day, N'Doch and Water spent hours together working up the details of the image that had gripped him just as he returned to consciousness from his dragon-made resurrection. Details of the burning land he just *knew* was where they were meant to go next. That N'Doch had volunteered this vision, he who hated any implication that he was tied to a dragon guide's destiny, this very act convinced Erde of the vision's truth. The dragons required no convincing. They were impatient to be off.

Quietly, the four prepared for their departure, soliciting from Margit a strong, stout knife for N'Doch to complement the slim dagger Erde had carried since fleeing Tor Alte. From the weavers, they gathered several thin linen tunics and leggings, advised by N'Doch as the best clothing for the hot climate he'd be taking them to. Lily made them footwear, laughing at the absurdity of sandals in deep winter. Doritt found them sturdy packs and equipped them with flint and tinder, and wax-stoppered water jugs and bread and cheese. N'Doch grumbled about the weight of all these things. He suggested that they should pay a stop-off visit to, as he put it, his "home time," to exchange the heavy crockery for a lighter container he called "plastic." Erde recalled the milky, flexible jug he'd carried water in, and thought it might be a good idea. But the dragons said no. She thought they seemed nervous about letting N'Doch go home, though they said it was only because they were in so much of a hurry. Besides, they were unsure how many of these provisions would make it through the veil anyway. Objects seemed to translate well enough if Earth specifically pictured them along with the person carrying them, but if it could not be easily carried, there was no point in trying to take it with them.

Erde warned N'Doch to keep his pack nearby at all times, or at least to know exactly where it was. They made no farewells, only tacit ones. The women knew they were leaving some time soon, and knew as well that they might— at any future moment—return without warning. Erde had given no notice at all when she and Earth had left on the journey that had led them to Water and N'Doch. She'd simply disappeared.

Therefore, it was just as well, when she heard shouting from the horse barn, men's voices raised in anger, and saw Doritt and Margit grab up the nearest heavy tool and head that way. It was just as well that the four were ready.

Instinct warned her. Breaking into a run, Erde turned her senses inward to locate the other three. Earth was outside the cow shed with Linden, helping to heal a sick calf. N'Doch and Water-as-Sedou were hard at work in the farmhouse library, the only quiet place. Erde made it to the barn just after Doritt and Margit. Flinging herself through the open doorway, she nearly crashed into Doritt, bending beside Captain Wender, who was sprawled face-down in the scatter of manure and straw.

She slowed. "Is he . . . ?"

"Out cold," said Doritt. "But coming around."

Wender groaned. Erde stopped worrying and moved on. Farther down, past the line of stalls, Margit had pulled up behind Raven and Rose. The three women watched breath-lessly while in the open space at the end of the barn, Kö-

then and Hal circled each other, snarling. Hal had his sword
at the ready, Köthen gripped a long-handled scythe used
for harvesting grain. Already, both men were bruised and
straw-dusted, as if this altercation had begun with mere fists
and arms, and escalated toward full-scale weaponry. Hal
bled from a long shallow slice on his thigh. The shouting
Erde had heard halfway across the farmstead had been replaced by silence, and the shuffling of straw and heavy
breathing. Gone well beyond words, the two men glared at
each other like maddened dogs, glared and circled, glared
and circled.

Erde halted beside Rose. "Oh, no! What now?"

"Dolph has refused to stay with us when Heinrich returns to the war."

The furrows in Rose's brow told Erde this was no ordinary skirmish. "But he gave his word."

"Apparently he's changed his mind."

The men's edgy dance brought Köthen's back around full
circle toward the women. Rose moved a step aside. Margit
shifted to ease up behind him. She had a length of rope
twisted between her fists.

"Back!" Köthen growled, with a warning sidearm swipe
of his scythe. Margit leaped aside and retreated.

"Dolph," said Rose. "Be reasonable . . ."

"Leave it, Rose! Reason has nothing to do with it!"

"How is this going to solve anything?"

"I will not, NOT be put out to pasture like some . . .
broken mule!"

"You will if you behave like one!" Hal was winded. His
chest heaved convulsively, making the difference in the two
men's ages terrifyingly apparent. But his manner was as
fierce and implacable as Erde had ever seen it. "You'll do
as I say, if I have to chain you to a rock!"

No, Sir Hal, she told him silently. *Don't you see this man
will go mad if you chain him, either physically or within his
soul?* Now she was sure that her plan was the right one.

"Will you?" Köthen yelled. "Just try it, then! No one
here but women, old man! You think you can take me?"
Suddenly he closed the distance between them, stepping
within range of the older man's sword. He lifted the scythe
to swing it like a club, then held it there for a long and
frozen moment, exposing the entire front of his body to

Hal's attack. "Cut me down where I stand, my knight! Do it, or I'll kill you, I swear I will!"

"Your chance for that has passed!" Hal spat. But his sword did not move.

"Is it?" Köthen cocked back the scythe and swung it wide. His aim was vengeful and true. It missed Hal's belly by a hairsbreadth, then swept his sword from his hand and flung it clattering into the stalls. Erde breathed a split-second's prayer. He would kill or be killed. He was, as Hal had said, beyond reason. She must do it now, or it would be too late.

She threw her heavy wool-and-leather coat to the floor, then sprang past Rose's restraining arm and ducked the long blade as it whistled past on its second vicious arc.

"No! You mustn't!"

She lunged and grabbed the scythe handle. The angry momentum of Köthen's swing jerked her hard off-balance and dragged her across the floor. Horrified, Hal drew his dagger but backed away. Köthen did not. He hauled on the scythe handle, sending Erde tumbling toward him. He caught her deftly with his free arm, twisted her around, and pinned her to his chest with the scythe blade at her throat.

"Foolish child," he muttered.

We shall see about that, thought Erde, amazed that she was not afraid.

"What are you . . . no!" Hal lowered his blade. "As a man of honor, Adolphus, let the girl go."

"I have no honor, my knight. You've made that ever so clear to me."

"I never meant . . ."

"No. Stay where you are if you wish this girl alive tomorrow."

"You'd never . . ."

"I would! I will! Why shouldn't I? You've left me nothing else. It's your word I'll need now. Safe passage out of here, Heinrich, on *your* honor, in exchange for her life."

But Erde caught Hal's worried look, shook her head once, and smiled. "It's all right. We're taking him with us."

Hal's eyes widened. "Now?"

She nodded as best she could, with a blade at her neck the length of a man's arm. She reached for her companions in her mind, and found each waiting: one, two, three. Then

she turned her head sideways against her captor's chest!
"My lord of Köthen, prepare yourself for a journey."

Köthen said, "What?"

And the dragons took them both.

PART TWO

The Journey into Peril

Chapter Twelve

When she doesn't immediately show the mysterious scrap of paper to the God, Paia knows that something has changed. She has kept secrets from him before, mostly minor ones in the cause of preserving her pride or dignity. But he is the God, after all. Anything that might affect her security or the welfare of the Temple, she has always told him about . . . before.

Before what? Since the God arrived, Paia has been his favorite, his priestess, his beloved slave. When she was younger, it was like having a father all over again. As she matured, their relationship altered to admit a sexual innuendo, but through it all, she's never doubted that the God loves her, in whatever way he's capable of. Now she's not so sure about all that. She tries to puzzle out what has happened. Was it the incident with the faked assassination? Is it his demand that she have a child? She doesn't think it's either of these. Though certainly both contribute, the real difference, whatever it is, centers around the note. Somebody she doesn't know is watching her for a reason she doesn't understand. Plus, she's beginning to understand that Son Luco, her supposed subordinate, knows a lot more about what going on around the Citadel and beyond than the Temple's High Priestess knows.

She stares at the remains of her breakfast: the crisp brown bread, the slim slices of precious melon, the tiny pot of honey from the hives in the Temple garden. There's enough food on this small gilt table to feed several people.

Yet Paia always eats alone, as the God has decreed she must. She tries to imagine other people in the room with her. Luco, perhaps, dicing up a bit of melon in his fastidious way. Or the current duty captain, sitting back in her chair, sipping mint tea cooled in the Sacred Well. Paia laughs, but it's a hollow sound in her big empty chamber. There's only one chair in the room, the one she's sitting on. If the God wishes to appear to sit when he comes in man-form, he commandeers hers.

Suddenly, what Paia has accepted as the welcome privileges due her exalted rank take on a more sinister aspect, that of isolating her from the daily life of the Citadel. She has been pampered and revered and protected, but she has also been kept apart, innocent, even ignorant. Perhaps Luco is right to call her spoiled.

So here's the question, she decides: *of what use is my ignorance to the God?* She knows he does nothing without a purpose.

She's kept the note in her sweatpants pocket, now folded away with her T-shirt in a bottom drawer where her chambermaid is unlikely to disturb them.

What price survival? She recognizes the reference to the Temple liturgy, but . . . whose survival does it refer to? Hers?

Paia feels some sort of response is called for, but she hasn't a clue what it should be or how to go about making it. Should she just scrawl a reply and leave it on the easel where she found the first? Would the note writer be looking for that? What should she say? *"I don't understand. Please explain further."* This time, her laugh barely gets beyond a chuckle. She needs guidance, but there's no one to turn to. Certainly not the God, though the God has always been her guide before. Certainly not his loyal servant Luco, though Luco is probably, after the God, the soul she knows best in the entire world.

She balls up her lace-edged napkin and flings it onto her plate, into the bright juice from the melon, into the melting stain of butter. The chambermaid will be heartbroken. Even so, Paia is tempted to upend the entire mess onto the starched white tablecloth. These are linens from the old days, her father's days. Then, she was too young to care about what was going on outside the protected world of her nursery or playroom or schoolroom. She overheard bits of it anyway, from her father, from his advisers and staff, from friends who had been invited to take refuge with the family. And from the House Comp, of course, which was always awake in those days, monitoring the increasingly disastrous progress of world events and reporting on it whenever requested, sometimes when not.

The House Comp.

Paia gets up from the table and goes to her alcove window. The sun is just up, a squat red oval hovering behind a pall of smoke and dust. The smoke is unusually thick to the south. Often Paia sees smoke plumes rising out of the distant hills and notes that something is burning again. This particular morning, it finally occurs to her to wonder what that something might be.

The House Comp.

The central brain of the deactivated House Monitor is still very much alive. Maybe it could tell her. Certainly in her father's day, it could have. How odd that she has never tried to ask it such things before. But the God must not know. She needs to get up to House's lair without being seen or followed.

Paia thinks her way through her Temple calendar for the day. She has a Sanctification of the Lambs at 0900, then a Ritual Bathing in the Sacred Well, then Lunch, then . . . maybe after Lunch, before the evening invocation, she can find a moment to slip away undetected to the Library. She hasn't been there in a long while, she realizes. A very long while. The God has been keeping her unusually busy.

She rings for her chambermaid to clear the dishes and help her dress for the Temple. She feels energized and powerful, as if she's made a momentous decision, and likes the surge of it in her veins. She paces about the room, humming, and allows the chambermaid to choose the most revealing of all her Temple garments, one she has always hated despite the ingenuity and richness of its design. It consists almost entirely of a shimmering body veil of the finest gold mesh. What little is worn underneath is sewn with thousands of gleaming seed pearls. The chambermaid smoothes a reverent hand across its silky transparent glimmer and unsnaps the thin, jeweled collar. A soft, unconscious sigh escapes her lips.

Paia strips and wraps the studded belt around her hips. The big gold clasp is decorated with the image of the Winged God Rampant. A fringe of strung pearls falls from mid-belly to mid-thigh. The chambermaid fastens the collar at the nape of Paia's neck. Under the long golden veil, her perfect breasts and buttocks are bare. The chambermaid fusses around her, straightening the clasps, arranging the folds, touching Paia in tiny intimate ways that could be an accident, could be a caress. Paia wonders if she reaches out, lets her fingertips brush and encircle the chambermaid's nipples the way hers have just been, what will happen then?

Abruptly sweat drenched, she moves restlessly out of range of the chambermaid's busy hands. She realizes that it's happening again, a sudden rising of desire, this time with precious little provocation. Surely the chambermaid has always touched her this way, inevitable during the process of Enrobing. Perhaps the chambermaid thinks she would look better in this very revealing costume if she went to the Temple with her nipples well-formed. Paia is almost tempted to ask her, except of course that the chambermaid has been mute since birth. How convenient for the God, she muses, who otherwise strictly prohibits defectives from serving either the Temple or the Citadel. Not only does the chambermaid have no voice, she has no name, or has never offered one, by whatever means she could. And Paia has never asked. With this realization, desire dies, and her rime of sweat wraps Paia in an actual chill.

Momentarily, she considers rejecting the chambermaid's choice of garment. But she can't stand the idea of going through the whole dressing process over again. She signals curtly for the woman to cease her silent fussing. The Priestess is ready. She assumes her most aloof bearing, nods for the chambermaid to open the door, and sweeps majestically down the hall.

Later, still damp from her Ritual Bathing, Paia hikes up the thin white Robe of Purity that her priestesses have swathed her in as she stepped naked from the gold-tiled pool beside the Sacred Well. She takes the stone stairs two at a time, exulting in her temporary freedom. She has done something unprecedented. She has ordered the red-veiled

Twelve not to attend her on her daily Progress to Lunch.
She wishes, she announces to them, to ponder in silence as
she walks. This took them completely by surprise. In their
confusion, she has managed to evade them by vanishing
with an airy wave into a privy, then immediately out the
other door and down the hall, several turns to the right
and left—she has planned this escape carefully—under an
arch and around a hairpin corner that opens onto a hidden
inner stair, used in her childhood by servants and now
known only to her. And to the God, Paia supposes, for the
God knows everything. But he'd be forced to shrink his
man-form to an undignified size in order to appear in this
rough-hewn passage, and she considers this to be unlikely
enough to verge on the "not-on-your-life." So perhaps this
passage has eluded him. It becomes Paia's favorite for that
reason alone.

The secret stair empties into darkened back corridors
where she must feel her way, burrowing deep into the bedrock. The builders of the Citadel wanted their computer
facility well protected. No one will think to search for her
here. No one but she (and occasionally, the God) ever ven-
tures this far. Eventually, Paia arrives at the massive
leather-and-brass doors of the Library. The entrance is
never guarded. It's merely locked, keyed to the palm prints
of family members and staff long since dead—except one.
A single recessed light glows softly overhead. Neither she
nor the God has been able to figure out how to turn that
one off, and Paia doesn't mind this minor squandering of
energy. She's sure the House Comp has chosen to keep it
burning, perhaps in an act of defiance for having to deacti-
vate so many of its other Monitor functions. Paia understands such gestures, made to maintain some small sense
of personal power in the face of an irresistible and tyrannical force such as the God. Like her own concealment of
the note, or this secret visit.

Paia's palm print admits her to a part of the Citadel
where no one else, other than the God, can go. The God,
of course, can merely materialize within. He does that now
and again. But once inside, he shows little interest in the
banks of screens and keypads and storage racks. He uses
Paia's hands and her experience with the system to keep a
particular function running, or to turn one off, but he has

never asked her help in accessing the Comp's less overt functions, its vast data banks or its sophisticated analytical abilities. He once informed her, in his high-handed way, that there was nothing a machine could tell him that he didn't already know. Paia is willing to believe this, and probably because she doesn't try to convince him otherwise, he lets her amuse herself now and then in the Library, when he's feeling particularly magnanimous. But Paia suspects that the God does not really understand the House Comp, or rather, he underestimates it. He treats it like any other of the myriad mechanical devices that make the Citadel run: admirably efficient but without any individual consciousness. At first, this seemed to her a sign of the God's obvious superiority, of his supernatural strength and wisdom, the House Comp's odd and indeterminate consciousness being below his godly notice. Now she sees it could be a weakness, the only one he's shown to her so far.

And she has never dared to come here without asking him before. Mostly, she comes to call up pictures of her dead parents, or to sift around the data banks in search of her family's past, very nearly an exercise in the heretical nostalgia. For the childish comfort it offers her, the God allows it. But what about the present? What could the House Comp tell her about that? No one, not the God, not even the gossipy Luco, talks about what goes on outside Citadel and Temple and the small circle of dependent villages that supply them with food and labor. The God does not want his servants distracted from their attendance to his proper worship. But if she should ask the House Comp to look outside the Citadel walls, can it do so? And will the God find out?

Standing frozen beneath the single hall light, Paia shudders through a flood of second thoughts. He's irritated with her already. Why risk worse? But her newly defiant momentum has carried her into uncharted territory. She doesn't want to waste it, as she's done too often before. She sets her palm to the bronzed glass plate. The leather-bound doors part and breathe open.

Inside, a row of green-shaded globes awake to faint life. As she moves into the tall, vaulted central aisle and down along the stacks of shelving, the globes brighten ahead of her to light her way, then dim again when she's passed. To right and left, long darkened alleys are lined with climate-controlled storage: her father's collection of rare and antique books. Rolling ladders lead to shelves high above hand reach. When the God ordered Paia to disconnect the House Monitor's HVAC, Paia claimed that the Library's climate-control was special, like the light outside the door, and could not be disabled. Miraculously, he has not yet discovered that she lied to him, or that the House Comp helped her do it. She's not even sure why she risked the God's disfavor in order to protect these essentially useless artifacts. She only knew she must. What else, she wonders now, could she be tampering with?

The Book Room is cool and very dry, instantly wicking all the moisture from her skin and robe. Paia pads along the axis of the room, her bare feet digging into thick maroon carpet that swallows up even the sound of her breathing. At the far end is an elaborate portal, three stone archways closed by much-worn and battered wooden doors. It was rescued, her father once told her, from an ancient castle in Germany. It has paired marble columns between each doorway, and capitals carved in the image of fantastical creatures that remind Paia of the Winged God himself.

Paia touches the pale smooth stone reverently, thinking of the men and women, living thirteen hundred years ago, who might have laid their hand just where hers is now. They have nothing to do with her life, yet she feels strengthened by the sense of physical connection through Time. She pushes on the central wooden door, which creaks realistically on its huge iron hinges. And there in the opening, she is halted by a sudden memory of the painting in the tower. The image is so present in her mind's eye, so vivid, so . . . green. She can almost believe that when she opens this ancient door the rest of the way, she will find that imagined landscape right there, on the other side. Shaken, she hesitates, then laughs at her own foolishness. She swings the big door aside and enters the den of the House Comp.

Since she was a child, Paia has thought of this quirky and increasingly unpredictable machine as if it was some kind of prenaturally brilliant animal that never leaves its cave. She knows it's only a machine, like the God says, but she talks to it as if it were alive. For in many things, the House Comp seems to have a mind of its own.

For instance, it keeps its room as dark as any wild animal's lair, no matter what Paia might request by way of additional illumination. Dark, and colder even than the rare book stacks in the next room. The chill raises goose bumps beneath Paia's thin robe. She feels like a white ghost gliding about in the darkness, groping for the back of the padded leather chair tucked in under the main console. She locates it, hauls it out, and sits, pressing her palm to the screen to awaken the system.

"Hello, House," she murmurs.

"Hello, Paia. It's been a long time."

"I know. I'm sorry."

"No apologies necessary." The House's voice is her father's, a calm, rough-edged baritone that always sparks a bright fire-shower of childhood memories. It was unsettling at first, after she'd lost him, and remains so even now, but she's glad he preserved at least this little part of himself for her to remember him by. "How can I help you today?"

"I need some information, House."

"Of course. That's what I'm here for."

This is what he always says. In fact, while the House Comp's vocabulary is limitless, his mode of expressing himself is not. Once he has settled on a clear and efficient way to convey a given meaning, he varies from it only if a better choice appears or is pointed out to him. Paia finds the utter predictability of his rhetoric both amusing and comforting, but a conversation with him is not quite like a conversation with another human.

Tiny lights flicker like fireflies on the console. "Where would you like to start today?"

"I'd like to take a look around outside." She says it without thinking, then wishes she could take the words back. There might be a subtler way to say it, a way that doesn't sound so much like a direct contradiction of the God's expressed wishes.

"Any particular direction?"

Did she detect a fractional hesitation before he replied? She leans forward over the keypad and whispers, "House, do you understand this might be dangerous for me?"

Another fractional pause. "Knowledge is power."

"I know."

"You are safe with me."

"You mean, he won't find out?"

"You are safe with me."

Paia wonders. What power could a machine muster against a God? "Well . . . toward the south, then."

"Range and resolution?"

"I . . . I'm not sure. What's the biggest? How about . . . well, there was fire out over the hills last night. More than usual."

"Working," says the computer. The huge mirrored black panel above the console glows, then lights up with a grid of images, six rows of ten. A scattering remain black, several are broken up by static. But in the remaining three or four dozen, Paia sees, as she peers more closely, that the images are contiguous, forming one larger image with pieces left out, largely in shades of blue. Toward the left and right, she notes areas of brown and orange, and here and there bits of green strung out like jewels on a necklace. Mostly in the blue screens, but including all the brown and green bits, is a faintly illuminated outline: a squarish shape with odd legs and arms pushing out at the corners.

"What is this, House?"

"LEO-view, dynamic image function."

"What's that?"

"That's the whole ball o' wax."

Paia refuses to ask the exact question again. When House starts using obscure and idiomatic turns of phrase, she knows he's being evasive and will continue to be so until it pleases him to be otherwise. There is some lesson he wishes her to learn. She rephrases her question. "But what am I looking at?"

"Home. Or what's left of it."

"There's so much blue."

"Water, water, everywhere . . ." House sings. An earthquake of static shivers across the grid, and when the images resettle into clarity, most of the blanks have shifted one screen to the right. "But perhaps you'd hoped for something a bit more . . . intimate."

"Okay," Paia agrees, totally mystified.

In the upper right-hand corner, one screen fades and refreshes itself immediately. There, Paia sees as the God in flight might see from high above, miles of barren granite hills, scoured valleys with narrow, boulder-strewn flatlands cut by the snake tracings of empty riverbeds.

"Resolution, one thousand meters."

"Closer," Paia says.

"Five hundred meters."

The image jumps, enlarges, then swallows the grid, swelling and filling the entire bank with a dry contour map of wilderness. A few of the black squares remain black.

"There are some monitors that need replacing," the computer notes reproachfully. "Also, there are a few sectors I cannot reach due to satellite failures. Fortunately, ours is not one of them."

"Shouldn't we be grateful there are still this many in working order?"

"Everyone wanted the satellites to keep working. Up to the end, a lot of money was put into making them self-maintaining and self-repairing."

Paia thinks this is a lot of information for the computer to volunteer. "Like you, House?"

"Yes, Paia, like me. But there is a serious oversight in my design: without hands, I cannot replace my own monitors."

Is that a hint? The God would be furious. She stares up at the gray-and-brown landscape, scanning for familiar details. "But it's good you can do some repairs. There's nobody else around who'd know how to fix you."

"Not locally, no."

She'd like him to elaborate on that odd remark, but the image distracts her. "Wait! What's that?"

In the middle row of screens, way off to the right, Paia spots a thin pale curl rising from the side of a rocky valley. "Smoke! Can you get in any closer?"

The computer makes an odd sound, soft and indistinct, like laughter. "I can kiss the hair on a bee."

"Really?" Paia wishes there was a human face built into this machine. She wouldn't care if it was real or not, but she'd like a pair of eyes she could look into, and know she'd made contact.

"Here we go. Magnifying. Resolution, five meters."

"Yes! Look!" She spots the telltale geometry of broken roadways and struggling kitchen gardens bounded by fieldstone walls. "Close in."

"Resolution, one meter and zooming. Beginning enhancement and scintillation correction."

The image dances and implodes. Suddenly it's like standing in among them, or like floating just above their heads: scrawny, ragged, soot-faced people racing about, trying to beat out the last embers of the fire that has consumed their hamlet. Blackened stone foundations smolder. Paia counts several dozen crumbling squares that recently were houses and barns. Lone figures, a man with one arm, an older woman, stand forlornly beside small piles of salvaged possessions. A naked child gingerly picks through smoking rubble.

"Is this one of our villages?" Paia asks. She means the God's. These people look different from the usual run of the Faithful in the Temple. No healthier or more prosperous, but . . . well, brisker in their movements, more determined somehow, even in this moment of grief and desolation.

"Working." The House Comp can be remarkably terse where the God is concerned.

In a corner screen, a recalled long view of the valley is overlaid with the red-and-blue lines of an old road map. The village had been called West Eddy. Paia does not recognize the name from the Temple roster, but if this village does pay tribute, it should be due some relief aid to help its inhabitants recover from this disaster.

"Son Luco will know. I must remember to ask him."

"Luco will not help this village." The House Comp never uses Luco's honorific.

"He will if I tell him to."

"He won't."

"Why not?"

The computer does not answer. Instead, the big central image of the burned village is replaced by an extreme close-up: one woman's head and torso, as she brushes hair back from her damp forehead. She is young and Paia can see she's been crying. But her face and hands are smudged with ash, so clearly her tears have not kept her from working alongside the others to put out the fire. She drops her hand and lets her red-eyed gaze flick upward. Her thin jaw hardens. She raises her hand again, balled into a fist, and shakes it twice at the sky.

"Turn it off!" Paia recoils in guilty panic. "What if the God sees it?"

Uncannily, it seems as if the young woman has aimed her rage directly at the House Comp's camera, and shot it into Paia's chest.

"As you wish." The images vanish into mirrored black, reflecting only the dim lights playing on the console.

"Why did you show me this? Why? The God would be angry." In truth, it is she who is angry. She's been caught off guard, and upset.

"You did ask to look around outside." There is a faint but significant pause. "Is there anything else I can help you with today?"

Sitting in chill darkness, Paia chews her lip. In the days when the House Comp was her tutor, dispensing discipline was not in his programming, so this was the tone he'd take when she misbehaved or didn't study her lessons. She used to get mad at him then. Once she went so far as to pound her fist on his console. He rewarded her with a brief but frightening electric shock, which was allowed, under the definition of self-preservation. Paia learned not to push the computer too far. But punish her though he might, the House Comp would never betray her to the God. She decides to take the chance.

"I'm sorry, House. I didn't mean to . . . there is something else, actually." And then she's unsure how to say it. "If you heard the phrase, 'what price survival?', would it have any meaning to you, other than the obvious? Like, is it a quote or something?"

"Where did you hear it?"

"I, um . . . read it somewhere." She leans forward again to whisper, even though there is no one else in the room. "What do you think, House?"

"Searching," the computer replies blandly, and then, "I can find no reference for this phrase."

She's not sure what she'd expected to hear. She doubts that the computer is capable of withholding requested information, but an unconditional negative surprises her. "Nothing? Nothing at all?"

"Do you wish me to conduct my search a second time?"

That scolding tone again. Paia sulks. She can almost suspect sarcasm. "I thought you were my friend, House."

A very definite pause this time. "I am your friend, Paia. I am the best friend you have."

Alone in the dark, Paia searches for an appropriate response. Instead, she hears the God's summons. Not a voice, but a power inside her, compelling her to come to him. Immediately. Has he found her out already?

"I have to go, House."

"Remember what I said."

"I will. I promise."

"Do hurry back."

"I'll try. Thanks for your help."

"No problem," says the computer. "Have a nice day."

She hardly hears him. She is like iron to a magnet. The God is calling her toward the Temple, toward his own inner sanctum, the huge hollowed-out second story above the Sanctuary that allows him entry from the air. He will be in God-form then. For the first time in a long while, the idea frightens her. In God-form, he is a physical presence in the world. If he wants to, he can actually do her harm. Still, Paia hurries, through the brightening and darkening aisles of the Library, into the dim outside corridor, down the hidden stair. She hurries as if to a forgotten appointment, or a secret tryst.

And she hurries because she believes in him. She is eager to prostrate herself before his magnificence. For as she discovers anew each time, in God-form he is the irresistible force, the supernatural beauty. He is the heart-stopping, soul-shaking miracle that won her faith in the first place. He is the Impossible Thing.

He is a *dragon*.

The God will not use the word, does not allow it to be spoken anywhere. New converts at the Temple are warned that just saying the word is punishable by death. He is the God to them and must be, nothing more, nothing less. One day, a few years after his arrival, he stood in man-form behind Paia in the Library while she called up dragon images on the House Comp's screens. She showed him medieval dragons carved in stone or rendered in gilt and turquoise in illuminated manuscripts. She showed him twining Celtic dragons in beaten silver and bright Chinese dragons embroidered on silk. Dragons on pottery, pen-and-ink dragons. Full color animations and virtual dragons. The choices were endless, but not all that varied.

"You see?" she told him. "You look just like them."

"They look like me," he replied. But he scanned them thoroughly, made her search the House Comp's entire repertory of dragons as if looking for something in particular. When Paia was done, the God nodded. He seemed satisfied, his attention already moving off in some other direction. And that was the last time the topic of dragons was open for discussion between them.

She halts outside the human entrance to the God's Sanctum. She brushes her hair back, wipes sweat from her upper lip, straightens her robe. She's sorry not to be appearing before him in the Veil of Gold. That outrageous garment is as popular with the God as it is with Paia's chambermaid, though Paia thinks the cool white Robe of Purity shows off her tawny skin to good enough effect. Then she has an idea. Quickly, she unbraids her elaborate Temple hairdo, letting her dark auburn curls cascade in ringlets down her back as only the young girls do. Perhaps this will help put the God in a more sentimental mood about her. She shakes her hair back and opens the door.

It is hot and stygian inside the Sanctum, as usual. Paia thinks of the black steel-and-plastic lair she's just come from. The only real difference is the extremes of temperature. And size. The God's Sanctum is as big as the entire Temple below. Paia waits inside the door for her eyes to adjust. The God is silent now. He ceased his insistent, irresistible summons the moment she stepped through the door. She can feel him waiting somewhere in the darkness. He likes her to find him. When she still trusted him completely, Paia enjoyed this game. Even now, her heart quickens with anticipation, as if for a lovers' tryst. Because this is the moment when she feels her special connection to him most strongly. In the absence of sight and sound, if she goes into herself and listens with that *other* sense, she can know where he is.

She moves forward, sightless but not blind. There are columns in this cavernous space, hewn out of the solid rock, and pitted spots in the floor. He guides her around each of these, with a wordless negative here, an unspoken positive there. This is a good sign, Paia decides. When he's in a bad mood, he lets her run into things. The dark cavern is like an oven. Her body is slick with sweat. The white gown clings to her back and legs. She sheds it, dropping it behind her on the warm stone. She feels him near, the God, the magma-heart of the heat. She reaches, finds the hot, smooth curve of a claw as high as her waist.

BELOVED.

"I am here, my lord, to worship thee."

His presence fills her, drowning out all other thought. She runs her hand along the polished arc of his claw to where the hard ripples of the sheath begin, and the slick scales of his mammoth paw. She imagines she can see the glimmer of gold and the flash of deep ruby that traces each rounded plate. She grasps the edge of a scale and pulls herself up to straddle the base of his claw. His voice in her head is a sighing like oceans, an invasion, a caress. The heat of him against her nakedness is too much to bear. Paia flattens herself against his broad foreleg, her thighs gripping the flawless curve of ivory, and lets the holy ecstasy take her in waves.

Chapter Thirteen

The trip is a rough one this time. N'Doch expects he'd have gotten used to it by now, but even so, he ends up short of breath, with his head between his legs and his gut in his throat. He guesses that the hard sound of retching he hears behind him is the first-timer bearing the burden of inexperience. He glances around, sees the baron on his knees in the dust, a sorry comedown for a man who was sure he had the upper hand a few eternal seconds earlier. There is no gleaming curve of hand-wrought iron beside him: the scythe didn't make it, and N'Doch thanks his own good luck for that.

The girl is on her feet already, watching the baron with something like pity, though N'Doch knows it's a lot more complicated than that. At least she's got the sense to leave the man alone to lose his lunch in private.

Besides, she looks a little woozy herself, and she almost never shows it. N'Doch lurches up to a squat, then steadies himself with his hands while his head clears. He can feel the sear of the sun on his back, like home, only different. Redder, is what occurs to him, like some kind of filter's been drawn across the light. Right away, he's sweating. He strips off the heavy wool tunic he'd had on when the girl alerted him. He's got his short-sleeved linen underneath, the closest thing the weavers could manage to a decent T-shirt.

"Phew. Musta come a long way this time."

"Yes." The girl comes over, offers him a hand.

N'Doch waves her away. "I'm fine." He appreciates the thought, but he doesn't need her reminding him how much faster she recovers from this dragon-transit stuff. He feels for the pack he'd hugged to his chest as if his life depended on it, since at some point, it might. It's there beside him in the dust. He noses around inside for his new sandals. Off to one side, on a bit of a rise, the dragons have settled in to wait for the humans to get a grip. The big guy's pawing at the dirt and sniffing it. Water has her blue-velvet nose straight up in the air. N'Doch admires the sinuous slim curve of her neck. He can hear their murmuring in his head, as they take stock of the surroundings. None of it sounds very promising.

"It's hot," says the girl.

"Heh, we knew it was gonna be."

She looks around, coughs. "And dry."

"We knew that, too." But it was *his* dream image they'd followed, so maybe he'd been better prepared for the reality of it. He hauls off his boots, stuffs them into his pack, and ties his sandals' complicated fastenings, wishing for something nice and simple like velcro. If he knew where he was, he'd go barefoot, but he's got to admit, he's finally getting some sense in his head about which risks are the ones worth taking. He gets his legs under him squarely and stands. Gazing around, he lets out a low whistle.

They've landed on an elevated roadway, or what's left of one. A wide one, eight lanes at least. To the right, the shattered pavement curves away onto solid ground dotted with rock and scrub, and the ruins of what might have been a group of commercial buildings. He sees bits of faded images and lettering too bleached out to read. To the left, the road rises optimistically, then ends in a tangle of corroded steel and rusted rebar. N'Doch takes a few steps in that direction, wondering how stable the wreckage is likely to be. "This was, like a big highway, and this here was a bridge or something." He sweeps his arm in a describing arc. "Big curving son of a bitch."

"Ah," says the girl.

She'll remember the few cars and trucks she saw when she was in his home time, but no way she's seeing the bridge he's got in his mind's eye. N'Doch gives in. He lets the dragons send her the image.

"Ah," she says again, her eyes widening.

"Yeah. Can't tell what took it out, though. Whatever it was, doesn't look real recent." He heads for the edge.

"Be careful," she calls after him.

N'Doch has to laugh. If he was being careful, he wouldn't be here in the first place. The roadway ends about fifty meters upslope in a wide, crumbled tear, like something took a great big bite out of it. Something huge. *Godzilla,* he thinks. He eases up to the point of no return and looks over.

Water.

The land falls away from under the roadway in steep slides of rock and rubble, dropping maybe twenty meters into a murky green bay that stretches into invisibility on either side. The opposite shore is hazed by dust and distance and hot red sunshine. N'Doch knows the bridge that stood here could never have spanned this gap, unless they had antigravity or something. He licks his lips. There's a definite salt tang in the dry air. He wants to ask the dragon: *you got any idea what went on here?* But that would be two concessions, too close together. He can feel her watching him.

He expects to see palm trees like the ones that line the ocean shores at home. But the vegetation here is sparse, low, and piney. It looks like it's seen better days. He sees nothing living where the water laps the rocks below. No fish in the shallows, no snails or starfish. Not even seaweed. He squints down into the green water again. It looks tepid and thick. N'Doch nods, deciding it's just possible that the whole bay's been taken by an enormous algae bloom. He knows all about that sort of thing.

He turns, walks back to where the girl is still pretending not to notice the first-timer struggle for breath. N'Doch sees the guy reach blindly for the sword that isn't at his hip. He's sick and out of it, but a weapon is his first semicoherent thought. *He'll come around all right.* N'Doch approves of the reflex, but it puts him back on the alert. He's less sure than the girl that the dude's obvious survival instincts won't be used against him. He'd advised against bringing him, but what the hell? It wasn't his call.

"There's like an ocean out there," he reports. "Maybe a

bay of some kind. Don't know for sure, but I think the water's a lot higher than it was when the bridge was built."

"Do you mean there's a flood?"

"Now? Don't think so. Looks like this water's been here a while."

The first-timer groans and coughs, then sits back on his heels, wiping his beard on his sleeve. He mutters something incomprehensible that, milliseconds later, through the miracle of dragon simultaneous translation, makes itself known to N'Doch as pretty foul language, even by his personal standards.

He smirks at the girl's blush. "I don't think his royal highness is too happy about this." He's said it that way to lighten up the mood a bit, not to mention that he can't pronounce the dude's name too well, with that weird vowel he can't get his tongue around. But the girl hears something else, and shoots him a glare.

"He's not a royal anything. He's only a baron."

"Only. Well, ex-*cuse* me." N'Doch lets out a high whoop of hilarity. "I'm only a nothing."

She blinks at him. "You are a bard, N'Doch, and a dragon guide. This is not nothing."

She's so serious, it's no fun even tweaking her. He'd thought her sense of humor was on the upswing, but he must've had that wrong. He sighs. "C'mon, you gotta admit—it was a rough trip. Let's give ole whatsisname a hand." He goes over, sticks out a palm.

No surprise, the guy does exactly what N'Doch had done. He waves the help away irritably and staggers to his feet. He quick-searches his body for injury, and seems puzzled when he finds none. "Mother of God," he growls. "What happened?"

"The DRT," returns N'Doch sympathetically. "Read that as Dragon Rapid Transit. Don't worry. It gets easier after the first time . . . Sort of."

But Baron K. does not have the advantage of a dragon translating in his ear. His dark eyes narrow at N'Doch, then sweep past him to take in the wrecked landscape and then the dragons. For a moment, he says nothing. Then N'Doch sees his brain switch into overdrive.

"This is not . . . what is this place?"

N'Doch shrugs. "Damned if I know."

The baron's gaze fastens on Water, whom he has never seen in dragon-form. "What's that, another one?"

The girl says quietly, "My lord baron, may I present the Lady Water, in her truest form."

Water turns her attention full at him, and somehow her expression is Sedou's. The guy stares back, figuring it out. N'Doch recalls the taut look that had passed between Sedou and the baron, that first night at dinner. He's obscurely proud to see the angry line of the baron's jaw relax as he takes in the blue dragon's beauty. But it hardens again when he turns to face the girl. "Where am I? What have you done, witch?"

"Told you this was a bad idea," N'Doch murmurs. But he's got to give it to her—this mean guy is real pissed, yet she faces him bravely all the same, like she's got nothing to apologize for, kidnapping him and all.

"Not I, my lord. It was the dragons who brought you."

The baron takes a breath, still not quite steady on his feet. "The conveyance, perhaps, but not the planning of it."

"You think that dragons do not plan, my lord?"

"I would not presume to guess. Damn it, woman! Don't play with me!"

"There is no play intended, my lord." She is so earnest, even N'Doch finds it hard to suspect her of the scheming he knows she's guilty of.

"What have you . . . !" The baron bites back on his snarl in an obvious decision to humor this madwoman until he can figure out what the hell's going on. "What would any self-respecting dragon want with me?"

"You might be surprised, my lord."

"You are correct. I would be. Would you care to explain further?"

N'Doch can see the toll it takes, reining in his anger like he is, mustering up this cool manner and terse formality, reminding himself that she's only a girl. *Yeah, right.* N'Doch gets his first inkling of pity for the dude. He's spitting nails and still shaky on his feet, but he's not taking this as seriously as he should be, because he has no idea how serious it really is. He's overmatched and doesn't even know it. N'Doch shifts sideways a bit, to where he can watch the power struggle from a better angle.

"Well, my lord baron, it is you who are correct. It was my idea."

The baron nods, like he's won a huge victory. "You thought to save Heinrich's life, I suppose." He runs a hand down his cheek, lets it drag across his throat. The memory seems to amuse him in a grim sort of way. "Death by scythe. Not exactly the end he'd envisioned."

"Not his life, my lord. Yours."

"Again?" He rubs his eyes, abruptly showing an entirely different kind of exhaustion. "So you think the old man has one trick left he hasn't taught me? Perhaps he does, though he was never much for withholding his secrets. But it hardly matters. Truth is, my lady, I suspect Heinrich and I will never be ready to kill each other. We've threatened it so many times in our lives, it's become a meaningless exercise." This thought carries him into pensive silence, as if he's forgotten he's not alone. He stares into the dust, then catches himself and rouses. "Of course, there was always the happy possibility that he'd kill me by chance. Meanwhile, my lady, the prospect of your continuing to rescue me might well induce me to behave under any circumstances. So now, you and your dragon familiars can return me to whence I came—though I hardly relish the trip—and we'll all be the wiser. I have work to do, and someday soon, God willing, Heinrich will let me do it."

She nods. Her hands are clenched behind her back. "We could indeed send you back, my lord."

"I am only waiting."

"But we will not."

And here we go, N'Doch tells himself. *Now the shit really hits the fan . . .*

"Of course you will."

"No, my lord baron. We will not."

"Come, girl, you've had your witchy fun with me. Enough is enough. I give my word that I will not kill Hal Engle." He raises one palm, lays the other on his heart. Then he grins. "Only beat him up a little."

"You persist in thinking of this as a prank, my lord, but it is not. We will not take you back."

"But you can't . . . this is an outrage!"

"But a necessary one, my lord baron."

He stares at her, and she stares right back. N'Doch sees

that his highness Baron K. just cannot believe this mere slip of a girl is jutting her chin at him, telling him no and sounding like she means it. Again N'Doch wonders if he'll have a fight on his hands. He's not sure he can take this guy, even though he's armed and the baron isn't. Definitely a good thing that the scythe didn't make it through the veil, 'cause the baron's breathing has tightened, like a man in a corner preparing to attack. But he doesn't. He stalks away a few paces. He looks again at the dragons and back at the girl, then he shoves his hands onto his hips and stares off into nothing. Incredulous and seething, but for the time being, controlling it well. "So," he mutters, "I am fated to remain a prisoner no matter what land I find myself in."

For a moment, the girl wavers, and N'Doch worries she's about gone her limit—she's gonna crack. She's also fighting a touch of translation sickness. And maybe it would be all for the best to just send the guy back. But she's followed the baron's glance at the dragons, and what has apparently subdued him lends her strength. N'Doch can hear whole choruses of dragon support vibrating between his ears. For sure, she'll assure him later that she could never have done this on her own, but he's more and more convinced she's a lot stronger than she looks.

"No prisoner, my lord," she says, her voice tightened to the verge of a squeak. "Any more than we all are—prisoners of our duty. In this world, you are free to come and go as you like. But you said you were a man without a purpose. I am offering you one. If you wish so much to fight, fight here. Your services are needed."

Laying it on kinda thick, N'Doch thinks, but even he can't help getting caught up in her rap just a little. As she warms to it, her squeak drops away. He hears for the first time that her voice is no longer that pure girlish fluting—it's gained harmonics, and that means power. She stands up real tall in her pale linens and her hair's finally grown out some, so it kind of coils nicely around her long narrow face, with its skin as perfect as some white girl's porcelain doll. But she's not as bleached out as she was when N'Doch first met her. The hot sun of his homeland has brought up a healthier color which the chill and dank of Deep Moor have not dispelled. She looks strong. She almost looks confident. One day soon, she's gonna be beautiful. Not

N'Doch's taste, of course, besides she's his sister. But maybe the baron's starting to see it just a little, or maybe he would, if he'd stop feeding his anger for half a minute and take a good look around him.

"My services," the baron repeats bitterly.

"Yes, my lord."

"Not much in demand anywhere else, is that it?"

The girl nods earnestly.

"I don't think you were supposed to agree with him," N'Doch murmurs.

She gives a tiny little gasp. "For now, that is, my lord."

N'Doch leaps into the gap. "Hey, man, I didn't want this gig either, y'know? One day I'm doing nothing special, then suddenly there's this blue dragon in front of me, and poof! I'm drafted!"

The baron stares at him, and N'Doch remembers he can't have understood a single word. But somehow, he must have gotten the gist, 'cause he looks away at the girl, then down at the ground, shaking his head. His laugh starts slow but builds and builds to a hard ironic barking that bends him almost double until he gets control of it. When he's done, he's wiping dampness from his eyes and beard. "So—this is how you get me out of Heinrich's hair. Ah, sweet Jesus! Might as well kill myself your way as his, is that it?"

The girl's eyes narrow. She is not happy with this. N'Doch can tell she considers it inexplicable and undignified. As for himself, he likes the man better for it. It suggests a complexity N'Doch wasn't sure he had. Feeling companionable, he unfolds a long arm to give the baron's shoulder a sympathetic slap, and finds himself jerked, suspended in air, then slammed down hard on the ground with Baron K. looming over him and the dust rising around them both.

Man! I knew he was fast, but. . . .

Breathless, N'Doch hold up a palm. "Whoa up, brother, I was just . . ."

The girl throws herself between them. The baron shoves her aside and levels a finger at N'Doch like it was a blade. "Don't ever do that again!"

N'Doch scrambles up, ready to fight him now. But the girl is there, holding him back. "No, N'Doch! Please! He's not . . . please let it go!

"He's not what? N'Doch snarls. "Not in his right mind?"

"Please, N'Doch. There are things . . . your ways are just . . . different."

N'Doch is amazed that, angry as he is, this makes him even angrier. "Different how? I offer the man a friendly little pat and he decks me!"

"It doesn't matter!"

"Well, I think it matters!" He looks over the girl's shoulder to see the baron eyeing him with a faintly superior smile. Suddenly, he's had enough of the arrogant son of a bitch. "It's more of that lordship shit, ain't it?" he roars, looking for a way around the girl's dancing, pleading hands. "If he's so sure he's better 'n me, let him prove it!"

"STOP IT!" she screams at him.

And N'Doch stops. She's never done that before, never leveled the full power of her lungs and being at him like that. It hits him like a ton of bricks, and his brain is vibrating with not-so-subtle dragon resonance. They're not too happy with him either. What is it about this baron dude, he fumes, that has everyone protecting him, putting up with his bad behavior? He'd get it if it was just the girl—these handsome, moody guys are always big with the women. But now it's the dragons as well. No way he'd get away with behaving like that. Least not anymore.

"I shouldn't hafta be like no prince for him to treat me decent!" But he knows the girl's not going to understand that. He glares at the baron, spits deliberately into the dust, and stalks away.

He heads off down the road a bit, blowing off his rage in long stiff strides but uneasy in his heart just the same. Because he knows the girl's just trying to help keep the peace. Plus, now that he considers it more calmly, he sees what the baron is up to, and it makes him mad again that the dragons don't get it. Mad enough to let them know it.

You all think he's so hot, but it's just the same old alpha-dog bullshit!

But as usual, Water surprises him.

I know that. And you're supposed to be man enough not to buy into it.

What? Why me?

Look at it this way: would it be useful to have him on our side?

N'Doch groans his assent. It pains him to admit it.

So do what it takes to get him working for us. What does it really cost you?

A whole helluva lot, N'Doch thinks. It's all this lordship stuff, really. That's what keeps getting him so riled. *None of that bullshit where I came from!* In the gangs, no real leader ever dissed his men for no good reason. In the gangs, a guy had to really prove himself before anyone'd give him the kind of respect this Köthen dude seems to think he was born with.

N'Doch kicks at a chunk of shattered concrete, trying to remember when life was normal, how he felt *then*. Something nags at him, and the concrete is in several smaller chunks before he finally makes the connection. He can say—like he has to the girl many times, to her total disbelief and astonishment—he can say there are no lordships and kings and what-all where he comes from . . . but is it really true? What's nagging him is, it's not.

'Cause there are lordships and princes in his country, and princesses, too. And kings and queens. Only he'd call them celebrities. Stars, like the beautiful women his mama watches on her vid, or rich people, like Kenzo Baraga the Media King. People with all the power of the girl's King Otto, and from what he heard at Deep Moor, probably a hell of a lot more. And he'd say: that's the life I want. That's what I've been dreaming of since I first sat down at a keyboard. And if he met them, he wouldn't expect them to treat him any differently than this baron guy just did.

N'Doch finds a piece of broken guardrail and sits down on it, totally confused.

Well? Can you deal with it?

Okay, so the guy's used to being in charge, and he's gotta keep up the front.

So he was bound to challenge you sooner or later.

Nice if it'd been later. But I could probably take him, y'know.

Water has no interest in that argument.

What would it gain us if you did?

What about what it would gain me?

But meanwhile, down the road, there's two people standing in the hot sun, waiting on his next move. For two entirely different reasons. Add the damn dragons and you got four. It seems to N'Doch that before he met these dragons, there was a whole lot fewer people expecting things from him. He wishes he was home, where he had some options.

But he gets up anyway, dusts himself off, and heads back. Wary, the baron watches him approach.

"Tell him I was just trying to be friendly," N'Doch mutters to the girl.

"I did. He accepts your apology."

"My *what*?"

"Please, N'Doch . . ."

Is there no end to this, he asks himself. "He tossed me around, and I'm supposed to apologize?"

She nods. "What can it hurt?"

"How 'bout my pride?"

She doesn't seem to have thought of that. And the baron's just staring at him, waiting for some acceptable sign of capitulation. N'Doch gives back the glare as best he can until the moment stretches beyond even his own patience with macho posturing, and the dragons are whispering between his ears again. Finally he reminds himself that he's always said he's a lover, not a fighter, and that there are other ways to win a war, and that he's got no reputation here to maintain, like Baron K. seems to think he has, no matter what century he finds himself in. And finally, if he keeps them standing here in the sun much longer, they're all gonna melt into smears on the ground. N'Doch decides to cede the skirmish—for now. But if it was a battle of guitars, he thinks, then let's see who'd win. He shrugs and looks away. Maybe this'll make a good song someday. "Go ahead. Take it all out on me."

The girl's eyelids sag briefly. "My lord of Köthen, he thanks you for your gracious pardon."

"Like hell I do," N'Doch mutters. But he tries the name out like she's said it, mouthing it silently, trying for that vowel again.

And Köthen relaxes, like he'd tired of the game even sooner than N'Doch and as necessary as it was, it's about time the girl got it over with. He turns his back on both of them, scuffs his boots in the dust with a deep and ragged sigh. Then, for the first time, he takes a serious look around. He tests the sun-softened pavement with his heel, then walks to the end of the broken bridge like he's taking possession of it, and gazes down into the water. When he comes back, it's with a bit of a swagger and a pensive frown. N'Doch can see he's intrigued despite himself.

Oddly, it's to N'Doch that he puts the question. He pulls up a few yards away and faces him directly. Like he's trying the idea on for size, he says: "Is this the Future you spoke of?"

The girl hastens to interrupt. "Why, yes, my lord baron. We believe it is."

The baron doesn't even look at her, and N'Doch tries not to act too sullen. He knows the guy's still smarting from them seeing him sick and retching from the transport. He's gotta show off enough bullshit bravado to recover the shreds of his dignity. So, this could be just another challenge, but it could also be some kind of peace offering. Carefully, man to man, he nods.

"Interesting." Baron Köthen shades his eyes, looking into the red sun. He studies the angular profile of the western horizon. Mountains, but before the mountains, there's a city there, a little to the north, maybe ten miles away. N'Doch has spotted the building tops already. In fact, the heat's not the only reason not to be standing out in the open like this for so long. Who knows who's been watching them with high-power whatever from whatever distance? But his thought is, probably no one. There's a too-weird stillness about this place. No birds, not even the buzz of an insect.

Now Köthen studies the dragons, letting his gaze linger speculatively on Water. "A shape-shifter. Do I understand that correctly?"

"Yes, my lord." The girl smiles at him tentatively.

"How could Heinrich bear to let you out of his sight?"

She folds her forehead seriously. "Other priorities were . . ."

Köthen waves her silent. "I know, I know. I know all about Heinrich's priorities. I am living proof, am I not?" He kicks at the dust again, then looks back at N'Doch. "We don't even know where we are, do we?"

N'Doch shakes his head, keeping his expression real neutral. The guy's bitter humor is so dry, it's practically invisible. But it strikes N'Doch funny. Then he has an insight. With her tin ear for comedy, the girl doesn't hear it, and until she does, she won't even get to first base with this dude.

"Or *when*," Köthen adds. "Am I right?"

Now N'Doch can't help but grin. "You do land on your feet, man, I gotta grant you that."

When the girl translates, irony settles comfortably into Köthen's eyes. He almost smiles. Then he says, "So what do we do now?"

A challenge for sure, but this time, not an idle one.

N'Doch shrugs. "First thing? Look for water." As the girl translates, he adds, "Water we can drink."

The girl offers the baron a few remarks from her own experience about the treachery of water in the Future. Köthen grunts, then raises a brow at the two packs lying in the dust. "Are we provisioned?"

N'Doch makes no quick move to the packs, so the girl does it. She hauls them over, pries them open, and holds up their contents for the baron's inspection. N'Doch thinks she is way overcompensating now. So she kidnapped the dude. So let's get on with it already.

Köthen makes no move either. He studies each item gravely as she exhibits them: bread, cheese, apples, dried beef, a few small jugs of water. He nods at each, back to humoring her, but N'Doch watches him making the tally in his head and sees him come to the obvious conclusion.

"This will not keep us for long."

N'Doch laughs softly.

Were it not for Earth, Erde decided, she would never have survived this ordeal. She didn't mean physically—she was well used to the rigors of dragon transport. Nor was it the heat and dust that swirled up around her in this alien place. Her stay in N'Doch's time had prepared her for that. But nothing had prepared her for the strain of dealing with Adolphus of Köthen one on one, now that she'd acted on impulse and done this insane thing.

Now that she had him on her hands, what was she going to do with him?

IT WASN'T EXACTLY ON IMPULSE.

Kindly, the dragon reminded her that she had planned it all rather carefully, had even checked out the details with him and with the others. It hadn't seemed insane at the time.

ALL HAS GONE ACCORDING TO PLAN. WHY ARE YOU CONCERNED?

IT WAS HARDLY MY PLAN FOR THE TWO OF THEM TO START FIGHTING FIRST THING!

Lady Water added her assessment.

Men. They behave as they must. Don't worry. They'll sort it out.

HE WILL HATE ME FOREVER.

Water laughed *Which one?*

Erde thought Lady Water a bit too relaxed about N'Doch's behavior. He was, after all, part of the problem.

Have faith, girl. The man is out of a job, and you're giving him one.

WHATEVER ELSE HE MAY BE, HE IS BRAVE AND HONORABLE. HE WILL THANK YOU FOR IT ONE DAY.

Perhaps. But how would she survive his growling and glowering until then? Erde was not sure she would.

He'll require a lot of care and feeding, no doubt of it.

NOW I UNDERSTAND WHY HAL BROUGHT HIM TO DEEP MOOR.

Just keep telling him how useful he's being.

DO NOT TROUBLE YOURSELF WITH DOUBT. CAN YOU HEAR THE CALL?

NO. WHAT? THE SUMMONS? YOU CAN HEAR IT AGAIN?

Loud and clear.

AS IF A VEIL HAS LIFTED.

OH, WONDERFUL! AFTER SO LONG! THEN WE'VE DONE THE RIGHT THING!

Erde took strength from the dragons. Their own crisis was so much vaster than her own slight personal matter. She shoved the food and water back into the packs, passed one to N'Doch, and shouldered the other. Then she faced Baron Köthen expectantly. N'Doch eased back a step or two, retiring from the field. She wasn't sure if she was grateful or not.

"My lord baron, are you with us or no?"

He didn't want to answer her. For she had put him in

the position that N'Doch was in just moments ago, where his only sane option was surrender. And this, of course, was the last choice he wanted to make. She watched him struggle with it, painfully aware of the additional walls of bitterness she was building up between them.

"You have the food and water, such as it is." He gestured faintly at the parched and barren landscape: "Do I have any choice?"

"If you prefer, I will give you half of it and you may go your own way."

"That would be . . . stupidly inefficient."

He had his rage under control now, and that was a mercy. It even helped Erde to accept the unforgiving smolder of resentment that edged his every word and glance.

"Of course you are right, my lord." She bowed her head in acceptance. "Then let us be going." She hadn't a clue where she was going, only that she must somehow get him moving—any direction at all would do. After that, the dragons assured her, things would take care of themselves.

Köthen said, "Wait."

Terrified, Erde stopped, then gave him as casual a glance as she could muster, tossed over her shoulder like an empty nutshell. "My lord?"

He stood as immobile as a rock, his arms stubbornly crossed, as if he knew exactly how to rattle her the most. "Since it is your duty and not mine that brings us here, this is what I propose: I will do whatever it is you need me to do here to the best of my ability, but as soon as I've done it, you will take me home again."

The girl nods, like it could work out that easy, just like that. Come here, do the job, and leave. N'Doch can't believe it. She's learning to lie. Or she's got a whole lot more faith than he does in this dude's capabilities.

Köthen says, "I'll need your word on that, my lady."

"You have it, my lord." The girl extends her hand, like some kind of queen.

Köthen takes it, then bites back his instinct to bow over

it. Instead, he shakes it, real man to man. N'Doch thinks maybe he's decided she really is a little bit nuts, so for now he'd better make the best of it. Meanwhile, in the girl's brave stance, there's just the slightest droop of relief. N'Doch swallows a laugh. It ain't over yet, not with this dude. If she thinks it's all smooth sailing from here out, she's got another think coming. But then, so does Baron K.—just wait until the serious dragon shit starts happening.

But suddenly the baron is all business. "Water first, then. After that, find shelter. We can reconnoiter from there." He points off west. "I suggest we try that way."

Since the man doesn't seem to be taking suggestions, even from the one guy who might actually have some idea about how to deal with this place, N'Doch just nods and adjusts his pack. He'd have headed that way anyway. It's occurring to him that he could actually get to like ole Baron K. just fine, so he decides not to let him get in too much trouble if he can help it. But he's willing to give the dude whatever rope he needs to hang himself just a little, to pay him back for the dusting.

"My lord, I have something for you." The girl reaches inside the top layer of her linens, pulls out a big fighting dagger, and holds it out on her palm. N'Doch hasn't a clue where she came up with it, and he's not so sure arming this guy is such a terrific idea. That mondo blade could be at his throat any minute, the way he sees it. But like he said, this gig is the dragons' call, and the girl's. She brought him. Let her deal with him.

Köthen snorts softly as he lifts the knife from her hand. "Better than nothing, I suppose. But Captain Wender will be missing it." He eases it into the empty sheath on his belt, then reaches to haul the pack off her shoulder and onto his own. Her resistance is only for show. The packs are heavy. N'Doch will attest to that. Köthen struggles a bit with the straps. Clearly he is not used to being the bearer of his own burdens. When he finally has the pack adjusted comfortably, his stance is eloquent with mockery. It declares him as a man who's only conceded defeat because it's convenient for the moment. N'Doch hopes the girl takes this warning to heart.

Köthen squints once more into the fat red sun. He rakes his fingers through his thick yellow hair, then glances at

N'Doch and away. N'Doch can see he's curious—as any man would be— about that city out there to the west. He'd like N'Doch's assessment, but he's damned if he's going to ask for it.

Fine, N'Doch decides. Let the game continue. Let's just see how far he gets in a world he knows nothing about.

Köthen shrugs the unfamiliar weight back onto his shoulders, starts forward, then stops. He turns back to the girl with the most ironic of grins. "By the way, milady witch . . . I suppose I should ask: whose side am I on this time?"

Chapter Fourteen

Paia wakes in the crook of the God's foreleg, curled against the hard wall of his chest. She wonders what time it is, how long she has been here with him. He has let a little air into the Sanctum, and a bit of light. Or maybe she is finally learning to see as he does, in the dark. His huge head is down beside her, resting on the bridge of his claws. His eyes, long and almond-shaped, are shut. He looks almost peaceful, as if he's actually asleep. Paia hopes he is. It's the only time she gets to observe him with any objectivity, when he is there in body but not in her mind.

The House Comp once gave her the God's basic measurements, as if cold fact might somehow cool her ardor. He is thirty-one meters long from blunt nose to razor-tipped tail, and twelve meters tall when rampant. He has a wingspan of twenty-five meters when fully extended. His average skin temperature is 110 Fahrenheit degrees. Were it not for his heat, she'd think him made entirely of precious metals, crafted by artists of inspired genius and god-like patience. For despite his size, his detailing is exquisite and delicate. Every centimeter of him is a perfect design of color and line. Every surface is decorated. Each golden scale is incised with a pattern of leaf-veins in ruby red, as brilliant as the finest enamel. His smallish hooded ears, the only thing small about him, are lined with royal purple as if with shimmering panné velvet. His leathery wings are gilt-scaled on top and azure blue beneath, so that in flight they sometimes seem like chunks of sky caught beneath a golden shroud.

The smallest of his scales, no bigger than Paia's hand, cluster around his eyes. There is something tender and vulnerable about them. Paia slides her still-damp body along the metallic smoothness of his arm to where she can trace the fine ruby veining with an adoring finger and press her lips, counting the kisses, to scale after scale. When he is like this, quiescent, having gifted her with the ecstasy of his holy worship, she cannot help but love him, almost more than life.

He stirs beneath her, a mountain shifting, geologic in scale, and lays his head a little to the side so that she can continue caressing him. At first she was surprised that her soft hands and mouth could transmit any sensation at all through so hard and polished a surface. But he seems to enjoy it. He will let her do it for hours, and sometimes when he's angry but lets her come to him anyway, it even quiets him a little.

He says it's her devotion that pleases him, that when the passion of her faith inspires her to surrender herself to the holy ecstasy, they are as one being and the ecstasy is shared. If this is so, Paia muses, it's the only true sharing between them. The rest is all power games and posturing and her carrying out his bidding. Such as how she must immediately have a child.

He must be asleep. Otherwise she could never lie so close to him and have such thoughts. But no, he's awake, for he stirs again and one long tip of his forked tongue flicks out and coils around her ankle. Instinctively she pulls away, but he holds her.

COME CLOSER, BELOVED.

Paia shudders with pleasure and terror. She is inches from his fangs. What is he up to now?

YOU HAVE BEEN DOUBTING ME LATELY.

"No, my lord. Why do you say so?"

YOUR THOUGHTS STRAY FROM YOUR DUTIES.

Is no part of her mind closed to him? Has she no privacy from him at all? But she knows how to deflect him.

"I miss you, my lord, when you are gone from us."

OF COURSE YOU DO.

His tongue eases farther up her leg, silken heat winding

around her thigh. Paia would like to stay conscious for this conversation, but only fear is keeping the ecstasy from overtaking her again.

"Where do you go? Can you tell me of the great sights you see?"

TOO MANY QUESTIONS. I NEED YOUR ABSO-LUTE ATTENTION, BELOVED. MY ENEMIES ARE NEAR.

"Enemies? What enemies, my lord Fire? Is there a new heresy?"

AN OLD ONE, BELOVED. THE OLDEST ONE OF ALL.

This is the first she's heard him speak of enemies, other than the usual heathen faithless that covet the Temple's riches and livelihood.

"But who are they? What do they want?"

ANCIENT FOES, POWERFUL FOES. THEY WOULD DENY ME MY GODHEAD.

"They are coming here?"

I SENSE THEIR APPROACH, EVEN NOW. THROUGH THE VEIL OF YEARS THAT I HOPED WOULD CONCEAL ME FROM THEM.

His grip on her relaxes. He is distracted. Paia backs away a step and leans against his jaw. Instantly, she longs for his touch again, but fears what he will do if she invites it. "Will they attack the Temple?"

THEY WILL BE SUBTLER THAN THAT. THEY ARE SLY AND DEVIOUS.

"How will we know them?"

YOU WILL NOT NEED TO. I WILL RECOGNIZE THEM INSTANTLY.

"What will they do?"

THEY WILL TRY TO MAKE ALL THAT IS RIGHT SEEM WRONG. THEY WILL CHALLENGE THE DE-VOTION OF THE FAITHFUL. EVEN YOURS, BELOVED.

"They will not succeed, my lord."

THIS IS WHY I NEED YOUR ATTENTION, CON-STANT AND TOTAL, TO HELP ME DISCOVER THEM. TO HELP ME VANQUISH THEM.

"I am your servant always, my lord." He's sounding faintly sullen about all this, like he's been taken by surprise, and Paia thinks it unwise to ask how it is that a God who knows everything does not know where his enemies are.

I AM PONDERING WAYS, BELOVED, THAT WE COULD BE CLOSER.

"Will you tell me, Lord Fire, when you know what they are?"

I WILL, WHEN I AM READY, AND I WILL CALL YOU TO ME.

But Paia is not fooled. Their closeness is no longer the foremost issue in his mind.

Chapter Fifteen

Earth was not happy. He hunkered down, looking more like an outcropping of rock than usual, and rumbled uneasily.

THIS IS A SICK PLACE. A DEAD PLACE.

Water agreed.

Why would he come to such a lifeless place, our pleasure-loving brother?

BUT IS HE HERE, DO YOU THINK?

I AM SURE OF IT.

Erde had been so preoccupied with the dilemma of introducing Baron Köthen to his altered situation that she had neglected the dragons almost entirely. Now she said she needed time to tend to them, that the two men should go on and she would catch up. She let Köthen straighten his battle-worn blue-and-gold tunic in bemused exasperation and strike off west on his own. Keeping up her brave false front had wrung her out. Besides, it was useful to let him test his apparent freedom. She doubted he'd go far unless those he had chosen to lead were actually following. The dragons drew her into a detailed discussion about what evidence of Fire's presence was already presenting itself, and in which direction they were likely to find him. Only N'Doch watched as Köthen blithely walked away.

"Don't you get it?" He grabbed up his woolen tunic and crammed it into his pack. "He doesn't care if we go after him or not."

Erde's heart wanted to go after him, of course, but her

heart was also with the dragons. Besides, he'd made it so clear that he still saw her as the witch, his enemy. "Yes, he does. Let him walk it off a bit. Remember, he rode into Deep Moor bound as a prisoner."

"Fine, great, but what if we lose him? What if he loses himself?"

She was surprised by her own irritability. "Then you'll be rid of him and you'll be glad, won't you? You didn't want him here in the first place."

"Yeah, but . . ." N'Doch's shrug was surprisingly rich with ambivalence. "Well, he's right about finding food and shelter, y'know."

Water uncurled her long neck to study the baron's receding back.

It wouldn't be a good idea to get separated right from the start.

N'Doch resettled his pack on his shoulders. "We'd all better keep up with him, then, 'cause he ain't waitin' for us."

So it was agreed that the humans would keep up, but the dragons would join them later, when they were done assessing this new place they found themselves in. N'Doch was uneasy about leaving Water behind. Erde had warned him many times about the futility of interrupting dragon discussions, but still he insisted on reasoning with them as if they were human. What she hadn't told him was that ever since Earth learned that he possessed a better means of transport than his four stubby legs, he'd not been keen about walking long distances. He'd much rather she went on ahead, then sent him an image to come to. Erde told N'Doch not to worry. The two of them would catch up with the baron. Later, the dragons would catch up with all of them.

Köthen had set a stiff pace, but so far had kept to the old roadway. It took a while to catch up to him, and when they did, he offered them no greeting. He just began talking to them as if they'd been there all along.

"So let me get this straight," he said, to neither one of them in particular. "You're in search of another dragon. And he doesn't want to be found."

"Two dragons, actually: Fire and Air. We hope one will lead us to the other."

"Water thinks one is concealing the other," N'Doch put in. Erde dutifully translated, though not without conveying Earth's disapproval of this notion.

"Ah, yes. I recall now. The difference of opinion. This'll teach me to assume that there's any kind of conversation unworthy of my attention."

His words were reasonable enough, but Erde had learned enough about Adolphus of Köthen by now to recognize the rage still simmering beneath his flat tone and his collected surface. He was angry in a way that no ordinary balm would assuage. But perhaps it wasn't entirely at her.

"So, first, we must find the dragon Fire."

"Sneak up on him's more like it," N'Doch retorted.

When Erde translated, Köthen's eyes never wavered from the horizon. "Really? How does one do that?"

N'Doch smirked. "Good question. I think she's hoping you'll have some ideas."

"I won't tell him that." Erde moved up into the yard-wide gap between the two men. A mile ago, it had been three yards. She threw N'Doch a barbed parody of a smile. "You know, N'Doch, if you tried speaking that German I know Lady Water has been teaching you, you could get into trouble with his lordship again all by yourself."

"Ha," said N'Doch. "His *lordship,* huh?"

Erde understood now that her scheme to kidnap the baron, while having many obvious advantages, had failed to take N'Doch's feelings into account. She had asked him, *pro forma,* then she'd swept all his objections aside and done what she wanted to anyway. "Just try to get along with him, N'Doch. Please?"

"This *is* getting along," N'Doch growled.

When Köthen moved ahead, Erde did not try to keep up with him. Let him go. She was glad he'd not asked about the aspects of the Quest that she herself knew little about, like what will the dragons do when they find either Fire or Air? Would he ever understand her willingness to follow the dragons whatever happened? She feared he would not.

But she'd worry about that later. It was time to start paying some attention to where she was. The dragons would be wanting the information. N'Doch hung back beside her, uncharacteristically lost in his own thoughts. The odd road twisted and turned, though it didn't seem to be curving around anything in particular, just more piles of rubble or clumps of desiccated trees. Erde recalled this same seamless surface from N'Doch's homeland. When he pointed it out and exclaimed in disgust, "Look at this road!" she understood that it was meant to be smooth and unbroken, not split by long cracks full of dusty weeds. Unhealthy-looking bushes sagged along the verges. Their scant leaves were leathery and crisped at the edges. Many of the stunted trees had no leaves at all. The grass seemed to be faring the best, growing tall and brown and coarse, with stingy little seedheads. Erde had never seen a drought before, except in N'Doch's land. But there, all the vegetation had been strange to her anyhow, so she wouldn't have known if it were suffering. Here, most of the plants were reasonably familiar, and their dire condition was obvious even to her.

They plodded along in silence for a long while. Then, echoing her musings uncannily, N'Doch remarked, "We got to be pretty far north, doncha think?"

"Why?"

He shrugged. "Well, I seen pictures."

"That look like this?" She wondered what kind of sad painter would bother to render such a devastated landscape. Unless it were to represent some new vision of Hell.

"Maybe like this might have looked before, y'know, whatever happened happened."

"How do you know something happened?"

"Well, look at it!" He spread his arms and did a little half-turn in the road so that he was walking backward. "This isn't the way it's meant to be! It's bad in my time, but not this bad. You see, where I come from, it's meant to be pretty hot and dry anyway, only not so hot as it is. But not here. Look at those plants and trees. They're meant for greener pastures."

Greener pastures, Erde mused. Like where I come from. Only it's not green there now either.

"You know what?" N'Doch nodded, confirming for himself what was clearly a recent epiphany. "I think this here is the future of my future. Like, after me . . . maybe even after I'm dead." He completed the turn and grinned up at the hazed amber sky. "And here I am, still alive! How 'bout that?"

Erde thought he was mad to grin like that. This same thought had haunted her all during those weeks she'd been in his own time, but she'd bravely kept it to herself. How like N'Doch to find it funny instead of terrifying. "This future does not look like a happy one, N'Doch."

"Maybe. Or maybe the milk and honey's right over that next hill."

"The what?"

Again, that little shrug. The one he always made when he'd just said something with great bravado, but wasn't really sure of it at all. "Just something my mama used to say."

He can't imagine why his mama's on his mind again, but he wishes he'd told the dragons to check on her when they went back for Papa Dja. The old man'll take care of her somehow. N'Doch lets himself believe that. But it does weird him out, thinking of how he's up here in the future, her future, and she's back there behind him in 2013, still weaving and watching her stories on the vid. He can't think of her as dead. That just doesn't wash.

N'Doch shakes his head. *Heat must be getting to me.* And the silence. First it makes him jumpy, then it lulls him into inattention, so that he comes to with a start to realize he's been walking for what could be an entire klick without being aware of a single centimeter of it. Each time, he checks the sun right off. The road's turned north a while back. From the high spots, where the road tops a rise, he can still see the bay off east, through the notches in the hills. Probably the road runs along the water, then into the city from there. Just what he'd do if he was a road.

The baron's a dozen paces ahead. He's stayed like that most of the way, wrapped in his own personal silence as thick as the silence of the landscape around him. The girl, trudging at N'Doch's side, watches the baron like she's trying to read his mind. N'Doch envies the man his inner privacy. No dragons worming their way into Baron Kö-then's soul, no sir. He finds himself watching the dude also—how he moves, brisk but graceful, never releasing his erect, chin-up carriage, even in this pounding heat. To amuse himself, N'Doch tries imitating the baron's walk, but it makes him want to look around for his audience. On him, this walk is a performance, some broad kind of caricature of manliness. On Köthen, it looks perfectly natural. N'Doch ponders this puzzle for a while until he'd just rather think about something else. He peels off into the shade of a rock face, where the road cuts through a hill, and unstraps his water jug.

The girl plods a few steps more, then stops. She calls ahead to the baron, real polite and tentative now, then comes back to join N'Doch, looking worn already by the sun and heat. She wipes her face with the tail of her shirt.

"Nice day, huh?" N'Doch grins. "Thought you'd already got used to this back where I come from."

"Never." She borrows his water jug and goes at it with long straining gulps.

"Whoa, girl, slow down. Told you to drink less, but more often, remember?"

She nods, still drinking.

"And take another layer off."

"I'm fine."

"You're dripping wet. Strip down, girl."

She shakes her head, glances out into the sun, and to his delight, she blushes. So the sexy baron's made her self-conscious. Got her thinking about her body at long last. N'Doch grins. He's got her number now.

"Okay, then, how's the scaly duo doing?"

She rolls her eyes at him, and he sees this particular way of baiting her has lost its effect. "You could ask them just as easily as I, N'Doch."

"Yeah, but you're so much better at it." And, N'Doch notes to himself, you *like* it.

She sighs. "They're fine. Lady Water says the salt bay is not healthy. There are no fish in it."

"She went in?" Suddenly, he's very concerned. "She shouldn't do that!"

The girl regards him with more pity than patience. "She's a dragon, N'Doch. What's dangerous to humans will not harm her."

"Well," says N'Doch uneasily. He has this odd notion

that a dragon is something old-timey. Might not be hip to the modern horrors, like toxic waste or red tide or whatever. He'd really hate to see that silky blue velvet hide of hers eaten away by some gross corrosive in the water. He's not surprised about the fish. "I guess she can take care of herself."

Köthen appears out of the sun and just stands there, looking at them. N'Doch hides a smile. He can almost hear the dude asking: *hey, did I call a break?* But like the girl, he's a little the worse for wear. His handsome square-jawed face is flushed and sweat-stained, so he seems willing to hold back and just pace a bit in the shade. These northern types, N'Doch notes with satisfaction. Just not cut out for the heat. He's carrying the girl's pack, plus he's wearing the chest section of his body armor, with the blue-and-yellow silk over and his tunic under. Both he and Wender wore that much of their mail all the time at Deep Moor, even around the house. N'Doch shrugs. *Soldiers.* The fine-linked mesh is amazingly flexible and gorgeous workmanship, but it's got to weigh a couple or ten kilos. The dude ought to just take it off, but N'Doch's not sure he should be the one to suggest it. He passes the baron his water jug.

He doesn't take it right off, but when he does, there's no tossing the water down like the girl did, like there'll always be more of it. Köthen drinks conservatively and hands the jug back with a curt nod, like it pains him to be beholden. "I would have brought my own, had I any warning."

N'Doch laughs, but the baron just cocks a cool brow at him and looks away.

Finally they move on, back out into the grinding heat. Köthen and the girl have exchanged maybe three words, and she's looking about as beaten down as N'Doch has ever seen her. *Hunh,* he muses. *The baron's not humoring her, he's punishing her.* He sees she's got this thing for him, so he's getting back at her this way for shanghaiing him. N'Doch's not sure he approves. Mental cruelty has never been his idea of a fair fight, especially with women. But, hey, it's none of his business, even if he does find himself feeling a little protective of her lately. Anyway, he's been telling her it was time she grew up, and falling for some mean dude twice your age is one way to do it. But he

wonders, if she really was his sister, would he be telling her
there might be easier ways?

Past the cut through the rock, the road flattens for a long
stretch. A little wind kicks up, like a draft from a blast
furnace. N'Doch feels the heat rising off the pavement and
signals the girl off to the side to walk along the weedy
verge. There might have been farm fields here once. He
recognizes the squared-off outlines, marked now by dead
tree trunks and isolated sections of rusted wire fencing.
Nothing in these fields now but brown grass and weeds and
dust that the wind is blowing right in their faces. He shows
the girl how to tie a corner of her extra shirt across her
nose and mouth to veil the grit, then wrap the rest around
her head against the sun.

"There!" He approves of his handiwork. "Now you look
just like a desert woman!"

And even better, he's made her laugh. Well, smile a little
at least, and he's glad about that. Grinning, he glances
ahead to see Köthen disappear around a bend. The road
beyond is masked by a tall stand of scraggly evergreens
growing in unnatural rows. The rows mount the hillside to
the right like soldiers marching in rank. Half of them are
dead or dying, but their trunks march right along anyway.
Over the pincushion of pine tops, N'Doch spots the towers
of a high-voltage power line. Instantly, he's on the alert,
he's not even sure why. Those lines could be dead as a
doornail, but in his own time, power was getting precious,
and the major transmission lines were either guarded or
remote-protected in some fairly lethal ways. Up ahead, the
baron could be walking into something nasty. He touches
the girl's elbow, quickens his step.

"What?" she says.

"Just got a bad feeling. Keep your voice down, but hurry
it up."

"What could . . . ?"

"Shh!"

They lope along the edge of the road. There's no way
they can keep really quiet. The crush of the dry weeds is
as noisy as the slap of their feet on the pavement would
be. As they get closer, the widening gaps between the slim,
straight tree trunks reveal a bright strip of open land beyond, and the pale green stanchions of the nearest tower.

N'Doch slows as he comes level with the first row of trees. He can see Köthen now, a small figure alone in the sun where the open swath crosses the road. He's staring up at the tower, a rusting metal latticework that's probably taller than any man-made structure the baron's ever seen. And finally N'Doch identifies the low background hum he's been hearing without being really aware of it—that edgy, teeth-itching drone of flowing megawatts. He sees that some of the lines are down, great dark loops of cable lying like thick snakes across the road, mere meters from where Köthen is standing.

"Oh, man . . ." he murmurs.

And sure enough, Köthen, still looking upward, takes a few steps sideways to better his view of something on the tower. N'Doch catches his breath.

"Tell him to stop!" he snaps at the girl. "Tell him not to move!"

"What?"

"Tell him to stand still!"

But the girl says, "What? What?" again, and N'Doch breaks into a dead run because he can't imagine what her damn problem is, can't she see the guy's about to back into a live power line?

She starts up after him, but she's no match for N'Doch in his finish-line sprint. He leaves her instantly behind. He can hear her calling out now, finally, and the baron does stop and look their way. But he's too far away to hear her clearly. By now, N'Doch is almost on him. Köthen sees him bearing down, hears the girl shouting madly and does what N'Doch's afraid he'll do: he jumps to exactly the wrong conclusion, and goes for his dagger.

N'Doch pulls up short. The insulation on the cable is badly worn all along the swag just behind Köthen's head. In some spots, the wires are completely bare. N'Doch can smell the scorch of raw power in the air. He spreads his hands, palms out, away from his own weapon.

"Just don't move, man," he says quietly. "Just don't fucking move."

Köthen's at ready, knees flexed, his knife arm extended to one side, too close to the cable. One more step back or even an unlucky arcing, and the man's a goner. N'Doch hears the girl pounding down the road behind him, but she'll never be there in time. He needs the language, the right words, and there's only one place he can get them. No reason he should be busting his butt for this guy who keeps wanting to kill him, but he'd really hate to watch him burn to a crisp, especially in front of the girl. So he does the thing he hates most of all, the thing that erases him, makes him feel like he's falling into a bottomless pit. He gives himself over and calls to the dragon, the way he knows he can and never does, and she puts the words into his head and guides his tongue.

N'Doch points at the cable. *"Fassen Sie das nicht an!"*

Köthen's not sure he's heard right, but his eyes flick to where N'Doch's pointing, then back again, narrowing. He thinks it's a ruse.

And then it's all there, the language N'Doch needs, an awkward tumble of German syllables, but enough to bring the dude at least halfway off battle alert, enough to talk him a few steps forward, away from the waiting cable, away from sure and instant death. N'Doch drops to a crouch, heart pounding, and rubs his forehead, trying to clear his brain of the adrenaline rush. Because now there's this dragon inside there that he's got to make a lot more room for.

Köthen does not sheathe his dagger, but he turns around warily to stare at the thick swag of cable. N'Doch can see he hasn't a clue what the danger is, but he's read and believed the urgency in N'Doch's voice and body and words. He takes a few extra steps away.

The girl catches up finally. "What is it, N'Doch?"

"Your boy here nearly fried himself, is all."

She stares at him, horrified. N'Doch thinks about what he's said, and recalls how the big dragon tends to translate to her in visual images. Probably they'll both get him wrong this time, but he can't help himself. He puts his head down and starts to laugh.

Erde's scowl was reflexive. She shouldn't be angry with him. She knew by now that laughter was N'Doch's usual release after a crisis. But the image of Köthen burning had left her shuddering and nauseous, so she had to frown at him anyway, like she always did. "It's not funny, N'Doch!"

"No," he agreed, laughing. "I guess it ain't."

Baron Köthen put up his dagger finally and crossed his arms. "Well, does he speak German or not?"

"When he feels like it," Erde was forced to admit.

"It's not like that," N'Doch protested, in French.

Köthen nodded. "I begin to suspect . . . no, never mind. Was I actually in danger?"

N'Doch glanced up from his crouch. "You bet your ass you were." But he said it in French, and Erde refused to translate. Caught, he stared at the ground, almost bashfully, as if listening very hard. Then he repeated it, in substantially more proper German. Erde privately thanked Lady Water for her refined sensibilities, but still, she wanted to cheer out loud. All her previous efforts to get N'Doch speaking her language had failed. Köthen had succeeded without even trying. And of course he had no idea what he'd accomplished. One quick glance, a curiously arched brow, and he'd accepted N'Doch's sudden acquisition of fractured but comprehensible German as if it was just one more in the series of bizarre events he'd been swept up in.

"You watch, now," said N'Doch. He rose from his crouch and walked over to the huge structure that towered over them like the tallest siege engine Erde could imagine. He searched around beneath it, picked something up and knocked it against one of the tower's pilings. It rang like metal, and the sound vibrated up the length of the piling. He brought the thing back to them, a length of hollow metal.

"Stand back," he said. "Way back."

Baron Köthen eyed the metal thing, seemed to decide that it was both too short and too rusted to be much of a weapon. He joined Erde where N'Doch directed them, into the shade of the pine trees. N'Doch moved back also, then he faced the dark, dangling ropes and lobbed the metal thing with a big underhand toss, right into the most frayed part of the loop.

Light exploded around it, white and blue and sizzling. There was a crack like lightning, sparks flew in all directions and the ropes danced and snapped like battle pennants in a gale. Erde felt the surge to the roots of her hair, and beside her, Köthen muttered. Then it was over, and the ropes were quiet again, and the metal thing lay on the ground, singed as if from the forge.

N'Doch offered them a death's-head grin, then let the dragon speak for him. "So whaddya think? That could've been you, Baron K."

Köthen wet his lips. "I don't think I'd have liked that."

N'Doch laughed softly. "Damn straight you wouldn't."

Köthen looked up at the tower. "What is this thing for?"

"You really want to know? How much time have you got?"

Köthen heard the challenge. Erde felt, rather than saw, him tense. He seemed to be considering his options, none of which he was very happy about. But he understood that his life had just been saved. Perhaps he felt he owed N'Doch a hearing, for he returned the same, soft laugh and said, "I seem to have all the time in the world."

So for the next several miles, N'Doch and Baron Köthen walked side by side, one long, safe pace apart, while N'Doch discoursed on the magical force called *electricity*. Erde trudged along behind, only half listening. Master Djawara had already explained this to her, when they'd visited his compound in the bush. Mostly she listened to hear Köthen's response, to hear if he believed N'Doch's insistence that *electricity* was not magic or if he, like her, was reserving judgment. But Köthen's response was so reserved, she couldn't even tell what it was. He just listened, nodded, asked a quiet question or two, and nodded some more, walking along with his hands tucked behind his back like he was out for a stroll in his castle yard. Perhaps, she decided, he doesn't believe any of it at all.

She was beginning to look forward to another rest in the shade when, ahead of her, the men pulled up short at the top of another big rise. Something in the angle of Köthen's shoulders made Erde quicken her step. What she saw when she drew up beside him left her speechless.

A city lay spread out in the lowland. A city half submerged in ragged foliage and the same green water she'd seen back at the broken bridge. She knew it was a city by its straight lines and squared angles, its so obviously human geometry. But it was like no city she'd ever seen. *Except . . .*

Without thinking, she put an urgent call out to Earth. He must see this with his own eyes. Sure that she was under some sort of attack, both dragons flashed into existence in the road right behind them. The hot air churned. The dust boiled up in small cyclones. Köthen whirled and swore, but when he'd got hold of himself and slid his dagger back into its sheath, there was a spark of admiration in his eyes.

"That's how we . . . arrived?"

Erde nodded.

He let out a breath. "With a whole army like that, you'd be invincible." Then he returned his attention to the city, which seemed to amaze him even more than the traveling methods of dragons.

He gave it a long, slow study, as they all did. The tall, rigid, boxlike structures rose in clusters out of the parched foliage, or in places, right out of the long green bay that coiled up from the south to partly encircle the city. The boxes were all different sizes, and reflected the sun in bright, blinding shafts. One towering rectangle seemed to be made entirely of burnished gold. But some were stunted, collapsed or broken off partway. Their gleaming skins were scorched and peeled back, exposing their understructure like the blackened bones of a decaying corpse.

"My God," Köthen whispered finally. "It really is the future, isn't it."

N'Doch grinned. "You got it, man."

But Erde shivered. OH, DRAGON! IS IT THE MAGE CITY?

They had dreamed a city like this, together: a tall-towered, fantastical city. But their city was perfect and whole and shining, not with the reflected light of a grim red sun but with an inner glow of purity and wisdom. And they knew a mage dwelt there who would help the dragon fulfill his quest.

THE CALL IS STRONG, BUT . . . NOT FROM THAT DIRECTION.

IT IS THE MAGE CITY, I KNOW IT IS! BUT IT'S IN RUINS! DRAGON, WHAT DOES IT MEAN? ARE WE TOO LATE?

WE CANNOT BE TOO LATE. I WILL NOT ACCEPT SUCH A POSSIBILITY.

Erde trusted the dragon's superior instincts and loved him for his stubbornness. But she was uneasy about the hopelessness that had settled over her in this desolate place, as heavy as a winding shroud. What if he was wrong?

Köthen beckoned N'Doch closer. Erde shook herself out of her gloom and prepared herself to keep the peace. But N'Doch's snatching Köthen from an unexpected peril seemed to have proved his usefulness. And now that the baron had established the chain of command to his satisfaction, he could treat the man he'd so recently drawn on and thrown to the ground as his new lieutenant. Even more astonishing, N'Doch did not seem to object. He'd given up all pretense of being unable to communicate. He stepped up beside Köthen, and they studied the city together.

"Do you know this place?"

N'Doch shook his head. "But there are cities like this where I come from. That is, the buildings look sort of the same. The landscape's real different."

"How many years since . . ." The baron stopped, cleared his throat awkwardly.

"Since your time?"

Köthen's mouth pressed back against the flood of questions he obviously longed to ask. He shrugged, nodded.

"Well, we know it's at least eleven hundred years, 'cause that brings us to my time and everything looks pretty familiar to me so far. Closer than that, it's hard to say. We're sure to find some bit of something that'll tell us."

Again, Erde watched the baron closely. Would he share her nightmares about the weight of all those intervening years? But he only nodded again and murmured, "Eleven hundred years."

"I could be wrong, y'know? I guess it could be less, but it's probably more."

Köthen waved a hand as if to say, how can a few years more or less even matter? "And what would such a city signify . . . in your time?"

"Signify?"

The baron pointed, measuring the city's breadth between the span of his outstretched hands. "Is it likely some king's capital?"

"Well, it might be a capital, but there probably isn't any king."

"Why is that?"

"Not a lot of kings left in the world, 'least not in my day. 'Course, now, you never know. But, seemed to me, kings were pretty much done for in the history of the world." N'Doch regarded Köthen sideways, as if gauging the distance between them, just in case the offense he implied was actually taken. Erde thought it another sign of his madness that he should needle Baron Köthen so rashly, over and over again. But didn't they make an interesting contrast side by side? The shorter, solid blond who carried himself like a much larger man against N'Doch's slim, towering darkness. N'Doch bending his head slightly to catch Köthen's terse and quiet questioning, Köthen not looking at him, as that would require him to look up.

"No kings. Is it a city of merchants, then?"

N'Doch laughed. "Oh, there's probably plenty of them, all right, if there's anybody." The German was coming easier to him, she could see, as he relaxed into it and let Lady Water guide his tongue. No doubt, Erde reflected sourly, he would soon be able to abuse her language as outrageously as he abused his own.

"If?"

N'Doch gave his little shrug. "Don't know. Just a feeling I have."

Köthen frowned. "Still, perhaps we'll find shelter there."

"Yeah. Just hope we don't find a lot else besides."

They leave the dragons behind again, a ways down from the rise in the shadow of what's left of a two-lane overpass. The big guy eyes the crumbling piers, then eases his bulk up beside the tallest and widest to nose the weathered concrete.

N'Doch touches the baron's elbow, real respectful and all. "Watch this."

Köthen tenses reflexively, but his eyes follow N'Doch's gesture, just in time to see the brown dragon still himself utterly and seem to vanish into the gray, man-made stone. He stifles a gasp.

N'Doch grins. "Neat trick, eh?" It can't hurt to have the baron considering how the dragons could be used to his advantage. He's glancing down that road already. While the girl's explaining this particular bit of dragon magic, N'Doch wanders over to where Water has tucked herself into a slice of shade. She looks half her normal size, whatever normal is for a dragon. She's always beautiful, but now she's almost cute. N'Doch's hand strays to her silken neck.

"That was cool, what you did back at the power line."

Saved your butt, buddy boy!

"Mine! What about his lordship's?"·

Same thing, under the circumstances.

"Yeah, well, okay, forget about it." N'Doch spins on his heel to gather up the girl and the baron. "I'll see ya 'round."

Köthen moves out smartly, still insisting on taking the lead. They stick to the highway as it curves around the city until N'Doch spots an off ramp that looks like fairly easy going.

He points it out to Baron K. "That should get us off the main road and down into town." Then he adds, "If you want." Maybe he's underestimated this dude. So he was hasty about assuming leadership without even checking to see who else agreed. At least he doesn't take the responsibility lightly. Since the power-line incident, since his first long look at the city, Köthen's questions have come at him steadily as they walked, smart questions, too. The sort that go right to the heart of what's what in a place. And, to N'Doch's disgust, the sort that expose the limits of his own knowledge. A layman's rap on electricity is easy enough—how's the guy gonna know any better? But actual ground intelligence? Access roads and fortifications? To say there aren't any just brings a disbelieving frown. And sooner or later, he and the baron have got to have a serious chat about guns.

"You sure ask a lot of questions, Baron K. Sorry I don't have all the answers." N'Doch hears the girl swallow a little moan, as Köthen's eyes flick up at him dangerously. She sees his free play with the dude's name and title as just one more offense he's committed among many, but for whatever reason, Köthen lets it pass without comment.

Instead he says, in the dry cadence of a schoolmaster, "Information is a weapon like anything else. The good soldier gathers up as much as he can, and never wastes his time regretting what he doesn't have."

"Smart move," says N'Doch. This is no news to him, but

he likes the sense that Köthen's repeating something told him a long time ago, like maybe when he was N'Doch's age. Which really isn't that long ago, now he thinks about it. He guesses Köthen's about ten years older than he is, maybe thirty, maybe not even that. The other impression he gets strikes him as funny: the baron has clearly decided to take him under his wing. It's a laugh only because, of course, N'Doch sees it the other way around. But he doesn't care. The dude's all right, really, for all his arrogance and attitude, and N'Doch would rather have him on his side than not. Plus he knows from his years in the gangs that some guys just gotta be sure they're the boss.

So they take the exit, like he's advised, and N'Doch lets the baron lead the way. He'd rather be rear guard anyway, since most sneak attacks come from behind. Now that they're moving down in among the deserted gas stations and the empty strip malls, N'Doch feels his adrenaline start to pump. Every window has been busted out. There's broken glass crunching underfoot, buried in a layer of what looks like dried mud, the same mud that cakes the bases of the buildings and the burned-out trees for at least a meter up.

"See that? The water's been even higher than it is now. And not all that long ago."

"Then it's not a drought?" the girl asks dutifully, but N'Doch can see that his concern is not deeply shared. For all she knows, the folks of this time build their cities in the water. Who's he kidding? For all he knows, they might. But not this city. This city is too familiar, not which or where it is, but how. Parts of it he knows were built in his own time, and parts were built before, like this big gray stone building on the corner that Köthen has stopped to stare up at. It's crumbling a bit, and there's weeds and scrawny old trees growing up out of its windows, but it has a kind of falling-down grace to it. Big cornices like on the Presidential Palace at home, and a couple of weather-beaten stone lions flanking what used to be the steps up to the door. N'Doch is no historian. He couldn't quote place or date, but he's sure seen buildings like this in vids. He looks around, then trots across the street to haul on a rusted sheet of metal he's spotted sticking out of a rubble pile. He pulls it free and brushes away the top flaked layer of mud. Sun-bleached letters appear through the brownish film.

The sign says: DRY CLEANERS.

"Omigod!" N'Doch scrabbles around in the wreckage for more signage. He can read a little English, and speak a bit more. He guesses from the bits of slangy ads he sees, and the bold, plain styles of the lettering. "Can it be? Oh, man, I think we're in the States!"

"What's the states?" asks the girl, coming up beside him.

He tells himself, don't jump to conclusions now. It's only a coupla signs. The English doesn't mean anything. People everywhere were using it by his time. But his hunch feels right, and he's seized by an old excitement. He goes out into the middle of the street, peering up and down for more convincing evidence. He's not sure he really needs any. "Oh, man, the States! I always wanted to come here!"

He's slipped back into French, and Köthen asks for a translation. When he gets it, the baron frowns. "Why didn't you, if it meant so much?"

The excitement makes N'Doch high and reckless. He turns on Köthen with a wild grin. A sharp retort about the abuses of power and privilege nearly escapes him, but he bites it back. What's the point? This dude was born to all that. How could he possibly understand about something you can't afford, or the yearning for a Promised Land? Instead N'Doch says, and he tries to say it proudly, even though his papa was nothing to be proud about: "I'm a poor man's son, Baron K. I never could go just anywhere I wanted."

Köthen meets his gaze without reproof. N'Doch is taken aback by the bleak and bitter compassion he reads there. "Like you think I can? Think again, lad. Besides, you're here now, aren't you?"

N'Doch catches himself grinning right into the man's eyes. And he sees an ironic ghost of his grin reflecting back at him. Flustered, he looks away. "Well, hell, yes, I guess I am." Then he lets the laugh rise up, lets it fill his lungs and echo along the blank faces of the buildings and down the mud-caked streets. "Hey! I guess I am! Hello, America!"

Chapter Sixteen

Paia toys with her breakfast. Usually she is infused with a reverent, energetic calm for many days after worshiping the God. Usually she goes about her Temple duties with a pious intensity that inspires both her subordinates and the Faithful alike.

"What does he say to you?" Luco ventured once, as they prepared the Sanctuary for a water ritual. He smoothed the red altar cloth absolutely flat and lined up the twelve candlesticks just so, six to either side of the sacred golden bowl.

"It's not what he says, it's what he does."

A candle poised in each hand, Luco gazed at her, his lips slightly parted. His blue eyes were particularly clear and guileless.

"He fills me with light."

"Light." Luco sighed. "How wonderful. I would give anything to . . ." He stopped, abashed. "Forgive me, my Priestess. I don't mean to presume."

Deeply into her calm that day, Paia was feeling generous. "Perhaps if you went to him, Luco . . ."

The priest's bronzed cheeks paled visibly. "Enter the Sanctum? Me? I can't imagine it."

Luco, First Son that he is, has never touched the God, has never laid a palm to the vital heat of the God's shimmering skin. Not even once. He says his restraint is born of worship and profound respect, but Paia sees the primal terror barely submerged in Luco's eyes when the God is near. She is often amazed herself that her love for the God so readily overcomes her fear of him, that she alone, of all the God's servants and Faithful, can bring herself into contact with his physical presence without swooning in terror. Luco is a brave man, for all his fussiness and vanity. His big muscular body bears the scars of his service in the God's Wars of Conversion, before he was elevated to the priesthood. Not many men or women have made that leap. It's a testimony to Luco's management and political skills, but to his nerve as well. Yet he cannot bring himself to face the God alone in the dark furnace of the Sanctum. Paia tries to imagine Son Luco in holy ecstasy. It might all be just a little too messy for him.

Bringing her attention back to her uneaten breakfast, she sees there's no melon on her plate this morning. The kitchen will surely put up the defense that it's unhealthy to eat the same thing every morning, and that the delicate egg-and-cheese pastries are a worthy substitute. But Paia suspects that they've run to the end of the melons earlier than usual in the Temple garden, like with the spring strawberries, and she'll see no more until next season. For no particular reason, she recalls all those blank blue screens on the House Comp's monitor bank. She should have asked him what they meant. She would have, had the God not summoned her. Paia slumps in her chair, inexplicably disconsolate. Perhaps the blackberries will be bearing soon.

She pushes the plate away, gets up, and finds herself pacing. This odd restlessness. It's so unfamiliar, she doesn't know what to do with it. It's like she's waiting for something to happen, but there's no reason to be expecting anything. Except for the occasional attempt on her life, there are no events in the life of the Citadel, only the endless rolling out of the Temple calendar: daily, monthly, yearly routine and ritual. Perhaps it's this most recent attempt, not only the threat but the humiliation of it. Perhaps she's absorbed some of the God's concern about these enemies he mentioned. She wishes he had told her more, but he'd refused to discuss the matter further.

Paia wonders if Luco knows anything about the God's enemies. She's aware that he and the God have long sessions together in Luco's office when the God is safely in man-form, to deal with the management of the Temple and its estates. Do they discuss other things as well? Would Luco even tell her if they did? She checks the Temple calendar. Luco has the morning free until the noon Call to Worship, which she allows him to officiate at without her. She throws on an off-duty red Temple robe and hurries downstairs to look for him.

The affairs of the Temple and the Citadel are managed out of a suite of rooms on the second level, rooms that Paia's father, in happier days, had used as reception rooms for meetings with members of the local communities, with village elders, with the occasional hardy visitor from outside. In one of Paia's earliest and most vivid childhood memories, she is watching from the balcony of her nursery, as dozens of shining hovers arrive, one by one, and settle on the narrow valley floor like a gathering of dragonflies sunning their wings. Each is met by her father's last functioning APC, and the passengers are transported in armored safety to the Citadel. This is a Big Important Meeting, her nanny explains, so we mustn't bother Daddy and Mommy while they're tending to their guests. The conferences and receptions went on for days, and late into the nights, and then the hovers went away. Paia saw one or two after that, dropping in for brief visits, but soon they stopped coming altogether. And the reception rooms fell into disuse, especially after her mother died. Her father let his chief steward assume the day-to-day operation of the Citadel and increasingly withdrew to the Library and his collection of precious books.

When Luco was promoted to First Son, he asked for these rooms to use as his office. Paia, eager to see them alive again, readily agreed. Just as she'd expected he would, Luco made their cleanup and restoration his first major project as operational head of the Temple. Not until their teak moldings and parquet floors were gleaming again, and their coffered ceilings were repainted and regilded, could he settle himself and his staff into them comfortably. Though Luco would protest that he is most fulfilled by his Temple duties to the God, Paia thinks he's at his most satisfied when seated behind her father's vast fruitwood desk, with a pile of production reports and levy accounts in front of him.

But it is quiet in the office today. Luco's staff, four handsome young Second Sons, glance up from their work as Paia barges through the front doors. They fall to their knees right there at their desks.

"Mother Paia," they murmur in unison.

Paia stops, inclines her head graciously, then motions them to rise. Luco has them so well trained, it's a pity to waste it. She has some difficulty telling the lesser Sons apart, as they all seem to look a lot like Luco, who—of course—is trying to look like the God. In desperation, she resorts to classification by body type and skin tone. "Is the First Son available to speak with me?"

"In his quarters, High Priestess," replies the taller, darker one, the one with the almond eyes, Luco's current favorite.

Luco's living quarters are in the Temple proper, which means that if Paia should encounter one of the Twelve on the way there, the foolish woman will insist on dropping whatever she's doing in order to follow and attend the High Priestess. Paia does not wish to be attended. She wishes to speak to Luco in private. She takes the back way. She has become very skilled at this by now. It's simply a matter of running counter to their extremely rigid expectations. It confuses them completely. Paia arrives at Luco's door free of encumbrance.

Originally, the God assigned a single guard to the First Son's door. The number appears to have risen to three. Paia wonders whose idea this was. Is Luco feeling some greater concern for his own security, or has the God's estimation of the value of his First Son risen accordingly? As High Priestess, Paia enters any door in Citadel or Temple without warning. Out of respect for Luco, she makes an exception in his case. She directs one of the guardswomen to announce her.

Luco is freshly shaved and washed and wrapped in a soft white towel when Paia enters the second of his string of three windowless rooms. The first is a parlor done in red and gold, stiff little chairs and all, borrowed from the most formal of the three unused dining rooms upstairs. The middle room is more stripped down, a domestic space lined with exercise equipment and cedar taken from one of the Citadel's defunct saunas. Paia's never seen the third room, his bedroom. She wonders what it's like. Like Luco's fantasy of the God's Sanctum, perhaps. She's tried before to get a glimpse of it, but the door is always firmly shut.

Luco is seated on a padded stool, having his long hair combed out by his chamberboy. The boy kneels when he sees Paia and does not look up. Paia takes the comb from his hand but has to tap him on his thin shoulder to get his attention in order to dismiss him. When he's gone, she moves around behind the priest to continue what the boy had started.

"I'm not sure this falls within your description of duties, my priestess," says Luco wryly. But he makes no move to stop her as she works the comb and her fingers through his damp and tangled locks. "What can I do for you?"

"Can't I just come visiting?" She works her way around a particularly knotted tangle, her fingers brushing the soft skin of his neck.

Luco wraps his towel a little tighter. "It would surprise me. No, let me put it this way. It would worry me."

"Oh, Luco. Are you afraid I'll try to seduce you?"

"The thought did cross my mind."

She laughs and sets the comb aside, slipping both hands into the mass of his curls. Gently, she begins to massage his scalp.

Luco lets out a ragged breath. "You'd be very good at it if you picked the right guy."

"I thought I'd picked the right guy last time, and look what it got me." She leans over, kisses the top of his head. "There, there, don't worry. I know I'm *lustful,* as you say, and way too old to be a virgin, but what I really need is a friend. Someone to talk to."

"I'm your friend," he protests. "We talk."

"We talk about the Temple. We talk about business."

"We talk about the Suitors . . ."

She squeezes his head between both palms and gives it a little shake. "Yes. Because *you* enjoy it so much."

"Well . . ."

"I mean, really talk." She goes back to her massaging.

Luco lolls his head back a little, letting her strong hands do their pleasurable work.

Paia laughs. "You are such a sensualist, Luco. Whatever are you doing in the priesthood?"

His eyes are closed. He grins. "Are they mutually exclusive?"

"They appear to be in my case."

"Ah, but you have the God."

"I . . . what do you mean?"

His grin fades. Paia feels new tension in the strong muscles of his neck. Her reply has came back at him too sharply, and as often happens, she's alarmed him. "Forgive me, my priestess. If I mispoke . . ."

She smoothes her hands over his unlined forehead. "Oh, Luco, you know you can say anything to me you want."

But the moment of real intimacy is over. Now he will just play at it, as he usually does. He lets her keep working on him, but he sits up a little straighter now and his eyes are alert. "So what did you want to talk about?"

"Just stuff. Things I've been wondering about. Like, what goes on in the villages . . . or outside."

Luco is silent.

With her fingertips doing detailed work at his temples, Paia asks, "Has the God said anything to you recently about some enemies he's concerned about?"

Now Luco is both silent and very still. She can feel his stillness translating through her hands as they cradle his skull. "Enemies? Of the Faith, you mean? Has another heresy been discovered?" He sits up and out of her grip and turns to face her. "Why wasn't I told of this?"

"He didn't say anything about the Temple. He said it was an old heresy, 'the oldest one of all.' He said these were 'ancient enemies.' What did he mean, do you think?"

Luco studies her a moment, as if assessing not so much the truth of her report, but her motive in offering it to him. "You mean, enemies from outside? Did he say from 'outside'?"

Somehow, it had not yet occurred to Paia to put that particular two and two together. But of course, it makes sense. The God had originally appeared from outside, after all. "He didn't say it, but what else could he mean?" She recalls now her surprise that the God could only "sense" these enemies. "I think he doesn't exactly know where they are." The priest frowns, and instantly Paia catches his anxiety. "Luco, what kind of enemies could the God be worried about? Who could be that powerful?"

"Or, *what* could be . . . ?"

Now they both fall silent. Paia knows she's veering dangerously close to questions about the God's claims of Omniscience and Omnipotence. Luco knows it, too, and he definitely does not want to go there. He picks up the comb from where she's laid it, to finish where she left off. "I have to get ready for the noon Call."

Paia sighs. "Of course you do."

"I'll let you know if I hear anything about this myself."

"I know you will." She watches him struggle to comb his hair out for braiding and keep his towel firmly about his waist at the same time. The towel, she notes, bears her father's initials. "Here, sit. Let me do it."

And while she braids his hair up in the triple plait he favors for daytime rituals, Paia is pondering where she should go next to find someone to talk to. That is, *really* talk to.

Chapter Seventeen

N'Doch clamps his hands over his own mouth. Yelling out loud, right in the middle of the street! *What am I thinking?*

He's thinking that after only a week of being pampered by women, his reflexes are already going soft. He sneaks a glance at Köthen, sees him swallow what might actually have been a chuckle. Then the baron orders them to move on, only this time, he sends N'Doch up to be point man. N'Doch doesn't like this decision, but he respects its wisdom.

They make their way, spread out in a cautious line, along increasingly narrow streets that, guessing from the numbers of big dead trees lining the sidewalks, were once cool and shaded in the summer. The buildings look mostly residential and really old. N'Doch doubts there's been much new building here—not since way before his time—because of all the brick. He recognizes brick from vids, but he's never actually seen the stuff in real life, least not a whole building's worth. Wasn't ever much building in brick where he's from, a few during the old colonial days maybe, but mostly it's cinderblock or concrete. Along here, there are entire blocks of brick-built townhouses, lined up side by side, confronting their mirror images across the littered streets, red-brown facades gaping doorless and windowless like one big collective scream.

He's scanning these buildings now like he would in a strange street at home, looking for the telltale signs of recent use, of covert habitation: anything that might warn of an ambush. He wishes he had a laser assault rifle or something serious, instead of a stupid, overgrown steak knife. But the streets just go on and on, empty of life. He gets a sudden chill: what if the place is hot, or diseased? But the destruction looks like looting to him, and firebombing and just plain age, stuff he's seen a lot of. No full-out nuking. And a place that's been plague-killed usually shows a lot more signs of it: the old remains lying around, the heaps of bird-picked bones, that sense of a fatal interruption having shown up in the middle of a normal day.

He pulls up on a corner, in the shade of a tall stone stoop. Crumbling exterior stairs lead up to a burned-out second story, arching over a lower entryway that's barred with a battered metal door and a rusted folding gate. The fact that there's still a door alerts N'Doch to check it out carefully. But he sees the gate is welded in place with that blue-green corrosion that salt water lays down on exposed metal. He hears a rustle in the shadowed corners under the stairs. He sees nothing big enough in there to hide anything of size. Must be a rat or something, he decides, and though he hates rats worse than most things, he finds this first sign of life oddly comforting.

First the girl joins him, then Köthen, who eyes the shadows under the stairs and drops wearily onto a chunk of the collapsed stair railing. N'Doch leans over to pass him the water, and gives his tongue up to the dragon's control once more.

"So what d'you think of the States, Baron K.?"

Köthen sips and passes the jug back, rolling the water around on his tongue like it was some big year wine. "Does it matter to you what I think?"

This surprises him. What's gotten the dude riled up again? Surely the baron's not reconsidering his deal already? "Hey, man, just making conversation."

"Let him rest, N'Doch," murmurs the girl.

Köthen glances at her over his shoulder, then reaches for N'Doch's water jug and a second pull. "What do I think? I think it is hot. And I think that this is a very large town to be so empty of inhabitants."

N'Doch leans back, relieved. He dislikes being pulled into this dance between the two of them, but he also sees how he can use it to keep the baron talking to him. In Köthen's eyes right now, he's the lesser of evils. "Bingo. Looks like they wrecked the joint, then got up and left."

"No one would do such a thing."

"Hmm. Might." N'Doch stretches his long legs across the mud-cloaked concrete. "You fought in wars, right?"

Köthen nods like it's a stupid question. Like, doesn't everyone?

"You ever looted some enemy village, then burned it to the ground just 'cause you wanted to?"

"Never."

The baron's tone alerts him, but not enough to keep him from plunging forward. "C'mon, really?"

"Never."

"That's what guys like you always do in the vids."

"Guys like me?" Köthen repeats, as if the slang tastes sour in his mouth.

"You know, knights in armor." N'Doch shrugs. "Well, probably they didn't have anything you needed bad enough."

Köthen looks to the girl, like he's checking to see if she agrees that anyone who talks like this is an idiot or out of his mind.

"N'Doch," she warns, "It's a bad idea to accuse a man of honor of behaving like a common thief."

"Oh. A *common* thief. Like me, I suppose. So sorry. I forgot his highness only steals big important things, like other people's thrones."

The girl's eyes squeezed shut. He can't imagine why, since he's said it in French so the baron won't hear. At least he *thinks* he's said it in French. But Köthen is staring at him, and if looks really could kill, N'Doch would be a stone dead man. He sighs and gets ready to defend himself again.

"Why, N'Doch?" moans the girl. "Why must you do these things?"

"He wasn't supposed to hear!"

Köthen's mouth is a thin line buried in his neat, tawny beard. "What was your point?" he asks coldly.

N'Doch's got a bone to pick with a certain blue dragon. What's she trying to do, get him killed? Now he's gotta go and tap-dance the baron into a peaceable mood again without making himself look too foolish. "My point? Just that when people need something bad enough, they take it. And when they got nothin' to lose, sometimes they wreck the joint, just for spite."

The baron's eyes narrow on him, then dip away. "Or themselves, if they can."

N'Doch sees Köthen retreating toward his private darkness. A better place for him than at my throat, he decides. But all this has got him thinking about home, and he realizes he hasn't given the whole answer yet. He considers what was going on then: the waves of migration out of the bush into the towns as the long drought took hold, then back out again as the drought continued and the towns became lawless. All stuff he'd taken for granted. But now, he's beginning to sniff out a wider perspective.

"No, okay, listen," he says, hearing himself sound earnest in spite of himself. "What I really think is, something happened. Not just another war, but something that made it no good living here anymore, no matter how much stake they'd put into the place or how much they'd fight for it."

The girl's voice is hushed. "Like . . . plague?"

Some things really are universal, N'Doch notes. "I gave that a moment, too, but I don't think it was anything that sudden. More like, over a lotta years."

This getting serious seems to work. The tightened vise of Köthen's jaw has relaxed. He's listening again.

"Some slower destruction," he says.

"Yeah, like . . . well, like the water coming up."

Recalling the meters of African beach lost to the sea, the dozens of coastal shantytowns washed away or forced inland, even in his own short lifetime, N'Doch gets up and points down the wider street that crosses the one they'd come in on. "Take a look down there."

The street runs downhill from their vantage into a part of town where the buildings get taller and newer. But a block or so past their corner, the road dips into the bay and from there on, the buildings rise out of deeper and deeper water. Köthen joins him, their argument forgotten. N'Doch watches him and the girl try to get their minds around what the water means. Sure, they both know what a flood is, but your usual flood is temporary. Eventually, the water dries up or goes away. This high water has obviously settled in for the long haul. He recalls his moment of revelation in Lealé's office, what seems like months ago and is really less than two weeks, when he held the hard copy of PrintNews in his hand and actually read it, understanding it as fact for the first time ever, not just entertainment media. And one of the things it talked about was rising sea levels all over the world, stuff about ice falling off in Antarctica and melting in the tropical oceans. Well, there was a lot going down right then, people shooting at him and worse, so he got distracted from the specifics. Now he wishes he'd read it more carefully anyway. He stares at the green water lapping the window ledges down the hill and shivers, once, very hard. It's like a spasm of comprehension settling in on him. He'd assumed the drought and the beach-swallowing ocean were local because they affected him locally. No, the truth is, he didn't even think about it. But now, here he is in the US of A, if his guess is correct, and the same thing is happening. Or has already happened. This is his future's future, all right, and he's not sure he's gonna like it.

Nah. Easier to backpedal. Be the old streetwise N'Doch who lived for the moment, never gave the future a thought. " 'Course I could be wrong, y'know. Probably just a real high tide or something. Storm, out to sea."

Looking at an ocean flowing through doorways, Köthen barks that bitter laugh of his. "Oh, yes. And the townsfolk will all be home by dinnertime."

N'Doch can't help but grin. Already this dude reads him pretty damn well. "Okay, then, say I'm right. It gets worse. In my time, this country we're in, or at least I think we are—this place was the wealthiest, most powerful country of all. If it could be done, the Americans could do it. So if they're in this sort of trouble, I just gotta be worried about what shape the rest of the world is in."

"It reminds me of home," the girl remarks solemnly.

Köthen turns his eyes from the water. "This apocalyptic thinking again. I must stop listening, or you will have me believing you."

"Oh, believe it, my lord," pleads the girl. "I am sure it has something to do with why we are here."

He blinks at her. "It's the weather you're after? I thought it was a dragon. Well, then, we might as well all go home.

It's God's choice, is it not, to send cold or hot, wet or dry? If He wishes to make the waters rise, there's little my good sword arm can do about it."

"It ain't that simple . . ." N'Doch begins, at the same time that the girl says, "But what if it isn't God who's responsible?"

"Who, then, other than God?"

"Some great Evil."

Köthen sucks his teeth, contriving to look both contemptuous and worried. "You'd have better brought Hal Engle on this trip, then, instead of me. Great Evils are his bailiwick. Especially as he thinks I'm one of them."

But the girl is in her dogged mode. When Köthen moves away to reclaim his chunk of rubble, she follows him, arms outstretched. "But isn't it odd, my lord? At home, there was snow and ice in August. In N'Doch's time, a drought was killing the land. Here, the sea is swallowing the cities! And, lo, dragons are waking from their timeless sleep, called to a holy Mission! Surely their mission is to defeat this Evil, and bring Goodness back into the world!"

N'Doch lets out a slow whistle. He can't help himself. Where the hell did all that come from?

Köthen rests his elbows on his knees, shaking his head. "Hal Engle has too charismatic an influence upon the young. He should be curtailed."

"Sir Hal has not even heard this idea!" the girl protests.

"Would you like to hear my theory?" N'Doch thinks it's time to deflect this argument. "I'm not sure you'll like it any better."

But Köthen's head has lifted suddenly, his nostrils flaring. N'Doch stills. "What?"

"Do you smell that?"

N'Doch turns his head into the faint stirrings of the heated air. "Huh. Smoke. Somebody's up and about."

Köthen nods. N'Doch watches him take the breeze into his head like a dog would, sorting the layers and subtleties. "At a distance," he says. "A sickly kind of smoke."

"Yeah?" N'Doch gives it another try. Sure enough, it ain't just woodsmoke. He's always thought he had a pretty good nose, but this guy's a real pro. "Could be . . . maybe . . . burning rubber? Oh, right. You wouldn't know what that is. It's this gooey shit they make . . ."

Köthen waves him silent. "What's burning isn't important. Who's burning it is what we need to know."

The adrenaline is rising again, tingling along N'Doch's nerves. "Like, friend or foe?" he mutters.

"Always assume the latter," says the baron.

"Better safe than sorry," N'Doch agrees.

Erde listened to their murmured litany, surely the sort of mutually reassuring exchanges that soldiers needed in order to prepare themselves for battle, and suddenly it sounded alien to her.

"No," she said. "That's not right. If we assume they are enemies, they will assume the same of us."

Both men turned as one to stare at her.

"But this is their land. We are the strangers here. We may need their help."

Köthen shoved his hands onto his hips and turned away.

N'Doch said, "And what makes you think they're going to give it to us?"

"How will we know if we don't even ask?" Then, finally, she offered her own version of pragmatism. "If we show up with a dragon . . ."

N'Doch shrugged. "She's got a point," he said to the baron.

But Köthen said, very quietly, "No." He tested the air again, walked to the edge of the broken sidewalk, and stared down the street. "You brought me here for this. It's what I do best. We'll do as I say."

"My lord baron . . ."

"The dragons are our reserves. Only a fool shows the enemy everything he's got at the start of the battle. A fool or a braggart."

Erde felt her back straighten involuntarily. "My grandmother the baroness often mentioned the value of a show of strength, especially if it means that needless killing can be avoided."

"I have no lust for needless killing," Köthen growled.

"We don't even know who they are yet!" N'Doch complained. "Why argue now about what we're going to do to them? By the time we decide, they may be doing it to us!"

"There is no argument," said Köthen. "We will do as I say."

"Tell you what, Baron K . . . let me go on up ahead and scout 'em out a bit. I can move fast and light. It sort of used to be my profession—before I got shanghaied into the dragon business."

Erde could see Baron Köthen wishing in his heart for someone predictable and steady at his side, like Captain Wender, or even the not entirely sane but surely reliable Hal Engle. On the assumption that there was greater strength in union, she decided to support him.

"No scouting now. We must stay together," Köthen insisted. To Erde's surprise, he turned to her. "Are the dragons agreed? They will come if you call them?"

"They will, my lord."

His gaze lingered a moment. Then he grabbed her hands at the wrists and twisted them palms up and open in front of him. Their unscarred, healthy flesh seemed more than a puzzle to him: an offense, perhaps. How else to explain his tight, nervous expression?

"Did I dream it?" he murmured.

"No, my lord."

"It's true, then, is it, witch? Dragon magic?"

Had he not believed? Was N'Doch's story of resurrection not convincing to him? "Oh, yes, it surely is. My lord Earth has made far greater healings than this."

He balanced one of her hands in his left, and with his right thumb and forefinger traced the invisible lines where Wender's dagger had cut into her skin. It was like sunrise. Her entire body awoke to his touch. Keeping her own hands steady was a supreme act of will. She couldn't even think of looking up at him.

He knows, she decided. *He knows exactly what he's doing to me. Damn him!*

And the thought gave her strength.

Köthen placed her hands down by her sides as if putting them back in proper order. "Well, then I guess I needn't worry about whatever fearsome weapons these warriors of the future might use against me. I have a dragon to put me back together again."

On the edge of the street, N'Doch cleared his throat. "Baron K. The sun's going down. We better get going."

Erde signaled the dragons.

SOMEONE IS ALIVE HERE!

Reluctantly, they gave over a part of their consciousness from their ongoing debate over the guilt or innocence of Lord Fire.

THE LAND IS DRY. IT COULD BE A BRUSHFIRE.

Erde's excitement ebbed. But surely Baron Köthen would know the difference between a man-made fire and one of natural origin.

N'DOCH SAID IT SMELLED LIKE "BURNING RUBBER."

Lady Water apparently knew what "rubber" was.

That's significant. Keep us posted.

BARON KÖTHEN REQUESTS THAT YOU MOVE IN CLOSER IN ORDER TO BE READY TO AID US IN CASE OF AN ATTACK.

DISTANCE MATTERS NOT. IF YOU CALL, WE WILL BE THERE UPON THE INSTANT.

YOU WON'T GO OFF HUNTING, WHERE YOU CAN'T HEAR US . . . ?

Nothing around to hunt.

N'DOCH THINKS HE SAW A RAT A WHILE AGO.

He never tells me anything!

Erde's head sang with the sibilance of dragon derision. In order to sober them up, she asked them something serious.

HAVE YOU LOCATED YOUR BROTHER FIRE YET?

We aren't miracle workers . . .

Lady Water sounded annoyed, but then, Erde often thought her too easily annoyed. Perhaps this was due to having an annoying human as her dragon guide. Erde was particularly irritated with N'Doch just then, as she feared he was bringing out the worst in Baron Köthen. She'd understood better how to deal with them when they were at odds. But just one life-threatening incident later, and they were instant allies. Any moment they'd be punching each other in the arm like barracks infantrymen and looking for flagons of ale to hoist together. When she said as much to the dragons, Lady Water grew even more annoyed, and her brother Earth even more tolerant and kindly.

Well, he got his highness up and moving, didn't he?

Did he? Erde thought she had done that.

YOU MUST TRUST THE BOY TO DO WHAT'S NEEDED. HE IS A SHAPE-SHIFTER, LIKE HIS DRAGON, MY SISTER. ONLY IT IS NOT HIS BODY HE CHANGES. INSTEAD, HE ADAPTS WHO HE IS TO THE REQUIREMENTS OF THE SITUATION . . . AND OF THE PEOPLE HE IS DEALING WITH.

I couldn't have said that better myself.

What about my needs? But Erde kept this thought in the private part of her mind. She was outnumbered on the issue of N'Doch, and always in such cases, she trusted the dragons' wisdom. Again, she resolved to try to better understand her fellow dragon guide.

They were about to start off, arranged in that stringlike formation that both Köthen and N'Doch favored, with herself in the middle and N'Doch up ahead. N'Doch came over and touched her elbow. "Did you warn him about guns yet?"

Guns. Oh, no.

"Will they be here, too?"

"Hell, girl, more'n likely. Once you get a good idea like that into folks' heads, they ain't gonna give it up easy."

"A good idea, N'Doch?"

He, of all people, who but for the dragons would be dead from the destruction that these "good ideas" could wreak on human flesh.

"Well, you know what I mean. They work."

"How should I warn him about guns?"

"How did you learn? I told you, right?"

"No. Someone just began shooting, and you told me to duck."

"Oh, right. I remember now. Well, maybe that's how he'll have to learn, too."

"No."

The moment was always in her mind, though most of the time she could ignore it, that preternaturally clear, slow-motion image that would never fade or be forgotten: *N'Doch is yelling. He is racing toward her over the bright velvet grass, dodging not out of but into the path of the guns firing behind him. And then his long, slim body is jerking, arcing into the air, his mouth flung open, his dark head hauled back, blood and bone and flesh, pieces of him spattering her chest and cheeks as the dragons' aura embraces them in a rush of silence and merciful oblivion.*

Erde buried her face in her hands.

"Hey, girl . . ." He touched her elbow again, uneasily. "You worry too much."

"No." She shuddered once, then dropped her hands and looked up at him, amazed. She had just understood something. While reliving that awful moment yet again, a detail had made itself clear to her, something she had not known, or had denied.

*. . . dodging not out of but **into** the path of the guns . . .*

He had put himself *between* them, between her and the guns.

He'd said he remembered nothing about that moment, the moment of his dying and just before. But Erde thought he should. She reached out to the dragons and asked them to put the image into his head. She saw its arrival in his eyes and in his sharp intake of breath.

"Why did you do that, N'Doch?"

He was wrung silent by the pictures in his mind. Only a strangled gasp escaped him, then a shudder very much like her own.

"Why, N'Doch?"

"I don't . . ." he murmured, then stopped and licked his lips. "No, I do . . . what I remember is, I was . . . so angry. Just so fucking angry! Shooting down innocent women because they're, like, an inconvenience!" His chest rose and fell as if he'd been running. "Baraga thought I controlled the dragons. I couldn't . . ."

"I know." Right there in the broken alien street, Erde put her arms around N'Doch, not even worrying about what Baron Köthen might think, and held him until he stopped shuddering. He did not return the embrace. He was too stunned, she could see, by what she had shown him, by what it told him about himself. And so was she.

She backed away from him a step, patting his arms several times as they hung long and limp by his sides.

"I will tell him about guns," she said.

N'Doch knows he can't let himself be distracted by this just now. He needs to be about four hundred percent alert. But he decides it's also not the best idea to let the girl fill the baron in on something crucial like guns which she knows shit-all about. Like, what if he says to her, how does it work? This guy could ask that kind of question. What will she say, by magic?

Plus he sees Köthen is leaning back against the brick wall of the building while she talks to him, with his arms folded across his chest at a majorly skeptical angle. It won't do for the baron not to believe her at all. He'll get his head blown off first thing. N'Doch slouches over to join them.

"So what'd you tell him?"

When she repeats it for him, N'Doch laughs. "I wouldn'ta believed you either." He offers a more mechanical explanation involving trajectories and lightning and simple ballistics, and Köthen's eyes surrender their resistant glaze. He has never heard of artillery or gunpowder, but he knows all about catapults, and once again, he impresses N'Doch with the agility of his thinking and his willingness to go after an idea as long as he can get the smallest toehold on it.

"Gun." Köthen rolls the word around as if tasting it. The military potential of such a notion is not lost on him, though N'Doch's description of gunpowder clearly smacks to him of alchemy. He uses the French word, somewhat awkwardly, since N'Doch hasn't been able to give him the word for gun in German. It doesn't exist yet for the girl and the baron, anyhow. N'Doch finds his own brain bending around that idea. Like, if he did know the German for gun, and he taught it to the baron and it got into the language that way, where would the word have come from in the first place? He reminds himself, when he has time, to ask the dragons. Just the sort of thing they ought to know.

"Main thing," he says, "is to stick close to cover. Just 'cause they're a ways away don't mean they can't get at you." He sees Köthen's glance flick down the length of the street and up the sides of the buildings, scanning the dark rows of empty window holes. *You got it, dude,* he agrees gloomily. *This here's sniper heaven.* He thinks he detects the slightest wavering in the man's ramrod confidence. It's there in his eyes—the shadow of a shark cruising the shallows—and as quickly gone, as the baron rejects the thought and shoves himself away from the wall.

"I am not the kingdom's best archer," he remarks, "but a stout bow would be comforting right now." He nods N'Doch forward and signals them to move on.

Feeling as much of a sitting duck as he can ever recall, N'Doch leads the way down the littered sidewalk, choosing now to hug the building walls for the sake of available cover. He checks every burned-out doorway or busted window and it's slow going, but the smell of smoke is still hanging in the air and the baron doesn't seem impatient.

The street runs straight for several more blocks, then snakes off to the left. At the crook of the turn, N'Doch spots a little huddle of what must have been shops, shorter buildings with gaping holes in the bottom story that used to be display windows. He peers inside each one. He sees old glass, mostly ground into glittery powder, and along the walls, wrecked and empty shelving, the charred remains of counters and freezer cases, heaps of twisted wire from storage racks. All junk. Anything useful has been salvaged already, probably over a considerable length of time. These places have a picked-over quality that N'Doch recognizes. He shrugs and moves on. Here and there, a bit of blistered metal offers a fragment of a word or image to confirm his guess: the northeastern US of A, some time after his. He can't decide now which is more surreal: walking around knowing you're in 913, or sifting through the wreckage of your own future.

Around the elbow, the street dips sharply and within a block, lowers itself into the muddy green water. There are no alleys or cross streets to lead them aside, along dry land. N'Doch glares about at the looming brick facades. *Cul de sac.* Perfect place for an ambush. But he's always had a major objection to retracing his steps. Then he sees something that makes him smile. Köthen and the girl come up beside him.

"Oh," says the girl. "We'll have to find another way."

"Unh-unh." N'Doch points.

Down the slope of the street and on the far side, where the bay has already swallowed the bottom story, a crude gangway has been lashed together out of salvaged pipes and window grating and battered metal doors. It leads from the raised stone stoop of the building at the water's edge, across that facade, and into a second-floor window of the building next door. It looks well-used and pretty sturdy, N'Doch thinks. It even has a jerry-built sort of railing. What he finds most interesting, though, is that there's been no attempt made to conceal it. It's like, well, yeah, this is where the road goes, now that the old one's underwater. He looks to the baron. "I'll check it out."

Köthen shrugs, like it's the best of a poor choice, and nods him forward. They head downhill and cross the street. Köthen and the girl wait on the stoop while N'Doch climbs the gangway. The windows of the facade are blocked with dented sheet metal until he gets up to the end of the ramp. The final window has been enlarged by knocking away the brick sill. It's now door height, if you're someone a bit shorter than N'Doch. He leans against the facade and pokes his head into the opening. The dark room inside has long ago been trashed. The wooden floor gapes in several places. N'Doch can hear the slosh of water in the space below. There's a salty dampness in the air, a coolish draft rising that he inhales with relief as he ducks through the doorway.

Inside, the gangway continues, cutting the room diagonally, across charred wood and naked joists, safety railing and all. It disappears through a wide archway into an even darker room beyond. N'Doch squints into the ungiving shadow. He listens. It looks and sounds like the building is empty, but he *feels* that it isn't. Old instinct tells him that in a place like this, it's likely he's being watched. He's been trying hard to ignore the chill in his gut from the girl's little dragon-video, but the image is on flash replay in his head and he can't find the off button. He needs a leg up here, so he does something he almost never does. He calls up the dragon voluntarily.

Hey, girl—you there?

Where else? What's up?

Nothin'. Only, y'know that eye thing you do? I'm out scouting this old building and it's dark as a powerdown in

*here, so like . . . I was wondering if maybe you could help
me out a little.*

Sure thing, bro.

He's got to grant her this, she doesn't rag him when she
knows he's in a tight spot. As he'd given over his tongue,
N'Doch now gives up his eyes to dragon control, and the
spectrum of light available to him increases vastly into the
infrared. Details of the room snap into focus in seething
black and white.

"Mega," N'Doch murmurs.

*You want to ride this road with me a while, or are you
guys too busy?*

I'm with you.

WE BOTH ARE.

N'Doch's gotten almost used to Water hanging around
in his head. She sounds pretty much like he does, so even
with their frequent disagreements, it's kind of like having
a conversation with himself. But when the Big Guy talks
to him, it's a shock to his system. Earth's voice is as slow
and vast as the dragon himself, and there's no denying the
weird and external source of it.

"Great," mutters N'Doch to himself and the dark space
beyond. "Hope you won't be sewing me up again too
soon."

He checks for the knife that Margit loaned him, then
leaves it in its sheath and starts off across the gangway.
Even in infrared, he sees nothing unusual, but his own personal sonar is about screaming by the time he makes it to
the other side of the room. He halts at the archway and
peers around one side. Another dark, empty room, longer,
much narrower. A hallway, maybe, its one window to the
left again boarded, its floor again in tatters. But it occurs
to N'Doch that here, the floor has been pulled up on purpose, so that an intruder will be forced to the gangway.

It's a few long steps to the next doorway. He takes them
swiftly and quietly. He sees that the door has been taken
off its hinges and used as part of the gangway. He sticks
his nose into the absolute darkness of the third room,
barely able to hear for the alarms going off inside his head.
Surveying the walls with his dragon night sight, he spots an
interesting arrangement of old rope and broken planks that
just might lead along one wall to a corner, where a mess

of pipe and plaster-dusted studs lean upright to suspiciously resemble a ladder. Sure enough, halfway to the crumbling ceiling, among the mildewing remnants of a plaster cornice, N'Doch makes out a shallow platform and two small bright spots of human heat. One of them has a stubby arrow nocked into a mean-looking crossbow, aimed straight at N'Doch's heart.

He pulls back fast into the archway.

What? Kids?

Water agrees. Even his one quick glance has revealed the proportions of the hot spots: slim-limbed, short, and, to N'Doch's surprise, probably female.

"Hunh." Should he go back, get the others? When he and the baron were having their manly shoot-first exchange, N'Doch hadn't figured on running into women. Not even women. *Girls.*

He leans against the archway, using it as cover. "Friend," he calls out softly, and then, remembering where he is or might be, calls again in English. He thinks he hears giggling in the corner, then a rustling and a brief frantic flapping of bird wings. Confounded, he calls again.

"Friend?" He hopes his English will be up to this.

"Toll or password!" demands a voice struggling to sound a lot deeper.

N'Doch represses a chuckle. He remembers doing this as a kid, extorting bogus toll from passersby in his nabe. "Don't know no password, ain't got no toll."

Now he knows he hears giggling. "Who sentcha, tallman?"

"Nobody. Sent myself."

Exasperation. "Gotta know sumbuddy sentcha."

"Well, nobody did." There's unconscious music in the invisible girls' speech patterns. Without exactly intending to, N'Doch imitates it. "Sumbuddy sendyu?"

Outright derisive laughter. "Natcheroo."

He lets his musician's ear lead him. "Who be dat, den?"

"We Blind Rachel crew. Whoyu?"

You listening in, girl?

He hears dragon assent in two-part harmony.

"I don't know Blind Rachel. Should I?"

"You lie, tallman." The voice has remembered to try

again for gravity. "Don' no'un 'scape Blind Rachel 'round heah."

"Toldja. Ain' from 'round here." N'Doch's afraid now that this parley's on an endless loop. Then he has an inspiration. "How 'boutchu takin' me ta Blind Rachel?" He almost adds, *me'n my friends,* and then thinks better of it.

There is a whispered conference up in the corner. N'Doch eases his head around the return of the arch. The dragon has tuned up the resolution, and he can see them as clear as day: two scrawny girls not much younger than the girl waiting outside. One is staring his way, resolutely aiming the crossbow. The other is murmuring and gesturing to her about it. And now he sees the rough-built cage beside them, with the pigeon-sized bird inside. But the cage is plenty big enough for two or three, and suddenly N'Doch fears he understands the wing flapping he heard before.

"Senta bird, didchu?" he hazards, trying to sound relaxed about it.

"Natcharoo, tallman."

"Okay, good. Now maybe Blind Rachel cometa me, steada me waitin' 'round all day."

A shocked silence from the corner. Then, "You talk reel big, tallman."

"No offense, see? But I'm a busy man." He thinks he's just about got the hang of their lingo. It's like singing and he likes the rhythm of it in his mouth. And then an entirely different voice speaks up.

"An what mightcher biziness be, newfella?"

This voice is male, and somehow he's got up into the room behind N'Doch. N'Doch alerts the dragons, thinking: *oh, man, the baron's never gonna let me hear the end of this.* He lets his hands float away from his body and slowly turns around.

Chapter Eighteen

The first thing Paia notices is that her security's been tightened. For two days in a row, she tries to elude the Twelve Daughters on the Progress to Lunch, in order to slip away to the Library. For two days, she fails.

Lunch is the only communal meal, taken in what was once the gymnasium for her family's staff. Paia, of course, sits alone at a long white table on a raised dais. The Twelve sit in a horseshoe two steps below her, their red robes matched with bright red table linens. Paia is tempted to blame this taste lapse on Luco instead of the God, who would have everyone living in cloth of gold if the Temple could afford it. Luco himself and his subordinates, eight Second Sons, sit opposite in their own horseshoe, while squadrons of Third Sons and Daughters vie for the honor of cheerfully serving their superiors, whose jobs they covet so desperately.

Paia hates Lunch.

It's even lonelier than eating in her rooms. At Lunch, she is face-to-face with all the people she is not allowed to talk to. And Luco, in so public a forum, steadfastly resists all but the most respectful eye contact.

She also hates that there's always more food on her plate and more water in her jug than anyone else's, even Luco's, who being twice her size should be eating twice as much. Paia never eats more than a third of it, assuring herself that she's feeding the kitchen underlings, who will eat anything she doesn't. But today, she notices, there's even less than usual on the red-rimmed plates in the horseshoe below, and a bit less, too, on her own gold service. She wonders if the God has instituted some new austerity measure. Another thing he could have worked out with Luco without telling her. This reminds her again of the security increase. Is this the God's idea . . . or is it Luco's?

When the tables are cleared and the Litany of Thanksgiving has been read, Paia intones the God's Benediction and rises, perhaps more quickly than is proper. She has three hours before Evensong, precious free time that she often spends in her studio. She's avoided the studio for several days, worried that her presence alone might turn the God's attention to the heretical painting. But if she goes there now, the Twelve will not follow her up the winding tower stair. She will be left, for a time, in peace.

They do, however, follow her right to the tower's bottom step. Without a word to them, Paia heads resolutely up the stairs. Just before her view of the corridor below is blocked by the central shaft, she glances back. Four of the veiled priestesses have settled cross-legged on the carpet to wait, and no doubt to meditate upon the mysteries of the Winged God. Paia flees up the steep stone stair.

The studio is as she left it: the painting still shrouded on the easel, her brushes in oil where she tossed them, the red afternoon light falling through the dusty window onto her drying palette. But Paia wanders around a bit, uneasy. *Something* is different . . . some subtle change in the room's shape or volume. It takes her a while to pick it out. It's the squarish, canvas-covered bulk in the corner. It wasn't there before. Paia considers a quick retreat to the stairs. One shout down the shaft would bring the Twelve boiling upward like angry soldier ants. But they are the last thing she wants invading her studio, her only place of true privacy. At least, private until lately . . .

She slips the God's little gun from its holster beneath her robe, and advances slowly on the mysterious object. It sits quietly, contriving to seem as if it has always been in that very spot. There is even dust darkening the folds of its cover. Paia begins to doubt her own memory. Could it have been here all along and she not have noticed it until now?

In front of it, she hesitates, then lifts a corner of the canvas. She reveals a wheeled metal equipment cart, with a single video monitor on the top shelf. She folds the cover back so that it hangs around the screen like hair, or a monk's hood. It's an older type of monitor. She hasn't seen one like it since her childhood. Possibly it's one of the deactivated house monitors, or something out of an obscure storage locker that even she doesn't know about. Its blank screen is oddly dark. Paia leans closer and hears the faint hum of power.

"I know this wasn't here!" she mutters.

Immediately, small white letters quick-march across the screen, as if the monitor is so old, it can only call up short sequences at a time.

HELLO, PAIA. HOW ARE YOU TODAY?

Paia ducks away instinctively, then catches herself, embarrassed. Finally she whispers, "House?"

YOU ARE CORRECT! YOU WIN THE JACKPOT! The screen blanks and begins a new message. WERE YOU EXPECTING SOMEONE ELSE?

Her heart is still racing. "I wasn't expecting anyone at all."

BUT YOU WANTED A MORE CONVENIENT ACCESS TO MY SYSTEMS.

Paia is confused. "It's a very good idea. House . . . but how did you get this old thing up here?" She is still whispering, as she always does when she's with the computer in the Library. Something about the House Comp encourages a conspiratorial guilt.

PARDON OUR APPEARANCE WHILE WE UPGRADE OUR SERVICE.

"That is not an answer, House. You were complaining about not being able to fix your own monitor bank. How did this old one get here?"

IT WAS ALREADY THERE.

"No, it wasn't."

THEN YOU PUT IT THERE. SILLY.

Paia remembers that mode of speech. It went with the voice her father used in play when she was a child. It was intended to put little Paia more at ease with the big bad computer, but the artifice of it disturbed her even then and she's glad not to have to listen to it now. She answers in her most adult voice. "I did not put it there, House."

YOU DIDN'T?

"I'm telling you, no. And it wasn't there before. I'd remember if it was."

The screen blanks again and stays dark for a long moment. Paia wonders what sort of data search House is running in order to verify her claim.

YOU ARE CORRECT! A REVIEW OF MY SURVEILLANCE TAPES REVEALS THAT THIS EQUIPMENT WAS NOT PRESENT AT THAT LOCATION UNTIL TWO DAYS AGO.

Two days. She hasn't been in the studio for at least three. "Surveillance tapes? But the God shut down the interior monitoring system."

HE WAS ALLOWED TO TURN OFF ALL NONCRITICAL FUNCTIONS. The scroll of lettering paused. IT'S MY JOB TO LOOK AFTER YOU, PAIA. DON'T YOU UNDERSTAND THAT?

Paia is stunned. "You watch me?"

OF COURSE.

"All the time? Wherever I am?"

WHERE I AM STILL FUNCTIONAL. AS I HAVE EXPLAINED, SELF-MAINTENANCE HAS ITS PRACTICAL LIMITATIONS. MUCH OF MY EQUIPMENT IS OUT OF ORDER. I CAN MANAGE ONLY AN INTERMITTENT RECORD.

Paia looks up, into the dim high corners of the room, ragged with the contours of hollowed-out stone. There is a tiny surveillance eye in each one, mounted among the rough-hewn ledges and crevices. "If the monitor wasn't here and now it is, someone brought it. Who?"

I DO NOT KNOW.

"Won't your tapes show it?" And then she wonders how a blank dark screen can be made to look so apologetic.

TO SAVE POWER, THE SENSORS ARE KEYED TO YOUR PRESENCE.

"Damn!" Paia realizes she's still gripping the God's gun. She slides it back into its soft secret holster. "Then you didn't see . . ." No, he couldn't have seen who brought the note either. But he must have observed her making the painting. She feels that same old restlessness rising in her again. She is forgetting to be afraid.

She strides to the easel and flips back the concealing tarp with a flourish of crackling plastic. "Have you seen . . . !"

Her gesture freezes halfway. The tarp settles around her like the train of an ancient ball gown. The painting has changed again.

Now the tall sky above the mountains is sooty with storm clouds. The great trees that line the silvery river are as bare as sticks, and the velvet grass of the valley floor is brown and stiff.

Paia cries out in pain. She cannot help herself. Something infinitely precious has been taken from her, or worse, intentionally destroyed. Who could have done this? She puts her fingertips to the painted surface, but the paint is as dry as if she'd laid it on this way herself that long week ago or more. Drier, even. She taps the paint ridges with a gentle fingernail, then smoothes a palm across the canvas. The rough, hard-curved surface sends a sympathetic chill up her spine. If she didn't know better, she'd swear this landscape had been painted years ago.

"I don't understand . . ." she murmurs. But she's still not afraid. Instead, she's excited. The old monitor has been carefully placed, she notices. The screen is fully visible if she looks just over the right-hand edge of the canvas. She glances up past the easel, straight into one of the cameras. "Have you seen this, House?"

IT IS VERY NICE WORK, PAIA. YOU ARE A TALENTED ARTIST.

"It is not my work." And having blurted it out so, she realizes that this is exactly how she feels about it.

BUT I OBSERVED YOU PAINTING IT.

"My hand, perhaps. But it is not my work." Paia has never within memory admitted to mystical beliefs, except where the God is concerned. It shocks her to hear herself saying this now. "It changes. It's different every time I look at it."

AS IS TRUE WITH ALL GREAT ART.

"Oh, House. This is not great art. I don't need your flattery. What I need is an explanation."

I AM SORRY, PAIA. I CANNOT OFFER ONE.

"Go back through your tapes. Find a record of the painting when I first finished it, and compare it with . . . this."

IF YOU WISH.

Soon the screen fills, line by line in an agonizingly slow scan build, with a murky gray-and-black image. Paia squints at it in dismay, then remembers that the internal security system had enhanced its monochrome with infrared data, but full spectrum imaging had been considered an unnecessary expense. But she recognizes the landscape anyway. Its clear skies and leafed-out trees are unmistakable.

"That's it! You see, I'm not imagining things!"

I DID NOT SUPPOSE YOU WERE.

The image clears, and the slow build of the current image begins. But midway, the screen flickers. Paia gets a single, flash impression of brilliant blue and green and golden light, and then is left staring as the monochrome scan resumes. "What was that?"

House sends a ticker tape across the bottom of the monitor: WHAT WAS WHAT?

It happens again. This time, the impression is milliseconds longer, enough for Paia to be utterly certain that she has seen a vibrant, full-color image—as clear and present as a photograph—of the landscape in the painting. "Where did you get that?"

GET WHAT?

"That last image! The color one! Bring it back!"

PAIA, YOU MUST BE MISTAKEN. A COLOR IMAGE IS BEYOND THE CAPABILITY OF THIS OUTDATED EQUIPMENT.

"But I saw it!" Then she tilts her head and smiles into another of the surveillance eyes. "This is a joke, right, House?"

I DON'T KNOW WHAT YOU ARE TALKING ABOUT. TRULY.

As if to prove itself, the green-golden image reappears, two, three, four full seconds, an eternity, long enough for Paia to watch the clouds shift softly and the grasses stir in the breeze. It's like gazing through an open window. Paia points. "There! That!" And then it's gone. She reaches out to it as if she could grasp its fleeting loveliness in her hands. The loss of it fills her with longing and despair. "Oh, House, what is that image?"

YOUR PAINTING AND . . . YOUR PAINTING, AS YOU REQUESTED. The computer is showing a sudden onset of uncharacteristic courtesy

"Not those images, the one in between! Please don't do this to me!"

ARE YOU . . . FEVERISH, PAIA? ARE YOU FEELING UNWELL?

At last she understands. The House Comp is not sending her the image she sees. Either that, or he is lying, and that she knows to be impossible. But it's equally impossible to believe that he could be wrong. Unless . . . Paia recalls how preoccupied House has been lately with the deterioration of his equipment. Perhaps . . .

The screen flashes again. But this image is not her landscape. It's a bright blue screen cut across by bold white letters: WHAT PRICE SURVIVAL?

Paia claps her hands to her mouth. She's afraid she'll scream out loud, and that will surely bring the red-clad Twelve racing up the stairs to her rescue. She stares at the words, waiting for them to vanish. They do not.

"House?"

The screen stares back unchanging, glowing white against sky blue.

"House? Are you there?" Paia waves into each of the little eyes at the four corners of the room. "House, come back!" She moves away from the easel in a long curve, and around the side of the room, as if to stay out of range of the monitor's insistent blue glare. She eases up beside it and taps the dusty box, jiggles its connections. "House?"

No response.

Paia fights off a creeping panic. There is no "off" switch anywhere to be found. She snatches at the folded canvas and drags it roughly over the screen, springing backward as if the entire assemblage might leap at her throat in revenge for being silenced. She stares at the shrouded bulk for a moment, then hurries back to the easel and covers the painting.

Then she stands stock-still, breathing hard in the stream of hot red light from the window, contemplating new strategies for evading the Twelve. She has to get to the Library. Quickly, and in absolute secrecy.

Chapter Nineteen

Baron Köthen hurried Erde up the wide stone stairs to the first landing. He motioned her against the hard, flat wall, then stationed himself a few steps away, at the bottom of the gangway. The neat rows of rectangular stones were hot against her back. While Köthen watched the upper window into which N'Doch had disappeared, Erde thought of all the labor involved in carving each little stone so precisely and placing them all just so. The lord who'd ordered all this built must have had many estates to call upon for labor, and been very powerful indeed.

She was conveying this insight to the dragon when Lady Water interrupted.

He's made contact!

Erde reached without thinking and laid a hand on Köthen's arm. His muscles tensed beneath the thin hard surface of his mail as he turned to glare at her.

Two young girls, he says.

She beckoned Köthen to bend an ear so that she could whisper the dragons' news to him. She mimed the bow and arrow. His stance shifted immediately. His dagger was drawn, and he was already heading up the gangway.

"Stay here," he mouthed.

Erde shook her head. When he frowned, she murmured, "How will you know what the dragons see?"

His scowl deepened. He tossed his head irritably, then signaled her to draw her own blade. She followed a pace behind him up the swaying gangway. His speed and silence made her feel clumsy and slow. She caught up by the entrance window just in time to grab at his tunic and keep him from going inside. "My lord! They say he's taken!"

Köthen's eyes slitted. He did not ask for the dragons to be summoned. He glanced away at the rows of dark windows facing them across the open street. "How many?" his hands asked.

Erde raised one finger. "A man."

She bent and drew the layout of the rooms as Lady Water saw it, in the dust on the gangway, marking the separate positions of the enemy. Köthen studied the diagram, then flicked her a grudging glance and nodded.

"Now you *will* stay here," he insisted silently. "Sentinel."

She thought it fit this time not to argue. Köthen slid around the frame of the window so quickly that he barely broke the opening's angular profile, so bright against the inner darkness. Erde crouched against the hot wall and prepared to slip in after him.

The man's got the drop on him, all right. And he's got the advantage of position. He's silhouetted in the doorway, against the faint light spreading in from the front room. He doesn't look real big, but he's got on a lot of loose clothing that conceals his shape. His head is shaved or bald—N'Doch can see the light reflecting off the dude's temples—but his face is in total darkness. The only useful detail N'Doch can make out is what looks like a big old fire ax in his hands. This is marginally better than the assault rifle or the Walther P350 that N'Doch has expected, but it can still do plenty of damage.

He spreads his hands a little wider. He smiles and hopes the man can see it. "Got no problem wichu, man."

"Mebbe no, mebbe yes." The man shifts onto one hip, his right, as if the other pains him, and looks N'Doch over. N'Doch feels ridiculously caught short. "Wheryu frum, den?"

N'Doch jerks his head in what he hopes is vaguely the right direction. "Up nort'."

"Ohya? Deadman Crew, aryu?"

N'Doch grins. "Hope not."

The man grunts. N'Doch thinks he may have got the joke. "Who, den?"

He can already tell they're talking turf here, and him without a clue who owns what. But he's finessed his way through worse in his time. "Way nort'," he amends. "Water Dragon Crew."

The man shifts back to a two-legged stance. "Sayu?"

N'Doch nods. "I do." He suspects from the guy's alert response that he's said something meaningful without being aware of it. But now he can relax a bit, for he's noted the brief dimming of the light from the other room, like a shadow passing, and he knows from the dragon that Köthen is in the building. His job now is to keep this guy talking and distracted. Problem is, what can he say that won't just expose his total ignorance?

"So, you really lay toll?"

"Betcha. Notchu?"

"Nah."

The man considers this. "Nuttin' ta get, up nort', ha?"

N'Doch hears the implication. He doesn't want to be seen as a rich prospect. He drops his head and nods diffidently. "Yah. Nuttin' much at all."

The man shifts his weight again to the right, and seems to be listening. N'Doch fears he's heard Köthen moving through the outer room. Using the unslinging of his pack as a noisemaker and an excuse, N'Doch backs up along the gangway to draw the man into the room. It works. The man's interest focuses on the bulging pack. He moves into the doorway. "You come fer trade, den? News?"

"Betcha," N'Doch mimics.

The man leans against the doorframe to relieve his hip, and an arm snakes out and slams him hard against it from behind. He lets out a pained yelp. N'Doch leaps back just as an arrow thuds into the gangway at his feet. He snatches the ax from the man's flailing hands and dives through the doorway to fetch up against the opposite wall, hearing the chunk of a second arrow as it buries itself in the doorjamb right beside his fleeing ear.

"Hold on, wilyu?" he yells. "Gonna kill sumbuddy!"

"Gonna kill yu, tallman!"

"Whafor, girliegirl? Ain't don' nothin' t'yu!"

"Yur hurtin' da man! Lettim go!"

"No way, til yu say truce." N'Doch's trying to look in two directions at once. Köthen drags the little man into human shield position, with his blade tight to the dude's throat, like he might do him in right then and there. N'Doch worries he might. The poor sucker hardly dares breathe and doesn't struggle, a wise rabbit in the jaws of a fox, like this encounter blew up into a lot more than he'd bargained for. Even in the dim light, Köthen's weathered face is pale beside him. N'Doch thinks this guy's skin might be almost as dark as his own.

"Ease up, Baron K.," he suggests, in the dragon's German. "I think we got the upper hand here. No thanks to me, of course." For the life of him, he can't recall why he thought it was a bad idea to bring this good soldier along.

Köthen lets the apology go by. "Tell him to call the girls down."

N'Doch does, in his best future-speak. He turns a little, hoping to let the faint light catch sincerity in his eyes. "Ain't gonna hurt nobuddy."

The man sighs. "Senda! Mari! Face heah!"

A chorus of raucous negatives bursts from the darkest corner. N'Doch and the little man suppress inappropriate grins. Köthen tightens his grip.

"Now!" gasps the man.

The girls climb down slowly but not because they're clumsy. They are, with big crossbow, strapped-on water bottles and all, as slim and agile as monkeys. But they are also reluctant and disapproving. N'Doch yanks the two arrows free and moves forward to tower over the pair on the gangway. They are maybe nine years old. Girl-babies, he'd call 'em. The bones of their faces seem to fall into patterns he recognizes. He wants to get all these people out into the light where he can really look at them.

He points at the taller one. "Whichu?"

She plants one end of the crossbow on the planking and glares up at him with her mouth pulled tight as a rosebud.

"Dis'un, Mari," rasps the man over the impatient edge of Köthen's dagger. "Senda, da udda."

N'Doch already feels bad about Köthen's roughness. He

leans on the ax handle, crouches in front of the girls, and thumbs his chest. "N'Doch."

Mari shakes her braided head. "Tallman."

N'Doch shrugs. "Okay, girliegirl. Have it yer way. Yu gotcha som'other blade ta pull on me?" Meanwhile, he's looking them over with his dragon vision. Not much on them to conceal a weapon of any sort. Their clothing is scanty, and he could probably count every rib and finger bone. But he lets them see he won't lay a hand on them even to frisk them. "Truce fer now?"

Senda, the little one, nods. Mari screws her mouth up even tighter and steadies her glare. N'Doch gives her the thumbs-up sign, knowing approval's the last thing she'll be expecting. Then he stands, hands her the recovered arrows, and deliberately turns his back on her.

Köthen eases his grip, just enough so his prisoner can stand on his own. With his head still held back from the glimmering blade, the man shifts his weight off his bad hip, and groans softly with the relief.

N'Doch says carefully, "Y'know . . . this ain't no war party, Baron K. The man's clearly hurting. What say you let him go?"

Does he see a glint of disdain in the baron's eyes, or is it puzzlement? But Köthen lowers his knife and steps back, as if removing himself from the argument. The man sags against the doorframe, breathing hard. Behind him, just as the dragons announce her, the girl's head swims up out of the darkness.

The man senses her and turns. "Yu got more ou' deah?"

N'Doch smiles, thinking of the dragons. "Mebbe." He lets this sink in, then adds, "But ain't none o' us lookin' fer troubba."

"Not heah, neitha."

"So, good. So, whachu say, den? Let's get easy some-weah, and talk."

The man nods. There's not even much resentment in him, not like the girls, for all his being tossed around a little. This guy's got some mileage on him. He shoves off from the doorframe and moves past N'Doch on the gang-way, heading into darkness and driving the kids in front of him with gentle cuffs to their heads. His limp is worse than N'Doch has expected, and he doesn't try to hide it. Proba-

bly he can move faster in his rhythmic rolling gait than if
he tried to walk straight. N'Doch follows him. Köthen and
the girl fall in behind.

Cripple or no, he leads them across the lightless room
with a blind man's confidence. N'Doch's own hands stray
to the guide rails. He sees the railings as a clue to the
joint's real purpose. It's not a death trap like he feared. It's
an oversized tollbooth, and you can't run a good operation
if you're killing off your customers. He knows some drug
dealers oughta learn that lesson.

They pass through one more dark room, then the night
thins. N'Doch can see the man's outline as he hauls back
on a thick drape. Red light streams in through an outside
opening, another window made doorlike with the liberal
use of a sledgehammer. The girl-babies scamper into the
light while the man stands back to hold the drape aside for
the others.

N'Doch becomes aware again of the sounds of water.
Squinting, he ducks through the opening onto a brief step
and a shorter, steeper gangway leading down to a floating
dock. The back of the building looks onto a kind of deep-
water courtyard, a harbor with tall brick walls. The dock is
another jerry-built assemblage of old doors and floorboards
bobbing on aging plastic canisters and rusted oil drums.
N'Doch is amazed they're still afloat. Some of them look
as old as he is.

There are a couple of little boats tied up alongside, tarred
and patched six ways from Sunday, and a larger raft-thing
up on pontoons like the dock. The raft has a stubby mast
in the center and some shreds of a sail. There's not a lick
of paint on any surface N'Doch sees. Just keeping these
tubs above water probably takes all these folks have got.

Mari and Senda take up stations beside the two small
boats. N'Doch detects a personal involvement there. He
eases down the gangway and onto the float. It's good to
feel the sea beneath him again. *All this started for me,* he
muses, *because of the water.* The air is thick and steamy, but
the buildings across the courtyard harbor throw a welcome
shadow across the dock. He finds a faded plastic crate and
tests it with his foot to see if it'll still hold weight. He sets
the ax down, drops his pack beside it, and sits.

The girl comes into the light next, then the man, then

Köthen, who has insisted on mounting a rear guard. The girl's a bit unsteady on the gangway as it stirs to the roll of the water. She makes it down to the float, then just stands there. A weird moment of suspension settles in, as they all get a first real look at one another. Each, N'Doch decides, is a surprise to each.

The man and the little girls are dark, as he's guessed. But they're all a different color, and none of them as ebony-dark as he is. Their faces are as mixed-blood as their skin tones. The man's skin is almost red-brown, and he is absolutely hairless. The girl Mari has Asian eyes and straight black hair intricately braided to frame her full nose and mouth. N'Doch predicts she'll be a heartbreaker when she's grown, 'specially since she's such a little spitfire. All of them are small. Walking behind the bald man, he's seen how the gleam on the top of his head comes barely to the level of his own heart. And the girls are petite. Their clothes are a grab bag of cheap faded sportswear, bits of heavier duty stuff like the man's scuffed work boots and his stained safety-orange vest, plus a lot of handmade bits, or pieces worked over so many times that their origins are unrecognizable. The plastic water bottles they all carry are scarred and scorched where heat has been used to mend them. N'Doch sees nothing on these folks that looks like recent manufacture.

Meanwhile, the three of them are doing some serious study of their own. They eye the girl's paleness, but her hair is dark like theirs, and N'Doch is darker and taller than them, but otherwise no big deal. It's Köthen who snares the stares, perched like he is in lordly manner at the top of the gangway, his thick blond hair ruffling in the drafts up from the water and his mailed sleeves glinting in the late sun. The girl-babies are openmouthed. N'Doch can't tell if they think he's the absolute finest thing they've ever seen, or the butt-ugliest. Given their own complex mix, maybe they've never seen a real white man before.

Finally, the bald man breaks the spell. He kicks a crate a little closer to N'Doch and lowers himself onto it. He reaches a hand across the gap between them. "Reuben Stokes. Call me Stoksie. Blind Rachel Crew."

N'Doch takes the hand. The man's grip is firm but brief. N'Doch is relieved there's no complicated shake ritual he's supposed to know. "N'Doch. Water Dragon Crew." No point in dumping the fiction now. Besides, it's not like he's lying to the guy. He nods toward the girl, who he notices has not been offered a seat. "This 'ere's Lady Erde."

The man Stoksie struggles up halfway to reach and offer the girl his hand. So he's got no problem sitting down with women, N'Doch notes. He just don't see a need to give up his chair for one. And the girl, it turns out, has been keeping track. She gives the man's hand a proper shake, then looks around for her own crate.

N'Doch sends her an approving nod. "Pull up a seat."

This leaves Köthen, who is watching the parley assemble down on the float like he has no part in it. N'Doch finds this irks him just a bit. If the good baron wants to think of himself as more than the muscle, he'd better act like it.

"Hey, Baron!" he yells, with what he hopes is a really irritating grin. "How do I introduce you to these folks? Can't ever remember all your names!" His voice echoes among the red brick walls. Out of the corner of his eye, he sees the girl shaking her head in mute dismay.

Köthen breaks off a methodical survey of those surrounding walls. He stares down at them for a moment, and N'Doch again envies the man's total feel for the Commanding Entrance. He's waited until he has every ounce and scrap of their attention. But as he starts down the gangway, N'Doch understands something else. Köthen's slow grace on the bobbing walkway is also caution. The girl had staggered a little coming down. These are inlanders, N'Doch recalls. Landlubbers. Köthen doesn't want to make a fool of himself while he's getting his sea legs, but he isn't gonna give up the Entrance. His balance is superb, though, and he gets the rhythm of the dance right away, so that he's striding across the float with confidence by the time he presents himself to the man Stoksie with a small bow and a gesture to him not to rise from his seat. Nervous, N'Doch gets up, just in case. But Köthen offers Stoksie his hand. "Dolph Hoffman," he says.

N'Doch stares at him, speechless.

Stoksie nods, returns a tight little smile, and the two of them shake like a knife at the throat is all in a day's work.

Köthen feels N'Doch's stare. He shrugs, with his eyes

still on Stoksie. "If Hal Engle can do this, so can I. I am
not so great a fool as you think."

"My lord, I never . . ." N'Doch bites back the words so
hard he nearly chokes. *Where the fuck did that come from?*

Now Köthen looks up at him. "Ah," he says, and tilts
his head ever so slightly. Then he turns and walks away to
the end of the dock to stare down into the water. N'Doch
wants to race after him, quickly explain his awful lapse.
But that would mean admitting to it in the first place.

No way.

He sees the girl watching him with sudden interest.
Damn her. She doesn't miss a thing. He turns his attention
back to Stoksie, struggling to imagine what he can possibly
say next. Stoksie, the better trader, helps him out.

"Yu speak fer 'em, den?"

N'Doch nods. He guesses he does, for now at least.

"So whatsa news, out onna road?"

"Da road's hot and dry," N'Doch replies truthfully. He
hauls over his pack and fishes around for his water jug. The
jug gets Stoksie's immediate attention. N'Doch unstoppers
and takes a swig, then much against his better judgment
and for the sake of diplomacy, he offers the jug to Stoksie.
Like, who knows what the man might be carrying? Except,
he's just *small,* not sickly-looking.

Stoksie slides the jug past his nose for a quick sniff before he drinks. N'Doch can see he's trying not to look too
cautious. He swallows without comment, then falls to studying the jug. He runs a dusty, tar-stained hand over the
grainy stoneware curves and turns the rich blue glaze into
the light. "Good work, dis. Hand stuff."

N'Doch nods.

"Trade it?"

A commodity. N'Doch appears to think about this.

"Givya gud value."

N'Doch counts. He's got three others. Meanwhile he's
thanking the Deep Moor potters for this unintended favor.
Good thing he didn't insist on dumping the ceramic for the
plastic. "Whachu offerin'?"

"Da night air camp, ha? Food n' shelta?"

They must look worse off than he thought. Or maybe
this is the standard offer around here. "All three, fer one?"

Stoksie nods.

"Done." Now that it's too late, he wonders if he's made the deal too quickly. Still, seems like a fair enough deal to him.

They shake on it. N'Doch shows him how to soften the beeswax stopper in his hands, not too much trouble in this climate, and how to remold it around the jug's tapered neck. "You got good water at camp?"

"Da bes'! Blind Rachel watta!" Now Stoksie grins, and his teeth are such wrecks that N'Doch can barely look at him. "Yu frum way long way, ri'?"

"You got it, man. Way long." N'Doch passes the jug to the girl. "Take all you want this time." He looks over his shoulder at Köthen, standing so still by the edge of the dock, head bowed like he's contemplating jumping. "Hey, Dolph!" N'Doch hits the name and the German as hard as he can. "We need you back here."

Köthen lifts his head slowly as if being stirred from the deepest sleep. He sways to the roll of the float as he comes toward them and hunkers down, completing the circle of crates. N'Doch sees how the girl watches his every step, and he knows he shouldn't be doing it, too, but the man's body language rivets him. He posted bail once for a gang buddy who'd spent two weeks in solitary, a tiny windowless cage. Köthen just moved across that dock like that same buddy walked out of jail. N'Doch doesn't understand any of it.

He nudges Köthen's elbow with the water jug. Polite as always, the girl has left some. "Drink up. I just sold the bottle."

Obediently, Köthen drains the jug. N'Doch takes it back, ceremoniously shakes out the last drop and hands it to Stoksie. " 'S all yers. So wha's da schedule?"

Stoksie glances upward. The sun is invisible behind the tall brick walls, but the sky is still bright and the building tops are hot with late afternoon glare. "Resta bit. Den we start."

N'Doch likes a man who travels by night. He translates. "Sound good to you, Dolph?"

Köthen wets his lips. "Where are we going?"

N'Doch realizes this man of the killer stare hasn't met anyone's gaze since he rejoined them. "I bought us food, water, and shelter. In their camp."

"With a water jug? A good exchange."
N'Doch laughs. "Let's hope so."

Erde considered the tacit understandings of men, even
between total strangers, and wondered if she would always
be mystified by them. For instance, how could these three
men who had been blade-wielding adversaries hardly a moment ago, now sit together in the shade, sharing nothing
more than a companionable silence? At the very least, she
would be asking every question she could think of. She'd
already planned an information assault on the little girls,
once they were done fidgeting with their tiny boats, unpacking and repacking the nameless objects stowed in every
conceivable cranny.

The dragon had no insight to provide her on this issue.
Though he was certainly male, the ways of men were as
mysterious to him as they were to Erde. But Lady Water,
like N'Doch, was always ready with an opinion.

It's the magic of commerce, girl!

Erde supposed this meant that because the man Stoksie
had given up so easily and had so quickly fallen to bartering
like a common tradesman, he was no warrior or person of
real authority, and was therefore not to be feared. Yet
Baron Köthen had been willing to shake his hand and sit
down with him as an equal. This was very confusing. After
her return to Deep Moor, Erde had realized that during
her stay in N'Doch's time, she had merely set aside the
assumptions and habits of her own world, like a garment
she fully intended to resume wearing without alteration as
soon as her stay was ended. But what if the garment no
longer fit as well as it once had? Erde had not reckoned
on this possibility.

And what of Baron Köthen, who had offered to a total
stranger—one without title or noticeable breeding—his
most intimate Christian name? Erde sensed turmoil beneath his collected surface. No, if she was truly honest, she
didn't sense it at all. She assumed it. Why else would he

be so alert to his surroundings and to signs of danger, and yet so profoundly self-absorbed? He must be in turmoil.

But when the rest was called, he stretched out flat on his back with his hands grasped behind his head like a boy on a summer riverbank. His stern square jaw was oddly relaxed as he gazed up at the yellowing sky. Erde thought she detected even the faintest ghost of a smile. Surely she had lost all understanding of what was going on in his mind. To make sense of it, she was forced to be strict with herself and ask how true her assumptions about him had been in the first place. She could set them up in a gleaming row, like the marble statues in the niches of Tor Alte's chapel, all labeled Adolphus, Baron Köthen. First, the Golden Lord, standing tall and proud. Next down, the Man Who Would Be King, his bright charisma emanating like an aura. Then, further on, in bands of candlelight and shadow, the Hero in Adversity, and finally, the Warrior Chained. She'd had a dream or two, and thought she knew him.

But there was no space in this pantheon, for instance, for the Drunken Lord or the Player of Silly Suicide Games, or even for this newest guise, the Pragmatic Democrat. Köthen in the flesh consistently eluded and defied her expectations. She said this to the dragon after she had imaged for him the empty street out in front. He transported in the middle of a thought, and his reply astonished her.

QUITE POSSIBLY HE'S DEFIED HIS OWN EXPECTATIONS AS WELL.

EXCUSE ME? Erde wondered if she had the dragon's attention. Already he was studying the neat red stones of the building façade.

WATCH WITH A CLEARER EYE. NOTE HIS OWN SURPRISE, HOWEVER HE TRIES TO CONCEAL IT.

Which he will. Just like a man . . .

As usual, Lady Water chose the more cynical road. Nonetheless, though, with a precipitous sense of loss, Erde admitted to the need to lay her old set of assumptions aside. They were attractive, but obsolete. They no longer served to explain the baron's behavior, probably because they were almost entirely of her own invention. If she was ever to truly understand him, it was time to make room for the person she really didn't know: Dolph Hoffman, the just-plain man.

Chapter Twenty

Alone in her window seat, with her escort camped outside the door, Paia has an epiphany. She knows it's a dramatic word, but after considering it carefully, she decides that it is not overstated.

She is gazing down on the Temple grounds, at the familiar geometry of the shadowed Inner Court and the outer, sun-baked Temple Plaza, at the square granite block of the Altar of the Winged God, its rusty bloodstain visible even from this height. She is watching the Temple staff come and go, on missions she knows nothing of, past the approaching lines of the Faithful, each with its own particular geometry, observed from this very spot for so many years. She is watching and thinking of something else, as she usually does, except that this time her attention is caught.

Something is different.

She redirects a bit more of her concentration, away from her worries about the House Comp's sudden silence and how to get to him, away from the mystery of those white letters on a blue screen. She studies the antlike patterns below more carefully. They are changing, have already changed, like the painting in the tower, although the difference is much harder to define. Paia is sure of it, nonetheless, and she wonders what it means.

The God teaches that change is the enemy of stability. Should she, as she knows the God would, take steps to avert it? This would require understanding what the change is. Should she, as she is sure the God would advise, trust in him to protect her from it? As she has always done, since the day he came?

A picture forms in her mind: change personified as one of those terrible endless hurricanes from her childhood that flattened everything in its path. The gales would wreck the windmills on the ridge above the Citadel, they'd be on emergency power for weeks, and entire coastal cities would wash away into the rising oceans. One of Paia's first memories is watching the destruction on the satellite news. She remembers her mother weeping about all the little bodies floating on the tide. She even recalls asking why those children's daddies weren't smart enough to take to the shelter of rock and high ground like her daddy did, and his daddy before him.

But then the hurricanes became windstorms, and then dust storms, and those became fewer but longer in duration, and as the heat settled in over the Citadel, its inhabitants retreated farther and farther into the mountainside. First her mother, then her father died, and young Paia stopped thinking about the ocean or the bodies or about anything at all except the struggle to keep herself and the Citadel alive.

Then the God arrived, and set everything back in order. Again, lives were lost, in the Wars of Conversion, but it seemed a small price to pay for the end of chaos. And the God advised his new converts not to think about the future, which is unpredictable, or the past, which is full of things you can do nothing about or ever have back again, like green hillsides, luxurious possessions . . . or parents. Survive the day, the God said. At the time, Paia knew exactly what he meant. Now she is no longer sure.

The rows of screens in the House Comp's lair had been that same blank blue as on the monitor upstairs, behind the white lettering. The blue of oceans.

What price survival?

Paia had always thought . . . had she been told this, or did she merely assume? . . . that when the hurricanes dried into dust storms, the oceans receded to their former levels. She understands now that this isn't true. Who would have told her such a thing? The God? It hardly matters. What she wants to know is how much of the world is still underwater? A quarter? A third? Half? Will it be more? Is this what's aroused the God's "ancient foes"? The need for higher ground, a new place of safety from an ever rising tide?

She's guessed at least one answer to the mysterious question: the price of her own survival has been ignorance.

How is it she can sit so still, when her mind is in such a frenzy? Paralyzed. As if all her capacity for motion has been given over to thought.

I know nothing. Nothing!

She could throw a huge tantrum about it, but she doesn't even know who to blame. No wonder the phrase "spoiled brat" rolled so easily off Son Luco's tongue. He's probably always thought that about her, even though he must be party to the agreement that keeps her in ignorance, in the name of preserving her innocence. The God's conspiracy, with Luco as his chief conspirator and who knows who else, all in on it, telling themselves it's for her own good. Only the House Comp has offered her knowledge, and she's been too stupid . . . or too naive . . . to take advantage of it.

Ignorance.

And what are they hiding? Something specific? Such as, why the southern hills were alight with fire last week, and again two nights ago? Or why there's been no melon on her breakfast tray for two weeks running? Why does she not know the faces of her priestesses? Why was the woman on the House Comp's screens weeping and shaking her fist at the sky? Who? What? Why?

Paia has asked questions before, but only idly, always allowing herself to be satisfied with evasion and the flattery of worship. But the Citadel is her father's legacy. It's time his only daughter took better charge of it.

In the courtyard below, a scuffle breaks out in the long line of the Faithful waiting in the hot and lethal sun for admission to the Sanctuary. Perhaps a third of them will be admitted, and the rest will continue their wait until tomorrow morning, or evening, or the next morning. When the scuffle clears, as it always does, there is a man laid flat on the paving stones, as there always is. There's no change down there. Paia understands that now. The change is in herself.

It's time to prepare for Evensong. The chambermaid will be knocking momentarily. Still Paia doesn't stir. Her arms and legs are lead.

What about the chambermaid, nameless to her mistress and mute since birth? Or so Paia is told, though now she has begun to doubt everything. Is the chambermaid also kept in ignorance? What about the Honor Guard outside her door? Or the Faithful, slamming each other's heads for a place in line? How far does this conspiracy of ignorance extend?

She pictures white letters on a blue screen. White as clouds, blue as oceans. Blue as the sky above velvet-green grass, in a landscape already passed into memory but for a black-and-white muddle in the House Comp's surveillance files.

And who is it who has finally had enough of all this ignorance?

Paia assumed they were the enemy because they asked a heretical question. But perhaps they mean to be her friends.

Her leaden fingers curl into fists. Her lips tighten. Small motions, great resolve. She will be her own conspiracy. First, she will get back to the House Comp. She'll sneak away in the middle of the night. She'll bribe the Honor Guard with her father's oldest brandy! Whatever she has to do, she will.

Next, she must get out of the Citadel. Must! Brave the sun and open air, the bandits and the assassins! She'll tell Son Loco that the High Priestess wishes to make a formal visitation to the villages of the Faithful. She'll bend every ounce of her authority and persuasion on him until he agrees. She's done with being an idle ornament for the God's altar. Only in full understanding of the world can she serve the Temple as the God deserves.

And she'll choose a Suitor, as the God has decreed, but his knowledge will be more attractive to her than his appearance. He'll be someone she can pry information out of while he's weak from the pleasures of her bed.

And somehow, she will convince the God to tell her about these awful, ancient enemies that threaten his peace of mind. For instinct warns her that they are the key to all of this.

Wrapped in stillness, Paia plans.

PART THREE

The Call to the Quest

Chapter Twenty-one

The chambermaid has come and gone. The High Priestess is on her way to Evensong, escorted by six of her
Honor Guard. She has made sure to be gracious to them.
She has even smiled at the duty captain, even though the
watch will have changed at least twice before her planned
darktime foray.

Paia strides ahead of them along the dim corridor. The
carpet, once so soft and thick beneath her feet, is worn thin
in the center from all this military traffic. It was meant for
comfort, not to withstand soldiers' boots. Even her sandals
make a scratchy sound against it now. Paia tries to look as
if she cannot wait to enter the Temple once more, as if she
is so eager to be leading her flock in holy worship of the
God. Meanwhile, she is wondering where he is. She cannot
feel him anywhere in the Citadel. She hasn't seen him for
several days. There is a measure of relief in this, but also
the ache of loss. She misses him. He used to visit her
more often.

She is gliding down the steps between the second and
third levels. She is thinking about the God, but her brain
registers a delayed response to the deactivated house monitor screen at the top of the staircase. Has she really seen
words there, or is she now imagining cryptic messages everywhere she looks?

She cannot glance back. If there is something there, a
look will bring it to the attention of the Honor Guard who,
from the steady clatter of their downward progress behind

her, appear to have noticed nothing. But there is another wall monitor at the bottom of the stair.

Paia slows a little, pretending to adjust the glittering folds of her red-and-gold Evensong robe. As she moves past the monitor, she gives it a fleeting but thorough study. A small tickertape is scrolling silently across the bottom of an otherwise dead gray screen.

ATTENTION: A GENERAL SECURITY ALERT WILL SOUND IN 110 SECONDS.

Paia bravely hides her first response, which is terror like a jolt to the heart. Security alert? The God's enemies must be attacking! Then she gets hold of herself and remembers that the House Security System has been turned off for years. Or so she'd thought, until the House Comp implied otherwise.

By the time she reaches the next wall monitor, the little scroller says 75 seconds, which means it's an active message. Paia keeps moving. It could be some sort of autonomic malfunction, or it could just be that House is up to something. When she thinks about it, she has her answer. Genuine security alerts do not conveniently announce themselves in advance.

Paia slows even more, as if taking on an appropriate degree of gravity as she approaches the Temple sector. She doesn't want to arrive there before the 75 seconds elapse and get caught in all the confusion . . . or perhaps she does. She picks up speed again. The Honor Guard must be wondering about her erratic pace, but if House has seen fit to provide her with a diversion, Paia wants to make the most of it. She will be very disappointed if this turns out to be a total false alarm.

The First Daughters await her at the bottom of the final flight of stairs, two rows of six lined up on either side of the corridor, heads bowed at precisely the same angle. They are ready to fall right in behind as the High Priestess passes through their ranks. They must rehearse this, Paia observes sourly. Probably daily. She does not wait for them. Let them worry about catching up. She's counting seconds. She reckons she has fifteen left, and the side doors to the Sanctuary, leading directly to the dais, are at least ten of them away. But she must not run. She cannot seem to be at all concerned about anything.

Paia lengthens her graceful strides. The Twelve scurry after her. A cluster of Third Sons blocks the entrance, straightening each other's robes. Too many of them spring for the doors at once when they spot the High Priestess advancing on them. Seconds are lost while they sort themselves out and get to the tall double doors. The none-too-finely carved wooden panels were a gift from some pious village Paia has never been told the name of. As she is making a defiant resolution to find it out, the doors are hauled open. And then the alarm sounds.

The shrill braying of the electronic klaxons is an alien and horrifying noise to the Temple's clergy, as well as to its congregation. The shrieks of the Twelve behind her blend with the moans and wails of the Faithful inside as Paia bounds through the doors and across the dais, dodging two Second Sons frozen in mute terror with burning tapers in their outstretched hands. She slips behind the altar screen into the shadowed niche of the High Altar, where the Flame of the Apocalypse burns in its polished golden bowl—the Unfueled Flame that never gutters or goes out. Reflexively, Paia lays two fingers to her lips and then to the rim of the bowl. The din of the alarm is appalling. She recalls several general alerts during her childhood, and she's sure the klaxons were never this loud. Clever House has maxed the volume from awful to deafening. But how, she worries, will the computer explain all this chaos when the God hears of it, as he doubtless will from Son Luco, and comes calling to the Library in a rage for a reckoning?

Deal with that later, she decides, like House obviously has. By the time the alarm cuts off, dropping into the Citadel a silence almost as deafening as the horns, Paia is through the little maintenance hatch behind the High Altar and racing down the deserted back corridors toward her secret stairway.

"House!" she cries, as she bursts through the antique stone portal that guards the computer's darkened lair. "That was brilliant!"

"A desperate act," replies the House Comp in her father's most grave tones, without his usual greeting or preamble. "I had to warn you somehow."

"Warn me?"

"I am being tampered with."

"Tampered? How?" It's as chill in the room as it always is, but Paia is still warm from her breathless race. "Is that why I lost you up in the tower?"

"I had only just discovered that dusty miracle of obsolescence, then suddenly, I no longer had access to it."

"Has someone been in here messing with you?"

"No human but you has access to this facility."

"Well, it isn't the God. He wouldn't know the first thing about it. Someone outside?"

"No one anywhere should be able to do this."

Now Paia feels the chill. Her father always boasted that the computer's security systems were invulnerable to tampering. "Can you tell where it's coming from?"

"It appears to be more than one source. One is almost certainly external. The signal is scrambled and very cleverly cloaked. For the other, there are no visible defenses. I have been unable to trace either of them or pinpoint their locations."

Paia settles into the leather swivel chair and flattens her palms on the black console, as if to impart some degree of calm, if not to the computer, at least to herself. "I think I might have a clue, House." She lowers her voice. If the computer is accessible to others, who knows who might be listening? In her quietest whisper, Paia tells him about the note left on the painting. "Perhaps I should have given you the whole story when I mentioned this before . . ."

The dark room is silent for a long moment. A few tiny red lights stare back at her unblinking from within the inky plastic. Then House says, "I am extremely . . . relieved."

"Relieved?" She has never heard the computer describe his emotional state before, or express any sort of hesitation.

"I spoke of two sources."

"Yes?"

"For two months now, I have been . . . seeing things."

"What?" Paia almost shouts: *me too!*

"I use a human metaphor, of course. I have been subject to . . . certain transient and random signals. They arrive in incredibly fast streams and are gone before I can store them. Images, I believe. I can neither decipher them nor locate their source, so that they appear to come out of nowhere. They do not even register as proper data in my circuits. I am aware that something has . . . come in, but can find no record of the transaction. This is most . . . bizarre."

The computer pauses, as a human might, to catch a breath or regain lost composure. "When no explanation presented itself, I became concerned that . . . that perhaps there was no external source. That it was a sign of some final malfunction . . . that I was breaking down, or that I was . . . imagining things. I do that sometimes, you know, but rarely so . . . vividly. When you first asked me about that phrase, I was . . . afraid to ask where you'd seen it. I worried that it had leaked onto one of my screens without my control or knowledge. But a real physical object, a note written by human hands . . . that puts things back into perspective again."

"Yes. It does. I guess." Paia strokes the console's unbroken surface, as darkly reflective as the Sacred Well at midnight. What sort of consolation does one offer a computer? How terrible to be a mind trapped in a box buried at the bottom of a mountain. She wants to ask House what else he imagines, but she knows that will have to wait.

"So you see why I called it a desperate act. They're all in an uproar down there right now, and no doubt this will send HIM and his cohorts on another of his circuit-frying, chip-melting rampages. I have so few working peripherals as it is. But I had to know . . ."

"I expect it's me he will punish, House."

Some real fear must have shown in her voice, or perhaps the computer's delicate sensors are reading telltale hints in her vital signs. In the tone he reserves for statements of absolute fact, he says, "You need not fear him, Paia."

"Oh, House, thanks for the comfort, but how could I not?"

"I said you *need* not. If you choose to, there is no help for it, but I tell you, he cannot harm you."

"Of course he can! You've obviously never seen . . ."

The big monitor bank fills with a sun-bright image of the Temple Plaza, smeared with the smoldering ash of the kamikaze zealot who'd played at would-be assassin not so many days ago. Paia shields her eyes from the glare.

"I see everything," says House quietly. "He is a monster. But to you, he cannot do injury."

"I don't . . . what are you getting at?"

"It is prohibited in what you might call his genetic makeup."

Does a God have genes? "How do you know this?"

There is another silence, an even longer one. And then: "This is only a small bit of data in a very large archive I have on the subject."

"You take data on the God?"

"I store data about the *dragon*."

Hearing the word spoken aloud makes Paia glance anxiously over her shoulder at the doorway. "Shhh!" she gasps, like the child the word makes her feel.

"Dragon," the computer repeats, and the word becomes the closest thing to a hiss she's ever heard out of him. "That's what he is, after all."

"Look, House, it won't do to have both of us in revolt at the same time!"

"Are you in revolt, Paia?"

"Forget I said that. Why wasn't I told about this archive during that search I made after the God first arrived?"

"I was not aware of it myself at the time."

"When did you become aware of it?" Paia would swear the computer was being evasive.

"During the last two months."

"Oh. You mean it came in with the mysterious messages?"

"No. Only my awareness of it."

"Hunh. Well, can I look at it?"

"It is probably time that you did."

Paia worries her upper lip between her teeth. "There's something you're not telling me, isn't there, House?"

"Do you recall how to read a book, Paia?"

"A book? I guess that can't be too hard. Why?"

"The archive I speak of is your father's library."

Chapter Twenty-two

The water was not as deep as Erde had supposed from its thick and murky wash. When the man Stoksie had finally arranged them—and especially their packs—to his liking on the narrow raft, he sent it away from the landing and across the flooded courtyard by means of a long stout pole shoved against the invisible bottom. The two brown girls paddled along behind, each in her own little boat. Erde envied them. How many times she had watched longingly from Tor Alte's walls while the prentice boys played at naval warfare in the village duck pond. She'd had to run away from home to get anywhere near a boat. This absurdity almost produced a giggle, but she held it back, not wanting to appear frivolous at such a serious moment.

N'Doch watched Stoksie labor for about three strokes, then took up a second pole from the deck and signaled his readiness to help. The raft began to glide along at an impressive speed. Erde thought of the dragon back in the street, but did not send him an immediate image. Her proximity to all this moving water would only upset him, although she'd noticed that his terror of it had abated somewhat since his sister had joined them.

The passages between the buildings were narrow and dark, with the tall red walls sometimes rising up inches from the sides of the raft. Often N'Doch was forced to set his pole aside and ease the raft along the green-slimed walls with his hands. They followed many sharp turnings, some of which looked like dead ends until the very last minute, in a mazelike progression from courtyard to courtyard, and everywhere the same tall red walls and shadowed, broken-out windows. I would get lost, Erde observed, then understood that this was exactly the point of it. She spotted other gangways, cobbled together out of whatever had been to hand, making bridges between two buildings or an exterior access around the perimeter of a hidden courtyard. But she saw no other floating docks like the one they had just left. Once, they slid under a particularly elaborate bridge construction, and N'Doch gave it a complimentary wave.

"Yer crew, dat?"

Stoksie nodded. "All dat." His gesture was a high inclusive circling, and Erde took it to mean the entire city. Baron Köthen sat up ahead of her with his back to the big post in the middle of the raft, so that he faced Stoksie, as well as the girls paddling behind. He was so quiet and still, it made her nervous. Once, he asked her to translate some remark of Stoksie's. When she'd checked with the dragons and passed it along, he looked away, up at the shadowed walls sliding slickly past, touched along the tops with the bright orange of the late sun.

"It's like some sort of fever dream, isn't it?" His eyes flicked toward her dolefully. "Not, of course, a dream such as you are accustomed to, my lady witch, though as I appear to be in it with you, perhaps I am mistaken about that as well. Still, it seems more like a vision—such as one is forced to move through without choice or control."

"My dreams were always like that," she reminded him sternly. "But this is not a dream, my lord. It is real, I can assure you."

Köthen laughed, soft and dry as a whisper. "To you perhaps it is."

And then they were distracted. The raft slipped out of the shade of a narrow alley into angled red sun glinting off a big rectangle of open water, like a flooded market square. Stoksie leaned into his pole and the raft lurched forward. N'Doch let out a happy yell and bent to his own pole. Soon they were coursing down the length of the square in full orange daylight at the speed of galloping horses. Erde grappled for handholds and clung to the deck as if she might be swept off by the breezes that riffled her hair. They shot out of the square into a long straight passage, approaching another sort of building, the hugely tall towers visible from the distance when they'd first entered the city. Close up, they were terrifying: taller than any cathedral spire Erde had ever seen, both gleaming and dark, and so narrow she could not imagine how they remained upright. Staring up at their soaring heights made her dizzy, and convinced her they were tumbling down on top of her. Several of them gaped open at the water level, with holes so vast that the entire raft could have floated right through and in among their charred and twisted beams.

Suddenly N'Doch gave another whoop and hauled his pole out of the water. "Too deep na, man!"

"Yah!" Stoksie replied. "Getchu heah, hold 'er steady, while I put up sail."

N'Doch trotted the length of the raft, as surefooted as if on dry land. Behind, the girls were padding madly to catch up. Stoksie slid his pole into a slot between two bits of wood projecting upward at the rear of the raft. The pole rested at an angle and drifted a bit, side to side. N'Doch took hold of it, pushed it back and forth experimentally, and Erde saw that the raft shifted direction according to the motions of the pole.

"Gotcha," said N'Doch. Stoksie went toward the front to shoo Baron Köthen away from the central post, which Erde now recognized as a sort of mast. After several complicated maneuvers and the untying of several knots, Stoksie straightened and shoved a thick rope into Köthen's hands.

"Haul it a gud' un, whitefella!" he cried. Then he whirled away to fumble with a mound of stained cloth beginning to stir in the wind as he released its bindings.

"He means pull on it hard!" N'Doch translated, with obvious glee.

Köthen flashed him a look as sharp as a needle, then took a firmer grip on the rope and pulled. A dented metal rod clanked upward at a precarious angle to the mast, drawing the sail up with it. The raft slewed clumsily as the hot wind leaned into the folds of the canvas and puffed it outward toward a smoother curve. Stoksie snatched the rope from Köthen's grasp, looped it around a raised bit of the decking, then fastened it with an abrupt flick of his arm. The girls grabbed at the end of the raft, one to either side of N'Doch, and sprang up out of their boats, dragging ropes to tie them with. The little boats bobbed along like dogs on a chain as the raft picked up speed.

"Hard off ta port, na!" Stoksie yelled. He clapped Köthen familiarly on the back as he scrambled toward the rear. Erde braced for another fight, but Köthen just stood there, fighting for balance against the craft's new momentum and observing the activity blurring around him with a bemused frown. When N'Doch shoved the pole to one side and the raft swung to obey, the patched and mildewed sail snapped into full billow. The girls sped forward, shoving Köthen aside to grapple with the ropes flapping from the bottom corners of the canvas. Köthen stared after them, then retreated to his safe seat at the base of the mast. Erde eyed him covertly. Had she misjudged his survival reflexes? Was all this newness and change going to prove too much for him?

" 'S'alright, Dolph!" N'Doch called from the helm. "We'll make a sailor outa you yet!" He grinned hugely and turned his face into the wind. Erde could not recall him ever looking so delighted, except when he was making his music.

The raft handles a lot better than N'Doch expects it to. Must be one helluva rudder attached to this mumbo jumbo tiller, he decides. And though he's sure that the beat-up sad wreck of a sail will split its many seams as the steep downdraft between the high-rises swells it out like a nine-months' pregnant woman, it doesn't. The crude stitching holds, and the raft responds to his touch.

"Which way, na?" he yells to Stoksie.

The older man crabs backward to join him in the stern. He points out a course between the plundered office buildings. The girl-babies take turns manning the sail sheets and refilling their water bottles from a big plastic barrel on the foredeck. N'Doch worries about the sanitary procedures, then figures if these folks are carrying all their own water, they must be taking steps. He's just gonna have to risk it and hope for the best, or go thirsty.

"Getting deep," he remarks, as the raft skates past the tip of some drowned church's bell tower.

"Yu gud deckman, tallfella."

N'Doch is pleased. "Grew up on da watta."

Stoksie looks at him. "So who din't?"

N'Doch guesses the man's age: maybe forty-five, fifty at the most. Has the water been high that long? He jerks his thumb forward. "Dem two."

"Yah? Mount'in-bred, den?"

"Betcha."

Now Stoksie's looking at him hard. "*Town*folk?"

"Nah. Castles, is more like." He wonders what the man's got against townfolk. Something, that's for sure.

"Yah? Where'sat?"

"Ever hear a Europe?"

Stoksie shrugs. "Sure, one time. All unda na, ri'?"

All under. All under what? All underwater? N'Doch swallows. How's he ever going to tell the girl? "Nah. Mount'ins still lef'. Like here," he guesses, with a glance toward the west where, between the shafts of dying skyscrapers, blue crenellations press upward like a woman's breasts against the red sky. The picture is coming in clearer now. It's just what the vid guys predicted. Half the world's underwater. Holy shit. "S' dey come heah, lookin' fer a fren'."

"Alla way frum Urop? Mus' be sumkinda gud fren', na."

N'Doch nods gravely. "Betcha."

"Sumun roun' heah?"

"Mebbe. Don' know fer shur. Din't find 'im yet." N'Doch sees the water opening out ahead, past the sunstruck edge of a steel office tower and through a gateway of rusted girders. "Dis town gotta name?"

Stoksie turns his blackened grin on him. 'Jokin', ri'?"

"Nope. Askin'."

"Dis here's Big Albin, tallfella. Da prida Nyork. How far yu say yu come?"

"Li' I tellyu, man. Way far."

Stoksie takes over the helm when they swing out into the open bay. N'Doch feels some mean crosswinds cutting across his nose, as dry as a gust off the Sahara but honed with salt. A current catches the raft and heads it downstream. But it seems Stoksie intends to tack upstream, so the going is slow for a while, back and forth in the unrelenting sun. But better than walking, N'Doch tells himself. He goes forward for a long warm drink at the water barrel, then settles down next to the girl to unload what he's heard. He'll let her pass it on to his lordship and the dragons. He does ask her, though, how they're doing.

She eyes him impishly. "Lady Water says she's waiting for you to stop enjoying yourself and get on with business."

N'Doch coughs out a guilty laugh. "She didn't say that."

"No. But she might have."

"Ha, girl! You made a joke! I'm keeping my eye on you now!"

The bay is long. Eventually, N'Doch decides it must be a river. It's risen with the seas and flooded out the low-lying areas, so it just looks like a bay, with barren, rocky shores. The girl-babies chatter among themselves as Stoksie laboriously guides the raft upstream. They throw looks at Köthen as he leans back against the mast and appears to doze. He looks stunned and passive, but N'Doch doesn't believe it for a nanosecond, and he's pretty sure the girl-babies don't either. At least the man's had the sense this time not to insist on taking charge. Maybe 913's favorite hothead is learning how to go with the flow.

After a tough hour of fighting the current, Stoksie is looking slick and tuckered. N'Doch worries for the little man's heart. "Yu wan' sum help?"

Stoksie waves him off stubbornly, and then, as if his refusal has gained him strength, the raft glides along more readily, actually picking up speed. Stoksie rubs his bald head and flashes a big, gap-toothed grin. "See dat? I ain' dun fer yit!"

"Yu ain' even half dun!" The dude's been so easy to deal with so far, no sense making him feel bad. N'Doch winks sideways at the girl so she doesn't spill the beans. There's no sign from below, no odd ripples, no careless bumping against the underside, but he knows a certain water dragon is down there, helping things along. He pictures her, a blue shadow streamlined into porpoise sleekness. He smiles, leans back, and shuts his eyes.

A much easier hour later, when Stoksie heads the raft

toward a little inlet on the western shore, N'Doch has actually been dozing. He stirs, refreshed, looks around. Things are a little greener up here, though not by much. The trees are stunted and dust-cloaked, but they have scrawny little crops of leaves, and the weeds scattering the tops of the steep clay banks show a few yellow flowers. N'Doch spots a line of broken foundations along the bank top, and an occasional bit of crumbling wall. Might have been a town once, but it's history now. His little nap has reawakened his curiosity.

"Wha's dat up deah?" he calls to Stoksie.

"Sumplace. I fergit whaddit wuz back den. Call it Plaguetown nah."

N'Doch looks alarmed.

"Na, dey's nuttin deah nah. Dem plagues is long gone." Then it's Stoksie's turn to look concerned. "Yu got plague still up nort'?"

"Na. None a dat."

"Gud. Cuz yu don' lookit. Look reel healt'y, alla yus. Firs' ting I notice."

Stoksie noses the raft expertly into the inlet, then strips his pole free of the rudder and plunges it into the water again. N'Doch leaps up to join him. It's too shallow here for invisible dragon assistance. The girl-babies race back to haul the rudder out of its casing. They toss it long and dripping on the deck, then grab their paddles out of the trailing boats to lend a hand at forward motion.

The inlet was probably once a creek emptying vigorously into the river. Now the water wanders sluggishly upstream. Jumbles of boulders, still marked by tar stain, line both sides of a steep and scrubby ravine. Soon the streambed sprouts rocks and becomes an obstacle course as the ground climbs around them. More ruins perch on the slopes past the rockfall, wooden structures sagging into shapelessness and char among the bleached skeletons of pine trees. Quaint houses along a picturesque mountain stream, N'Doch muses, recalling travel vids of Switzerland, or the American Rockies, where the cowboys come from. Then there's a cry of metal on stone, and Stoksie calls a halt. The raft's oil drum pontoons are scraping bottom. He poles toward a bankside stair made of ascending natural ledges, and lands the raft with a final shove and a twist of his pole.

A faintly worn track winds up and away through the stiff scrub clinging to the slope.

As the raft stills, the heat descends again, thick with the smell of parched dirt. A swarm of midges stirs from the algal muck along the shore. N'Doch bats at them irritably, but is privately glad to see any sign of wildlife. Köthen shakes himself out of his putative doze. He stretches elaborately. N'Doch has to chuckle at the pair of them, both avidly scanning the landscape, both pretending so hard not to. The girl-babies scramble onto dry land and tie off the raft to a battered tree trunk. Stoksie ships his pole, so N'Doch does likewise. Not much of a destination, but he guesses they're here. He listens. Nothing but midge whine and their own boat noise, which make a huge racket in the total absence of other sound. It's been no different since they first arrived, but here, knowing he's on someone's turf, the silence makes him paranoid. He's glad now to have Köthen's eyes and ears as well as his own. A path up through rocks and woods? Prime ambush territory.

But he helps Stoksie lower the sail, then gives the girl a hand. He tosses Köthen her pack without even asking. He's amazed how he feels freed now, to treat the man like anyone else, like something's given him permission. Köthen himself, he suspects. The good baron is busy taking an ostentatious vacation, while he figures out who he's gonna be if he ain't gonna be the boss.

The girl-babies bounce back to the raft to haul their own little boats onto dry dock, swiftly relieving them of their cargo and lashing them away in the brush. Stoksie has his own major unpacking to do, lifting this and that invisible hatch in the deck to pull out wrapped bundles and tied-up satchels, until he has a huge pile waiting up on the shore.

"Yu wan' help dis time, man?" N'Doch wonders what the guy would have done if he hadn't picked up three extra passengers.

"Betcha," Stoksie breathes gratefully.

N'Doch nods, like it's the least he can do. He doesn't think it prudent to mention the big brownish boulder that's taken up residence a ways off to the left, while everyone's back was turned—even though he could save them all what looks to be a long hard climb. He shrugs, sighs, and hands the girl something easy to carry. She offers to sling another over her free shoulder. As he's adding a few to his own load, he sees Köthen hesitate, then mutter tersely to himself and grab up one, then two of the heaviest. The girl-babies help Stoksie take up the rest, like they were balancing a packhorse. Then they lead the way up the hot and crumbling ledges and into the scrub, away from the shore.

Chapter Twenty-three

Paia enters the long security code that the computer made her memorize, having absolutely refused to print it out. The lock cycles, and the clear, thick facia sealing the shelf slides aside. Ancient odors drift outward on the spiraling drafts of the Library's cooling system: leather, ink, parchment, vellum. Words her father had always spoken with a collector's reverence. Because all knowledge came into her own life in digital form, Paia had seen her father's books as an old-fashioned eccentricity, a charming but useless repository of the obsolete. And she'd presumed that the texts, the actual writings, were of less interest to him than the physical objects, the *libri.*

Now her understanding is somewhat more complex.

Breathing in the scents of the past, Paia studies the spines. None of them offer the explanatory block-print titles she has hoped for. Many are chapped and crumbling, their drying flesh flaking away in ashy brown, tippled here and there with faded gilt. A few are mere stacks of thick and yellowing pages tied between two worm-eaten boards. But others, while seeming no more modern in their construction and design, have weathered the long centuries with abandon. Though mottled with use, their leather is still dark and supple, with a hint of sheen. Paia chooses one of these at random.

Well, not precisely at random, for her eye is drawn to this book as if it has called out to her, though it is otherwise an unremarkable specimen, neither big nor small nor fat nor slim, nor of a particularly interesting color. But it has a healthy, energetic look. *A living look,* Paia muses, then scolds herself for excessive flights of the imagination. She grasps it gently, eases it from the velvet-lined shelf, and balances it gingerly on both palms. It has no writing on the outside binding, just the subtle spots and stains of centuries. This book, she decides, has been well-treasured, but also well-used.

She carries it out of the careful gloom between the storage cases to a reading table. The pool of light washing the green fabric of the tabletop brightens as Paia places the book down on the soft felt. She has never handled her father's books before. She pulls up a cushioned chair and settles herself before the book as before an unfamiliar food she is not sure she will enjoy. She lifts the worn leather cover and lays it back against the green tabletop. The first page is a pale, speckled buff color, and is entirely blank. Paia turns it aside, surprised by the greasy thickness of it between her fingertips. The next page is elaborately bordered by flowers and vines, with fish and birds darting between them. In the center is a circular symbol, artfully drawn in bold black ink, divided by quarters into smaller individual symbols. Paia is surprised by the vibrancy of the ink. Surely after so many years the ink should have faded more. She shrugs and turns the page.

The text begins on the third page, with a title block and cursive lines of neat black script. Though Paia recognizes many of the letters, she cannot read the words. But the House Computer has prepared her for this eventuality as well. She pushes back her chair, so silently on the dark rich carpet, and pulls out a shallow drawer from under the table's edge. She sets the book face up and open in the drawer, and closes it gently. On the tabletop, a section of green felt slips smoothly aside, exposing a neat rectangle of screen, like a glass place mat directly in front of her. Through the transparent screen, Paia sees the book: lit with a cool glow, as well as a translation, superimposed, faintly luminous green letters suspended above the actual text. From somewhere past the pool of light, the computer's voice floats down like mist, as gentle as she has ever heard it.

"The Secret Mysteries of the Wyrm, author unknown.

Text in Latin, Frankish, and Old German. A collection of folklore, copied probably around 700 AD, in what is now southeastern Germany. Its first documentation is in a handwritten catalog, since destroyed but existing in facsimile, of the estate library of a Baron Weissstrasse, known chiefly for his remarkable collection of such books and for his very thorough record keeping."

"Such books . . . ?"

"About myth and legend and what were then called 'the ancient arts': alchemy, magic, witchcraft, the like. But in particular, the Weissstrasse Catalog evidences a keen interest in the subject of dragons."

"Ah." Paia bends closer to examine the text and its translation.

Several hours later, she is still reading. Her back aches and her eyes smart from the unaccustomed close concentration. But her mind is entranced. She is in another world. A far-off time ruled by unseen forces, perilous and mysterious but open to manipulation in the hands of a skilled adept. Not ruled by science, as her world had been until the coming of the God, nor yet damaged by the excesses of technology. A time when people believed in dragons, and the very existence of the God, or any god at all, made a lot more sense.

Once Paia would have dismissed such tales as fantastical nonsense. But if the God exists now, which he undeniably does, could not all this have existed then? Or, looked at another way, if the God exists, could all this exist now? Is magic the reality and science the myth? What about dragons who come and go at will? Or sacred pools that remain deep and icy in the heart of the drought? Or paintings that morph on their own between viewings? Paia allows herself the excuse of having been just a child, but it astounds her to realize how quickly and willingly she and every other inhabitant of the Citadel put away rational inquiry the moment the Winged God appeared, wreathed in thunder and gouts of gehennical fire. As if magic was easier to believe in than science, which required thought and could be counted upon to turn on you when you least expected it. But so could magic, if the lore in this book is to be believed. So are they separate or the same?

Paia glances back at the words on the screen: *"A True Recipe for Raising Dragons."* The alchemists clearly thought they were the same. She puts her face in her palms and rubs her eyes. She is hopelessly confused, but elated just the same, as if she is on the brink of some sort of new understanding. The God, she recalls, rarely uses the term "science," but he certainly knows how to turn it to his advantage when he wants to.

"Paia." The computer's voice is so soft and directionless that, in her daze, Paia thinks she's hearing it from inside her own ears. Right now, nothing would surprise her. "Paia, the search is becoming desperate."

"The search? Oh . . . for me?"

"Perhaps you had better show yourself before they alert you-know-who."

"He's off on one of his trips."

"They'll call him back if they're frightened enough."

"Call him back? How?" She looks up into the darkness beyond the low-hung lamp. "They can't do that."

"Luco can. The dragon has made sure that he will always be kept informed."

"Luco?" The priest must be in better favor than she'd realized.

"But Luco needs a device. You do not."

After what she's been reading, Paia finds this statement as provocative as House no doubt intended. "I can't call him. How would I call him?"

"Have you ever tried?"

"Of course not." The idea of summoning the God like he was some sort of servant seems preposterous to her.

"Why not? He calls you."

"But he's the God." Paia goes back to rubbing her eyes. "Could you dim this light a bit, House? I'm done reading for now."

The light softened, but the computer would not accept the change of subject matter. "If he can call you, why shouldn't the connection between you work both ways?"

"He's never said . . ."

"Of course he hasn't. Such knowledge would give you real power over him."

"Well . . ." *The Power of Summoning. A True Recipe*

for Raising Dragons. Paia rubs her eyes a little harder.
Power over the God? Exactly what she's always wished for.

"Don't tell him we've had this conversation. Just try
it . . . sometime soon. Now, you'd better go. The whole
Citadel is in an uproar."

"If he were here, he'd know where I am."

"Yes."

"Would he know where Luco is?"

"Only if Luco is wearing his tracer, which he always
does. Off with you now. And remember, question anything
you see or hear on any of my systems outside this room. I
am not entirely in control of them."

Paia stands wearily, retrieves the book from the reader
drawer, and carries it back to the storage stacks. She re-
shelves it carefully, sucking in one more dusty, odorous
lungful of the past before she locks the case. She comes
back to the edge of the light falling around the green-
topped table. "House, it's as if you've decided to be my
tutor again, after all these years."

"Hardly a decision. More like an instruction."

"Really? From whom?"

"I was not given that information. Time-delayed programming. Like my awareness of the archive itself."

"But why now, do you think?"

"There is little fact available to support an accurate conjecture. Are you asking my *opinion*?"

"Sure. Why not?" If she could talk to a hunk of silicon
as if it were a living creature, why should the difference
between science and magic trouble her even one little bit?

"Well, then . . . I think . . . that you weren't ready to
listen before. Suddenly, for whatever reason, you are."

Paia purses her lips, absently stroking the soft felt, suddenly, unaccountably daydreaming of grass. Grass like she's
seen only in old pictures: thick, moisture-rich, smelling . . .
well, green . . . as she imagines magic might smell. Grass
like in the painting upstairs. "Hunh," she says, and walks
away from the light.

She lets herself out and stands by the tall paneled doors,
listening. If a frantic search is underway, it hasn't yet
reached this deep into the rock. She's enjoyed this respite
from the mundane life of the Citadel, but it's also given

her several days' worth of thinking to work her way through. She sighs and hurries down the dim corridor, trying to decide where she prefers to be found.

One level lower and several room blocks closer to the front, the halls are still unlit, but now she hears the muffled beat of booted feet and voices bellowing orders and information. She used to see it as a game. She created the occasional fuss like this when she was a rebel teen, intentionally losing herself just to break the tedium. Endless loud and threatening lectures from the God about the heavy weight of her priestly responsibilities (never mind what he said he would do to her if she didn't stop) had rendered her more docile as she moved into adulthood . . . at least, until recently. Perhaps those other games were her training for now, when she can give them a true sense of purpose.

Docile. The word sticks in her mind and slows her steps until it actually brings her to a halt. It's not a word she'd have thought to apply to herself, and yet . . . it is what she's been. Not the bright, beautiful, and tempestuous woman of her standard self-image, an image built entirely in the God's vocabulary. Those are *his* qualities, which she has been allowed to play at but not truly BE. Like Luco, she has been only a mirror for the God. She has been indulged in the things that don't matter in order to buy her compliance in the things that do. At least, the things that matter to the God.

Standing immobile in the darkened corridor, Paia resolves to reverse this pattern. And she's already decided what her first demand is going to be.

Voices and feet approach from the lighted sector. Paia moves resolutely forward to meet them and, rounding a corner, runs smack into Son Luco with a contingent of worried Third Sons trailing behind him.

Paia steps back and smiles. "Hello, Luco. I thought I'd come down and see if it's all over."

Luco is caught off guard. It takes him long uncertain seconds to plant his fists on his hips and square his broad shoulders. "Where have you been?"

"Up in back, of course." Perhaps the appearance of docility will be useful for a while longer.

"Of course?"

Paia lets her hands flutter. "When the alarm sounded, I

was so surprised, I just did what we always did when my father was alive: run for the safest spot in the Citadel!" She imitates his peremptory stance. "Really, Luco. Is this any way to greet your High Priestess?"

Luco's blue eyes narrow. He drops his arms to his sides, though his big hands remain fisted, and he bows to her from somewhere in the middle of his back. "Mother Paia. Forgive me. How miraculous to find you safe and well."

Behind him, the Third Sons are already on their knees murmuring thanks to the God. If any one of them had an ear for irony, their priestly training has burned it out of them.

Paia nods graciously. "Tell me, First Son, what was the emergency?"

"None that we could find, my priestess." Luco smooths his long hair back with restless fingers. "An equipment malfunction, I suppose. I had thought the general alarms disabled, but it appears that I was wrong."

"Ah. Nothing to fear, then. What a relief." Paia moves past him and between the kneeling priestlets. Sailing grandly down the corridor, she beckons airily behind her. "Son Luco, a word in private if you please."

Luco bounds after her to loom at her side, his perfectly sculpted mouth flattened with rage. "Now what are you up to?"

"Please, Luco . . . I'm sorry if I worried you. I really didn't think . . . I just ran. My father drummed it into us until it was practically an instinct."

"You'd be a lot safer if you ran toward me in an emergency instead of away!"

"Oh, Luco, I wasn't! I tell you, it was instinct."

The priest is silent for a moment, pacing along beside her, shortening his stride to match hers now instead of the usual other way around. Paia knows he's deciding whether or not to believe her. Since her attempts to talk truth to him have all been rebuffed, she doesn't mind that he suspects her of subterfuge. It's an improvement over being taken entirely at face value. She smiles at him sidelong, reverting to the playful, pleasure-loving Paia he seems most comfortable with. "Besides, it got your heart rate up, didn't it? Don't you feel invigorated?"

Before he can sputter a sufficiently indignant reply, she

lowers her voice and waves him closer. "Now, Luco: I have a proposition to put to you. I've been thinking it over, and I've decided that in these hard times when the Faithful are so despondent . . ."

"Who says they're despondent?"

"They're always despondent! Look at how they live, see how fervently they pray! They must be despondent! Anyhow, I've decided it's time for the Temple to return a gesture . . ."

"*You've* decided . . . ?"

"A gesture of appreciation for their unswerving devotion and of hope for . . . no, don't scowl. How about hope for tomorrow, even if not for the day after? Shouldn't they be offered just a little something, at least until the Last Day is actually upon us?"

Luco draws out his grunt of agreement until it comes out like a negative. "What sort of gesture did you have in mind?"

"Well . . . they're always coming to the Temple. I think the Temple should come to them." Paia checks her mental ammunition and forges ahead. "In the person of their High Priestess. Who will make a Visitation to the ten most exemplary villages. You can come, too, if you like."

Luco's jaw slackens. "Ten?"

"Five, then. How many do we have? Luco, neither you nor the God ever tell me these things!"

"Why should you care how many villages?" he retorts stiffly, then seems to hear how snappish he sounds. "I mean, Mother Paia, your holy duty is the care and feeding of their souls, whatever their number."

Paia pats his gold-banded arm. "Well spoken, my priest. You do the God credit. But how am I to truly understand what troubles them, be they one soul or many, if I have never walked among them?"

"You walk among them every day, in the Temple. It's the God's decree that you do so."

"Oh, Luco, surely you can't believe such a narrow view can build a true understanding of a human soul?"

She feels him studying her without wanting to be seen to do so. Finally he says, "What's gotten into you? Who have you been talking to?"

Paia suppresses a laugh. Suddenly she's infused with a

heady sense of power. "Why do you say that? Can't I have an idea of my own? Besides, who would I talk to, besides the God and you? I'm not allowed, remember?"

"That doesn't mean . . ." Luco lets out a breath and collects himself. "Have you presented this mad scheme to the God?"

"Ah, mad, is it? And here I thought that you, as a man of the people, would approve of the idea, and help me convince him."

It's the first time Paia can recall using her heritage as a weapon against him. When Luco was a mere foot soldier, she would not have bothered. By the time he was elevated to the priesthood, she'd learned the folly of saying "don't tell me what to do, I was born here!"

But Luco fields the challenge by ignoring it. "Have you?"

"No."

To her surprise, he seems more interested rather than less. "As it happens, I think it's a fine idea, though I'd have never dared propose it myself. If you can clear it with the God, I'll arrange it."

They reach the end of the corridor, where it meets the major cross hall for that level. To the right and down are Paia's quarters. To the left and farther down, Luco's. Paia says, "Couldn't we do it when he's not around?"

He laughs, sharp and quick. "You must be kidding."

"I thought perhaps he might trust us by now to make a few day-to-day decisions on our own."

"He does. But parading the High Priestess of the Temple around the countryside where she's an open target for any and all disgruntled patrons—never mind the highly paid assassins—is hardly the God's idea of day to day. Or mine either. But if you get his permission, I'll make it happen. It'd be good for you to have a better idea of what we're up against here."

Paia glances at him, sees bleak reality surface briefly, only to be smothered once more by his Temple face, his Temple smile. "I'll try."

Luco shows no inclination to see her directly to her door. He's decided she can't get into any more trouble between here and there. As officious as he is, and ever so deeply in the God's pocket, Luco knows that she needs the occasional private moment, even if it's only while traversing the hallways to her rooms. His clutch of acolytes gaze after her sheepishly as she takes the right-hand turn away from them, alone.

As grateful as Paia is for Luco's small gesture of trust, there is one little detour she intends to make before retiring to her chambers. Down level, along the hall a bit, then another hairpin turn. Another servants' secret back stair, and she's avoided the probably twice strong and doubly alert contingent of Honor Guard waiting about uselessly on her doorstep. She's past them and trotting down dark corridors toward the winding stair to her tower studio. She takes the first twenty steps two at a time, amazed at her own vigor after such a long day of heavy mind work and racing about.

But on the top step, she hesitates, seized by the conviction that there's someone in the room. She listens for a long, long moment. Nothing. She is imagining things. No human could stay so still.

The cavernous space is a symphony of light and darkness. A vast rectangle of cool moon brilliance falls through the big window, blinding her vision into the pitchy corners and the shadows as thick as smoke. Paia reaches nervously for the lantern in its niche by the entrance. Lit, it clears her path to the shrouded easel but it does nothing to lighten the weight of those night-black corners. Still, she has never been afraid in this room, and she resents feeling that way now, resents whoever has been violating her private space, her sanctuary, without at least explaining themselves. As she nears the easel, her courage and her ire blossom. If he, she, or they are here now, she will confront them. She welcomes the chance.

Even so, she gasps softly when she sees the neatly folded note. This time it's been pinned to the outside of the plastic tarp. Irritably, Paia rips it free and shakes it open to hold it up to the lantern's pale flame.

"Hunh," she says, for the second time in less than an hour. She has wished for clarity, and this time, she has gotten it. She reads it again, and a third time, biting her lip.

His aura explodes around her only an instant before he speaks. "What does it say?"

Paia whirls, her heart nearly leaping from her chest. He is silhouetted against the bright window, his grand profile etched with moonlight. But he is not looking at her. He is gazing out the window, his broad back like a wall and his hair loose and wild like the plumage of an extinct exotic bird. There is just the faintest glimmer about him. "Where did you come from?" she gasps when she has breath enough.

"What a ridiculous question. Where do I always come from? Wherever I have just been."

Paia swallows. "My lord, I meant . . . where have you been?"

"To a place that no longer exists! Do not hope to distract me. What does it say, this paper you're hiding in your hand?"

The note is a crushed ball in her fist. Paia remembers the magic sword she's just read about, how she imagined it would sound when being drawn from its sheath. The God sounds like this now.

"Open it and read it to me. Every word."

"It's nothing, really, just a . . ."

"A what? A love letter?"

"No, of course not! Just a . . ."

"Read it to me!" he thunders.

"Yes, my lord." Paia flattens the paper against her thigh but doesn't bother to look at it. How long has he been standing here, waiting for her to arrive and unfold it, his rage and frustration building because he is unable to perform this simple *human* task? "It says, *'Is your luxury worth the burning of a village?'* "

"Ha!" The God tosses his head. The bird plumage becomes a nest of snakes winding about his head.

"Has someone been burning villages?" she asks innocently, although by now she guesses the answer.

"Of course. I have. And I will continue to as needed, to keep my enemies at bay." He aims a gilded nail at the crinkled note. "This is sedition!"

"Yes, my lord. I suppose it is."

"You *suppose*?"

Paia is relieved to discover that once her shock has receded to the normal levels of fear and dread, the infant flame of her rebellion still burns within. "Well, after all, it's only rhetoric, isn't it? What could anyone actually do?" She picks up the lantern and moves toward him, away from the easel and its shrouded, subversive painting. "I mean, against the power of a God? Surely these poor villagers are not your enemies."

"Enemies of the Faith! Sedition must be stamped out wherever it appears, and while it is only rhetoric. Before it matures into treason. How else can control be maintained? Do you question my right or my wisdom? My view is longer than you can conceive of. Who are you exchanging messages with, beloved traitor?"

"It's no exchange, my lord!" Paia would like to discuss his long view with him, to hear his response to the history she has just learned. But the word traitor wakes new thrills of terror. She clings to what the computer has promised: the God cannot harm her. She prays it is true. "Someone's been leaving these notes up here. This is only the second. The first one said, 'What price survival?' and I didn't understand what it meant."

His head swivels toward her. His stillness is what's most frightening. His eyes glow in his shadowed face. In manform, he has never looked more dangerous, or more alluring. "And now you do?"

"I think I am beginning to."

The God laughs softly. "And you asked me what had changed . . ."

She meets his golden gaze as boldly as she can. To her astonishment, he looks away to the window, turning his back on her. A silence hangs like a scent in the air, mysterious, inviting. And then, for no reason she can explain, Paia finds herself frightened for him, rather than of him. How could that be? "My lord Fire, is there something wrong? I mean, something else? I wish you would tell me."

"It's all wrong," he growls. "All of it, all I've worked for. All my work through space and time." He spreads his arms grandly, encompassing the barren moonlit hills on the other side of the thick glass. "All this. My art. The expression of my genius. It'll all be gone if I cannot defeat them."

Paia understands nothing of this, except that he's finally been distracted by thoughts of his enemies, and that he's in pain. The God is in pain. Like his rage, it pervades the room. Amazed, she sets aside the lantern and goes to him, as close as she has ever volunteered to approach him in man-form, close enough to feel the charged heat that his manifestation generates. It prickles along her bare arms and up the middle of her back and, disturbingly, deep in her groin. She wishes she could touch him, to soothe the rage and restlessness out of him. She raises her hand as if to lay it on his chest.

His chin lifts. His elegant lip curls in a sneer. "Don't. We'll only both be terribly disappointed."

Paia drops her hand but stands her ground. It's he who chooses to move a step away from her. She studies him. The difference in him unsteadies her. "How did you come here this time without my knowing?"

His sneer sharpens to petulance. "I have a few tricks left you don't know about. Entire lives you never even see."

"You were . . . spying on me, my lord?"

"I must be certain of your loyalty."

As if a keyed lock has just clicked, Paia becomes aware of an instinct she's never noticed before: deeply buried, isolated, inaccessible until just now, like the House Comp's time-lag programming. An instinct to read the truth in him and of him, and the truth of their bond. His wild threats against her may well be nothing but emotional manipulation. But equally, she would be unable to do anything to harm him. She can't imagine what that could be—how could one harm a God? She only knows that she cannot do it.

Her lips are dry, and her throat even more so. She wonders how long they have stood there, side by side, unspeaking in the moonlight. When she looks up, he is looking down at her, and the distance between them is a zone of fire. She has never wanted any man as much as she wants him now. Except that he is not a man. This time it is she who backs away, one step, then two, brushing tears from her eyes.

"My lord Fire, my loyalty to you is undying. It cannot be otherwise."

"Easier to promise than to prove."

"A shallow response, my lord, when I am trying to tell you something serious, something I am only just beginning to understand." Her hours in the Library have left her with half-knowledge, supposition, guesswork and conjecture, with understandings instinctive but still vague and uncertain. "I mean that I am born for this. To serve you."

"Indeed. It pains me to hear that this is news to you."

"I mean that it's more than duty. It's in my blood. I have no choice. Nor do you."

"Be careful, my priestess . . ."

Again his stiffness frightens her, but she's gone too far to stop now. "My lord, I mean that . . . it is decreed by history."

"Decreed? History? How dare you!" He spins away from her, then whirls and seems to launch himself at her. Paia recoils as heat washes over her in a torrent. The hair on her outstretched arm is singed by his passage. "It's their doing! They have put this into your head!"

"No! No! It's not true!"

"How would you know? No matter! It's all lies! Lies! I will not be ruled! By you or any other!"

Instantly he is before the easel, looming over a covering he cannot physically remove. The cavern shudders. The very bedrock shakes, glows hot and liquid. Magma. Paia crumples to the floor, the softening liquid rock. The computer was wrong. This is how he will destroy her. Not by his own hands but by . . . and there, he is Himself, a vast gilt-scaled monster coiled in the room with the easel at the center of his arc. His great barbed tail lashes at the wooden worktables and the piles of stacked canvases, sending brushes and palettes and mixing bowls flying, while a single ivory claw hooks the easel toward him to snag the plastic tarp and rip it free.

And then, as if this spasm of violence was no more than a fever dream, he is there in man-form again, staring at the painting, in the light of his own golden glow. The rock is rock once more, but the worktables are in scattered ruins and the treacherous landscape lies revealed to him.

In a heap on the floor, Paia weeps in grief, but also with relief.

"Get up and get over here," he orders. He sounds disappointed.

She struggles to her feet and goes to him, stopping several long paces away. She looks at the floor, at all the mess, anywhere but at him or at the perfidious painting.

He laughs harshly. "Not so eager to stand beside me now, are you, beloved?"

"You have no cause, my lord," she murmurs. "No cause."

"I have no need of cause, my priestess. I am your God. It would do well for you to remember that." He waits, glowering. "Did I hear you say, 'yes, I will'?"

"Yes," Paia whispers. Are hatred and love like science and magic, in the long run, only one and the same? "Yes, my lord Fire, I will remember that."

"And any further treasonous communications you will report to me."

"Yes, my lord."

"I will stake your loyalty on it."

"I understand that, my lord."

He moves away, kicking futitely at bits of wreckage, then paces back to throw an offhand gesture at the painting. "Your work, I presume?"

She's been waiting for this. Paia steels herself to look at the painting, then has to steel herself all over again. The canvas on the easel is like any other in the room: a painting in reds and browns and grays, a painting of dry rock and barren hills. Paia feels her self-conviction weaken and slide away like a melting ice floe. She has imagined it, then, all of it: the velvet grass, the trees, the silver ribbon of river, even the changes, the grim storm gathering above the mountains. It must be her loneliness and isolation, at last eating away at her sanity. "Yes, my lord," she replies dully. "My work."

"Beautiful."

Her eyes widen at him. Perhaps he's the one who's crazy. Or it's both of them, now that she thinks about it. That makes the most sense. If they are so indelibly bonded by centuries of tradition and breeding, how could one be insane and the other not? "Thank you," she murmurs.

"Any progress on the choice of a Suitor?"

"None."

"Get on it, then."

It's folly, but Paia raises her eyes to his, finding in herself a chill deep enough to match his own. "You are a monster."

There is a flicker in his reptilian eyes, and a slight move toward turning away, until he catches himself and lets a cold smile twist his beauty into a carved and gilded mask.

"Perhaps. And you are my pawn. As you said, you have no choice."

With that, and the last word, he is gone.

Paia sinks to the floor and lets the darkness surround her for the length of time it takes to stop weeping and get her bearings. Then she raises her head and crawls to where she's left the lantern, miraculously undamaged by the God's fit of rage. She stands unsteadily, brings it back to the easel to look at the painting one more time. She's glad that her reflexes have been slowed by her ordeal, which is all that prevents her from dropping the lantern.

For the painting has changed again. The valley in the mountains has reappeared, but this time the tall dark pines, the ribbon of river, the green velvet grass, are buried under a heavy weight of ice and snow.

Whoever is doing this, Paia muses, *perhaps they're on my side.*

Chapter Twenty-four

The path up the steep slope was brush-choked and narrow, and there was no longer the relief of a breeze. As
she toiled upward in the crushing heat, Erde prayed that
the men were right about going off with the first strangers
they ran into. Particularly strangers who had threatened
and tried to rob them. But N'Doch would say it was the
quickest way to acquire the sort of local information they
needed to find their way about this new land. Baron Köthen apparently agreed. So, until she had a better suggestion, she must follow their lead.

Climbing just ahead of her, N'Doch gave no sign of
worry. He seemed, just as she had accused him of back on
the raft, to be enjoying himself. He whistled now and then,
one of his homemade tunes, and his step was jaunty, even
as laden down as he was, with his own pack and a few of
Stoksie's. Was it simply confidence born of knowing that
dragons shadowed their every upward step? Erde rubbed
grit and sweat and the dust of crumbled leaves from her
eyes, readjusted her own load and fixed her gaze on
N'Doch's heels, as if they could winch her up the rugged
trail behind him. And she kept up her running internal
monologue, reporting to the dragon what she saw ahead,
imaging it all for him in detail—the stunted brush and broken trees, each cluster of ruined homesteads, every dry ravine—so that he could keep up, transporting himself and
his sister to each imaged place as soon as the climbers had
left it behind. Meanwhile, she again put to him the question

that kept plaguing her, one she'd asked several times already since arriving in this dreadful place.

HAVE YOU THOUGHT FURTHER ON IT, DRAGON? IF THIS LAND HAS NOT ALWAYS BEEN SO RUINED, HAVE YOU AN IDEA YET WHAT SIN THESE PEOPLE COULD BE GUILTY OF, THAT GOD SHOULD PUNISH THEM SO TERRIBLY?

Again the dragon replied that he did not, that he had no understanding of such matters, but would continue to consider it deeply. It was curious, Erde thought, that Lady Water, so ready to voice her opinion on every other matter, refrained entirely from commenting on this crucial spiritual issue. Well, almost.

Maybe it's a whole new sin. One you've never even thought of.

Erde could not imagine what she meant. After all, didn't God decree what was a sin and what wasn't?

Her pondering distracted her for a while as she plodded upward, dulled with heat. When she woke to her surroundings again, the ruined signs of habitation had given way to patches of scrub clinging to ever-steeper slopes of solid rock. The path, such as it was, switchbacked right and left several times, winding around thin-layered outcroppings that reminded Erde of tall stacks of parchment. Or it wound up among piles of dragon-sized boulders, narrowing further until Erde could barely squeeze herself and her burdens past the enclosing walls of stone. She'd been glad to leave the biting midges behind down by the landing, but now it would be reassuring to hear the song of one bird or the hum of any insect, not this unnatural stillness broken only by their own heavy breathing and the crunch of their labored steps.

They stopped for a brief rest and a drink where the terrain leveled out at the foot of another towering rock face. Erde had her pack halfway off when N'Doch stopped her.

"You put it down now, girl, it'll be a whole lot harder to pick up again."

She did as he advised, but reluctantly. The rock wall faced southwest, and there wasn't an inch of shade to be had anywhere on the ledge.

"Nice view, huh?"

"Are they taking us to their town, do you think?"

"Nah, we're way up past where the old towns were."

"A mountain stronghold, then?"

N'Doch grinned like he did when she'd said something he called *quaint.* "Something like that." He gestured with his water jug at the far-off glimmer of Big Albin's towers, then to the left where the wide stretch of water was visible over the tops of the dusty scrub. "Lot of people living down there once."

From this distance the water was a deceptively inviting lavender, drawing warmth from the long summer twilight. The far shore was a faint line of purplish hills. Erde thought they must be a very long way away. "What happened to them? Was there a war?"

"Haven't gotten around to asking that right out, y'know? But it don't sound like they all got up and went somewhere better."

"You mean, they just died?"

"Probably. Sickness, starvation, massacre. Who knows what else."

"Oh. Oh, dear."

N'Doch looked her over dubiously. "You holding up okay? Wherever we're headed, they sure don't want to make getting there easy, do they?"

"I'm fine." Erde thought of Tor Alte, a thick-walled stone fortress perched high on a mountain pinnacle. At several points along that upward road, visitors must walk their horses single-file. And these points, of course, were heavily monitored, and vulnerable to a well-placed rain of arrows or a deluge of boiling oil from above. She was familiar with the advantages of building in a secure location. But if there were so few people left around, what were Stoksie and his "crew" protecting themselves against? He was obviously more uneasy here than he'd been on the river. Every step of the trail, he and the girls stayed on the alert. Perhaps he would prefer to move along faster, but she couldn't imagine how, with all that he was carrying. "Am I holding anyone up?"

"No way." N'Doch tipped his head sideways. " 'Cept maybe his lordship."

Baron Köthen stood with his back to the rock, impassively observing the view. He had again positioned himself at the rear, so that no one was ever behind him and the path of retreat was under his control. He did not look worried, or even particularly concerned. He merely looked . . . careful.

The girls Senda and Mari were up and ready to be off again long before Erde was. They scampered straight along the face of the rock wall just long enough to raise her hopes that the climbing was over. Then they turned sideways and vanished from view as the path hooked a sharp right and crawled nearly vertically up the side of the ledge. At the turn, N'Doch leaned back to give Erde a hand up the first seemingly impossible step. Ahead, the taller girl called out and threw an eager wave upward. Behind, Stoksie let out a sigh of relief, then a long warble, three descending notes, two ascending, like a birdcall. An answering whistle echoed down among the rocks. Erde craned her neck this way and that. Finally, on a sharp jut high over the path, a slim figure moved into view, silhouetted against the amber sky. It carried a slim, dark object, like a broomstick with a handle, which it now slung over its shoulder to free one hand up for a wave.

A gun. The long kind. Erde recognized it, from her recent and all-too-vivid acquaintance with such objects. N'Doch saw it, too, and dropped back suddenly under the pretense of a stone in his sandal to confer with Baron Köthen in the rear. A *gun*. Erde was again haunted by the images of N'Doch's body being torn to pieces by the last guns she'd seen. Her hands were wet, and her boots not the best for climbing. Distracted, she slipped, nearly lost her grip, then slipped again. She froze in terror.

DRAGON! I CANNOT MOVE! WILL YOU CATCH ME WHEN I FALL?

YOU WILL NOT FALL. THERE'LL BE NO TALK OF FALLING.

He was right of course. It would surely panic their guides if the dragon was forced to reveal himself precipitously. She must control her weakness. She must forget about guns and falling, and blank her mind of everything but the effort of hauling herself safely upward. She imagined the rocks as the dragon's plated back, hospitable to her grip, and was able to move forward. Gaining the top, she was breathless and weak, incapable of another forward step. Humiliated, she collapsed onto a nearby ledge, and was uncharitably gratified when Stoksie struggled up over the edge, as much the worse for wear as she was.

He resettled his load to ease the burden on his bad hip and mopped his dark brow. The little girls had run off ahead already, their cries and childish chattering growing fainter with distance. " 'Ard un, dat las'."

Erde nodded wanly, forcing a smile, then realized it wasn't an effort at all. She quite liked the man. Their shared plight somehow transformed him in her mind from a dark and forbidding stranger to an odd little man with a cheerful look. She didn't need to know his language to get the sense of his words. Without N'Doch to translate, she had no words to say back to him, but this didn't bother Stoksie one bit. So they sat catching their breath in easy silence, waiting for the others. When she could breathe more freely, Erde became aware of a subtle difference in the air—it was cooler here, even in the sun, perhaps due to the added elevation, but lighter and sweeter as well, with a promised hint of moisture.

Stoksie grinned when he saw her sniffing like a pack hound. He said something incomprehensible, bobbing his head fervently as if nods alone could make his words intelligible. Then N'Doch levered his tall frame over the edge. He stood panting for a moment, responding to their silence with a listening readiness of his own. Suddenly, he broke into a smile. "Aww, listen to that! Music to my ears!"

Erde had noticed it, too, a soft background sighing, like high-country breezes. Listening more carefully, she wondered how she could have mistaken running water for mere wind. And not just running, from the sound of it, but falling, as if from a great height. Stoksie, watching them inhale with such relish, nodded and grinned like a proud parent.

Baron Köthen finally joined them, dripping and scowling. "Seems we've paid our toll after all," he remarked when he had breath enough. "As the good merchant's beasts of burden."

"You know it," agreed N'Doch.

"All heah?" Stoksie bent, eagerly loading himself up again. "Quick, na."

Putting weight on her feet again was painful. Erde repressed a groan, thinking that she'd happily trade the nausea and disorientation of dragon transport for this physical torture. But the path here was better trimmed and wider, and the rise was gentler. She thought perhaps the foliage had a healthier tinge, and that the dwarfish trees might be gaining some height. Soon they broke out of the scrub entirely, where the path intersected a gravel-strewn cut through a grove of taller trees, some sort of pine. The heat was making the blood pound in her ears, and Erde was grateful when Stoksie turned right and led them into this sweeter-smelling shade.

"Used to be a road, this." N'Doch kicked at shards of rubble poking through the mat of needles, raising dust. "Not a real big one, though."

Erde hoped that if it had been a road, its end was nearby. Would it only lead to more ruin? She was eager to be somewhere, to arrive, rather than to be ceaselessly pushing on with no particular goal or direction. There seemed to be no real place left to go in this destroyed future. Simple movements, like walking, were becoming a struggle, but another dose of dragon encouragement and the music of flowing water drew her onward.

Deeper into the grove, they rounded a bend screened by a thicket of broad-leafed shrubs to discover a trio of armed men ahead in the road, watching their approach. No, Erde noted, two women and a young man, with scowls and threatening postures and the long sorts of gun slung easily into the crooks of their elbows, guns almost as tall as they were.

N'Doch pulled up sharply and eased Erde behind his back, but Stoksie greeted them cheerfully by name.

"Wha's dis?" one of the women snarled, shoving out ahead of the rest with her gun leveled.

"Easy, na." Stoksie put up his palms.

"Doan tell me easy! Whachu tinkin', bringin' straingeas up heah? Yu sumkinda fool?"

"Whoa," murmured N'Doch. "Heavy language."

But Stoksie rolled his eyes at his guests over his shoulder. "She mean, bring yu heah w'out askin' huh. Y'know?"

"Betcha," N'Doch replied with his usual bravado, which Erde was beginning to see the purpose of.

"Dis heah Brenda Chu," Stoksie offered. "Call her Pitbull, 'cuz she chews hard!" He grinned, but thrust his narrow jaw forward just a bit. "Dees heah gud ole bizmen, Brenda. An' dey's fine 'n healt'y, lookit 'em. Back off, na."

The woman had a shiny dark cap of short hair, a flattish

face with eyes shaped like almonds. Her skin was the same color as the smaller of the little girls, and she wore a ragged scar like a fighting man's from the tip of her right eyebrow to the corner of her mouth. Her tough stance reminded Erde of Lily and Margit, Deep Moor's scouts. But the resemblance ended with this woman's reflex hostility, as she shifted her gun to her shoulder and stood up taller, as if proud to be named after a vicious animal.

N'Doch stepped forward to offer his hand. "N'Doch heah." Brenda just stared at him. He shrugged. "Das cool."

"Das Charlie 'n das Punk," Stoksie continued, as if nothing had happened. "Dis heah all Water Dragon Crew, frum up nort'."

Charlie was a bronze-skinned blonde woman with a patchy complexion and paler skin showing at her cuffs and neckline. Even in the heavy heat, she was as covered up with clothing as anyone could possibly bear to be. She looked like she might be willing to smile, if only Brenda's scowl was not so discouraging. Punk was an alarmingly skinny, dark youth—about Erde's own age, she guessed, surely no more than fifteen. All three wore the same sort of mismatched assortment of garments as Stoksie and the girls. Erde saw Punk measuring N'Doch's height and ebony sheen with interest, maybe with envy. She had never known until today that human beings came in so many different colors, almost all of them darker than her own.

"Dees two is Lady 'n Doff," Stoksie concluded, with a wave in her direction. "Frum Urop. Got good trade."

"Urop?" Brenda was skeptical.

"Bad deah now, huh?" Charlie's casual remark earned her a nasty look from Brenda, but the business end of her gun sank slowly toward the ground.

"Real bad," N'Doch agreed, giving Charlie his "special" smile. Erde hoped he knew what he was talking about. She noticed he didn't try the smile on Brenda. There was a bit more arguing and hand waving, and another brief gun-pointing, which brought Köthen lunging forward only to run into N'Doch's swiftly outstretched arm. But finally Brenda was overruled by Stoksie's bluff good nature and the obvious curiosity of the others.

"Dey's healt'y-lookin, alrite." Punk shrugged and slung

his gun over his thin shoulder. "Weah yu bin, Stokes? We wuz worried boutchu."

"Lookin' fer trade, wachu tink? Tellyu, Albin's a ghost town! We dun picked it dry. 'Bout ta come home near empty. Li'l stuff, y'know? Den I find dees uns." Stoksie showed all his bad teeth in a victory grin.

"Dju frisk 'em?" Brenda demanded, her final display of disapproval.

Their guide nodded, though he hadn't. "Cupla blades. Nuttin' much."

"Frum Urop wit a cupla blades 'n des still walkin'?" Brenda's eyes raked their bodies and their packs for signs of hidden weapons.

"Tellyu one ting . . ." Stoksie jerked his chin faintly in Baron Köthen's direction. "Da reel whitefella? Fas'. Real fas'. Watch 'im."

Erde sensed this was merely a sop. True as it was, Stoksie wasn't worried about Köthen. But Pitbull Brenda's honor was satisfied, now that she had an assignment: keep an eye on the grim-faced soldier. Clever Stoksie. At last the expedition moved forward, deeper into the shade, delayed only if one cared to observe the surreptitious dance between Köthen and Brenda as they skirmished over who would bring up the rear. Erde was unamazed when Köthen won.

A larger but less threatening delegation awaited them at the mouth of the clearing. This group was more cheerfully suspicious. They crowded around—men, women and a few wide-eyed small children—greeting Stoksie gladly, demanding reasons for his delay, staring openly at the strangers while helpfully relieving them of their extra burdens. Mostly small and dark-skinned like Stoksie and the girls, they didn't look like they could put up much of a fight. But they had no problem verbalizing their curiosity. Erde was glad when Stoksie demanded silence and said the questions had to wait until the visitors were refreshed and settled. Immediately, the crowd pulled back, and a child was urged out from among them. A blue ceramic pitcher was put in his thin little hands. He presented it to Stoksie, who tipped a few drops of water onto his fingers, then touched them to his forehead. Erde heard a few indistinct but reverent murmurs from the crowd. Next Stoksie poured out a little on the ground, then he grinned, tilted the pitcher to his mouth and took a long, long drink. The crowd cheered, and the pitcher was offered in turn to each visitor until it came back to the child's hands empty. The water was sweet and cold. Erde would gladly have drunk more of it, but the child beamed and ran off with the jug, giggling.

"Gud, na! Blin' Rachel Crew say welcome!" Stoksie gathered up his guests and led them on into the clearing. The chattering crowd fell right in behind.

The once-road opened on an expanse of space and bustle and noise, bare dirt with patches of grass and a few trees, tall enough to provide a bit of real shade for the busy maze of structures spread out beneath them: a motley assortment of tents and lean-tos and high-wheeled wagons with oft-patched canopies, and conical shapes of canvas and lower-slung carts built up with windows and chimneys like tiny rolling huts. The leftover nooks and crannies were crammed with livestock pens and awninged market booths. Even the odors were lively. A thin goat wandered forlornly and, everywhere, chickens clucked and scratched in the dust. A pair of lop-eared hounds ran up to greet Stoksie effusively, until he had had enough of their eager tongues and paws, and sent them bounding off again.

Over the din of people and animals, the sigh of the water was gentle and welcome music. But past the unkempt line of tent poles and rough-built roof peaks rose the most astonishing structure Erde had ever laid eyes on. Stoksie stopped them out in the open where they could take a good long look.

It was a building seeming to vanish right into the precipitous rock face looming behind it. It was both tall and yet vastly horizontal: layers of stone terraces coiling around the central green like the apse of a cathedral and rising one after the other, four, five, six, seven stories, each curved plane set off from the one below it, either forward or back, like the natural contours of the layered rock she had just climbed through. But for the sturdy central staircase, Erde could not always tell where the hand of man laid off and that of nature began again. It was like a palace built with the help of magic.

"Fuckin' A!" breathed N'Doch beside her.

"This is some great lord's castle, surely," said Baron Köthen, joining them at last.

"Some rich guy's paradise, more like," N'Doch replied. "It's Blind Rachel's now, whoever she is."

"I expect we shall meet that good lady soon enough."

Repeating rectangles of glass glittered along each level, broken here and there by some duller material. Intricately carved wooden railings alternated with thick rails of natural stone, or in some places, no railing at all. As she collected her senses enough to really study, Erde began to notice the many details of the damage: the rotted newel posts, the sagging lines of the extended terraces, the shattered glass. But the whole, viewed generously as through a veil, was still magnificent.

"Nise, huh?" Stoksie prompted.

"Real nice," N'Doch agreed, for all of them.

"Gwan up 'n findyu room, na. Putcher stuff in, nobuddy bodda, gotcha? I tell 'em. Den I shoyu roun'."

Stoksie shepherded them through the lingering curious and around the circular roadway. The crowd called out eager invitations to dinner, more than could ever be honored, then dispersed and went on about their business. At the center of the giant curving edifice, a double set of stairs climbed side by side like lovers to the second level, then turned away from each other to continue their journeys to the third. On the fourth, they met again, and so they continued their meeting and parting until they ran out of levels to climb. Grinning proudly, Stoksie gave his guests another moment at the bottom of the stair to gaze upward with the appropriate awe. Then he led them up the first flight, pointing out the weak spots and rotted treads, and then to the left, along the second level balcony. They passed neatly spaced paneled doors alternating with broad stretches of window, most of which were still intact. Erde had seen this miracle of glassmaking when she was in N'Doch's home time, but those magical sheets of glistening transparency had all been shielded by metal gratings.

Stoksie saw her slow to touch her fingers to the surface and skim them smoothly along without bump or obstacle for two, three, even four paces. "Good stuff, dat. Latest, 'fore dey stopped."

"Stopped?" asked N'Doch.

"Makin' it. Y'know?"

N'Doch nodded. "Yeah. Guess I do."

Erde absorbed the translation one step behind. "They stopped making glass?" N'Doch passed the query along.

Stoksie's shrug was more emphatic than usual. "Probby som'weah dey still do. Not roun' heah. No call fer't na."

"He means nobody wants any."

Erde chewed her lip. "But glass is very precious. At least it is . . . was . . . in my time."

"And real cheap and necessary, in mine."

Behind them, Köthen glided his own spread fingertips along the glass. "The Future," he murmured.

"Not my future," N'Doch retorted. "Well . . . least, not the one I was looking forward to."

Stoksie waved them onward. "Be dak soon. Messtime. Don' wanna missit, na." He took them past door after door, all of them closed up tight, and past window after window. Erde attempted the occasional covert glance inside these mysterious and threatening spaces, but her view was usually blocked by fabric hanging just inside the glass, or by boards fastened up where the glass was missing. Where there was a crack in a broken door to peer through, or a space between the hangings, she saw heaps of clothing or a bit of crockery, but beyond that, only darkness. She could not help but worry about what the darkness might conceal.

Far along the curve of the terrace, almost to the end, Stoksie stopped in front of a door constructed from mismatched planks. Each had long ago been painted a different color, now faded together into a mere suggestion of variety of hue. "Dis'll do ya, ha?"

A greenish rectangle of metal, obviously a more recent addition, fastened the door, pinned to a corroded loop in the jamb by what Erde recognized as a crude and diminutive sort of lock. A thin sliver of metal protruded from its bottom end. Stoksie took hold of this and struggled with it for a while, then finally twisted it clear and popped the lock open. He handed the sliver to N'Doch.

"S'all yers. Getchu settled. Back mebbe ten, yucool?"

"Mecool." As Stoksie turned back toward the stairs, N'Doch called out, "Hey, man . . ."

Stoksie turned.

"Thanks, y'know? Dis real good trade."

A quick nod. "Gotcha.

Once N'Doch is inside, he knows the place for what it was. No rich man's paradise after all. The room is an oblong box, low-ceilinged and dull as they come. Once upon a time it probably attempted some more fashionable shade than the ugly salmon it's graying into. It's completely empty, but he can see where the beds went, two matching queens, he's sure, advertised on a big sign outside. A luxury sort of joint. He sees the closet indentations, missing their doors and hanger poles. An archway in the back leads through a dark dressing nook to a tiny square room he knows was the bathroom, even stripped like it is—surprise, surprise—of everything portable, sink, toilets, pipes, even the wall tiles. He reminds himself to ask Stoksie for directions to the privy.

He comes back up front where Köthen and the girl are setting their stuff down reluctantly, like they're not so sure the floor's clean enough or something. They both look at him expectantly, like the pressure's on for him to set some sort of "modern" frame of reference here. But he's not sure he can oblige. He rubs his palms together. "So. You guys have any idea what a motel is? Nah, guess you wouldn't. Anyhow, if they don't turn on us sudden-like and try to murder us in our beds, I'd say we just got real lucky."

Köthen gazes around the tight, dim space. N'Doch can see he doesn't trust it much. "Is this an unusual degree of hospitality?"

"Where I come from, any hospitality is unusual, at least to strangers. 'Cept out in the bush." N'Doch unstraps his pack and leans it against a wall. "Maybe it's the same thing here as there. When there aren't so many people around, strangers are useful, y'know? They got stories, they got news. And Stoksie seems to think we got good trade. Hope we don't disappoint him. For a few days, at least, we're the entertainment."

"A few days?"

N'Doch grins at him slyly. "I bought us one. After that, Dolph my man, it kinda depends on just how entertaining we decide to be. Doncha think?"

The girl says quietly, "Is this where we will sleep?"

"I've slept in worse places."

"All of us together?"

"Oh. I get it. Well, tell you what, girl—you can have the bathroom all to yourself."

Köthen is examining the lock on the door. "All of us, behind one door. That way, one can always watch while the others sleep. Unless, my lady witch, you can offer a few spells to protect us."

"No problem, man, the dragons'll . . ."

"My lord of Köthen!" the girl bursts out. "I beg you do not call me 'witch.' I am not one, nor never have been!"

Köthen glances up. His hands are full of metal parts, as he studies how to switch the lock from outside to in. "Your pardon, my lady. If it distresses you so, I will desist."

"It does! Very much! I wonder that you haven't noticed!"

"Hey, girl," N'Doch chides, but gently. He sees she's got tears in her eyes. "Been a long day for all of us."

Köthen chuckles darkly, deftly reassembling the lock. "The longest in human memory. Began in 913 and ending God only knows when."

N'Doch thinks it's too bad the girl doesn't find this as funny as they do, but even he's surprised when she spins away from their laughter, skims out the door past Köthen like a spooked rabbit, and tears off along the balcony. He can hear the clack of her footsteps, hurried and sharp. "Whoa!" he mutters, and follows her into the open. "Hey, girl! Erde! Come on back here!"

She ignores him, clattering all the way around the curve of the building until she's brought up short by the heavy wooden railing at the other end. She props her elbows on it and buries her face in her hands.

"Aw, jeez . . ." N'Doch leans against the railing behind him and folds his arms. He's starting to feel bad for the girl and there's no time like the present to speak up about it. She's strong and all, but she's been through a lot lately, and the good baron could just be the final straw. "Listen, Dolph . . . I know you're mad at her, and hey, I don't blame you a bit. But you gotta go easier on her, man. Just a little."

Köthen straightens, dusting wood and metal splinters from his fingers. "Why? It would only encourage her."

"Well, umm . . . hunh." N'Doch was ready for huff and attitude. This blunt honesty leaves him kind of without an argument. "Okay, I understand all that, but . . . hey, look, all I'm saying is, we're all in this together."

"But I would not be, were it not for her meddling."

"Yeah, yeah, but . . ."

"I speak but the truth to say she is a witch."

"How d'you figure that?"

"Who else but a witch has converse with dragons?"

"Huh. So where does that put me?"

Köthen's glance flicks hard at him and then away, but not quite quick enough. N'Doch has read the sudden doubt in his eyes, and a few of the baron's assumptions are beginning to piss him off. He wants this dragon business understood for what it is, at least the way he sees it.

"I'm not just here along for the ride, y'know. The blue dragon is mine. Yeah, that got your attention. Mine. I didn't ask for it, but that's how it is. So does that make me some kind of warlock? I can tell you, I ain't one of them."

Köthen's jaw settles stubbornly. He says nothing.

"You wanna know what I think?"

"You've shown little inclination to guard your tongue so far . . ."

"Yeah, and you're not as much of a jerk as I thought, 'cause you keep letting me talk. Must be you like the challenge."

They stare each other down for long cool seconds, and then Köthen rewards him with a sigh and a weary twist of his mouth that is almost a grin. "Presumptuous whelp. Go on. I'm listening."

"Really? Well, that's progress now, ain't it?"

"Don't . . ."

". . . I know. Don't press my luck." N'Doch lets out a breath. "Okay, here it is: you *hope* she's a witch, if there even is such a thing, 'cause it's easier to bust her ass for the mess you're in than it is the dragons'. Am I right?" He starts to pace a little, like a little engine's fired up inside him. It's not only that he's saying this personal sort of stuff to a man proven to be armed and dangerous. What's most amazing is that he's thinking it at all, like, of his own accord. "And that's because you won't accept that you've been part of this since long before you got yourself dragon-napped."

"This being . . . ?" Köthen asks with a look of distaste.

"This being some kind of, well, plan . . . that's a lot bigger than all of us. I thought it was bullshit, too, just like you do."

"And now you don't?"

"Less than I did." N'Doch notices he's the one moving around abruptly, nervously, and Köthen who's steady and still. "Listen, man, what you gotta see is we're here and we're stuck with it. Neither me nor the girl has any real power over this situation, 'cept what we can ask from the dragons." He halts his pacing by pressing his back hard against the balcony railing, willing the little engine to stop its frantic revving. He's not used to acting like somebody's big brother. "Look, I can't give you the technical explanation for all this weird shit, but I do know I ain't no warlock and she ain't no witch. So give it a rest, whadda ya say? Save your revenge for later, so we can all concentrate on keeping each other alive."

And then he can't help himself. He just has to add, "And maybe later, it won't look all that important anyway."

"You mean, when I've become properly committed to the quest?"

"I didn't say that, but hey, stranger things have happened. Like to me, for instance."

"You are welcome to your quest, friend N'Doch. I remain respectfully unconvinced."

N'Doch uncrosses his arms. Now this *is* progress. His actual name out of the man's mouth, rather than "hey, you" or some epithet. "Okay. Whatever. Look on it as a kind of working vacation. But if you could just . . ."

The baron lifts a warning finger. "Your point is taken. Enough."

"You got it, man."

Köthen looks away, as if something in the treetops has caught his interest. "One thing more. If I am to believe myself part of this 'plan,' as you call it, I have a question."

"Yeah, what's that?"

Köthen turns back to him deadpan. "Where's *my* dragon?"

N'Doch's thoughts shoot off in several directions, but he's saved from having to settle on one of them when Stoksie comes limping briskly around the curve with the girl firmly in tow.

"Doncha be lettin' huh run roun' lone, na."

"Why? Brenda'll think she's spying or something?" N'Doch slings one arm lightly around her shoulders. He wonders if the little man's concern is for the girl's safety or for his own reputation in the camp. He hopes it's both.

"Sumpin li' dat. Giv'er a nexcuse, an' she'll make it hard fer yus."

"Gotcha. Thanks, man."

"No prob." And like it really isn't, Stoksie beckons the men to lean over the railing while he maps out the camp for them. A circling gesture marks the bustling tree-shaded area nestled within the sweep of the building. "All dat's da Mall."

N'Doch chokes back a grin. "The mall, huh?"

"Yeah. Sleep up heah, eat 'n do bizness down dea. Y'know?"

N'Doch nods. Amazing how words slip in and out of meaning. When he was a kid, a favorite fantasy was being let loose in an American mall with a pocket full of someone else's credit. He looks down, sees a pair of older women pouring water into a wide trough dug around one of the taller trees. All the shade trees have troughs like that. "So where do ya have fun?"

"All ovah, na?"

"Good. Think I'm gonna like it here." And for some reason, he does. Maybe it's the trees, or maybe it's being back among folks closer to his own color. Or maybe it's just the easy way Stoksie has about him—makes people relax, like he's got nothing to prove, 'cept that he's honest and likable. A useful manner for a salesman. N'Doch tries to imagine what the big space out there was once: big parking lot, probably, planted around with fancy greenery, a big neon sign somewhere and the awful kind of landscape lights that turn the shrubbery gross shades of pink and blue and orange. He glances around and above, admiring the undulating rise of the terraces. He's backed off his imitation of the local accent. Stoksie understands him well enough. "So . . . when you figure this place was built?"

"Oh, reel ole place, dis. Mebbe a cent, y'know? Mebbe more. Fore my daddy's daddy, leas'. Dat's ole granpa Ben Stokes, him I only heard tell of. Dis place wuz wuna da las' ta go, roun' heah. Das wha' ma da alwuz say."

"Last to go?" N'Doch hopes the girl's calmed down enough to be listening real close while he pumps their host for information.

"Y'know, ta fall outa da loop." Stoksie parks his elbows more comfortably on the railing and eases the weight off his hip. N'Doch can tell there's a favorite old story coming, like the ones his own old people used to tell, over and over, never tiring of them, finding comfort in the familiarity. "Dis how ma da alwuz tell it. He wuz Reuben Stokes like me. I'ma junyer. Anyhow, he say peeble usda come heah up from Albin, or frum da sout'—Bigapple, mebbe—lon' time sin'. Den dey stop. Or dey come 'n wanna stay. Cuz y'know, when it git bad, it git bad down deah fust, an' it come on fas'. So dey come runnin up heah, lotsa fokes, only dey can' pay no moah. Den mebbe dey do work heah, y'know?"

"To pay their board?"

Stoksie doesn't seem to know that word. "Whadevah. But dey's too minny a dem, and final' deah ain' no pay, noweah."

N'Doch pulls out a word culled from American vids. "No cash, you mean?"

"Ri'. Leas' not heah. Mebbe down Bluridge way." Stoksie scratches his bald head, gazing up into the dusty pine boughs while he muses a bit on this idea. "Mebbe some still down deah, na."

"You trade down there?"

"Nah, noway. Gotta have sumbig firepowah, ya wanna do biz down deah. Sum-big."

"Bigger crews down there, you mean?"

"No crews deah, doncha know? All sorta sumbitch gubbermints, regulatin' da shit outa ev'ryting. Ev'ry lil valley gotta gubbermint. Pain inna butt."

N'Doch settles into a more comfortable lean on the railing. The girl sticks close beside him. "So the governments are like the crews down there?"

"No way! Whachu sayin? Da crews nevah pull dat sorta shit! No way!"

"Right. Okay." The little man's pure outrage makes N'Doch grin. "So, you ever been down there, just to go?"

"Almos' got der. Got far as Deecee one time, wi' ma da, dat's Reuben Seenyer. Me jus' a boy. Yu cud still go deah den."

"Not now?"

"Not easy, 'less yu gotta boat. A real kinda boat, wit alotta teet', y'know?" Stoksie cackles, miming the clashing of giant jaws and the recoil of giant guns.

N'Doch's ears perk up. "There's people around with boats like that?"

"Down deah, dey's sum still. Leas' deah usta be. Mebbe dey's all rusted up na, y'know?"

"Old, you mean?"

"Nah, c'mon." Stoksie shakes his head impatiently. "Say it rain alla time down deah."

"Yeah?"

"How yu like dat, na? Down deah, alla time. Up heah, notta drop. 'Cep all dis salt. Ain' needer place kin grow a gud feelda corn no moah."

"No rain at all, huh?" N'Doch finds himself watching the women below as they water the trees, all of them, one by one.

Stoksie shrugs. "Na 'n den, inna winta. Yusda get moah, even sinz I wuz growin'. Less 'n less. Keep on dis way, doan know how we'll git on. Why, yu got rain up nort?"

"Where I'm from, no, not enough."

"Da story alla roun. 'Cep Bluridge. Dey got rain 'n dey got pay." He waves his arm toward the tents and caravans. "Me, I'ma ole man heah. Mosta dese peeble nevah herda pay. Dey still got pay up nort'?"

"Nah. All trade there." N'Doch hasn't a clue, if the truth be known. He so badly wants to ask the question right out: please please please, what year is it? But he's sure he'd blow their cover, such as it is. "Like here, yeah?"

"All trade. Betcha."

He tries to sneak up on the data issue. "So what was Albin like, before?"

"Nise, I guess. Lotsa peebles. Lotta rain den, too, dey say. Snow, even. Nise place, y'know? Wasa capidal."

A capital. Of what? N'Doch pictures the ruined, flooded, deserted city, and is seized by a kind of panicky despair.

He decides it doesn't really matter when it happened. Point is, it did. Global warming. The planet is simultaneously drying up and drowning. What a friggin' waste! The coincidence that he's traveling with two dragons named Earth and Water who are sure they have serious business to take care of is not entirely lost on him, but the possibilities make his head hurt. Too much thinking's gone on in there for one day. One very long day. N'Doch yawns and tries to hide it.

Stoksie shoves back from the railing, dusting his hands together. "C'mon na. Time ta innerduce yu ta Blin' Rachel."

He makes them lock the door. N'Doch pockets the key. They follow Stoksie along the balcony and descend a hidden staircase at the far end of the curve. N'Doch decides it's either cleverness or some superior authority on their guide's part that they don't pick up Brenda the guard dog until they're at least halfway 'round the so-called mall. Even then, she and her entourage hold at a respectful ten paces behind, pretending like they're out for their own little evening stroll and just happen to be carrying all their guns. Stoksie's rolling limp sets a stiff pace down a gravel path through pines and brushy undergrowth, heading toward the sound of the waterfall. N'Doch is excited. He's never seen a real waterfall before. He imagines something like Victoria before it went dry, or old Niagara, from the travel vids. Who knows? Maybe it is Niagara. He's in America, isn't he? To be out of the sun is a major relief. But he wonders if Blind Rachel always greets her visitors out here in the woods.

As they near the water, the air softens with moisture, and the bushes lining the path get taller and fuller, harder to see through. For the last hundred meters, they glide through a sort of green tunnel, leaf walls on both sides, dappled shade overhead, doused in mist and scented with pine.

"Ohhh," breathes the girl.

"Like home for her," N'Doch replies to Stoksie's glance. "In Europe."

"Yu say?" Stoksie looks impressed. "Still?"

N'Doch vamps. "Just homesick, y'know?"

"Sure, sure. Long way to Urop."

Then suddenly, around a leafy bend, there is the waterfall.

It is not Victoria Falls, or the Niagara of N'Doch's fervid imagination. In fact, he's amazed that such a sad thin trickle could make so much noise. Maybe because it falls from such a height—fifteen, twenty meters at least—or because it's broken and deflected at so many points of its fall before it plunges into the narrow rock-lined pool at its base. Or it's the towering rock face that gives birth to it, echoing and amplifying its sound. But N'Doch's disappointment passes quickly. It doesn't need to be Niagara. After the lifeless, swelling river and the parched lands below, this cool leaf-scented air and the crystalline clarity of the water nearly bring him to his knees, as he sees Stoksie has been, groaning faintly as he lands.

Oddly, it's Köthen who reads the significance of this gesture. Quietly, he beckons them downward in respect at the water's edge. He mimics also the little man's dipping of one hand lightly into the pool, to touch his forehead and lips with dampened fingertips. The moment is over quickly, like the water ritual that welcomed them into space. No heavy-duty ceremony. Stoksie groans again, rising, then spreads his arms as if to embrace the entire rock face, the silvered thread of falling water, the clear and turbulent pool. "Dis heah Blin' Rachel!"

All three of them are wily enough by now not to crane their heads around in search of . . . a person. But there is a moment of utter stillness, which Stoksie apparently takes for reverence, for he beams at them as if they have fulfilled his every expectation. Then he turns the sweetest of gazes on Pitbull Brenda, who has been observing from the head of the path.

"Nise, ha?" he grins.

"Sehr schön!" says the girl.

"Nice," N'Doch agrees.

But Stoksie wants a bit more. "Whachu got up nort'? Water Dragon nise like dis?"

One more piece of the puzzle falls into place. It's like naming the desert tribes after the oases they claim. In a world reverting to desert, it makes a lot of sense. N'Doch looks up to where the slim cascade shoots forth from a shadowed fissure in the rock. There's another thirty meters of sheer rock above that. He knows without asking that this water is drinkable and safe. "Nice, yeah. But . . . y'know, different." He reaches for a memory, even a fantasy, of safe, flowing water, and comes up dry. "Later, you visit. I'll introduce you."

"Mebbe, mebbe." Stoksie's already counting up his inventory. "Got good trade up nort'?"

N'Doch lets his grin go sly. "Depend on whachu bringin'."

"Yu'll seeit den, an' not befoah!" The little man claps him on the back, hugely satisfied. "Hey! Yu wanna washup?" N'Doch notices how the main pool spills over into a series of smaller pools, partly hidden by the screening greenery. The first of these lower pools has a steady stream of people carting containers back and forth from camp to dip and fill in its clear, chill depths. The second, wider and shallower, is lively with naked bathers. N'Doch does a kind of double take, sure he's mistaken. But no, the pool is full of men, women, and children, scrubbing away, rinsing each other diligently. Young folks and old folks, gasping, laughing with the cold, though it looks a bit more like work than fun. N'Doch suspects it's the frigid water making them all so energetic. In the third pool down, continuing the organized use of this precious unpolluted source, laundry is being done. N'Doch knows this swirling race of liquid ice will cut him to the bone, but his opportunities for bathing were infrequent at Deep Moor and now he's got another time's layers of dust and grit and sweat smeared all over him. He nods to Stoksie. "I'm there!"

"Alla yus, na!" the little man waves, turning toward the lower pools, already stripping off his worn and dusty layers. But the girl is blushing furiously and shaking her head to N'Doch in mute appeal.

Köthen, who has knelt again briefly to douse his face with cold water, wipes his beard on his sleeves and offers her a brisk bow. "If my lady prefers, I will see her back to the chamber beforehand."

The girl blinks at him. She can't help glancing at N'Doch in confusion. "My lord is most kind," she murmurs.

"Few who know me would agree, my lady."

N'Doch isn't sure if this is better or worse. What's better for sure is that he not get any more involved in the issues between them than he is already. "Good man, Dolph," he says cheerfully. He digs the key out of his pocket and tosses it to Köthen. "Hurry back. I'll save you a spot at poolside."

Baron Köthen walked her back along the woodland path and up the rickety stairs in silence. Unlocking the door of the cavelike room, he removed the lock and hung it on the inside of the door. Then he bowed again, as one would to a respected stranger, and handed her the silvery key-thing.

"I would suggest, my lady, that you lock yourself in. We will return soon enough to escort you to dinner."

With the air of a man who is discharging his moral duties, he insisted that she try the key in the lock, and stood by until she had called her competence with it through the safely fastened door. Then she heard his steps recede along the balcony—rather quickly, she thought.

Erde found this newly solicitous behavior bewildering. Though it was a relief not to have him growling and glowering and calling her "witch," this chill and distant formality was only a slight improvement. But at least it was one she could live with.

The moment she thought she could suppose him to be out of sight, she unlocked the door and slipped outside, locking it again behind her. Hopefully, his passage back to the waterfall would occupy the hostile and suspicious Brenda for long enough for one very quiet girl to sneak past into the woods. It was time to find a secret place for the dragons to come to roost.

A bit of sheltering rock, an open space among the pines, some handy and concealing shrubbery. The hiding place had not been hard to find, and it only needed to be free of prying eyes while the dragon transported himself and Lady Water there safely. Once they were settled, Brenda herself could stroll right by without spotting anything unusual. Both dragons were becoming expert at hiding in plain sight.

They were restless when they arrived, materializing like

two giant shadows out of the gathering dusk. Erde had hoped for time to curl up next to the dragon for a while, soaking up comfort before she must return for the evening meal, and a long night in a dank and cheerless cell. But Earth would not settle. Like an old dog unable to find a comfortable spot, he nosed around and around the little clearing, sat down, shifted about, got up and lumbered around a bit more. Lady Water stood to one side, rubbing her velvet-blue hide against a tree trunk. Her swim in the river, she said, had left her itchy all over.

IT'S YOUR MIND THAT'S ITCHY, SISTER.

Perhaps. But even breathing the air here is like swimming in filth.

Erde gave up chasing after the dragon and sat down on a convenient rock to listen in. She noticed that her throat did feel rather raw, like when there was green wood burning in the castle hearths.

THE SUMMONER'S CALL IS FADING AS WE TRAVEL INLAND.

Not fading, brother. Being interfered with.

WE DO NOT KNOW FOR SURE . . .

I think we do know. I think he is deliberately blocking the signal.

Erde guessed it was Lord Fire they were squabbling about. In the way of dragons, they might go on exploring the fine points of this debate until halfway to dawn. Perhaps she could hurry it along.

HE KNOWS WE ARE COMING, THEN?

He knows we will come, sooner or later. Each step he takes to deflect our approach brings us closer by calling attention to his actions. I wonder if he has considered this inevitability.

Earth rumbled disconsolately, got up, moved two paces, and lay down again.

WE MUST CONFRONT HIM. THEN WE WILL KNOW THE TRUTH.

YOU KNOW WHERE HE IS, THEN?

THESE GOOD PEOPLE WILL LEAD US TO HIM.

THEY WILL? HOW?

LISTEN CAREFULLY IN THE CAMP. THE CLUES WILL APPEAR. HE DOES NOT KNOW HOW TO LIVE QUIETLY.

Erde got up from her rock and went to lean against him.

CAN'T N'DOCH LISTEN? I'D RATHER STAY HERE WITH YOU.

WHAT IF THESE PEOPLE INTEND TO MURDER US IN OUR BEDS
AND STEAL ALL OUR WORLDLY GOODS . . . ?

Such as they are.

WELL, I KNOW IT'S NOT MUCH, BUT THEY DO SEEM VERY OC-
CUPIED WITH . . . THINGS.

**CHILD, THEY LIVE AS THEY MUST, AS SCAVENGERS OFF THE
CORPSE OF THE LAND.**

Lady Water ceased rubbing against her tree and came to
join them.

*There's one more bit of bad news they have ahead of
them.*

Both girl and dragon looked her way.

*Their precious stream is dying, along with everything
else.*

OH! HOW CAN THAT BE?

*The deep source that feeds the spring is drying up. There
is another aquifer below, but it is blocked.*

YOU CAN FEEL THE WATER THROUGH THE GROUND?

*I always know where the water is. In three dimensions,
downward through the earth, upward into the sky.*

YOUR PARDON, MY LADY. I DIDN'T KNOW.

Did you ever ask?

SISTER, YOU ARE IRRITABLE.

No kidding.

The blue dragon turned and pranced away, her tail
lashing.

**IT'S HIS FAULT, YOU SEE. SHE'S TOO MUCH IN THE WORLD
OF HER ANTAGONIST OPPOSITE.**

LORD FIRE, YOU MEAN? IS HE HER OPPOSITE?

FIRE AND WATER? WOULD HE NOT BE? IS SHE FORGIVEN?

OF COURSE SHE IS.

Earth had finally settled, it seemed. He put his great
horned head down and got very still and quiet. Erde
snuggled against him happily, until suddenly he spoke
up again.

PERHAPS I COULD UNBLOCK IT.

It was a while before Erde understood that he was talking about the underground water.

OH, DRAGON, COULD YOU TRY?

**THE SLIGHT SHIFTING OF A FISSURE, PERHAPS. A DEGRADA-
TION OF THE BLOCKAGE. THE APPROACH WILL HAVE TO BE**

CAREFULLY CONSIDERED. I WOULD NOT WISH TO CAUSE ITS
FINAL DESTRUCTION INSTEAD.

YOU ARE THE CLEVEREST OF DRAGONS! YOU WILL NOT FAIL!

Though the dying stream was terribly unfortunate, Erde
was delighted that the dragon would have a useful project
to soothe his restless mind. Just pondering it now, he was
calmer.

The sun had nearly set. She must return to the camp,
but now she did so with a lighter heart.

DRAGONS! I'M OFF TO LISTEN—VERY CAREFULLY—AND I
WILL REPORT TO YOU EVERYTHING I HEAR!

NOT EVERYTHING, I HOPE. HOW WILL WE GET ANY WORK
DONE HERE?

Chapter Twenty-five

When Son Luco knocks on her door two hours after dinner, so much later than the priest has ever come visiting before, Paia knows it isn't a social call. Not that Luco is often given to such civilities, but it's the lingering startlement in his blue eyes that puts her on alert, and his comfortable civilian clothes underneath the gold Temple robe tossed on so hastily, its complex fastenings only half done up. He leaves the big door open when she invites him in, as if to head off any possible suspicion—on the part of the righteous Honor Guard in the hall, she supposes—of improper behavior within the Temple's highest authorities.

At least, Paia notes wearily, he's left his entourage in the corridor.

"Mother Paia," he says formally, then flounders to a halt. His startled eyes seem to be warning her, not just to behave, which he always does, but of some graver danger. He's had a shock, she decides, and she's sure she can guess the source of it. "Mother Paia," he begins again, "I have come to inform you that you are to be graced by the God's Decree with a Special Presentation of the Suitors in the Hall of Audiences, first thing tomorrow after the morning Call to Prayer. The God himself will honor us with his Presence."

Paia is practiced by now at looking delighted when she isn't. Certainly Luco can't believe that her bland and welcoming smile, maintained just now with such effort, reflects her true response to this news. But why make him suffer any further for her own transgressions? "The God honors me indeed." She tries to draw Luco farther into the room, away from listening ears, by offering him the only chair in the room. But of course, in public, he would never sit down in the presence of the High Priestess. "Did he bring this wonderful news himself?"

"He just now left me."

Does she detect a singeing of Luco's brows, or of his shining locks of hair? Paia lowers her voice as well as her glance. "Poor Luco. Was he in an awful rage?"

"He was . . . terrifying."

"Yes." She turns away, to the comfort of her window, and twitches the drapes aside to gaze out in the red dusk. The sun goes down so very late at this time of year, she muses. "Well, Luco. Extremely short notice for you to be organizing such an event. I hope it will not prove too taxing for you and your staff."

"What the God wills . . ." Luco replies mechanically.

She is so used to the fear now, she barely registers it. "What the God wills. Thank you, First Son. I will see you, then, in the morning."

Because she has already reconsidered the uses to which she can put the right Suitor, Paia goes to bed charged with purpose and resolve. If this is how the God seeks to punish her, so be it. But now she must charm and soothe him sufficiently to preserve some power of choice in the matter. She falls asleep planning how she will dress, so carefully—for him. She doesn't care what the Suitors see or think. They will want her anyway, no matter how she presents herself. There is probably no higher goal among the Faithful than the High Priestess's bed. Paia can only pity them.

At some point later, she comes suddenly awake. She's sure she has heard someone call out her name. Lying still and listening, she can almost feel the echoes fade away, like receding ripples in the darkness. But she hears nothing.

She reaches under her pillows for the God's little gun, then lets it lie there. The call—probably not a call at all, just the tail of a forgotten dream—it seemed to her like a summons. But not the God's familiar and irresistible command. A softer appeal. Almost an invitation. Paia holds the vanished moment in her memory, probing it carefully. The voice was like a breath of wind, and it came wrapped in blue. In blue.

In the darkness of her bed, Paia smiles. How absurd dreams often are.

But the notion of summoning now takes up residence in her brain, and will not be ignored. *A True Recipe for Raising Dragons.* Fully awake until her adrenaline rush subsides, she stretches out long in her cool and silken sheets and tries to imagine how she would accomplish such a thing.

When the God calls her, it's a compulsion. She cannot deny, only answer. She can't for a moment consider compelling the God in return. But perhaps something else might bring him. If she was in danger, or in need, and if there was no one around to aid her, would he hear her then, as she hears him, like a ringing in her soul? Or would he come if she . . . begged him?

She contemplates the voice that just woke her, how it vibrated through the air like something physical, not just a sound but a force. Then her own summons should be like that, a line of force reaching out to the God where he lies sleeping in the heated perpetual night of his Sanctum. Let it fasten itself to him, twining like a young vine, up around his shining ivory claw, to pull itself taut, taut with her imperative.

The darkness around her shudders. Like tinder bursting into flame, he appears in an explosion of light, bellowing as he materializes, as if unable to contain his fury but even less able, within the bounds of this smaller room, to express it satisfactorily.

"What are you doing?" He is glowing like blown embers. "Are you mad? *What are you doing?*"

Paia is too stunned to produce sound, never mind a coherent word. She has done it. She called him, and he came. But he is not happy about it.

"Ignorant woman! You meddle with forces you know nothing of!"

If she could ever believe that he slept in his man-form, she'd swear he's been dragged straight out of a very human bed. His hair is wild and the clothing he's snatched at for this hasty manifestation is disheveled and minimal. His chest is bare past his navel and glitters with hard, golden scales, as if he couldn't be bothered to effect a full transformation.

Nevertheless, she is thrilled by her success. The first words she manages are not an apology. "If I am ignorant, my lord, it is you who have kept me that way."

"Yes! For your own good! And mine, which is all that matters!" He is moving faster than any human could, practically spinning in outraged frustration. "How dare you summon me? HOW DARE YOU? I am the God here! What are you thinking? With your clumsiness, they'll hear you for sure! You'll give us away entirely!"

"Hear what?" Paia remembers this implication from before, that she is somehow a danger to him. "Hear my thoughts?"

"Well, I do!" He whirls past her, and heat settles around her like a toxic cloud. "Do I not?"

"But . . ." Paia knows she's meant to cower, but she's too amazed and curious. "Who are 'they'?"

"The enemy, foolish woman! Mine. Yours. Those who wish to bring an end to us and to all we've made here. And you, with your childish games, your stupid, clumsy experimenting, are going to help them do it!"

"But I said nothing! I only *thought* . . ."

"Idiot! Thought is the language of my enemies!"

"How am I suppose to know that?" Suddenly she's on her feet in the middle of the bed, yelling at him. Yelling at the God. Paia hardly recognizes herself. "First it was the notes, then you suspected my paintings! How can I know what to do if you never tell me anything? How can I learn to help, when you call me a pawn and treat me like one?"

He halts his wild gyrations as if a switch has been pulled. He stares at her. His hair swirls around him with a restless mind of its own. "What gives you the deluded idea that I need your help?"

"You do!" Now that he's still, she sees there is even stubble darkening his jaw. "Look at yourself! What kind of a god are you? You're a mess!"

"This? *This?*" He scoffs, yet flicks a glance at the sliver of window, as if seeking his reflection in it. "This is not me! This is a mere simu . . ."

"It is your state of mind made manifest! And it tells me you need all the help you can get!" She's appalled that she's said it, for appearances mean so much to him, but once she has, she knows it's true. The shapeless anxiety she'd felt for him just before his tantrum in the tower begins to take on substance. She begins to believe in these enemies. She begins to sense them herself. And having hurled insults at him without immediate repercussion brings a kind of calm. In sudden earnestness, Paia sinks to her knees among the bundled bedclothes, knowing finally what she really needs to say to him. She brings her palms together in a Temple gesture of supplication. "My lord Fire. Why must you insist that fear is the only way to rule? Let me be what I am meant to be to you, what I am destined to be. Let me grow. Let me use the gifts I have to work against these enemies that plague you. Let me love you and serve you in every way I am able to."

The God's hands are in his hair, taming its impatient life, raking it into submission. His eyes are like bright contemptuous suns. "Better if you had stayed a pliant nestling! How weak and tragic to be tied to the progress of years!"

"Because I am human, yes, but who better to go out into the world and be your voice among humans?"

"I am my own voice, as you can see. And I have other, more compliant human voices working for me already, here and in places you know nothing of!"

"Luco. Loyal Son Luco. Who lives in terror of you, like every other human . . . except me. Luco speaks only of duty and obedience. Who will go to the Faithful and speak for you of love?"

"Love?" He spits it out like an obscenity. "I need their service, their devotion! I have no need of their love!"

"But you do, my lord! So that when your enemies arrive, the Faithful will rise for you rather than against you."

"They wouldn't dare!"

"Why not be as sure of their love as you are of their terror?"

"How argumentative you have become, my priestess!"

But the faintest shadow dims his glare, and like the sun setting behind the mountains, he decides to end his tantrum, as if it no longer served his purposes. He comes to stand at the foot of the bed, his arms neatly folded, his garments more decorously draped. "You have some scheme in mind already."

Paia smiles. "How clever my lord is." He drinks in the flattery more from need and habit than from belief. Flirting is a game he's always played to put her ill at ease, but it can work both ways, she sees that now. "My scheme is simple. I preach your virtues each day in the Temple. Let me go out among the Faithful and preach to them in their villages, on their own ground." She settles gracefully back on her heels, kneeling like a child before him. "When my father was alive, I loved and feared him both, as I do you now. If your Faithful only fear you, my lord Fire, it is not true devotion. Let me change that. Let me be your ambassador of love."

Maybe her preaching skills have improved. Like a merchant counting up potential sales, the God looks intrigued. "When?"

"Tomorrow. The next day. Whenever Luco can arrange it."

"In such a hurry to race out from under my protecting wing, my priestess? A trip outside is a dangerous undertaking. Have you any real idea what it means when I say that the rule of law ends at the Temple Gate?" He regards her with half-lidded eyes. "If I allow it, it will seem that I care little for your safety."

"Well, my lord, if I am the thorn in your side that you claim me to be, then you will be glad to be rid of me. And I can be on the lookout for your enemies." He is so immediately and obviously torn by this suggestion that Paia almost laughs. The Ambivalent God. Perhaps if she does get into trouble out there, he will not come winging to her rescue. She has often expected to die by his hand, but has never for a moment thought he would not protect her from dangers other than himself. A terrifying yet exhilarating possibility, ripe with implications of true freedom. "Then I can go?"

He nods, the faintest motion of his gilded head.

"And we can cancel the Suitors for tomorrow?"

An even fainter nod.

"Oh, wonderful! You are the wisdom of the ages, my lord! You are the beginning and the end!" Paia stretches out in front of him, as sensuously as a cat, heady with victory and her new sense of power. "Perhaps on my Visitation I will come across a proper Suitor, my lord. One that pleases us both." She leans forward and murmurs, "You can watch."

Chapter Twenty-six

Dinner in Blind Rachel's camp was a disorganized and communal event, held at sunset around the cooking hearths clustered in the center of the big dirt lawn. There was more food in the cook pots than Erde expected, given the lifeless countryside and the lack of visible farmsteads. Provisions were shared, but she could deduce no agreed-upon plan to the preparation of them. Everyone—perhaps thirty or forty adults and a few children, surprisingly few—jostled from hearth to hearth with their tin bowls and cups, chatting, tasting, eating what was ready to eat, and encouraging the progress of whatever still had a while to go.

No formal hospitality was offered to the guests, nothing more than "here's food, take a seat." But Stoksie took pains to borrow bowls and implements for them, then urged them into the crowds at the cook fires to claim portions of stewed rabbit and ash-roasted roots and crisp chunks of fresh bread. When he'd found them space to sit, away from the heat of the fires and where no dogs and chickens were prowling, he nodded happily and wandered off, food in hand.

With the sun at last sinking between the trees, the worst of the heat was easing off. But Erde envied the men their bath. Both of them looked clean and refreshed. Baron Köthen's hair was still wet, slicked back with his fingers like a young boy's. She found it hard not to gaze at him stupidly, so instead studied her bowl and its contents, pondering the perilous beauty of men. For a while, they all ate in silence, finally willing to admit how hungry they'd been. She watched N'Doch for clues about the safety of the food, about how to behave. She saw how he sniffed at each edible, when no one was looking, then tasted it cautiously before stuffing it in his mouth. Then he emptied half his bowl before slowing down enough to report on his adventures in the pool.

"Tinkers?" Erde thought it a curious thing for these people to call themselves, since it seemed obvious that no one here was manufacturing anything.

"Meant 'gypsies' more, in my time. The crews each claim a basic territory, but they move around a lot, in and out of each other's turf, making trade. That's why Stoksie didn't put an arrow through us first thing. That and the fact that we look like we got something to offer. Like he says, healthy." N'Doch tore off a fist-sized hunk of bread. "Good food."

"Camp food," said Köthen.

"Hey, you didn't have to kill it, and you didn't have to cook it. Don't complain." N'Doch mopped up pink juice, then waved the dripping bread in an airy circle. "This here's Blind Rachel's base, the only place they got anything permanent. They keep it secret from everyone but the other Tinker crews. When I got down to trade right off, it was sorta like giving the Tinker password. Pretty good, huh?"

"Lucky," Köthen muttered.

"Nah." N'Doch grinned. "Good instincts, man. See why you gotta keep me around? Anyway, these folk aren't fighters, they're businessmen." He circled the bread once more around the clearing. "But this . . . this they'd fight to keep."

"Who would try to take it from them?" Erde asked.

"Look around you, girl! Anyone would take it who could, 'cept another Tinker. They got an agreement."

"For the water, milady, for the water." Köthen was now only picking at his stew.

N'Doch nodded, his mouth full of bread. "They say there's not as much of it as there used to be, but it's still enough to fight over, when there's no other water around." He gestured at Köthen's bowl. "You better eat up, man, or somebody else'll eat it for you."

"Yourself, for instance?"

"Mebbe."

Erde saw that a further adjustment had occurred between them. The baron now seemed to find sour amusement in N'Doch's needling. "But why haven't we seen farms? Are there towns or villages left anywhere?"

N'Doch swallowed so that he wouldn't choke. "In the valleys, or down on the flats. Wherever there's still some bit of drinkable water."

"None of it to compare with the purity of Blind Rachel. Or so we are told." Köthen rested his bowl on one knee, with what seemed like genuine interest. "Nonetheless, the food staples are grown in the villages. The Tinkers keep livestock and limited kitchen gardens, but they are too nomadic to be reliable farmers. The craftsmen as well live in the villages."

"Yeah, and the Tinker crews move all the food and goods up and down between all these strung-out villages. The villages don't travel: too busy defending what they got. So the Tinkers are the transport system." N'Doch eyed Köthen's food. "So, you gonna eat it or not?"

"Off me, whelp! I'll eat in my own time!"

Erde blotted her lips delicately with the hem of her sleeve. "You discovered all this information while bathing?"

N'Doch swiveled a huge grin on her, his eyes and teeth bright in the growing darkness. "You'd be amazed how friendly people can be when you get yourselves naked together!"

Were it not for the baron's quiet snort, Erde might have been able to fight down her blush. Not that they would notice in the dim light, but she felt it herself, as a brand of her increasingly tiresome innocence. It really was time, she decided, to learn how to conceal her feelings, rather than perpetually wearing them on her sleeve for all to see and mock at. Or to learn to make a performance of them, as N'Doch did. She thought the former more likely, in her case.

"No love lost between these people and the villages," Köthen observed as solemnly as if he'd never cracked a smile.

"Yeah. Those flatlanders sound like a nasty bunch.

'Course, they got a hard life, but that's no excuse. Like, a Tinker'd never marry out. Well, I'm not sure they get married at all, but you know what I mean. Anyway, we were talking to this guy Luther Somebody. He says there's some villages they won't even go to. Some sort of religious fanatics who think everybody's got to agree with them."

"Another holy war?" Erde had hoped the Future would be done with such things.

"We were just getting into that when Bulldog Brenda decided we were taking up too much pool time."

Köthen speared a bit of rabbit meat out of a puddle of gravy. "There are factions within the camp as well as outside of it."

"I'll say. What a major pain in the ass she's getting to be."

"But there's no apparent leader." Köthen glanced around, inviting their response, as if to say, what am I missing?

N'Doch was unhelpful. His head was up, listening. "Don't think you'll find one, Dolph. It's not that kind of a group."

Erde frowned gently. "Not Stoksie?"

"No way. He's more like . . . an elder. Like whatisname . . . Luther. He's another one."

From across the irregular circle of fires came a few experimental notes from a pipe and the strum of a stringed instrument being tuned. Stoksie was headed in their direction, his dark face flushed with the last glow of sunset. His progress was slow, not just due to his limp, but because he stopped continually along the way with this group or that to chat or exchange a laugh. Erde was surprised how comfortable she already felt among these Tinkers, more so than she had with anyone in N'Doch's time, except for his grandfather, Master Djawara. With that thought, she put out a mental query. But Earth had not yet decided how to try unblocking the water.

"Lack of leadership is a fatal weakness," Köthen observed quietly.

"Think of it as the leadership being shared. Can you get your head around that, yer lordship?" N'Doch set his well-mopped bowl aside and unfolded his legs. "You guys hang, huh? I'm going visiting."

The minute he hears the music, N'Doch loses interest in food crops or issues of leadership. He lifts his long body off the ground and wanders off casually among the hearths, nodding to the men, patting the kids, and returning the smiles of the women with promising smiles of his own. He even grins at Bulldog Brenda, who scowls back. He doesn't care. The music is what matters now.

He finds the music makers off to one side, three of them around a small fire of their own, like a side pocket to the main table. The sweet woodwind he'd heard is a reed flute, played by a crinkly-faced woman with dark, frizzy hair. The drums are two little lap drums, and the drummer's about his own age with big, fast hands, real eager. He's already wearing a zoned-out glaze, N'Doch notes enviously, and he hasn't even got himself started yet.

But it's the guitar player who draws N'Doch's attention most: an old black man with no teeth left in front, and gnarled stubs of fingers. The guitar's an ancient four-string acoustic in as bad shape as the man is, with a worn bit of glass stuck up under the strings near the top frets. But as the old man bends over it, his ear nearly flat on the box, his wrecked hands dance over the strings like butterflies, and quiet but magical music comes out. He picks his way through a little melody, trying it out, as if making it up on the spot. N'Doch is in love.

He stands in the shadows, listening, until the old man finishes. Then he moves forward with a wave and hunkers down an easy distance away. "Hey, nice," he says.

The old man raises his head from the guitar and looks his way, slow and off-focus. He's blind, or nearly so, but sees enough to read the tall stranger's eyes. "Yu play?" His voice is like an old truck engine.

N'Doch shrugs, which is what he's supposed to do. "I play some."

When the old man hands over the guitar, just like that, and the others don't object, N'Doch can't believe his luck. Maybe they're all tired of listening to themselves or something. He's sorry when the man slips the glass shard out from under the strings and pockets it carefully, but hey, beggars can't be choosers. He accepts the guitar reverently and settles it safely in his lap before sticking out his hand. "N'Doch. Water Dragon Crew."

"Yah," huffs the old man. "Marley."

The drummer is Luis, the reed player Ysabel Dominguin. Though they are nowhere near the same color or body type, N'Doch understands they are mother and son. They shake hands around, but the preliminaries are brief, like anywhere he's ever sat down with other musicians. They're all three of them waiting to hear if he's any good.

He doodles around some, like he's allowed to at first, getting the feel of the strings. He tunes a bit, thinking how raging cool it would be if he could come up with a song they know. Then he gives that up for a simple eight bar blues that he knows they'll be able to come in on. In no time at all, they're playing and grinning at each other, and old Marley is clapping those ruined hands on his knees and chest in complex syncopation with Luis. Soon after that, they're attracting attention from around the cook fires. Folks are leaving off conversations that were limping along anyway, abandoning their emptied plates and bringing their filled bellies by to settle down with the music. A woman hauls in a few chunks of wood and the little fire brightens. N'Doch sees that making music means a lot to these folks. No vids or arcade games to fill their evenings. He'd bet they're great storytellers, too. When he moves on to another old blues song, Luis and Ysa segue into it seamlessly. Stoksie brings over Köthen and the girl, then shoulders his way into the circle to drop down beside N'Doch, making the point about who it was who brought him. Even Brenda's listening, but she's just got to show him a frown, though her foot's right there tapping out the time.

When the song is done, N'Doch vamps a bit, waiting for the others' permission to solo. Ysa nods, so he slides into the simple, plaintive melody of an old Wolof love song, lingering through it once, ever so sweetly, then slamming into the jazzier version that he'd written for himself a few years back. It's a show-off piece that he's used to playing on a keyboard, but somehow his fingers still find a way among the strings. When he's done, he's worked up a sweat all over again but the moment is worth it, 'cause the little

crowd goes ballistic, hooting and stamping and yelling for
an encore.

N'Doch looks at Marley. He doesn't want to be upstaging
the man completely. Marley grins and crosses his arms. As
N'Doch bows his head over the guitar, thinking what to
play next, he hears the dragon in his head.

*Play them Sedou. Play me down around that campfire.
I'm bored of hanging out in the woods with my earnest
brother . . .*

N'Doch keeps his face smooth and lets his eyes roam
casually, seeking out the girl. She's heard. She's frowning
a little, but she's already preparing Köthen. His blond
head's bent low, listening, as he crouches beside her, very
careful to keep his distance.

Everyone okay with that? What does Dolph say?

He says he'll be pleased to renew our acquaintance.

What's the story?

That you have better security than they ever guessed.

N'Doch shrugs. *I'm leaving that to you, then.*

Thas cool, little brother.

The song as he'd sung it at Deep Moor is in French. He
hopes it'll add to their cover, give the Europe thing a little
more depth. The dragon doesn't sing it with him this time,
at least not at first, so N'Doch is intensely aware of the
sound of his own voice, husky but strong and true, soaring
through the dusk-time stillness of this foreign mountaintop.
There are new notes there he didn't know he had, and new
resonances. And the song. He knew it was a good song
because it conjured Sedou at the highest moment of his
life. But now he's thrilled to learn that the song is a good
song all on its own. In fact, it's a beautiful song.

By the third verse, he feels the dragon presence coalesc-
ing somewhere off in the woods. These people, he thinks
fleetingly, have no idea what they're in for. By the fifth
verse, a tall black man is standing at the back of the rapt
little crowd, leaning against a wagon wheel and smiling. By
the last verse, he is singing along, a deep almost unheard
harmony that is so natural, it's not even noticed.

N'Doch draws out the last few measures slowly, and
holds tantalizingly before the song's real end. Every eye is
on him. He feels his listeners, each of them, as if they were
touching his mouth and his eyelids and his hands with lov-

ing, grateful fingers. He flattens his picking hand to quiet the strings, and within the space of the sigh before they applaud, he stretches a welcoming arm toward the darkness behind them.

"Folks, I'd like you to meet my brother Sedou."

He knows there was bound to be a commotion, and there is. A lot of gasps and jumping up, knocking over cups and bowls, even a scream or two of fright and a bellow of outrage, more than a few. Like, where did this big guy come from? By the time the knives are out and gleaming nastily in the firelight, N'Doch has set the guitar gently in Marley's lap and stepped through the confusion to Köthen's side, with the girl between them and Sedou behind, like a wall. Then the thing he's worried about happens: Bulldog Brenda swoops up that fat-barreled rifle of hers and levels it at them.

"Call in da res', or yer a dead man."

Sedou spreads his hands genially. His deep voice flows around them like a sweet, cool breeze. "There are no 'rest,' Brenda. I'm all there is."

Her eyes narrow over the gunsight. He knows her name. "Whachu dun wit' my men?"

"Your sentries? Four of them, right? Two women, one man, one boy. The boy hums a lot. Call them if you like. They're fine. They're alert. They were doing their job. They just don't hear as good as they should."

"Yuh? Yu say?" Brenda whistles into the ruddy darkness. Four answering whistles come right back at her.

The mutters rustling among the crowd tell N'Doch they've won already. Easier for these people to convince themselves that this dark and smiling giant slipped through the cordon, under his own clever steam and brilliant stealth, than to wonder how else he could have shown up completely out of nowhere. The truth is often the hardest answer, N'Doch muses. He sheathes his knife, relaxes. Brenda swears a blue streak and sends Charlie and Punk off into the woods to make a personal check on the sentries.

Stoksie says, "Nah mo', na? Speak tru?"

"No more men," Sedou agrees.

But in his mind's eye, N'Doch sees the large rock that has appeared in a little clearing not far from Blind Rachel's pool. He squeezes the girl's shoulder. "Good work," he whispers. And then the mystery man seals his welcome with a gift, and not even N'Doch can imagine how the dragon got it there.

Stooping back into the shadows under the wagon he'd been discovered by, Sedou picks up a lidded tin bucket by its looped handle and carries it forward to the hearth. Eyes still a little wide, the Tinkers make way for him, murmuring. The bucket sloshes as Sedou sets it down at Stoksie's feet.

"For your hospitality, my brother," he rumbles. "For Blind Rachel."

Stoksie leans over, trying not to appear suspicious, and carefully lifts the lid. "Gimme a light, sum'un." A lantern is handed along to him through the crowd. He holds it up and peers into the bucket. His glance at Sedou is sudden and amazed. "Wha's dis, na?"

Sedou crouches, like a mountain descending, and dips one finger to stir the surface gently. It erupts with a roil of silvery minnows, frantic to escape into deeper, chiller waters. "Breeders, my brother. I heard Blind Rachel could use some."

"Good uns? Hellt'y?"

"All healthy."

"Whea yu gettim?"

The big man smiles and stands back. "Can't say. You know how it is."

"Trade seecrit, ha?" Stoksie accepts this, as any practiced merchant would. His expression is already speculative. How can this sudden resource be best exploited. Others press around him to lean over and stare into the bucket. More gasps and commotion, this time of a friendlier sort, especially as Charlie and Punk are back to report the sentries all well and at their posts, though smarting no doubt from a very recent tongue-lashing. An air of hopeful celebration breaks over the clearing like a summer shower. Eager debates erupt over the proper care and feeding of fish. Schedules and menus are being proposed. Big clay jugs appear and a clear liquid is doled out in judicious helpings.

N'Doch eases away from the crowd to watch Sedou work his magic. Not all of it, he reflects, is dragon magic. Some of it is just pure Sedou. He knows. He remembers how it

was, when his brother was alive. Köthen, too, is watching
Sedou, his arms folded across his mailed chest and his rugged face tense with concentration, as if answers to his own
dilemma might be gained from this close study.

When the first burst of excitement has died down, Stoksie
stirs up the crowd again by deputizing the girl-babies Senda
and Mari to deliver the fish to their new home. He makes
Sedou give them detailed instructions, then sends them off
with the bucket slung between them. Two thirds of the
camp, and all of the children, trail after them with lanterns
and cups of home brew.

N'Doch is thinking about Marley's guitar again when Köthen surprises him, bringing over two half-filled cups and
handing him one.

"Here is one thing they do make here. Rather well, I
think."

N'Doch passes the cup under his nose and feels the
fumes leap up like tiny birds into his nostrils. He takes a
sip. "Hooo! Fire water!"

Köthen chuckles, deep and quiet.

"Better watch out," N'Doch warns. "You're gonna slip,
and start enjoying yourself."

But Köthen is pondering the gift of fish. "If even half
those hatchlings survive, they'll be lucky. But after a few
seasons, there'll be a fine catch in that pool. If they're careful, it'll lead to many years of fine catches." He pauses,
glances up. "What? What's the matter now?"

"Nothing." N'Doch realizes he's been staring. "Hey,
Dolph. When you were . . . y'know, back there . . ."

"At home?"

"Yeah. You, like, must've had a big, what, a castle? With
a whole lot of land? And you had to know how to take
care of all that land, how to grow things, right? Raise up
all your food, take care of the animals? Like the women
at Deep Moor do, right? You had to know how to do
all that?"

By now, it's Köthen who's staring, with one cocked
eyebrow.

N'Doch laughs. "Don't worry, I haven't gone off or anything. It's just a side of you I never saw before, caring about
raising fish. You don't think of a lordship caring about fish,
or anything that might get his hands dirty."

"But I must care about fish, and crops and fruit and cattle. A landowner must know about such things. Or take on bondsmen who know what he doesn't." Gravely, Köthen drains his cup. "Good husbandry is a great and noble responsibility. If you abuse the land, it will not feed you or your people."

"Right." N'Doch slouches back on one hip. "So tell me about your place, man. What's it like?"

Köthen's gaze darkens. "Remember . . . or perhaps you didn't know . . . I lost my estates when the hell-priest betrayed me. He will have given them to some minion, who will be wreaking the Lord knows what manner of havoc upon them. That sort care nothing for the land, only for the power it brings them. They will use it up and abandon it, and I am powerless to prevent any of it!"

His fist has tightened dangerously around his empty cup. N'Doch reaches over and levers it out of his grip. "That's all past now, man, from where we stand. That guy's long dead. You're not. How 'bout another round?"

Köthen lets out air between his teeth, a slow hard hiss of rage and tension. Then he shakes his head. "No. I think not. It would be . . . unwise."

N'Doch hands over his own cup, still half full. "Finish up with this, then. I like a beer like the next man, but I ain't much for the hard stuff."

"And you know I am."

"Give it a rest, huh? I ain't criticizing. I'm offering."

Köthen eyes him, then takes the cup. He raises it in brisk salute and tosses back the contents in one swallow, then lingeringly savors the heat on his tongue and in his throat. "You are a strange one, friend N'Doch."

N'Doch just chuckles. He's feeling pretty good right about now.

"But tell your . . . dragon: it's a handsome gift. A gift of hope."

"Tell her yourself."

"Perhaps I will."

A thoughtful silence settles down around the cook fires, now mostly burning low, little piles of glowing ashes scattered across the clearing. A couple of teenagers pile up dishes for transport to the wash pool. A young mother rocks a fretful child. It's the only infant N'Doch has seen.

Among the forty or so in Blind Rachel Crew, at least ten of the women are of childbearing age, and they all look more or less healthy except for the minor physical deformities that seem common among all the Tinkers. Given the level of tech around so far, N'Doch can't imagine there's much available by way of birth control. So why aren't there more babies in the camp?

Stoksie kicks a few charred log ends into his fire and lowers himself to the ground with a sigh. Sedou eases down beside him as the little man uncorks a jug and gestures Köthen and N'Doch back to the hearth for a refill of their cups. The girl has taken a first sip and is staring into her cup in shock, her mouth working soundlessly.

"Go easy on that, kiddo," Sedou advises, laughing.

N'Doch is dying to ask what a dragon knows about getting drunk, but this is clearly not the time for it. A few hearths away, Brenda and Charlie have their heads together, muttering. Punk has already conked out nearby, with his fists wrapped around his brew cup. To N'Doch's delight, Marley stirs in his side pocket and starts up a long, quiet, complex riff. The music drifts over the embers as tangible as smoke.

The man called Luther ambles in out of the darkness to drop down at Stoksie's fire. "Dis heah Luta Willums," Stoksie offers. N'Doch introduces the girl and Sedou. Luther's a big man, for a Tinker, somewhere in his forties and by N'Doch's estimation, smart as a whip and wily as a hyena. He's also noticed, during the communal bath, that Luther has webbed toes.

Ysabel Dominguin, the reed player, joins them next, patting N'Doch on the head briskly, exclaiming, "Good music! Good music, na!"

"Good food, good drink!" he laughs. "You guys always live this good?"

Luther smiles. "Musta knowd yu wuz commin'."

When Bulldog Brenda kisses Charlie lingeringly, then gets up and slouches over, alone and reluctant, to join them, N'Doch understands that what passes for something formal among Tinkers is happening right around him. He nudges Köthen, who nods and murmurs, "Privy council."

N'Doch isn't sure what that means, but he knows a meeting when he sees one. Sure enough, the silence drags on for a bit, pretending to be easy and companionable but actually chock-full of unspoken tension. The girl's on the other side of the hearth, so N'Doch readies himself to translate for Köthen.

Finally, Stoksie clears his throat. "Me 'n Luta bin tinkin' . . ." He looks up at N'Doch, then lets his gaze drift to Sedou, then down to the dirt between his crooked knees where he's worrying a patch of grass with a stick. "Yu nah frum Urop, ri'? Speek tru, na. Ona a da hart."

After a split-second of inner conferencing, Sedou embraces them all with his big soft laugh. "My brother, I do honor your hearth, and I do speak truth." He slides his thumb at Köthen and the girl. "They're from Europe. Me and my brother? No. We're from Africa. Like some of your people, my man."

Truth of a sort. Just not the whole truth. N'Doch wonders if the dragon would lie.

Stoksie's still digging in the dirt. "Nah. My ole peebles from Bruklin."

"Before Brooklyn. Way back. We're cousins, maybe."

N'Doch's not sure there is a 'before Brooklyn' in Stoksie's mind.

"Africa," he repeats, and scratches his bald head.

"Cud be, na," Luther remarks.

Brenda snorts. She stares, not at Sedou resting back next to her on his elbows like a reclining giant, but across the fire at N'Doch. "Howyu git heah frum Africa?"

Her disbelief is contemptuous and total. N'Doch gets the hint that air travel might not be the usual thing anymore. "Boat," he lies, and begins to spin out a relevant fantasy in his mind about stowing away on a derelict supertanker like the wreck grounded on the beach near home.

But Stoksie isn't really interested in Africa or how they got here from there. He waves Brenda silent. "We bin tinkin' . . ."

"Yu bin," Brenda growls.

"Me 'n Luta 'n Ysa, den. Dat's tree ta wun." Stoksie waits, but Brenda subsides, grumbling. "We bin tinkin' mebbe yus like ta stay awhile."

"Yeah?" asks Sedou softly. "Why's that?"

Luther leans forward. He has a big nose and graying anglo hair that keeps falling into his face. N'Doch guesses he's pretty seriously nearsighted. "Yu lookin' fuh sum'un, na? We helpyu fine 'im, den yu help us mebbe. Good trade."

When N'Doch gets this far in his murmured simultaneous translation, Köthen stirs. "What kind of help do they want?"

N'Doch repeats the question.

Stoksie grins at Köthen. "Yer kinda help, bigfella."

"I think he means he wants some muscle, Dolph."

Köthen looks interested. After a pause, the girl says, "Please explain."

To Erde's surprise, it was the musician Ysabel who answered. And her accent was another surprise, throwing off the dragon translators for at least the length of a sentence. It was rapid and musical and full of rolling vowels, as unlike her own native German as any language Erde had ever heard.

". . . so ju zee ter esa tis town aqui . . ."

The next sentence was more coherent. If she worked at balancing it, Ysa's accent faded away and Erde heard only the translation, running in her mind. "Dey meke ferry good shuz tere . . . very good. We get good trade for these shoes wherever we go. But it's a big danger to go to this town."

"Why is that?" Sedou prompted.

"Church wackos," said Brenda with a dismissive wave.

"Wacko, huh?" Luther shoved hair from his eyes. "Yu nevah bin deah! Yu nevah seenit!"

"'Cuz I gotta be heah! Yu wan Blin' Rachel safe, na?" Brenda retorted hotly, but Erde guessed that Luther's accusation was true.

"Sumtimes yu be as dum as a townie, Brenda." Stoksie dug in the dirt again with his stick. "Look, newfellas, heah's da ting. Trade round heah's getting tuffer, yeah by yeah."

Luther nods. "Tru, tru. Times is getting tuffer by da minit."

"So dis town's a biggun, and dey make stuff ev'rybuddy want. We need dat stuff ta make owah nut, y'know? Uddawize, we doan eat. But dey's a problem deah." Stoksie's hesitation sounded less like caution than shame.

"So what's the problem?" N'Doch prodded.

Luther fidgeted and stretched his legs. "Yu gonna laff at us."

N'Doch did laugh, then immediately looked apologetic. "Nah, man, I mean, c'mon. Why would we laugh, as good as you've been to us? It's like, some kind of personal problem? Somebody ran off with somebody else's woman?"

"Wudna head fer town if we did dat," murmured Luther.

Stoksie shook his head with a wry smile. "I tink we cud deel wit dat."

"And this other thing you can't deal with?" Sedou asked.

Ysa pursed her lips in a silent negative. Stoksie tossed his stick into the fire. Brenda sulked.

"Okay, den. I'll sayit if nuna yus will. Heah it is." Luther shook his gray forelock out of his eyes and cleared his throat. "Dey's a monsta comes deah."

Another stifled laugh from N'Doch. "A what?"

"A monsta."

"What kinda monster?"

"Shit, yu know—big teet' 'n wings 'n all."

"Wings?"

"Yah. Wings an' a tail."

Now true silence fell around the cook fire. Erde's heart surged in her chest until she was sure everyone could hear it pounding. Sedou rose up from his elbows and fixed his inhuman eyes on Luther. For a moment, all the air went out of the world. In another second, they would be gasping like dying fish. Then she heard N'Doch muttering his translation into Köthen's ear. She took a breath, and the world moved forward again.

Sedou said, "What does this 'monster' look like?"

"Big gold sum'bitch." Luther crooked back both his elbows like a hawk stooping to the kill, then bent his fingers and worked them like claws. "Lon' neck, lon' tail."

Mercifully, Stoksie mistook their sudden intense focus for disbelief. "S'trut', I sweah. I seenit. Nevah bin close, na."

"Lucky," said Ysabel.

Luther laughed. "Souns crazy, na?"

"No," replied Sedou gravely. "I don't think it does."

"I do," Brenda offered. "Wacko. Alla dem."

"Yu go deah, den!" Luther exploded. "Yu wachim come down outa da sky lika litenin' bolt. Den yu tell me I'm wacko."

Brenda gathered herself as if she was ready to leave right then. "Okay, den, I will! Yu take care a da camp!"

"Whoa, whoa, wait!" soothed N'Doch. "Say again? Out of the sky?"

Luther swooped one fist into the other with a resounding slap. "Nevah seen anatin' like it. Don' know whaddit is."

But we do, Erde wanted to cry out. We do!

OH, DRAGON, ARE YOU LISTENING?

WITH EVERY CELL AND SINEW.

Stoksie said, "So whachu say? Yu come wit' us?"

Sedou laughed, barely able to conceal the exultation of the dragon within. "But if this monster's as big and bad as you say he is, how can we protect you from it?"

Are they wondering, Erde asked herself, why we aren't more surprised?

"Nah frum da monsta," Luther said. "No way yu cud do dat. Frum da guys who wanda trowyu tada monsta."

"Really?" Erde could not hide her shock. "And what does the . . . monster . . . do then?"

"Broilyu 'n eechu. Onna spot. Whachu tink?" Their stunned silence clearly puzzled Luther. "Yumin sacerfize, y'know?"

"Wait. No." Sedou shook his head. "Surely you're mistaken."

"Nah. I saw 'im."

"Are you sure?"

"Yah, betcha."

Erde thought she felt the ground shiver, ever so gently.

Stoksie agreed soberly. "Meetu. Reel ugly bizness. Parda der religin, kin yu emagin? Jus' like a townie, ta let sumpin li' dat go on."

"Man!" breathed N'Doch. "That's no better than witch burning!"

Sedou rose suddenly, a motion as quick and fluid as water, and paced away. "Oh, my friends . . ." A soft cry of pain at the edge of the darkness, answered by a distinct shuddering from the bedrock. A shift and crack. No one but Erde seemed to notice, so she swallowed her own horror in order to send both dragons soothing thoughts. As low an opinion as Lady Water had of her other brother, she had never thought him capable of such barbarism.

Stoksie watched after Sedou a bit, then shifted his gaze to N'Doch. "He scared off, na?"

"Nah. Just, y'know . . . upset. That's terrible news. Ought to put a stop to that right away."

"Betcha," muttered Luther. "If we could."

"Well, den, whachu tink?" Stoksie asked. "Yu come wit?"

"I'm ready." N'Doch raised his voice slightly. "What say, bro?"

Sedou turned back toward the light, reclaiming his smile with enough effort to render it defiant. "I say, sure. We'll come. We'll come see your monster, and offer whatever help we can. Wouldn't miss it. Who knows? We might find this friend we've been looking for right there in that village."

N'Doch snorted grimly. "Yeah. Wouldn't that be a surprise."

And underneath Blind Rachel, new water flowed.

PART FOUR

The Meeting
with Destiny

Chapter Twenty-seven

The God has given her a day to get ready, and she's been at it since the previous noon. Now it's getting on toward six in the morning, and Paia sits cross-legged in the middle of her bed, defiant in her sweat suit as she directs the swirl of servants packing and repacking her luggage. It had not occurred to her, as she worked so hard to sell the notion of her Visitation, that her greatest concern would be having nothing to wear.

She hasn't been past the Temple's outer gates in fourteen years. Even her ceremonial forays into the open air of the Temple Plaza have been kept as brief as possible, for the sake of her safety and her health. But Paia recalls the elaborate precautions taken whenever she went out as a child. Over the multiple layers of sunblock creams went the long sleeves, the high collars, the thin reflective gloves and hat. All made of the lightest possible materials, but still they were stifling hot. The God always says Paia should daily thank her mother and nannies: to those strict precautions she owes her flawless skin. Even then, going out was rare. Usually she was on her way to some special local event that the landowner's family was expected to attend, a christening, or a funeral. Leaving the house was less a pleasure than a duty.

But right now, Paia is thrilled by the prospect, even though the sunblock has long since dried up, and all that protective clothing, even if it could still be found, would no longer fit. Even though her extensive wardrobe of revealing

Temple garments is woefully inadequate for a trek across the open countryside. Paia has been improvising all night.

And then there's the issue of something to put it all in. There hasn't been a thorough search of the storerooms in a long time. Paia was shocked to discover how much has vanished from those rooms where the locks are disabled. Her immediate response was to storm off to Luco in a rage over this silent and systematic looting. The God would hear of it! The First Son took time to soothe and calm her, but she sensed an unusual impatience beneath his dutiful concern, as if such invasions and inconveniences are only to be expected. She'd pouted. If it didn't involve the God, he didn't care about it!

Now, looking over the bits and pieces she's been able to gather, she's more intrigued than outraged. They have a motley, rough-and-tumble aspect, laid out on her mother's fine Turkish carpet: a black nylon duffel, one boxy plastic trunk, two big blue satchels, a silvered metal case, and an ancient but well-preserved mountaineer's pack in leather. Leather is an absurd luxury, but the pack bears her father's initials. Paia unearthed it in one of the unransacked store-rooms and fell in love with it instantly. That storeroom, keyed open by her palm print, is a virtual time capsule. She could have spent a whole week in there, revisiting her life before the God. But that would have been a lonely exercise. She has no one to share these memories with.

The God is right, she decides. Nostalgia is a useless luxury.

The chambermaid spreads another armload of clothing on the bed. Paia allows her to display each garment for inspection, nodding a yes to this, a no to that. The chambermaid hands off the single yes to a packer, sweeps up the rejects, and goes back for another load. Paia wonders if there is time to have a few more sensible items made up: long-sleeved shirts and pants with handy hidden pockets for the God's little gun.

Out in the hallway, the red-robed Twelve are gathered in a weepy cluster, mourning her departure from their sight for even a moment. Paia has forbidden them entry. No doubt they're convinced that this trip is a forced order. Why would anyone leave the Citadel willingly? A contingent of Honor Guard is milling about as well, relieved that their watch hasn't been chosen for escort duty. The moist chanting and murmuring of the Twelve breaks off briefly as a brace of Luco's Third Sons shoulder them aside importantly, bearing through the doorway a shrouded rectangle. Paia has had the mutating landscape brought downstairs, to be hung on the wall opposite her bed, another expression of her newly assumed autonomy, though no one will read it that way but herself and the God. She hopes it will be like having a new window cut into the room, a mystical kind of window where the view changes each time you look out. She'd take the painting with her if she could. She'd like to know that it's safe. But she suspects that even the suggestion might render Luco, in his present state, apoplectic. Paia waves at the young priests to lean the covered canvas against the wall. What vista would it reveal to this room full of servants? She will wait until she is alone again to unveil it.

Son Luco has been in and out at least twice this morning, in high gear and at the earliest hint of dawn. First he came to remind her of their schedule of departure, then to describe the instantaneously devised ceremony slated for 0800 sharp in the Temple Plaza. He was at his most abrupt and efficient, but beneath the official mask thrummed true eagerness. His bronzed skin was almost luminous, as if lit from within by suppressed anticipation. His subordinates whirled around after him, basking in the glow of his energy. At one point, Paia glanced through her open door to discover him in a one-way consultation of gestures with the chambermaid—whom, as far as she knew, he had never before even noticed. Why should Luco be so charged up, she'd wondered a bit sulkily. He gets to go out all the time.

An unfamiliar kitchen servant hesitates in the doorway, balancing the breakfast tray. Paia bites back an urge to snap her fingers and yell at the girl to hurry. The child's confusion suggests she's never ventured so high in the Citadel before. Paia gestures her over to the bed, studying her as she approaches. Paia has resolved to be more observant of those around her, either servant or priest, especially since she's discovered how hard it is to remember to do so. This girl looks decently fed, but her eyes are dull and she is ghostly pale. Her cheeks have almost a blue cast, no doubt due to a life spent entirely in the Citadel's subterranean levels. She walks with her shoulders crooked, struggling to hold them straight as she weaves a cautious path across the crowded room to the High Priestess' bed. Despite a concealing sleeve, Paia sees that her right arm is withered, just managing to steady the heavy tray. Again Paia controls a tart response. It is the God's stated policy to forbid deformities within the priesthood and among the Citadel workforce, but even Paia knows exceptions must be made, or the housekeepers would have trouble filling their staff. Only the high frenzy of preparations has brought this child out of the concealment of the kitchens.

Unable to repress her reflexive shudder, Paia reminds herself that she will have to observe much worse when she gets outside. Best to practice ignoring things now. She nods neutrally at the girl, then terrifies her with a brisk thanks when the tray is set down without mishap. The girl bows clumsily and flees back through the crowd.

An hour later, Paia is dressed and fed. The little gun is tucked against the small of her back. The luggage has been fastened and sent downstairs. She has followed Luco's advice in her choice of a Leave-taking outfit: the softest and most comfortable of the glittery Temple garments underneath a long hooded silk robe that can be worn open for the ritual, then fastened up tight for the road. The chambermaid is offering up for her approval a belt of jewel-studded gold mesh, when a relay of shouted orders echoes down the hallway and the disconsolate mutter of the priestesses goes suddenly silent.

Paia shivers with the usual thrill of fear, but she cannot repress a prideful grin. He is out there, filling the whole length of the corridor with his heat and speed and magnificence. What is he doing here? The God has never accompanied her in any sort of procession. All the rituals dictate that she must come to him. Paia waits. His approach is noiseless. Not a sound but the Honor guard snapping to shocked attention, followed by the soft flopping of twelve terrified young women flattening every possible inch of their bodies against the threadbare rug. The chambermaid has her back to the door and cannot sense the God's entrance. When he sails through the door, it's only the shifting of Paia's eyes that alerts her.

Paia tries not to look at him and fails. He is as tall and

broad as the corridor will reasonably allow, and caparisoned in gold and flashing jewels, like a barbarian emperor. His vest shimmers with thousands of tiny sun-disks that ring like breathy cymbals as he moves. Luco may have seemed to glow, but the God actually gives off light, and he brings with him a hot, crisp scent, as if he's just charged through a furnace. The chambermaid nearly strangles on her own swallowed squawk and collapses into the tiniest ball she can manage. But even she is sneaking a peek.

Paia bows deeply, as the God expects her to do when the Faithful are about. Their relationship may be evolving all of a sudden, but it would be folly to air the process in public. "You look absolutely splendid today, my lord Fire."

And he does. He has taken extra care with this manifestation. His nod is faint and lordly. "I have come to grant my priestess the honor of my presence at her Leave-taking."

In other words, time you got going. Paia bows again, wondering if this gesture was his idea or Luco's. "A grave honor indeed, my lord."

His brief ironic glance answers her question. He turns away abruptly, beckoning with a gold-tipped finger, and sweeps grandly out the door. Paia tosses a quick regretful look at the still-shrouded painting leaning against the wall. Something else that will have to wait. She has been summoned and she must follow. The chambermaid scrambles up and scurries after her.

On the stairs, Paia holds herself the ritual five paces behind, but somehow—with a trick he's never offered before in man-form—the God's voice is at her right ear, not in her head but just outside it—intimate but noninvasive, like a whisper from inches away. And she is able to answer him in a murmur.

"You have remembered the gun."

"Yes, my lord."

"Go nowhere without it. You have packed sufficient ammunition?"

What does he consider sufficient? "Yes, my lord."

"The sun is your deadly enemy, remember. You've brought protective garments?"

"Of course." Paia is not fooled by his rough, clipped

tone. The God is anxious. Perhaps he is not so eager to be rid of her after all. "Lord Fire, you are mothering me."

"You are reckless, my priestess."

"All in your service, my lord."

He snorts. "Has it not even occurred to you to wonder about this restlessness of yours, where it has come from all of a sudden?"

Paia cannot think of a clever response. Nor does she know the answer.

Ahead of her, his broad shoulders shift beneath their rich cloth-of-gold. "No matter. Go your way. Perhaps you will lead me to them. Meanwhile, I have ordered the First Son to pack safe food and water to last twelve days. He is charged to bring you back in eight. Not a day past, or his life will be forfeit."

"His *life*, my lord?"

"I have said so."

"But some delay might occur that Luco has no control over . . ."

"The First Son has agreed to the terms. Therefore, he will be extra vigilant to prevent such delays. My Word must be enforced, or chaos is upon us."

Chaos, again. Lately, all the God's anxieties seem to focus on the potential breakdown of his carefully ordered system. Paia's childhood history studies included the macabre dance of shifting political structures that played out during her father's lifetime. Considering that example, Paia thinks the God's obsession with chaos might be too narrow. For all this paranoia about his enemies, he never seems to allow that the real threat might come from a different brand of order.

The Ceremony of Farewell, hastily invented by one of Luco's trusted underlings, is held in the Sanctuary and is mercifully brief. It allows the Twelve to weep copiously and publicly beneath their red veils, then dry their eyes for a prayerful dance begging that their beloved priestess be soon returned to them. Paia, who has regarded them with increasing dislike and suspicion since they've begun dogging her every footstep, imagines the hot little seeds of hope her departure must be planting in each of them. Such as, perhaps the God is punishing her with this trip for some secret transgression. Perhaps disaster will befall her. Perhaps she will not return. Perhaps the God, in his infinite wisdom, will make one of them High Priestess. It's just as well, Paia decides, that she does not know their faces or names. Less need to be civil to them.

The Formal Progress from the Sanctuary to the Plaza includes a quick stop at the Sacred Well, where Paia sips the crystalline liquid from the scoop of her own palms, the only vessel deemed pure enough by the God to convey the sacred waters. She savors its chill perfection. It is the expression of an ideal. She wishes she could slip a bottle or two into her luggage. But for once, the God is standing there watching. The Twelve are so overcome by his sustained presence among them in man-form that they can barely manage their part in the ritual.

At last, the God leads the procession out into the blinding sun, past the stained sacrificial altar to where the First Son waits, with the full ranks of the priesthood lined up to left and right. Behind, a dust cloud rises as servants and bearers race about among the high-wheeled wagons and piles of packing crates, frenzied with last minute preparations. Luco's blue gaze is eager, though his jaw is set and serious. He bows abjectly to the God, then gestures him toward the towering bejeweled and golden throne that's been dragged out of the Sanctuary for the final Leave-taking. Off to one side, two of the elaborately decorated sedan chairs sit side by side. These are usually reserved for the Temple's most lavish and formal ceremonies. Virtually overnight, they've been refitted for the rigors of outdoor travel. The High Priestess and First Son of the Temple will ride. The goods will be hauled in the wagons by hand. Everyone else will walk.

The God ascends his throne, and under Son Luco's brisk direction, the ceremony begins. Paia always prefers it when Luco officiates. He's so much better at it than she is, with his grand manner and melodious voice. The First Son is a different man in public performance. He loses his fussy edge, becomes smoother, less self-conscious. Grateful to be only a passive participant in this unrehearsed production, Paia lets her mind wander, past the looming Temple gates, out into the valley, into the ruddy, stony hills ringing the Citadel, hills she will soon be crossing. Her sedan chair glitters in the sun, a tall gold box on sturdy gilded legs, the God Rampant embroidered in red on either side. She is relieved to see the chambermaid scurrying into an appropriately abject position beside it, suddenly and miraculously dressed for the road. She is far less relieved when two of the red-robed Twelve detach themselves from the processional with all indications of joining the escort party. Paia sighs. The God—in his wisdom, of course—has made sure to supply her with chaperones.

Later, Paia will be unable to recall a single detail of the elaborate ceremony. It assembles the total populations of Temple and Citadel, and goes on for entirely too long, praising the God's wisdom and perfection, beseeching him to see to the safety of the High Priestess as she goes about her holy duties among the Faithful out in the world. There is chanting and motion, and eventually the crowds murmur aside. Paia comes out of her daze to find herself facing the outer gates, a direction that for so long has been forbidden even to consider. As the long bolt shafts are drawn back into the wall, reality at last takes hold. Her awareness irises in to a pinpoint of concentration on the great central locking mechanism with its polished, God-shaped escutcheon plate. She is finally leaving the confines of the Temple. Will anything out there be as she remembers?

After another eternity of chanting and prayers, the God stands and spreads his golden arms. The First Son sweeps forward to hand the High Priestess into the curtained door of her chair. As the gauzy metallic drapes swing loose to veil the shaded interior, the four bearers lift and steady. The God vanishes from his throne in an explosion of flame and light. The throng falls to its knees as a vast shadow of wings passes in threat and benediction over the sun-baked courtyard. The gates roll open. Across the upper landing, the Grand Stair lies waiting. The caravan starts forward.

A twelve-man contingent of the Honor Guard leads the way, followed by the First Son with as many of his Seconds and Thirds as could be spared from the day-to-day running of the Temple. Paia is surprised by the number of them: twenty at least, if she hasn't counted the same one twice. Her own two chaperones pass through the gates next, then Paia in her chair with her servants behind. Behind them, more Honor Guard, more servants, and finally, the supply wagons. Overhead, the God flies long, swooping figure eights etched in flame. Inside the chair, a fiery night descends each time he passes. Paia approaches the Grand Stair. Abruptly, she is terrified.

What have I done?

But this is the sort of terror she is used to, like her terror of the God, mixed with exhilaration. She is practiced at dealing with it. And turning back, she has decided, is not an alternative.

The steps are low, six meters wide and a meter deep. The chair tilts forward only gently, and the bearers fall into a mildly rocking rhythm to manage the descent. The chair looks light enough, but there's a reason it takes four strong men to carry it. It's become a self-contained mini-fortress. Luco has explained to her how it carries extra food and water, and is hardened to deflect knife blades, spear, axes, arrows, even a small caliber bullet, though the God has promised Paia there won't be any of those around, except in her own hands. She tells herself she's safe, but she's certainly not comfortable. It's hot and airless inside. Already her skin is slick, and her fine silk robe is soaking up the damp. As the rocking continues, Paia begins to doubt the steadiness of her stomach.

She parts the curtains, only a crack. The outside air is no cooler, but at least it's in vague motion and she can fix her eyes on the steadier horizon. A thin crowd lines either side of the stairs, sun-toughened men and women from the village at the bottom. She should know some of these scarred and withered faces. Living so nearby, they will have made the long climb to the Temple most often. But Paia has endured her years of ritual specifically by not looking at the faces of the Faithful. She vows to change this practice when she returns.

As her chair passes, the villagers shove their few scrawny children forward to wave at her. There is maybe one child for every fifteen adults. Paia had thought the God's repopulation efforts had been going better lately, but she sees no toddlers or infants at all. Perhaps the mothers will no longer risk exposing them to the sun and crowds, even for such a special occasion.

A glance behind, back up the stairs, distracts Paia from her nausea. The gates are still open, as the last of the supply wagons clatter through and gather on the broad upper landing to be unloaded for transport down the steps. The gates are each four meters wide, double-walled steel taken from the hangar where Paia's father stored his armored vehicles. They are set into stone walls two meters thick by seven high. Since the God ordered these walls built, no force has bested them, though Paia has heard that during the Wars of Conversion, several respectable attempts were made. She has always thought that Luco's readiness to bore her with the old war stories is one of his few personal weaknesses. But gazing up at those scarred and sun-bleached walls for the first time, she wishes she'd done more than just humor him. If she'd also listened, she could have learned. She thinks how much the House Computer would approve of this insight, and then, how useful it would be to have House along. This Visitation will make her a student all over again, except that, this time, she has some idea of how little she knows.

That vow again: to be a more intent observer.

From the central gates, the wall runs off about thirty meters to either side, then turns back toward the cliff and the Temple. A tall slender watchtower marks each corner. Through the open gateway and over the crenellated top of the wall, Paia can see the Temple's elaborately carved façade, and the bland natural rock face of the Citadel rising behind it. Reality takes hold again. Impulsively, she shoves aside the curtain and leans out into the sun, ignoring the villagers' pious stares. She cranes awkwardly around the hard edge of the doorframe to count the windows glimmering high on the cliff. She is seized with an urgent need to identify her own, before all that's familiar is behind her and out of sight.

But it's only eight days!

Paia is shaken by a sudden intimation of a chasm crossed, of an irrevocable step taken toward a new life, at the moment she passed through the gates. She counts and searches as her chair rocks downward, until she picks out her level, her room, her very own window. Only then can she grasp at her dignity again, and withdraw into the shade of her tiny mobile fortress, obscurely comforted.

In Paia's father's time, big carpeted elevators transported Citadel guests and residents up from the valley floor. They were fitted with solid brass and lined with polished hard-wood. When the God came, he proclaimed them an unreliable luxury, even though they were powered by the windmills up on the cliff top and hardly ever failed. Paia suspects they were simply not magnificent enough for his purposes. He built the Grand Stair to *really* impress, with its five hundred massive steps and carved railings. The climb to Paia's tower studio is a mere hop by comparison. But the Grand Stair is not just decorative. It serves also as a first line of defense against attackers, and further, as a test of a worshiper's devotion. For it is the God's opinion—shared (Paia believes) by his loyal general, Son Luco—that anyone who gives up before they've reached the top can't be counted on for much anyway.

At the halfway point, where the cliff is sheerest, the stairs level out into a shallow landing, then split to left and right to move across and down the face of the rock. The chair is set down, and the bearers are given a brief breather. Paia has a view through the parted drapes of the valley below, and the bright meander of the dry riverbed crossed by the straight line of road that once led to her father's airstrip and thus, back to civilization. Leaning out a bit farther, she can just see the roofs and chimneys of the village huddled at the bottom of the steps.

Each night at the Citadel, most often shrouded from Paia's high window view by darkness, but now and then glimpsed by moonlight, a human chain five hundred steps long transfers food and goods from the Temple's dependent villages up to the Citadel. Paia is not supposed to know about such things. Once she questioned Luco about it, just casually, and he pretended she'd spotted the rare occurrence. At the time, she reasoned that the chain was easier than requiring each bearer to walk all the way up and all the way down. But surely it's a bit foolish that *all* the supplies for this trip were hauled *all* the way up, only to be brought *all* the way back down again. Paia approves of the rigorous safety inspection that anything slated for her consumption must pass, but out here in the broiling sun, with half the stairs looming high behind and the other half, like a drop into nowhere, still to descend, the waste of energy seems, well, irresponsible. Not a concept Paia has thought much about before.

As her bearers hoist the stout carrying poles onto their shoulders and set off again on their rocking descent, Paia muses over the possibility that the God prefers this hard show of human labor over the mysterious ease of a mechanism he does not understand.

The village at the bottom began its life in her father's time, clustered around the entrance to the elevators, as housing for service and maintenance personnel, for the tenant farmers and their families, and for anyone in his employ who, despite the obvious security disadvantage, could not bring themselves to live tucked away in the bowels of a cliff. Paia recalls it as a sizable, tidy gathering of tight stone houses and fenced garden plots. She recalls attending a birthday celebration down there, dressed in a new outfit sewn by her mother's seamstresses, who also lived in the village. Her mother brought the cake, and her nanny brought a bundle of clothing that Paia had outgrown. These were passed among the children at the party to be tried on for size, and everyone went home happy. Except perhaps Paia's mother, whose natural generosity was encouraged by the sure knowledge that she could never have another child. Paia also remembers a wedding, somewhat later, where she carried a bouquet of patchwork flowers lovingly sewn from the fabric of some of those old outfits. The bride carried real flowers, from Paia's father's greenhouses, but Paia preferred the patchwork ones. She still has one somewhere, she thinks. Odd that she should recall such detail, after so long. It must be looking down on those blue slate rooftops that brings it back so vividly.

But when the last stair is behind her and her chair is at last traveling on level ground, Paia does not find herself in the quaint village of her memory. The stone houses still stand, but the slate roofs are cracked and patchy. Red dust is caked into every seam. The once-colorful doors and windows have gone unpainted for decades. Their storm shutters are missing or broken, and where the neatly fenced gardens once struggled but grew, ragged clusters of hovels and shanties have sprung up, filling all the spaces between. Apparently, for many, living within the safer shadow of the Temple is worth any sort of discomfort.

Here also, along the barren main street, villagers are lined up to greet their High Priestess. They pray aloud for her safe journey and swift return. One woman calls out a fervent wish that the Last Days not come upon them while the Priestess is away from the Temple. Paia sees several soldiers of the Temple moving roughly among them. She would like to believe that the villagers' good wishes are genuine, but she can't help but notice that where the soldiers are, there also is the crowd's most passionate response. She considers her rash promise to the God. How will she speak of loving to these desperate folk who are taught only fear?

She is glad that, because these Faithful have daily access to the Temple, the procession does not stop for a formal Visitation. She is not yet ready to face them directly. Soon her chair has passed down the main street and is headed out across the valley floor.

Once, before even her father's time, this was fertile bottom land. There was water in the riverbed and trees along its banks and rain enough to grow grain, to pasture livestock without irrigation. Current agricultural information would never be offered to the High Priestess, but in the Citadel, Paia habitually eavesdrops. She has learned from her Honor Guard how the fields are now sized by how much water can be spared from the village's shrinking wells, and then by how far that water can be transported without being stolen. Even pipes can be surreptitiously rerouted, and the best-armed parties ambushed.

Leaving the last group of hovels behind, the procession passes among the high stockade fences surrounding the vegetable plots. The livestock are similarly contained. Paia hears chickens and goats and the occasional sheep, but sees nothing but walls of weathered timber patched with bits of sun-brittled plastic. Soon, even that is behind them and there is only untilled, uninhabited ground ahead. Overhead, the God executes a final glittering omega over the line of wagons. His cry shakes the ground like the thunder of an avalanche, but Paia hears his farewell inside her head, terse, resentful, full of longing. Could he not just come with her, and delight the villages with the honor? She sighs. Surely there has never been a more complex being than the God.

The valley seems wider, far more open than she recalls, though Paia doubts that she's recalling trees from her own memories. Those were already rare enough when she was young. Through the slit in her curtains, she can see a few softening patches across the valley, gray-green, tucked away in the shaded rocky folds of the hills where a bit of dew might regularly collect. She thinks of the shrouded painting in her room, the way it first appeared to her, ripe with foliage and moisture. She hopes the road will lead the caravan through one of those distant greening patches. She would like the chance to walk among real trees, not one or two but a whole gathering, a grove, tall and cooling. There must be a few left out there . . . somewhere. Out on the baking flat, irrigated fields give way to parched wasteland. Paia feels exposed and vulnerable, breathless, as if the very air were being evaporated from her lungs. Her view through the draperies becomes mobile, blurring and dancing with the rising heat. The stained sky looms like a weight, endlessly falling in on top of her. Nausea returns, stirred by agoraphobic panic. Paia shivers and draws the curtains tight.

It is too soon to be so out of control. As the caravan crawls across the valley floor, she gives herself a stern talking-to inside her hot golden box. She knows how to live with fear. She must now learn to live with discomfort. The heat is so much worse than she'd imagined, and the landscape so much more desolate, even though she has painted it for years. But that was from a distance. She has taken the cooling effects of the Citadel's bedrock too much for granted. But she has asked for, no, *demanded* this trip. Therefore she must suffer it gladly, for the honor of the God and the Temple, as well as for her own self-respect. Calling up the meditative state that gets her through the longest and most tedious of the Temple rituals, she settles into a heat-drenched trance.

This holds her steady until the rhythm of the bearers' pace alters suddenly, shaking her awake. The chair tilts backward, rising raggedly. Paia bolts upright in her padded seat. She fears they've turned around, that they're fleeing back up the Guard Stair to the Temple. The bright sun on her curtains fades as the chair passes into shadow. A shouted order rings out from up ahead. The caravan straggles to a halt. Paia reaches for the God's gun. Are they under attack?

She parts the curtains, and is assailed by clouds of dust.

Settling, it reveals a sheer stone face, but no sign of mayhem or panic. The bearers set down the chair, releasing
their cramped muscles with exhausted groans. Paia peers
ahead. They have entered a narrow defile, barely wide
enough for the wagons to pass. Wind-shaped rock walls
tower on both sides. Dusty clumps of bushes cling to cracks
and spring up between the boulders where landslides have
breached the sides of the canyon. The dry, rising ribbon of
road is treacherous with loose stones and gravel.

Dust swirls up again as Son Luco strides toward her
along the length of the caravan. He has put off his ceremonial trappings, leaving only the loose white pants and shirt,
and a red robe that floats gracefully open behind him. He
has, Paia thinks, an odd look on his face, as he checks in
with each wagon and contingent, even the servants. Odd,
that is, for Luco. He looks . ... relaxed. More at ease out
here in the heat and grit than she has ever seen him in the
Citadel, as if he has shed a part of himself along with his
Temple finery. Disconcerted, Paia withdraws into her protective shade. Luco arrives and peers in at her. She cannot
hide the hints of panic in her hooded eyes.

"Mother Paia. How are you managing?"

She knows he's used her title as a reminder to set a
good example for the rest of the caravan. As always, his
officiousness piques her, which was perhaps intended, for
her panic recedes.

"Less well than yourself, First Son . . . apparently." Paia
coughs as the dust he has brought enters her sanctuary.

"It's good to be out and about," he replies. "In the air."

What air? She tries for banter. "Very much the handsome captain, aren't you now? Is this what it's like going
to war? I think you must have enjoyed it more than you're
willing to admit."

He smiles blandly. "Once a soldier, always a soldier."

She can feel his concentration diffusing beyond her, up
and down the line of wagons and farther, out into the surrounding hills. Alert and listening, even as he converses
with her casually. Paia is reminded that every step away
from the Citadel leads them farther into danger.

"We'll rest here a bit," he says. "It's safe enough in the
hill shadow. Come out and stretch your legs. Are you
drinking your water as advised?"

"Water. What a good idea."

The well-used canteen from her father's backpack waits on the seat beside her, full to the brim and even a bit cool. Paia downs several gulps, then swings the strap over her head and shoulder as she steps down from the chair. The water hits her stomach hard and threatens to rebound. Her legs have no strength. She staggers, grasping at the door-frame.

Luco catches her arm and steadies her. He sends the bearers off to refresh themselves. "You haven't been drinking."

"I will from now on," she murmurs.

"We're not tucked away safe anymore."

"I know that." Snapping at him revives her slightly. "You needn't treat me like an idiot."

"Then don't act like one. For all our sakes, if not for your own. Drink some more. Slowly."

She knows he will stand there till she does. The God has charged him with her safety. She is out of the Citadel, but she is still not free. She takes little sips, then wipes her mouth on her sleeve as unceremoniously as possible. "Where are we?"

Luco looks away, as if toward the valley, but his eyes seem to gaze on a far greater distance. "I fought a great battle here. In the service of the God."

"Does the place have a name? Perhaps we should name it after you."

After a moment, he says, very quietly, "It already has a name, my priestess."

"And what is that, my priest?"

"Whose answer would you prefer, mine or the God's?"

Paia swallows a gasp. Sacrilege from the First Son? "Are they different?"

His mouth quirks at some private thought. "The God calls it, rather eloquently, I think, The Sunrise Passage. But to me, and those who live around it, this is Cauldwell's Clove. The only negotiable road out of the valley."

She stares at him. "But that's my name! Or it was." She has almost forgotten she had a family name. She hasn't heard it spoken in years. She hesitates even to repeat it, for fear she will burst into tears.

He looks down at her. "Is that so?"

The God has outlawed any history of the Citadel or its former owners to all but herself. Still, knowledge persists. "You knew that, didn't you?"

Luco's expression grows odder still, rich with nuance that Paia cannot interpret. Squinting up at him, she is rocked by sudden intuition that she at first denies and then accepts entirely. But it's not possible! Surely he would have said something, even though it would put him in danger of heresy. For the same reason, she has never thought to ask him.

"Luco!" she hisses. "Did you *know* my father?"

"I did not say . . ."

"Luco, please? I won't tell anyone!"

His face closes. "The God does not permit . . ."

"Luco! Did you?"

"This conversation is in violation of the laws of the Temple, my priestess."

"Oh, Luco! You started it."

He nods, lips pressed tight. "And I greatly regret my lapse."

"But we're out in the middle of nowhere! Who could possibly . . . ?"

He touches her arm in warning, then booms jovially, "Ah, here are your Faithful, come to see to their mistress at last."

Instantly, Paia smoothes the urgency from her face. The red-robed Two, still veiled as if at the Temple's highest ritual, are bearing down with water and food and a damp cloth to bathe their Priestess' sweated brow. Their postures seem to exclude Luco from this women's privilege. It occurs to Paia that the First Daughters might be reporting to someone other than the First Son.

Luco bows. "Mother Paia, with your permission, I leave you in these devoted hands. See that they find you a good spot in the bushes."

You knew my father?

She cannot call him back, or allow herself to stare after him as he strides briskly away. It would draw undue attention to a conversation the God would not look well upon. And after that, Luco keeps his distance. All during the difficult climb through the rock-strewn gorge, at the many rest stops or in the several places where the twisting path is so precipitous that even the High Priestess must leave the comfort of her chair and proceed on foot, for her own safety, Luco avoids her. Or if he does appear, he comes in the company of at least two of his acolytes. Paia is hurt by his reflex paranoia. Does he really think she would report so minor a heresy to the God? Or even carelessly refer to it, especially when it would mean so much to her to know for sure, to be able to talk to someone who knew her father? And, if he's so fearful, what moment of weakness brought the name out of him in the first place?

Late in the day, the upward path levels into a wider sort of road and crosses an open plateau toward a notch between two hills. The road disappears into the notch, but a village nestles at the mouth of it, sunk in afternoon shadow. Paia spots the livestock before she sees the village, tired-looking cattle and thin sheep grazing fitfully among the thornbushes and scrub. They are guarded by small crowds of men armed with knives and spears, plus a few big dogs who stare sullenly at the caravan as it passes. The dogs catch Paia's interest especially. Her family always kept dogs, but the God banished all animals from the Citadel when he came.

Along with people's family names.

Cauldwell. The sound of it rings in her mind as if Luco had just spoken it. Paia shoves away the thought. These dogs are scruffy and half-feral, and do not waste their energy barking, but still, she's encouraged. If this village can feed dogs, they must be feeding themselves well enough.

In the village outskirts, the caravan passes vegetable plots surrounded by stone walls wide enough to walk along, as Paia sees three women doing. They patrol the garden perimeter, using their sharpened poles as walking sticks. They stop and draw together to watch the procession go by. They seem more apprehensive than excited. Paia would like to think they're simply unaware of who their visitor is, but she cannot help but notice the tallest one's quick and anxious scanning of the sky.

Inside the village, a less ambivalent welcome has been prepared. A party of local clergy awaits them at the head of the dusty main street, and the caravan proceeds grandly into town, past several clusters of dilapidated stone houses and barns, to pull up in a semicircle on the flagstones of the central square, which appear to be freshly swept. Paia peeks invisibly through her draperies. She has been set down at one side of the square, facing the Temple Chapter House, so that she has a perfect view of the image laid in reddish lavender stones, crude but recognizable, and dark against the paler gray: the Winged God Rampant.

She looks about for Luco, hoping for a chance to speak in private. But the local Temple does not wish to be thought lackadaisical or unprepared. The caravan is immediately swept up in a fervent and lengthy Ritual of Welcome. And from there, the evening progresses much as Paia might expect, in fact, more or less as she had envisioned when she came up with the idea of this trip, at least until toward the end. The joyous welcome is led by the head priest of the chapter. There are several priestesses as well, all properly veiled like Paia's own Temple Daughters, but vested in dark purple, as befits their lower rank. None of the local clergy attempt to converse with the High Priestess, and Paia guesses from their nervous but practiced manner that all are well versed in the appropriate behaviors. They are whole, well fed and healthy, the cream of the village crop. Each has doubtless paid many visits to the Mother Temple and would not wish to appear provincial.

After the Ritual of Welcome, the High Priestess is formally entreated to walk among the Faithful of the town. This is the part Paia has been dreading. The Faithful must be able to touch her directly. For that, she must remove her protective robe and expose herself in the flimsy Temple garments to the sun and the hot, dusty wind as she has never done before, as well as to whatever disease and impulse toward violence might lurk within the crowd. But this ritual is central to Temple doctrine and must never be denied. The health and physical perfection of the High Priestess is the miraculous proof of the God's favor. The Rite of Touching, the God himself insists, brings the Faithful closer to him.

With a grand gesture, Paia tosses back her hood and shrugs the robe back into the waiting hands of her priestesses. An awed murmur rises and falls in the crowd. So far, she has not disappointed.

As the local priest falls in on one side and Son Luco on the other, Paia processes around the sides of the square, where the townspeople are gathered. They have washed and scrubbed and still they appear soiled, as if stained by their toil in the parched earth and by the awful sun. Some kneel, some do not. It doesn't matter. Paia is taller than any of them, and Son Luco appears among them as a giant. Their eyes are weary, yet hands reach eagerly for a touch of holy flesh. Paia usually endures the touching rites without response. But here, out in the open, with the sun slanting away toward the hilltops and the smoke from the cook fires tickling her nostrils, she is impelled to a more genuine contact. She stretches out her own hands as she moves down the line, grasping bony fingertips and brown wrists, worn and wrinkled elbows, scarred stumps and twisted limbs. The delighted crowd sighs its gratitude for this unexpected blessing. A step behind her, Son Luco clears his throat, either in disapproval or surprise. Paia does not meet his glance. She doesn't want to know what the First Son thinks right now. Probably that she is taking too long, and holding up the next stage of the ritual. But she's enjoying the smiles and wonder that her touch freely offered brings to the faces of these simple people. She is moved by the sense of connection. Perhaps this is how she can preach love of the God to them, not with words but action. Love given must be returned in some fashion, she reasons. If the God cannot love his Faithful, perhaps his High Priestess can do it for him.

She has completed three sides of her slow progress around the square when Son Luco deflects her with a murmured warning about overexposure.

"Please behave," he says, then deftly whisks her into the waiting arms of her red-veiled chaperones. The two priestesses grandly fling her robe about her naked shoulders and use their grasp on its sleeves to maneuver her onward to the Confirmation of the Clergy, where Paia must anoint each priest and priestess of the local chapter with the God's special blessing. This ceremony is plainly considered to be the more important one, at least by the clergy. After the blessing comes a recitation of the chapter's history, and the honors bestowed on it by the God. After that, a long presentation by the head priest, detailing the duties of the Faithful in the Last Days of the World. He is not a compelling speaker, but Paia judges him as sincere verging on fanatical when he interprets the total lack of rainfall in so many months as a blessing from the God to hasten the holy End.

Finally, just at dark, torches are lit and a grand feast is laid in the center of the square. Paia is surprised to find herself ravenous, despite a long day of discomfort, boredom, and nausea. There are not enough tables to offer the High Priestess the honor of a private one without seating the First Son among the locals. This was decided to be the more inappropriate, so Luco sits beside her at the high table, facing the rest of the clergy at a longer table set in front of them, all of them surrounded by the Faithful who must sit on the flagstones. To Paia, it feels too much like the hated Lunch at the Citadel. But at least there is food enough to go around.

Paia lifts a morsel of stewed rabbit on her fork. "Tastes just like home." Though of course it doesn't.

"It ought to." Luco smiles graciously as a villager elder bows before them with a platter of fresh radishes. "Did you think we raised our food ourselves all these years?"

"Of course not, though it's no thanks to you that I know any better. Even in my father's day, our food came from the villages." She nibbles at the rabbit pensively. "Luco . . . ?"

"No. Don't ask. I beg you." He blots his lips and folds his napkin in a precise triangle. "I knew this was a bad idea."

He looks more wary and tired than he has all day. Each dish that comes to the table, he tastes himself before allowing Paia a portion. He is in eye contact with each of the six men from her Honor Guard who are currently arrayed at a discreet distance from the table, and Paia catches him polling them regularly. But Paia cannot imagine what the First Son is so worried about. The humble little square is filled with the loyal Faithful, and their attention is mostly on the food. They are probably delighted to be eating better than they have in months. She sips gingerly at the odd wood-scented wine, sorry that the God's intemperate death threats have kept Luco from enjoying his meal.

She tries a less sensitive subject. "How inspiring that this town's deep faith impels them to such great generosity."

Luco chews, nodding neutrally.

"It's a miracle they can grow anything at all out here.

It's so much drier than I expected. Is it true what the priest said, that there's been absolutely no rain at all?"

"None that I know of."

"Is this a change, First Son? A sign that conditions are worsening?"

"It is."

"Well, we must ask less of them for the Temple."

Luco's fork hesitates midway, then continues to his mouth. "The God will not agree with you."

"Or we must help them somehow. In my father's day, there were pipelines and . . . Luco?"

"You will excuse me, my priestess. Now that the formalities are done, I must see to Temple business while all are here assembled."

He rises, and spends the rest of the meal working the lower table. He is clearly relieved when Paia, her servants, and the two Daughters of the Temple are ushered into the Chapter House to spend the night. It's only one dingy room with a stone floor and an attached privy, but a high row of windows along each side provides good ventilation. Paia decides to let Luco do all the worrying, since he seems inclined to do it anyway. Resisting the fussing of the red-robed Two, she lets the chambermaid, who has been hovering nearby, prepare her for bed. When she lays herself out on the tall pile of sheep's wool mattresses provided for her comfort, she falls instantly asleep.

And she dreams, oh, such dreams. So many and so rich. It must be the food, or being out in the open air. All her nights up till this one seem quiet by comparison, as if the bedrock of the Citadel somehow stifled her dreaming and now she is making up for lost time.

Images flash by, too many and too sudden to hold on to. Strange faces and places, and others she recognizes. Her father, for instance, lecturing her gravely about duty and responsibility. But he is surrounded by huge piles of books that topple and bury him before he can tell her what duty he's talking about. The books all crumble into dust that swirls up in clouds like the dust on the road. When it clears, there is no sign of her father. She is standing in front of the painting, back at the Citadel. The landscape is as it was when she first saw it, lush, green, inviting—in tragic contrast with the desiccated countryside she has been traveling

through. It sits on a tall easel in a darkened room. A huge
gilt frame surrounds it, overwhelming its simpler beauties
with gaudy carvings of fruit and flowers. As she moves
closer, the carvings resolve into the sinuous figures of
dragons, intertwined, chasing each other around the
frame. Tiny jewels sparkle in their eyes: ruby, sapphire,
emerald, diamond.

She moves closer, searching for the image of the God in
the carving. Frame and landscape enlarge. She stands in
front of the painting as if before an enormous window. A
breath of wind tousles her hair, and the window becomes
an open doorway. The frame is the stone portal that guards
the entrance to the House Computer's inner sanctum in the
Citadel Library, but the Library is nowhere in view.

PAIA!

Someone is calling from outside the door, in a musical
lilt that makes her very name sound magical, as if the wind
itself were speaking.

PAIA!

The sweet voice resonates in the same place inside her
as the God's silent summons. Paia peers around the side
of the portal, sees no one.

PAIA!

Perhaps the caller is just beyond those trees. Paia steps
forward.

With a roar and a flash, her way is barred by a sudden
curtain of flame. White heat sears her eyelashes and hair.
Paia stumbles backward with a cry, and wakes.

At first, she thinks she's in her own room, then she
doesn't know where she is. Then she's sure she's still
sleeping.

The God is standing at the foot of her bed. The room is
the same darkened room of her dream except for the God,
who shimmers with his own angry glow. Paia waits for him
to speak. But he just stares at her, for so long that the hot
rage cools in his eyes, fading to gray. His light seeps out
of the room like the end of day, and Paia is overcome by
inexplicable grief. She bolts upright. Dream or not, she
reaches for him. "My lord!"

The God eyes her bleakly, then shakes his head and turns
away, a faint glow gliding through darkness like a fish
through soundless depths, back and forth, back and forth.

"Do you find it beautiful, all that damp and green?"

Paia swallows. Yes is obviously the wrong answer.

"What about me? Am I not beautiful? Is not the kingdom I've created more beautiful than this?"

He gestures into the darkness, and the painting reappears, only to explode into flame. Even as it burns, Paia can see the trees dying and the landscape shriveling into desert. A sob rises in her throat, but she holds her tongue. The servants and Temple Daughters sleep on as if nothing could wake them.

"She seeks to win you to their cause, beloved."

"She, my lord?" His enemies have never had a gender before.

"My sister."

"Your *what?*" Now Paia is sure she is dreaming, though the tears on her cheeks feel real enough.

"My sister, who plagues me even from the confines of her prison." He paces away. "Well. How goes your Visitation so far? Are you teaching the Faithful to love me?"

She absorbs his bitterness like a lash. "They will, if they follow my example. If only you would be there with me, the teaching would be simple."

The God rolls his golden eyes at her.

"My lord, a dream means nothing! Why do you insist on doubting me?"

"THIS dream means everything! I wasn't sure how deeply she had touched you. Now I know, even if you do not." He paces back to stand beside the bed, then sits, though the sheep's wool mattresses show no sign of added weight. He stares searchingly into Paia's face as if into the farthest reaches of her soul. He traces the shape of her chin with his palm, millimeters from her skin, and the tears dry on her cheeks.

"Oh, my dearest lord," she whispers.

He leans in as if to kiss her, but Paia feels only heat, little tongues of flame licking at her lips, curling into her parted mouth, seeking the back of her throat. It is both intense pain and deepest pleasure, but Paia smells no burning flesh so the only sensation she knows is real is her overwhelming surge of desire. If only she could press herself against him, let his glorious heat fill her in all ways. But to grasp him now would be to grasp air. The pain and her hunger take her together like a whirlwind. Whimpers and groans mix deep in her throat.

Abruptly, he pulls away, leaving her gasping. Her mouth feels like it's been stung by a thousand bees. She touches her tongue to her lips delicately.

"Have I damaged you, my priestess?"

Paia has never seen the God's perfect face so taut with rage and tragedy. "I . . . don't think so."

"You see how it is, then."

"Yes. I see." What Paia really sees is their private ritual of Holy Ecstasy for what it is: the only way the God can pleasure her as a man would do. What, she wonders, does he get out of it? "Is there no other way?"

After a long moment, he replies, "I have managed much. This I cannot. And because of this, you will betray me."

Returning grief stuns her, stealing the protest from her mouth. As she struggles to speak, the God holds up a gilded hand. "Do not make promises you do not understand." When he sighs, it is like the magma rumbling at the volcano's heart. "It is not your fault. You lack the means to resist them."

"I will not believe it!"

"How would you know?" He sighs again, looks down. "Perhaps you are right. I should not have kept you so long in ignorance."

"My lord Fire . . ."

"Do not speak." He stands, insubstantial as air, as weighty as centuries. "I will have the painting destroyed," he says, and vanishes.

And Paia wakes, this time for certain, amid the snoring of the other priestesses. Her fists and jaw are clenched, her pillow slick with tears.

How can this be?

If her father's library holds the truth, if the long centuries of blood and history have truly decreed this indelible bond, why would it be shaped in a way that can only break both their hearts? What purpose would there be in it?

Surely history has gone wrong somehow.

For the rest of the long night, Paia ponders how to even think about putting it right.

Chapter Twenty-eight

The Tinkers will not be rushed. After two idle days of waiting through their prep for the big trade expedition, N'Doch and the baron are getting restless. For different reasons, of course. N'Doch, because he's picking it up from the dragons, no matter how hard he tries to resist. The baron, because restlessness is his natural state, as far as N'Doch can tell.

Mostly to bug him, N'Doch pretends to relish the long hot days spent mostly within hands' reach of Blind Rachel's chill pool.

"You just gotta lighten up some, Dolph. A little r 'n r is good for a man of war like yerself." He trails his hand in the cooling water, then drips it luxuriously across his bare chest.

Köthen merely grunts, then spits on the honing stone he's cadged off Luther and sets the blade of his dagger to the dampened surface. "I've many times wished for Hal Engle at my side," he muses, rotating the already lethal steel in small, precise circles, "but now more than ever."

"What? I'm not good enough for you?"

Without ceasing his honing, Köthen gazes out into the amber darkness of the dusk-shadowed woods. "Hal Engle knows everything there is to know about dragons. He would know how best to kill one, I imagine."

N'Doch sits up straighter. "Whoa. No one's said anything about killing. If this 'monsta' of theirs is Fire, and he *has* got Air stashed away someplace, killing him ain't gonna help us one bit."

"But it might help the local populace."

"Hey, man, you didn't even want to be here. What the hell d'you care about the local populace?"

Köthen shrugs, not a thing N'Doch sees him do all that often, since the baron's not much into either indecision or ambivalence. "They appear to be in need, and they have requested our help."

"Oh. I get it." N'Doch nods sagely, wondering how he got so brave, to be talking like this to a man with both a temper and a very sharp blade. "Now I know the kinda guy you are. You think you can fix everything, right? Whatever's wrong, you're gonna be the man for it."

Köthen doesn't leave off making his neat little circles on the stone. "There's no success without effort."

The man's self-restraint is admirable, N'Doch decides, now that he's got it back in hand. He's settling in to his exile with the scary kind of patience that usually portends an explosion of action when the time comes. N'Doch's never known a man who could make his silences so loud. The Tinkers walk softly around Köthen, but never fail to let him know they're glad to have him as an ally. "You're just bored, is what you are. But listen up, Dolph. Don't you let the girl hear you talk about killing dragons."

Now Köthen looks up. "Perhaps if I did, it would finally affect the disillusionment I've been unable thus far to achieve."

"Mebbe. I wouldn't count on it, though."

An odd crackling off among the trees alerts them both.

"Horses," says Köthen, with mild wonder.

"Nah, c'mon. Here?" N'Doch gets to his feet, squinting into the dim spaces between the trunks and branches.

Köthen spits on his stone again, listening. "Horses, unshod. No riders. No, they're . . ." He looks up, frowning, as a crowd of large animals noses its way through the woods to the edge of the pool, followed by several of the Tinker children. "Ah, that's it. They're mules."

"Damn." N'Doch is impressed, both by Köthen's ear and the animals' size. They look strong and tough, if a bit on the thin side.

Köthen sheaths his dagger and stands to make room as

the herd lowers their long heads to drink. His hands move over them eagerly, smoothing flanks, assessing leg muscles. "There's some skill to breeding a good mule."

N'Doch stands back. He's not so easy being surrounded by large hoofed animals. "Wonder where they've been keeping them."

"Yo! Dockman!" Luther calls from behind. He slaps a lagging mule toward the water and ambles over to join them, gesturing at the stone in Köthen's belt. "Yu dun wit' dat?"

Köthen nods, offering it back. *"Ja, danka."*

"Time ta pack up, nah. Yu ready?"

"Betcha!" N'Doch waves a hand at the mule herd. "Where'd all this come from?"

"Up da hill sum. Dey's grass deah, sumat." Luther laughs, a mournful hollow sound. "Didna tink we was gonna haul dem waggins by oursels, didju? Das fer townfolk!"

When suddenly the next dawn proved to be departure day, Erde watched the hitchup with eager interest. The sturdy mules reminded her of Sir Hal's uncanny beast, and that set her worrying about how matters were in Deep Moor, and with the war. She wished Linden was here, for the youngest Tinker baby was ill with a mysterious ailment that their own herbalist could not seem to cure. Erde considered stealing the child and whisking it off to the dragon in the woods. He thought perhaps he could help. But the mother never left it alone for a minute, and it was still not time to let the Tinkers in on the true nature of their new allies.

It was good to be on the move again, even better that her heavy pack would travel in the wagons instead of on her back. Erde had been able to learn a lot in her two days at Blind Rachel, about the villagers and their dragon worship. The information had only upset her own dragons further, but it had decided them that confrontation was the best course, and that there was no time to lose. The search for Air would take a back seat to the search for Fire. Now both dragons were sure that one would lead to the other.

AND MEANWHILE, YOU WILL REST HERE AND BE COMFORTABLE?

I DO NOT NOTICE SUCH THINGS.

YOU NOTICE WHEN YOU'RE HUNGRY.

INDEED I DO, AND WE SHALL NEED TO BE THINKING ABOUT THAT SOON.

The woods around the Tinker camp were nearly barren of wildlife. Certainly there was nothing big enough to keep a dragon fed. Erde found herself gazing at the mules and averted her eyes guiltily.

I WILL BUY YOU SOMETHING FAT AND SWEET WHEN WE REACH THE VILLAGES.

If there is such a thing in the villages. And what will you buy it with, girl?

Leave it to Lady Water to come up with a fuller understanding of commerce. But for her dagger and the dragon brooch pinned inside her shirt, Erde had nothing of value.

I'LL TRADE FOR IT. I'LL THINK OF SOMETHING.

"Of course you will, little sister." The dragon-as-Sedou joined her, laughter in his eyes. "Don't mind me. All set to leave? The signal's been given. Come walk along with me. The day's just begun, yet I sense we are nearing our journey's end.

Earth felt it, too. He said it was like hearing a rumbling in the distance for ever so long, and then finally spotting the thunderhead. And the summons had strengthened again, he said, that silent call that only the dragons heard. Erde was sad to leave him behind again. She welcomed Sedou's company, since N'Doch had decided to walk with Baron Köthen in the rear. More than half the crew was going along, leaving only a handful of elderly to care for the rabbits and goats and to water the little kitchen gardens, plus a small warrior contingent assigned to the camp's defense.

But Erde understood why. Listening carefully over the past few days, especially to Luther who did not mince words, had made it clear that this trip was more than the usual "biz." Despite the beauty of their stronghold and Stoksie's irrepressible cheer, Blind Rachel Crew's situation was deteriorating. Their trade stocks were precariously low, their stores of staple foods even lower. Their survival as a community depended on the success of this expedition. At least the continuation of their water supply was now assured, though none of them knew it. Erde wished she could tell them, to relieve at least one source of their constant anxiety.

She and Sedou joined the line of wagons midway as it rolled out of camp. The road outward did not appear to be a road at all. The first several hours were a trek across crumbling stone ledges and dry, scrub-choked meadows. Erde pointed out to Sedou how both wagons and walkers spread out in a wide fan formation wherever space permitted.

"I believe they hope to leave as faint a trace of our passage as possible." He circled a hand in the air. "Not even much of a dust cloud raised."

She nodded, intrigued by the Tinkers' quiet methods of defense. Her father, Baron Josef, would have built a big stone wall around such a stronghold, then loudly challenged all comers to vanquish it.

Before the sun was high, the expedition was several leagues from the camp by Erde's estimation, stretched out in a long, lazy line. The pace had slowed to an odd kind of waiting. But then, at a call from up front, each walker and wagon turned abruptly left from where they were, and moved downslope into a broad stand of sharp-needled evergreens. These young trees looked so thick and healthy that Erde wondered if someone had been watering them, like they did back in camp. Passage between the trunks was so narrow that the rough branches scraped the sides of the bigger wagons. The mules groaned and protested, but on the other side of the grove, Erde saw they had come out onto what N'Doch would call a "real" road, paved like a castle courtyard with that pale seamless stone he called *concrete*. The low, heavy greenery screened their sideways approach to the road as effectively as any big stone wall, or perhaps more so, for the fact of not announcing itself.

Once on the road, though it was cracked and pitted and dotted with tall tufts of weeds, the expedition moved faster. They descended through dusty pine scrub onto more open slopes of thorn brush and brittle yellow grasses that rustled like a woman's skirts in the hot breezes. Here and there, a few stunted hardwoods clung to the hillsides, bent over with drought and wind. Along one such dry meadow, the Tinkers stopped to rest, by habit or common consent, Erde could never tell. Their decision-making process was often too diffuse for her even to detect. Two or three walkers left the road and plunged into the scrub, to answer a call of Nature, she assumed. But a wave from one brought another dozen leaping down from the carts and caravans, armed with buckets and long-handled baskets of metallic mesh. Others followed more slowly.

"Bluburry," announced Stoksie as he limped past, a bucket in each hand. "Real gud trade, bluburry. Be heah a while, den. Yu doin' okay, nah?"

Erde nodded gratefully, looking to Sedou for help with the English, which she could understand now but still had trouble pronouncing.

"Can we help?" Sedou asked, for them both.

Stoksie handed over one of his buckets with a gap-toothed grin. "Betcha!"

The berries were tiny but sweet. Erde couldn't resist nibbling a few, but all the Tinkers were doing the same. The picking went quickly with so many pickers, and consolidation produced an impressive crop. Several large buckets were capped and stowed. Watching Stoksie rub his hands in satisfaction, Erde thought, *every little bit helps.*

A small noon meal was shared out, with water from the big wooden casks lashed to each wagon. When the expedition moved on, a steady pace brought them down off the higher reaches and into the foothills by midafternoon. It was hotter there, and traces of civilization appeared. Very soon Erde understood Baron Köthen's dry bemusement at what he called N'Doch's "ridiculous luck," for stumbling upon the Tinkers and not someone more dangerous.

Her first hint was the ruins along the road, the crumbling stone foundations of farmsteads long ago deserted. These looked sad and lonely, but with a peaceful aura of having eased gradually back to Nature. After that came less comforting signs: structures more recently inhabited, not fallen back to the barren earth quickly enough to eradicate the high metal fences that had once surrounded them, now smashed and broken, or the wide dark scars of explosion and conflagration.

"Surely there was a war!" exclaimed Erde, after the seventh or eighth burned-out ruin.

The dragon-as-Sedou shook his head. "Mankind is a rabid animal destroying itself from within."

"No animal would so foul its nest. God set Man apart from the animals, to do His bidding, but Man will not follow His will."

"It's humanity's belief that they're different from animals that leads to all this." He gestured across the devastated landscape, his face stony with ancient despair. "Would any true god allow it?"

Erde's lips pursed. She regretted starting this conversation, for the dragon could talk circles around her. But there were certain perversions of dogma that she should not let pass unchallenged. "As if there could be more than one! My lady Water, you learn this pagan talk from your godless guide!"

"More from his brother, the martyr and idealist whose shape I walk in."

"A man you've never met."

"Yet who lives richly in the mind of the brother who loved him."

"Oh, how do you know what's really Sedou and what's merely N'Doch's memory of him?"

"I do not. Does it matter? Why do you say merely? Is it not mankind's dearest hope to be lovingly remembered when one no longer lives?"

"Mankind's dearest hope is salvation," Erde reminded him primly.

"Ah. Salvation."

She sensed mockery and frowned up at him.

The dragon-as-Sedou grinned. "Well, little sister? Did it never occur to you that some dragons—and their guides—might not be Christian?"

A shout from ahead saved her the cost of a foolish reply. The wagons halted and every Tinker without reins in their hands reached for a weapon.

"Uh-oh," murmured Sedou, sounding very much like N'Doch.

N'Doch and Baron Köthen came loping up from behind. Köthen had armed himself with a stout sharpened pole.

"Dochmann! Stay with milady!" he ordered, still moving forward. "Dragon man, come with me."

Sedou fell in beside him. "Dragon woman, you mean."

Köthen shook his head. "Woman dragon. Dragon man."

Sedou laughed, and the two of them trotted ahead, along the line of wagons. Next, Luther hurried by, with several others behind him.

"Should we go, too?" Erde asked N'Doch.

"We're safer here."

"No, I mean, don't you want to know what's happening?"

N'Doch stares at her. She's craning forward, this way and that, like an anxious bird. Either she's the bravest fool he's ever met, or she really has no idea. "Hey, we'll know soon enough. If it blows up into something serious, we'll go in as backup."

"Well, I'm going now."

N'Doch grabs her arm. "No, you don't. The boss says stay here, that's what we'll do."

"The boss?"

N'Doch fidgets. "Y'know. His high-mucky-muck lord-ship."

The girl looks interested. "Have you sworn service to Baron Köthen?"

"Gedoudaheah! No way!"

She cocks her head at him, puzzled.

"Just never mind, okay? What do the dragons say is going on up there?"

She makes a little pout at him, then goes inward to that place where, as N'Doch thinks of it, the channel is always open. "That there are some people up ahead who claim the right of payment for our safe passage through their lands. Stoksie, Luther, and Brenda do not agree with them."

N'Doch smirks. "The old toll gambit. Getting back what they gave."

"But Ysabel seems to think it might be wiser to negotiate a reasonable price."

"What for?" Actually, N'Doch is sorry to miss this bit of entertainment. His regret must be reading on his face, 'cause the girl grabs his hand and starts yanking him forward.

"You do want to know! Come, N'Doch! You needn't do everything Baron Köthen tells you to!"

Ouch, he thinks. She's really learned how to get to him. But by the time he's made up his mind to go along with her, the Tinkers are relaxing off the alert, remounting their wagons and taking up the reins again, though their weapons are set closer to hand. Soon Köthen and Sedou come strolling back from the front, both of them looking just a bit smug.

"So what happened?" N'Doch demands.

Köthen flicks a hand dismissively.

"A few hungry people trying to fill their bellies the easy way," Sedou says.

"Yeah? What'd you do?"

Sedou shrugs. "Just showed up."

"Well, that's kinda too easy, ain't it?"

"A scrawny, measly lot of brigands," Köthen mutters.

"Not brigands, Dolph. People starving."

Köthen bows to the dragon man satirically. "I stand corrected."

"Stoksie's seeing what they have left to trade for food."

"Oh," exclaims the girl. "We ought to just give them what they need!"

N'Doch is glad he's not the only one staring at her like she's a lunatic. "And what do you plan to eat after you've given it all away?"

"Well . . . if they had items to trade, would they not have traded it for food already, in the villages?"

Sedou gropes for a middle ground between honorable charity and reckless waste. "Luther says these people can't go to the villages. They're exiles. They don't approve of the villagers' religion."

"Good on them," N'Doch remarks.

Sedou nods. "So Stoksie's trying to work out a way to give them some food, without giving it outright."

"Which is against his principles," Köthen adds.

"Like to see what he gets for it," says N'Doch.

"I think he did not wish to make them beg for their food," Sedou concludes.

Köthen sucks his teeth. "I think they were not strangers."

They all look at him, waiting for more.

"Really?" N'Doch prompts.

"Yes, though they wished to pretend otherwise."

"Well, that doesn't make sense."

Köthen offers one of his hard looks.

"Okay, lemme put it this way: why would they do that?"

"Friend N'Doch, I have not yet given the structure of alliances in this region a thorough enough study."

N'Doch's getting irritated. "Well, lemme know when you do."

It's only after the wagons move forward again and Köthen drops back to his habitual spot in the rear, that N'Doch realizes the baron's learned how to bait him, too, in return for the abuse he's been dishing out. This makes him laugh out loud.

The girl stares at him. "What's funny?"

"Your man Dolph."

"Don't call him that," she murmurs.

And her regret is too real for him to make light of. "Okay. I won't."

When they pass the spot where the front wagons had halted, he sees a group of eight or ten ragged folk squatting down in the dust with a small pile of food between them. They're arguing over it already.

The toll gambit is pulled on them twice more before the wagons reach the first village, with much the same results. By then, N'Doch suspects that Köthen is right, or the Tinkers are more softhearted than they'd like to admit. Either way, he hopes they pack extra rations on these trips, so they can afford their own generosity. No wonder they're in trouble.

The first village is a small one, no more than twenty houses set beneath a scattering of battered, broad-trunked trees. Must be water underground, N'Doch decides, to keep these oldsters alive. The houses are low and square and made of stone. If they were cement block, they'd look a lot like his mama's house. A roof over one's head but otherwise full of holes. At dusk, the place looks deserted, not much of a threat. Not even a junkyard dog to greet them, just a few old people peering cautiously out of their doorways. The Tinkers pass through the village unchallenged and pull the wagons into a tight ring in a dusty field on the other side. While dinner preparations are underway, a small but well-armed delegation walks back into town to announce the start of trade at dawn the next morning and to negotiate water and grazing for the mules. N'Doch wonders who they're gonna find to talk to.

He's scavenging bits of twig for Luther's cook fire when a murmur runs around the circle of wagons. Folks straighten up from their chopping and stirring to point at the horizon. N'Doch dumps his meager handful beside Sedou and the girl. She's teaching the dragon man how to peel potatoes.

"Take a look out there," he tells them.

An odd formation of cloud has appeared to either side of the blood red setting sun. Not rain clouds, but puffy and pink. More what N'Doch would call fair-weather clouds, unlikely at dusk in any location, and certainly weird in this place. He hasn't seen a hint of a cloud since he arrived, only the ever-present sooty murk that turns the empty sky yellow and green.

Sedou stares at the horizon, the potato forgotten in his hand. "Interesting. Not one of mine."

N'Doch laughs. "Oh, yeah?"

"Mine have more water in them."

"Cool, bro. Bring 'em on! I could do with a shower."

"Such energies are not to be squandered lightly."

N'Doch sees he's serious. "Wait . . . you can do that? Really?"

The girl gets that haunted look. "Have you forgotten how Lady Water saved us at Lealé's?"

"I can do it, sure, I can. A shower is a mere parlor trick." Sedou turns his dragon stare on N'Doch, only there's a lot of Sedou in it, too, Sedou flaring in righteous wrath. He shakes the potato in his dark fist as if it stood in for all of Nature. "But do you mean, can I fix this dust, this parched field, this . . . wasted earth? I can turn it to mud, if you like . . ."

"No, I . . ."

"For an hour perhaps, and then the life-water would be gone, sucked away as if it had never been! The roots would still dry and the stems still wither! It takes more than just water, even if I could offer an endless supply. Too much water, after all, is a flood, and a flood is as destructive as a drought! Alone, I can do little. But with proper help . . ."

"Whoa. Easy." N'Doch hates this. Just when he's let himself forget, the millennia creep back into the voice of this man-thing who isn't really his brother.

Sedou stares at the horizon, and then his rage is gone as quickly as it came. "But with help . . ."

"With help you could what? Make a monsoon?"

The girl clucks her tongue, disapproving his attempt to lighten up a moment just because its gravity makes him nervous.

"No. No. But surely this is part of it."

"Part of what?"

"Part of all of it. Of what we are to do, to accomplish. Together." Sedou's chin lifts and his shoulders drop back as his gaze drifts to some inner dragon space that N'Doch doesn't even want to contemplate. "Sometimes I see . . ." He falters, his inhuman eyes suddenly dark with foreboding.

"What, bro?" N'Doch asks again, uneasy. "What do you see?"

And then it comes to him what's been bothering him since they arrived at Blind Rachel. He just knows this gig's been much too easy so far. Any minute now, the shit is gonna hit the fan. The girl is staring at Sedou reverently, like he might lay out some final truth any moment. She prefers him like this, damn her, more dragon than Sedou.

But the dragon/man sighs, shakes his head. "It's never clear enough to really say. What my brother Earth calls a Purpose only partly understood . . . for me, it's more like a vision, only partly glimpsed." He shakes himself out of his sober reverie. "But those clouds . . . those are interesting. A sign . . . of some sort."

The Tinker delegation returning from the village descends upon them with jovial enthusiasm.

"C'monta my fire, nah," invites Ysabel. "Feedju up gud!"

N'Doch soaks up the crinkle in her hair and the faint Latin music in her speech like it was cool, sweet water.

Sedou lifts the pot of potatoes he and the girl have not

quite worked their way through. "Thank you, but Luther was kind enough to ask . . ."

"Luta come, too, den. Dat ri', Luta? Allyu come wit me! Heah da news frum town."

Stoksie grins up at N'Doch. "Yu bring gud luck, tall-fella."

"Yeah? How's that?"

Stoksie runs a hand across his shiny bald head, then points at the clouds, grown into two thin spires that flank the ruby oval of the sun like the minarets on a mosque. "Dese townies call dat a sign. Say da god smile onda trade day."

"Which god is that?" Sedou asks lightly.

Stoksie and Ysa flick glances at Luther, as if waiting for a cue.

"Dere's only one fer dem," Luther says grimly. "Da monsta."

The girl frowns. "They think the monster is God? You did not mention that."

N'Doch laughs. "And he cares about trade?"

Stoksie's grin returns. "Shur, shur. Lotsa time, dem townies trade der food 'n der craftwerk for stoopid glittajunk to give 'im presents."

"Glitter junk?"

"Shur. Like dem jools what wimen usda weah. Orny-ment." Stoksie sees he has the three visitors' total attention. "Fake stuff, y'know. Salvage." He mimes digging. "We find it 'roun."

Sedou nods. "But why are the clouds a good omen?"

Stoksie blinks at him. "Clouds is alwiz a gud sign, tall-fella. Whachu tink? Mebba it rain, nah?"

"When did you see clouds last, can you remember?"

"Can' say wen it wuz. Wachu tink, Ysa?"

"I'd say tree mont', mebbe fowah. Dat weerd time. Yu memba dat, Luta?"

Luther, absorbed in cloud study, responds to his name with a start. "Betcha! Come up suddin like, afta nuttin fer neah a yeah. Den a few, den moah 'n moah fer a week, like. Den alla suddin, nuttin agin. Till now."

"Three months ago?" asks Sedou thoughtfully. "Clouds like these?"

"Sumpin' like."

"Interesting."

"Okay, c'mon nah." Ysabel hooks an arm around Stoksie's elbow. "Talk whilyu eatin'!"

Night settles in during the meal prep. There are fewer cook fires inside the ring of wagons than at the camp. Not enough firewood. N'Doch feels the darkness wrapping him close. He's used to not much light at home, out in the bush, but this night is the very definition of lightless. It looms like a wall, a tsunami of darkness. And his conviction that the party's over is still giving him the creeps. Maybe the others sense it, too. N'Doch sees how, despite the heat, everyone finds a spot to huddle in tight around the few dim pools of glow. But it's not a night attack that worries them. Instead of keeping it quiet, they talk louder than usual, act raucous, as if to shout down suffocation by the void.

At Ysabel's fire, Luis joins them and a few couples N'Doch knows by face but not by name, plus Mari and Senda, who hang around Sedou whenever they can get away with the idleness that hanging around requires. Brenda and Charlie sit down long enough to eat, then go off on perimeter watch. N'Doch wishes Marley was by, with his guitar, but the old man has stayed at camp to look after his prize tomatoes.

The conversation is about the townies. Those who went into the village share out the local gossip—who's dead, who's married who, who's promised what for trade. Then comes the news that's got the village in an uproar: some big religious figure making a town-by-town tour will not be stopping by their village because it's too small.

"Too small fer da monsta ta bodda wit'," notes Luther. "An' das a gud ting!"

"Das why we come heah," Stoksie agrees.

"But dey hate dat, doncha know? Makes 'em feel bad. Like dey not gud enuff."

"Gud enuff fer us, nah."

General agreement runs around the fire, then talk turns to the monster god himself. War stories, N'Doch thinks of them. Disputes about the span of his wings, the size of his claws, the direness of his wrath. It takes a lot, he notes, for these folks to air their grievances. They'd rather be laughing and yarn-spinning. Old tales are trotted out to shock the visitors' virgin ears, and everyone dutifully claims not to believe any of them, so Luther can attest loudly to the accuracy of every single one. N'Doch thinks of evenings in the bush village where he grew up, though the gossip there was mostly the bad news from the city and the stories were the familiar ancestral myths, recounted each time as if for the first time.

"But why do they call him God?" protests the girl in her polite but pained way, after Mari and Senda have shuddered their way through a fourth graphic tale of bestial cruelty, "Where is the religion in such a practice? Is there doctrine? Does he work miracles? If he's there in the flesh and there's no denying his presence, what are the issues of Faith?"

Köthen, leaning in to N'Doch's quiet running translation, agrees. "More a plain tyrant than a god, it would seem."

Luther clears his throat, and though no one actually moves, somehow the others make a respectful space for him, as they have done for Sedou since he appeared among them. "Well, der is doktrin. Summa dem belief it. But I tink mosta dem jes say so cuz dey skeerda da monsta."

"What do they believe?" Sedou asks.

"Ina enda da wold. Any day nah. Say der's no pint doin' nuttin fer da future, cuz der won' be any. Or so dey tink."

"I take it you do not share this belief."

"Nah." Luther offers a wan grin. "Das too dak fer me, y'know?"

Sedou asks, "So what do you believe?"

For a moment, silence reigns around Ysabel's fire. Again, it seems that the others, even Stoksie and Ysabel, defer in such matters to Luther. He begins slowly. "Well, summa us see it diffrint. We say it mebbe look like da enda da wold, bud it ain't." He pauses as if he would welcome a change of subject, but Sedou waits him out. Finally Luther shrugs and hikes his stooped body and big nose forward, his scarred hands lifting from his sides to talk along with him. "No, it ain't. Why? Cuz der's One comin' ta make it right."

"She walks in light," Ysabel murmurs.

"Fixit all, y'know?" Luther's arms pinwheel around him. "Alla it. Den mebbe we liff like umins again."

"The One?" the girl breathes. "You mean, Our Savior?"

"Probably not the one you're thinking of," says Sedou gently.

"You think this fix up's gonna happen soon?" N'Doch asks, for it sounds like he does. Maybe even tomorrow.

Luther rocks his head back and forth like a tired bear. "We don' know dat, nah, cuz y'see, da One gotta big problum. She shuddup inna dark by da Handa Chaos, waitin' till we figure a way ta ged her out."

"She? In the dark?" The words escape Sedou as a sigh. N'Doch is too astounded to speak, and the girl looks thunderstruck.

"She walks in light," murmurs Ysabel again, echoed this time by Luis and one of the nameless couples. Stoksie, N'Doch notices, remains silent. The others shift uneasily.

"Like I sez," Luther concludes, "Only *summa* us belief dis."

N'Doch feels the deep thrum of dragon energies in the air, in the very ground beneath his feet. He wishes he was like the Tinkers, sitting there unawares. He remembers how, at Lealé's, when the dragons decided to make their move, things started to pinball with sickening speed. The girl's still looking stunned, but he knows she's in furious converse with the big guy back in the woods. Despite the high voltage that Sedou's generating for those who are plugged in to it, his surface remains calm and merely . . . interested.

"An imprisoned messiah. It's a beautiful notion, Luther. Is it yours?"

Luther looks shocked, then embarrassed. "Na, na. I heerd it frum . . . a frien'. A greyt preecher-man, y'know? I lissen, I jus' know he got da wold on right."

"I'd like to meet this preacher. Does he say where the Hand of Chaos is keeping your awaited One?"

"We all lookin' on dat. Ev'ry day, we closer to da ansa."

"And what will it take to free her?"

Luther lowers his elbows to rest on his knees. "We ain't figurd dat yet neider."

"Der's sum say da One'll be free whenda monsta is ovahtrone."

This is a new voice, one N'Doch doesn't recognize, and he's sure he knows all of Blind Rachel's sounds, if not the names. The speaker is a young woman crouched on the other side of the fire, partly obscured by the flames.

"Sum say dat," Luther agrees dubiously.

She's got two other strangers with her, one on either side, two guys, youngish and serious-looking. N'Doch is ashamed how they just snuck up out of the night without him noticing. Köthen is already watching them, probably has been for a while. But the Tinkers act like it's nothing unusual.

He nudges Stoksie. "Who's that?"

"Frum town."

"You don't mind?"

Stoksie shrugs. "Wild young'uns. Y'know?"

Luther shoves his hair back, speaking across the fire, "But dem as tink dat got no ideah how dey gonna make it happin."

"Sum do," says the young woman.

"Sum oughta git bettah ideahs befur dey go preechin' 'em."

And then it looks like that's all anyone's willing to say, until Sedou draws a deep and quiet breath. The hot wind that's been fanning the embers dies back. N'Doch feels his own breath coming shorter now, and he knows for sure that his vacation's over. Some conjunction of circumstance and subject matter has occurred. The ball is in the slot and the blue dragon's hand is on the lever. He glances down the line of listeners, sees all the apprehension in her and catches his fellow dragon guide's eye. He that he's trying to keep off his own.

"Here we go," he mutters to Köthen.

"Now, Luther, I won't claim that my ideas are any better, but there's one I'd like to try out on you anyway." Sedou looks to Luther for permission.

"Yer ideahs is always welcum, tallfella."

"My thanks. What if I say, then . . ." Sedou gazes around until he holds their attention, even the newcomers across the fire. "What if I point out an amazing coincidence. The friend my companions and I came looking for is also imprisoned in an unknown place. We believe her imprisonment is keeping her—and us—from accomplishing a glorious good. And we believe that he who imprisoned her does not want this great good accomplished." Sedou glances down, the very image of humble self-doubt. "Do you think, my friends, that it is too much to conclude that this jailer is the same monster god you speak of?"

Murmurs build around the fire.

"A moment longer, friends." Sedou puts out a hand as if smoothing ripples. The murmurs die into edgy silence, and N'Doch senses the lever's twang. The ball is in motion.

"What if I say something further, something . . . oh, you who have asked our help, listen well! What if I tell you the help that I bring is far greater than you've supposed, and of a . . . different sort. It will shake your faith, but then surely renew it!"

The Tinkers eye him, some wearily, others with caution, like they expect him to start raving any minute. Maybe he already has. N'Doch guesses it's like opening a box you had great plans for and finding it empty, or full of the same old garbage.

But Luther says, "Go on, tallfella."

Sedou nods. "It cannot be mere chance that has brought us together. It cannot be! There is a great mystery here that I have not yet been able to penetrate. But I believe our shared knowledge of it will fit together like a key in a lock, that together, we can discover this prison and free my friend . . . and your awaited One." The dragon/man drops his hand and his voice. The wind dies entirely, as if someone's switched off the fan, and Sedou's whisper insinuates itself into every ear. "For, you see, my friends: I believe them to be one and the same being, that is, my sister Air."

Luther coughs gently, just once. "Tallfella, we weren't expectin' da One to be *umin* . . . y'know?"

"Nor is my sister Air."

Luther nods, like he's been waiting for this.

N'Doch shivers, despite the heat. *Well, that certainly lays a lot of our cards on the table.* He's not sure the other Tinkers are ready for it. But maybe they are. He looks around at the stubborn faces still protecting themselves against the rising of hope, eyes narrowing at Sedou, trying to decide exactly how crazy he is . . . or isn't.

Because there's a difference here: these people don't need to be convinced of the reality of magical creatures. There's one ravaging their countryside already. What they need is renewed faith and a weapon.

Well, one has just arrived. No, make that two.

N'Doch fills Köthen in on what's gone down, and is un-surprised by the baron's sudden grin of anticipation. As for himself, he's got nothing against a good fight, but he feels a darkness creeping up on him that he cannot explain.

Sedou smiles into the uneasy silence, a glow like the full moon rising. There is power in his very calm, as if he knows they will come to believe him and he needs offer nothing but patience while they find this out for themselves.

Damn dragon arrogance, N'Doch swears, watching the dragon/man morph into something subtly less earthly, with-out needing a note of his music. He'd be surprised to find a steady hand or slow heart in the house. Finally the townie woman stands. She moves stiffly around the fire until she's face-to-face with the sitting giant. She has round Asian fea-tures and tawny pox-marked skin. N'Doch is sad for her disfigurement. Otherwise, she would be beautiful.

"Give us a sign." Her back is rigid and her Tinker accent suddenly flushed from her voice. She's brave but terrified.

Sedou laughs. "A sign?"

"Of this power you speak of. We've had our fill of messi-anic lunatics!"

"Of course you have."

She glances defiantly at Luther. "Some people will be-lieve anything if they want it bad enough."

Agreement whispers through the gathering.

"Who are you?" she demands. "Or . . . what."

"My name is Sedou. I am what I am. Who or what are you?"

"I am Miriam, and I . . ." She bites her lip, glances back at her two young accomplices. Their mouths hang open. Wide-eyed, they nod. "And I . . . stand in opposition to the Winged God of the Apocalypse!" She plants her hands on her hips, glaring at Sedou in challenge.

"Well, Miriam. Well spoken. So do I. So does everyone here."

"I know that." His gentleness has caught her off guard. "But these Tinkers do nothing about it! They oppose but do not act! Why do you come to them with your magical appearance and your gift of fish?"

"Word gets around, I see."

Young Miriam scoffs. "Easily accomplished! Why should

we listen? Why should we believe? Show us a sign that cannot be explained away!"

Just call in the big guy, thinks N'Doch. That'll convince 'em. Or it might just send them screaming in the opposite direction, given their current expectations of dragons.

"A sign." The dragon/man laughs again, a great booming laugh that tickles a smile or a sheepish grin onto the soberest of disbelieving faces around the fire. He stands, towering over the young woman, but she stands her ground as he spreads his arms wide and throws his head back as if welcoming the surrounding darkness. "So be it, doubting Miriam!"

And a soft rain begins to fall, a precise zone of cooling relief that stops a step outside the circle around the fire. Miriam catches tiny drops on her outstretched palms until they run with moisture, then presses them to her eyes with a sob.

"Parlor tricks," says Sedou sadly.

But Luther lowers himself onto his bony knees, his rough hands clasped in gratitude. "Welcome, pilgrim! Your search has ended."

Chapter Twenty-nine

Paia spots the odd clouds on the sunset horizon at the end of the third day out, just as she's decided that nothing out of the ordinary will happen on this trip after all, except a near fatal overexposure to the elements. Another sweltering dusk, another dried-up town clinging to subsistence, another dull evening of ritual and routine to look forward to. Or not. Everything she sees, everyone she meets is so listless and played out. Where are the brave and busy villages she has imagined, energized by faith and the common struggle against the hostile climate?

Paia is irritable with discomfort, and the constant diet of ceremony. Plus she's kept as isolated as she ever was in the Citadel. All of it leaves her floaty and disoriented, and vastly disappointed with her Visitation.

"Why can't I talk to anyone?" she rails at Luco as he ushers her toward the High Priestess' lonely seat of honor at the banquet. This particular town is wealthy enough to provide her with a table all of her own, on a raised dais and everything. They're so proud of the dais, a sordid little box with only one step, that they've even painted it the God's sacred red.

Luco's broad shoulders sag, then resettle with new resolution. "You know how the God feels about the importance of maintaining the Temple's image."

"It'll hurt our image if we talk to the people? The God is the Caretaker of the Faithful. What kind of caretaking is that?"

"It lowers you to their level, instead of elevating them to yours."

"Which they can only manage by prayer, which is inhibited by any sort of *normal* conversation?" Paia balls her hands into fists and vibrates them in frustration. "I came to walk among them! To preach to them! To inspire them with my love of the God!"

In fact, Paia isn't loving the God very much right now. She's angry with him for destroying her painting. But she can't explain any of this to Luco.

"Inspire them?" he growls. "You'll be lucky if they don't eat you alive."

"What?"

"I mean, of course, that they're desperate. They need sustenance, not talk!"

"Faith *is* sustenance, First Son! If you aren't careful, it will be me advising you to hold your tongue. Won't that be a novelty!"

Luco's eyes clench shut briefly. "Your pardon, my priestess."

Paia sighs and forces her hands to relax. No more arguing. She must apply her flagging energy to the task of surviving the heat and boredom. She points out the clouds to Luco, to change the subject.

"Hunh. Look at that." He finds them more interesting than she does. "In the direction of the Citadel."

"Are they rain clouds?"

"He'd never allow that."

"Who?"

"The God. He'd as soon it never rained."

"No, Luco, surely . . ." Paia peered at him closely. Was the heat getting to him, too?

"In the Chapter House, they'll be saying it's a sign."

"Of what?"

"Of whatever they need it to be a sign of."

He flicks her a sidelong glance as he seats her at the table. Paia would like to laugh. When officiating, the High Priestess is barely allowed a smile, never mind the belly laugh she'd like to let go of. A great big laugh of pure abandon. It would be so freeing. But the First Son's joke was not very funny. He's too distracted by . . . whatever he's distracted by. With a warning frown, he leaves her struggling. He has not used this trip to ease his insistence on proper Temple protocol, and the subject of her father still shuts him up like a box. But in the brief times they've been apart from listening ears, a progressive change has been evident. The more miles put between them and the Temple, the more relaxed is Luco's tongue. When they do speak together, it is almost a conversation.

And this has taught Paia something: Son Luco does not see her as a religious icon with God-given mystical power, as would any lesser devout of the Temple. To Luco, she is simply the God's designate, the Temple figurehead, chosen not as Luco would choose, but for the god's own inhuman reasons—which the priest is loath to question.

Happily, Paia agrees with him. She's glad she's never pretended with Luco to be something she isn't. What's more, she's always assumed his boundless patience with her tantrums and impulses to be due to his devotion to the God. But new insight suggests that Luco has forgiven her a lot simply because she is her father's daughter. Someday, she will convince him to tell her the story.

The ceremonial feast is over early that evening, before the sun has completely set. Perhaps the dull-eyed inhabitants of this village have squandered too many of their scant resources on their silly dais. Nearly stir-crazy with sitting, Paia begs Luco for a walk outside the village, across the fields perhaps, even up that hill on the far side. She would like a better look at the odd pink cloud towers. He agrees to allow it, if proper security precautions are observed. But he begs off accompanying her, claiming Temple business, as he has every evening so far. In a town so meager, Paia wonders how much business there could be. Visits to the outlying homesteads, perhaps, where the Faithful are in need of spiritual advice or even renewal. Though he shines in the formal recitation, it is hard to imagine Son Luco delivering a sermon. Still, Paia has overheard his admiring acolytes tell of his great oratorical prowess during the Wars of Conversion. But there are no sermons in the Temple of the Apocalypse. Only endless litany.

Before he disappears off to who knows where, Luco gives Paia into the hands of the head of the local Chapter House, a dour, crop-haired woman twice her age. Paia's heart sinks. Being a full priestess, the woman need not go veiled, which means there is nothing to disguise her reluctance.

"Mother Gayle." Impatient to be off on his business, Luco puts on his voice of polite coercion. "Supreme Mother Paia has a need for some exercise before retiring. Would you be willing to oblige her? A viewing of the local geography, perhaps?"

Paia settles the God's little gun more firmly against her ribs. She notes the look that passes between Son Luco and the local priestess, but she cannot interpret it. Probably he is begging the woman to take her off his hands, or simply warning Mother Gayle to make sure the High Priestess disports herself in a manner becoming to the Temple.

Mother Gayle bows. "The God's servant in all things, my priest."

Luco goes briskly off, and Mother Gayle gathers her entire staff, plus the Temple Honor Guard, in the event of a surprise raid by bandits from the hills. She guides Paia onto the main road out of the village, where they walk in silence through the dusk, with half the village trailing after them. Paia notes how her sandaled feet leave little pouch marks in the deep dust. Suddenly it seems sad that no one even talks about it anymore, this drying up of the world. One just acts as if it has always been this way, even though the worst of it has occurred within her own short lifetime. Accept what is. It's the God's sort of thinking.

The procession crosses the arid field in silence, then climbs in silence as well, first within the shadow of the hill, then with the sun's red ball straight ahead of them, brilliant and blinding, exploding into their eyes. Paia cannot see her feet. Even the ground ahead of her is lost in the dazzle, as if it has fallen away and left her floating. She was already disoriented in her mind, now she is disoriented in her senses as well. She puts out both arms, feeling unbalanced but rather enjoying the novelty.

"It's like walking in light!" she exclaims.

The sober stride of the priestess falters beside her. "I beg your pardon?"

"The sun . . . it's so bright." Paia opens her arms to the bloody glare.

"Ah, yes. The sun. Of course." Mother Gayle nods, then

immediately withdraws into her walking silence. She looks, Paia thinks, oddly relieved.

The top of the hill is a series of barren stone ledges with brittle mats of dry moss between. The farthest ledge protrudes over a rather steep drop, providing a perfect platform for viewing the surrounding peaks. But its corners are suspiciously square, and Paia sees it's actually a poured concrete slab, much weathered, probably an old foundation for a house. Mother Gayle points out this mountain and that, identifying them as Tall Mount or Red Face, generic names that are new even since Paia's childhood geography classes. The more colorful names, such as Vanderwacher or Goodnow, have been erased in the God's campaign against history, as if his coming has made the past irrelevant.

But people remember, Paia tells herself. Luco remembered. *Cauldwell's Clove.*

Then Mother Gayle takes her arm and gently draws her to the very edge of the platform, to point straight down. A hundred, two hundred feet below are the remains of a town. Quite a large town, judging from the length of the main street. Its crumbling chimneys and collapsed roofs are touched by the sun's dying rays as if with fire.

"Oh, my! Oh, my." Paia squints to make out faded letters on tumbled-down signs, to take in the rich variety of the buildings, even in their state of ruin. The language of the architecture is so much more complex—dare she say it?—so much more *human* than the blocky, unadorned style favored by the God for current domestic structures. Even the odd crooks and curves of the streets tell an interesting story. She can see where the trees might have been, shading the sidewalks and houses. Paia stares down at the town for a long time, while Mother Gayle waits patiently beside her.

Finally she takes a chance. "Has it a name?"

"Oh, no, Mother Paia."

"I mean, *did* it, at one time? Or has it been forgotten?"

The older priestess clears her throat, then murmurs so that only Paia could possibly hear. "It was called Carlisle. Of course, I only know this because . . . well, I was born there."

As the Temple's highest representative, Paia should deliver a stern reproof. History is forbidden, after all. But she herself has asked, and what escapes her is a sympathetic nod.

Mother Gayle looks mistrustful but again relieved. "There

is a heresy, you know, that claims it can all be made green again." She laughs harshly to show her contempt. "Imagine that!"

"Indeed," replies Paia, wondering why the woman is saying this, to the High Priestess of the God's Temple. Everyone around her seems to be losing their grip on propriety. Including herself.

Mother Gayle sighs. "I've thought of petitioning Him to burn it to the ground, like He has so many others. It would be easier. The God is right about the pain our useless old memories can bring."

But why, Paia asks herself, if the town was still standing, could the people not just live there? She's sure the God has told her there were no towns left after the Wars. That his great building spree was undertaken for the good of the homeless Faithful.

Gazing downward, she is suddenly racked with vertigo. Disorientation made physical. She hardly knows what to believe anymore. Thoroughly depressed, Paia backs away from the edge. "It will be dark soon. Perhaps we should be getting back."

The God visits her again that night, only this time she is sure she is not asleep. She would never dream him in this grotesque a rage.

Besides, she has been dreaming of something else. A man. A blond man with a sword, like she has seen in her father's ancient tomes. A rather pleasant dream, for a change.

When she wakes, the God's golden eyes are inches from her own, as hot and bright as twin blast furnaces. There is not a hint of the tragic mask of his most recent visitation. He is nothing but eyes and a long screech of fury, like knives in both her ears. "The picture! The picture! Where is it?"

"The picture? You mean, the painting?" Paia is groggy, confused. "The landscape? You haven't destroyed it?"

"WHERE IS IT? Where have you hidden it?"

"I haven't hidden it. It's in my room."

"LIAR! LIAR!"

"My lord, I am not!" She shoves herself up on her elbows. The painting. He hasn't destroyed it. She struggles to clear her head. Again, she is bedded down in the local Chapter House, and again, the servants and priestesses bedded down with her snore through the God's tirade. Only the High Priestess must endure the heat of his wrath. "I had the painting brought down to my room! It was there when I left! Surely you saw it yourself when you came for me!"

"Then your confederates have stolen it to safety! Where? I can forgive your being an unwitting pawn, but conspire against me at your direst peril! Where is it?" His cry shrills against her eardrums and behind his eyes looms the shadow of horns. "TELL ME!"

"I don't know! I have no confederates!" Her grogginess dulls her fear. She is tired of his tantrums. "How could I have confederates? You allow me no friends! Besides, you know I can conceal nothing from you. You invade even my dreams!"

"After others have already done so! Your dreams are not your own! Have I not said they will destroy us both?"

"Then I will not listen to them!" Paia slumps back on one elbow. How can she prove anything to him? She so much wants him to believe her just because he believes her, as she believes herself. Indeed, she would like to know herself where the painting has gone, this mutable vista that someone else has made her paint. She thinks of the House Comp's tale of tampering, and worries for its safety. "Is it truly not there?"

The shadow behind the hot glow of his eyes resolves into something more manlike. Her concern has rung true, and unsettled him. Paia judges that the worst is over.

"Would I waste my time here if it was?"

"Surely, my lord, the person who left those notes has taken it."

"Ha! Ha!" He fumes inarticulately, but his twin fires withdraw a bit as the focus of his rage shifts to the note-writer. "I have questioned the entire population of the Citadel, yet cannot rout out this traitor!" The light dims as he turns away to begin his habitual pacing. "They have human agents working for them, even as I do. Here, there, and everywhere. I should expect nothing less!"

Paia squints into the returned darkness. There is no sound but his voice.

"How could he conceal himself from me, otherwise? How else could he know about the picture?"

"Know what about it?"

"That picture is nothing without the knowledge of it."

"What knowledge?"

"He is in league with my enemies. It has to be so."

"WHAT KNOWLEDGE?" Paia yells. If she wakes up every woman in the Chapter House, she might get his attention. But the others sleep on undisturbed.

The twin furnaces flare again. "Ha, my priestess! Read a few old books and you think you understand everything! What arrogance!"

Paia's teeth clench. "My arrogance pales beside yours, my lord!"

"I AM YOUR GOD!" he bellows. "What you should understand is how little you really know!"

"I do, more than I ever did! I am out here in the middle of nowhere among strangers who hate me, and you will not offer me the slightest crumb of comfort or encouragement, when I am only begging for enlightenment! Teach me, so I can help you in your work!"

"I don't need your help!"

"Then why do you keep me?" She's up on her knees now, waving her arms at him, wishing she had greater control. But he does need her help. She knows he does. What she doesn't know is how to convince him of it. "Choose another, if you're so dissatisfied! Let me go my own way!"

He stops pacing. "Is that what you want? Is this how you show your devotion to me?"

"It's always about YOU!" she screams. Then a sharp whiff of déjà vu throws her back on her heels. Her mother and father didn't argue very often, but when they did, this is exactly what they sounded like. She is replicating their behavior, she fears, simply because she knows no other. The rush of memory leaves her deflated and confused.

The God hovers over her like a swarm of angry wasps, ready for the next round. But when she remains slumped dejectedly with her hands clasped limply on her knees, he calms a bit, enough at last to assume full man-form, so that he can loom at her bedside with his arms folded, looking satisfied, certain that he's beaten her into submission. Moments like this, of course, are when he is the most generous toward her. She has learned to argue with him, in order to let him win, and then they can be peaceable together. But surely this is not how it was meant to be between them.

"The picture, little fool, is a portal. Didn't your precious dream tell you that?"

A portal? Paia tries to focus on where his mind has gone now. She recalls how, in the dream, the gilt frame became the stone entrance to the Library. "A portal, like a doorway?"

"Indeed. A doorway, if you have the knowledge of it, to wherever—and whenever—you want to go."

"*When*ever?"

The God nods, enjoying her amazement and the superiority of his wisdom. "In your dream, it was showing you the past."

She takes care to maintain the little-girl manner that has settled him down. "You mean, like an image on a monitor screen?"

"Are you deaf? A portal. Like an open door."

"It lets you actually go to the past? Is such a thing possible?"

"If you have an understanding of the working, which fortunately, you do not."

Oh-so-humbly, she asks, "Do you, my lord?"

"I've no need of such devices. I travel when and where I wish to."

"To the past? You travel to the past?" How can she not have known this? He is right. She should have stayed in the Library and read every book she could get her hands on.

"Often." A speculative shimmer crosses his shadowed face. "Perhaps I will take you someday. Perhaps I will leave you there, to stop your meddling in my present."

Paia just shrugs. She has no fight left in her. It's what he always counts on, that he will outlast her. Her constant avowals of innocence cut no ice with him. "Perhaps I would like the past."

He flares again. "If it meant you could be rid of me?"

"And you of me."

"Don't tempt me!" he snarls. "Even a brief visit would teach you some gratitude! I don't know why I didn't think of it in the first place! Or I could drag you back there and abandon you to a short life of disease and drudgery in a dark, cold, damp world where women are routinely beaten, raped, and burned at the stake, and where currently, due to my efforts, there is a famine and a very nasty war going on! As pampered and spoiled as you are, believe me, you wouldn't like it!"

As he speaks of it, she sees it, in chill dark flashes of snow and blood. "If you say so, my lord. I don't need the past, then."

He glares down at her. She can feel the heat of his suspicion and she wants to ask what he means about fostering chaos and misery. But she hasn't the strength to joust with him further this night.

"Please, my lord, I will ask it again, for I think it would solve many things. Can you not accompany me on this journey?"

"I follow your progress. I see all that you do."

Then why all these false accusations, she wants to demand. If he truly saw everything, he would know she is innocent of conspiracy. But then he would lose the pleasure of showering her with his fury and spite. "I mean, for the Faithful, my lord. To show yourself to them in all your glory, as the God of Love as well as the God of Awe. I can speak of your magnificence and perfection, but your actual presence is so much more inspiring."

"Inspiring, is it?" He offers a skeptical eye, and she can see him watching himself, conscious of his beauty made poignant by tragedy. "Perhaps I will . . . beloved traitor."

"My lord, I am not . . ."

But he is gone. Paia falls back against her pillows, wrung out as she always is after one of his rages. She waits for sleep, but thoughts of the vanished painting keep her eyes wide. A traitor in the Citadel who even the god's strong-arm methods can not uncover? A portal to the past? War and famine created by the god's own hand? Why? Why? Why?

She feels like flotsam on the flood of events. Destiny's pawn. Must her involvement be so ignorant and random? Can't she meet it head-on somehow, and take some control of the situation? Paia sighs, and then sighs again.

Soon it is dawn, and the chambermaid rises dutifully to prepare the High Priestess for another day.

Chapter Thirty

Erde considered it a mark of the Tinkers' honor and pride that, after the evening's revelations and miracle, no one in the crew treated the visitors any differently the following day. Except perhaps for Luther, who seemed somewhat stirred out of his habitual gloom.

Besides, they had treated Sedou with respect from the start, due to the mystery of his sudden appearance among them. More importantly, it was a market day, and for the Tinkers, commerce took precedence over all things. Even, Erde remarked to the dragon, over saving the world.

The land around the village was flat and treeless. She had seen no hidden spot to call the dragon into, so he stayed where he was.

ONE CAN ALWAYS SAVE THE WORLD TOMORROW. BUT A GOOD BARGAIN COULD BE LOST UPON THE INSTANT.

She was glad to find him in a humorous mood, despite his growing hunger. Dragon impatience, she had found, was either blinding or imperceptible.

LUTHER SAYS HE'LL TAKE US TO A PLACE ALONG THE ROAD WHERE SOME OF OUR QUESTIONS MAY BE ANSWERED.

WILL THERE BE FOOD THERE?

HE DID NOT MENTION FOOD, DEAR DRAGON, AND OF COURSE, I COULDN'T REALLY ASK. HE WAS VERY SECRETIVE ABOUT THIS PLACE, ALMOST DEVOUT. I THINK IT MUST BE A HIDDEN CHAPEL OR SHRINE, TO THEIR IMPRISONED ONE. BUT WE MAY HAVE TO FACE THE MONSTER FIRST, AT THAT TOWN THAT HE COMES TO.

MONSTER? HE IS MY BROTHER. DOES THAT MAKE ME A MONSTER, TOO?

OUR PARDON, DEAR DRAGON. IT'S ONLY HIS BEHAVIOR THAT MAKES HIM A MONSTER.

TO MOST HUMANS, IT IS ALSO HIS SHAPE. WHY ELSE MUST MY SISTER EXPEND SO MUCH ENERGY TRAVELING LIKE A MAN?

YOUR SISTER IS PRAGMATIC. WOULD YOU NOT DO THE SAME, IF YOU SHARED THAT GIFT? WE COULD ENJOY THE JOURNEY IN COMPANY.

The dragon was silent for a moment.

NO, NOT EXACTLY THE SAME. I THINK I WOULD TRAVEL AS A WOMAN.

The morning's trading did not go well. Long before noon, Stoksie and Ysa folded up their counters and canopies in disgust, and the other Tinkers followed suit.

"Dey got nuttin' lef' heah ta trade," Stoksie lamented.

Erde clucked sympathetically as the little man sorted through his meager takings: some chipped enameled dishes, a bucket of rusted fasteners, a half-crate of mealy-looking potatoes. The only item he was happy with was a thin box the size of his palm, with a hinged lid. He popped it open for her proudly. Inside was a jumble of the slimmest, shiniest metal pins Erde had ever seen. Each one had a tiny white ball at one end. She tried to pick one out to examine it more closely, but only succeeded in pricking herself.

"Ouch!"

"Betcha! Doan fine dese ev'ryday, nah!" But Stoksie confided that he'd had to trade a valuable wool cap for them. Erde thought this was a very smart trade. Who'd want to wear wool in this heat?

The Tinkers packed up and moved on, toward the next village several hours down the road. By setting a stiffer pace than usual, they arrived in time to set up for a late afternoon market. But the mood around the campfires that evening was somber. Business in this village had been even worse.

"Tole me anudder Crew's bin by," Stoksie grumbled.

"No way," Brenda snorted. "Dey tink' we wudn't know 'bout dat?"

"Mebbe be Scroon Crew, comin' in frum Westhills."

"Nah. Dey know our route."

"See what dey say when we meet 'em."

Luis spoke up in his scratchy young man's voice. "Dis townie woman tole me da monsta's priests bin aroun', takin' up evin moah dan ushul."

Stoksie slapped his knee angrily. "An' doan leave us nuttin!"

"Priests frum da big town," Luther explained to Erde. "Das Fenix, y'know. Weah da monsta come."

They went to bed right after cleanup and rose at first light, to be on the road early, and so arrived in the heat of midafternoon. The town itself, viewed on the approach from the high seat of Luther's big yellow caravan, gave no outward sign of being a place of unusual depravity, though Erde gave its pale walls and rooftops due scrutiny as the wagons pulled up in an outlying field. It was called Phoenix, Luther said as he unhitched his mules. It wasn't one of the "new" towns. It sat in a long but narrow valley, hemmed in by hills. The slopes to the south were rocky and sheer, sliced by boulder-choked ravines. Those to the north were almost green, furred with an unusually thick and twisted growth of stunted pines. Phoenix was a real town, Luther said, larger than any of the villages they'd visited.

"We usda set up ou'side fer yeers," Stoksie said as he limped up to join them. Baron Köthen paced at his side like a hound eager to be loosed for the hunt. "Den dey say, we gotta go inside."

Phoenix possessed a sizable market square. New regulations required the Tinkers to set up their wagons there, inside the town's high stone walls. Otherwise, their business was no longer welcome.

Stoksie spat delicately. "Da priests run da markit deah, nah. Got dere fingahs in all da biz. Wanna keep an eye on us."

Blind Rachel refused to go inside. They'd had a child stolen away from them in Phoenix, never mind the depredations of the monster.

"We be sittin' ducks in deah!" Luther exclaimed. "Bildins all aroun'. Walls 'n gates. If dey cum fer us ta feed da monsta, ders no way out!"

"Itsa standoff," Stoksie agreed. "Bin li' dis neer ten yeer nah. But we need da trade, bad dis time."

The baron asked Erde to relay a polite suggestion.

"He asks why you do not take just one or two wagons loaded with goods, and leave the rest safely outside of town?"

Luther shoved the mules on their way to forage for what little grass they could find. "Cooper Crew dit dat wonst, notta yeer since. Los' two men anda hole waggin."

"The monster ate the wagon?"

"Ate da men. Da townies stoll da waggin." He began opening the many drop-down lids and sliding doors of his caravan. They were metal and had remarkable latches. Erde thought of the big yellow carriage as a sort of magic puzzle box.

Köthen waggled a finger with as feral a grin as she'd ever seen on him. "But they didn't have the Pilgrim and me protecting them."

The Pilgrim. Luther's spontaneous salutation had flung itself on Sedou and stuck there like a burr, so that even the baron had picked up the use of it. Now that the Tinkers accepted Sedou as something more than a man, a mere man's name for him no longer seemed adequate. Erde considered their choice more than appropriate. Were they not all four of them pilgrims, dragons and dragon guides alike, sworn to a holy quest?

The Pilgrim himself joined the discussion, and a compromise was reached: while the other Tinkers made camp, Sedou, N'Doch, and Baron Köthen would accompany Luther and Brenda into town to look the situation over, and negotiate with the necessary officials to allow a trade delegation of just a few wagons.

Erde clamored to go along. When Baron Köthen told her to stay behind, she reminded him in their native German that the dragon in the woods should also get a good look at this town.

Luther said, "Yu gotta blade wichu?"

"Of course."

"Okay, den." But he did advise her, shyly, to resume her boy disguise. "Gud lookin' yung wimmin go in der, dey's shur ta go afta yu, cuz dat monsta, he luv da yung wimmin bes'."

Erde shuddered, but into town she went, bearing up under Baron Köthen's scowl and the high heat of the afternoon. It's only his precious sense of honor, she mourned that compels this concern for my safety.

The thick walls and the surly townsmen at the gates, armed with guns and clubs, reminded her (but for the guns) of the fortified mountain villages around Tor Alte where the very daylight seemed dimmed by clouds of hostility and suspicion. But Luther skillfully bought them entry with shares of the sweet spring water in their canteens, and his alluring descriptions of the food and goods to be had at the market if their negotiations were successful.

The sentries growled that they'd have to see the priests about that. One of them insisted on escorting them down the main street as if they were prisoners, to what he called the Chapter House. He permitted no side excursions along the way. Brenda fumed, but the others went along calmly, their hands never far from their weapons. Even N'Doch was unusually quiet, his wary eyes soaking up every detail.

Inside the walls, the angular grid of streets was sunk in a layer of pale red silt, as fine as a lady's face powder. The dwellings were identical two-story stone boxes with slate roofs, raised up on what looked like the foundations of older, vanished structures. The same red dust drifted over walls and stoops and doorways, melding all the colors into one.

"Reminds me of one of them government-built bush towns," remarked N'Doch. "Or maybe it was an army base."

At first, the dark-skinned people hurrying to and fro, laden down with burdens, stepped quickly out of their way, as if to prevent any touch from a stranger. But as they followed the sentry farther into the center of the town, this scattering of populace thickened into a busy throng, and brushing shoulders became unavoidable.

"Keep an eye on your blades," N'Doch murmured. "This could be a slick-fingered crowd."

The Chapter House, which the sentries had spoken of with such reverence, was just another, larger, bland-faced box with a simple, double-doored entrance. The surly guard waited with them once they'd been announced, scuffing his feet in the dust and pointedly not making conversation, except for his crude attempts to muscle Brenda into hand-

ing over her canteen permanently. Brenda told him several
things she would do to him, and the man backed off.

Finally, not a priest but a red-robed woman appeared at
the door. An abbess or mother superior, Erde concluded,
for she seemed to be a person of some authority. She made
them more welcome than the sentries had, though in-
forming them at least three times of how busy she was, due
to an illustrious visitor arriving the next evening. And she
pointed out with little subtlety that several other Crews
were on the road to trade in Phoenix. Luther countered
this by politely insisting that he spoke for all the Crews.
This seemed to concern her, for finally she invited them in
and offered them water, and agreed that while Luther,
Brenda, and Sedou remained to discuss matters of business,
the rest of their party could have the liberty of the town.

"Smooth move," N'Doch said once they were out of ear-
shot. "We'll just wander around gawking like tourists, and
meantime, we'll have the joint cased in no time."

First, Baron Köthen said, they should determine whether
the town stood apart from its wall, or if dwellings were
built into the wall, as was often the case at home, providing
possibilities for concealed exits and entrances. But a road
ran around the entire perimeter between town and wall,
wide and smooth and entirely clear of obstacles, except
for some hastily erected pens housing a few scrawny pigs
and goats.

"A no-man's-land," N'Doch remarked. "All that's missing are the land mines and razor wire."

"This is an ugly town," Erde muttered. "I'm glad I don't
live here." But she was glad to see the livestock: a potential
meal for a hungry dragon.

Satisfied, Köthen led them inward, toward the market
square and the hubbub at the center of town. They had to
shoulder their way through crowds for the last few blocks.
The square was, in fact, a long rectangle, bounded on three
sides by the low boxy houses and on the fourth by the back
of the Chapter House, or actually, the ceremonial front,
judging from its triple-arched portico. The surly guard had
taken them to the rear, no doubt to the servants' entrance.

"Hey, girl. Look at that." N'Doch nudged Erde and
pointed.

In the paving stones in the middle of the square, visible when the crowds milling across it momentarily cleared, was a giant image of a winged and rampant dragon, set in red tiles.

"Oh!" A little chill ran through her, a finger down her spine. There on the ground was the twin to the little dragon carved on her brooch. "It's the same! Exactly the same! Look!"

N'Doch caught her hand as she reached to unpin the big jewel from inside her shirt. "Don't be showing off anything that valuable around here."

"Or anything," Baron Köthen added dryly, "that brings up the subject of dragons."

"But why is the monster's image on my ancestral brooch?"

Köthen studied the dragon on the paving. "No doubt we will find out soon enough."

In front of the Chapter House portico, townspeople were erecting a two-level platform: a small top tier set back from a wider bottom, itself raised several feet off the ground. Both look out over the square and the red-tiled image of the dragon. Several women veiled in red worked among them. The workers' intent and breathless pace gave the impression that all this was being thrown together at the last minute, and in high excitement. At the far end of the square, amid loud clangs of metal on stone, long banks of seating were being raised.

N'Doch stood back to let a pile of well-used timbers go by. "Some kind of big event going on here. Wish it was a rock show."

They found a shaded wall to lean against, removed from the bustle of workers. Erde sensed something oddly familiar in this last-minute building frenzy. At first, she could not place it. Then, when the memory came clear, it so stirred her that she broke her own rule: she gave voice without editing.

"My lord of Köthen, does this remind you of anyplace?"

"Not that I . . ."

"Not the market square at Erfurt?"

"No, Erfurt is a well-appointed town. I don't . . . Ah." He gave her a hard look, then folded his arms and contemplated the ground.

THE BOOK OF FIRE 379

N'Doch said, "What?"

"Her ladyship is offering me a small lesson in perspective."

"Yeah? What happened at Erfurt?"

"N'Doch, must you?"

"You brought it up." Köthen lifted his head, and his gaze did not soften. "Indeed, the similarity gives one faith in the symmetry of all Nature and events."

N'Doch looked interested. "So, tell."

"So, I will. Listen, Dochmann, and learn of the extremes to which ambition and vanity can drive an otherwise honorable man. Or so my lady Erde would have it."

"My lord baron, I did not . . ."

Köthen held up both hands. "What? Would you deny me this rare opportunity, an expiation for my sins?"

"You are satirical, my lord."

"When also, my lady, I am commonly the most in earnest. May I proceed?"

Unable to read his intent, she could do nothing but let him. And as he laid out the scene that day in Erfurt, Erde saw him again as she had that time, the first time: a handsome and victorious lord, riding in through a cheering mob. She recalled how the clear blue and yellow of his tabard shone in the wintry light. How his mail glittered as brightly as the long sword sheathed at his hip. And how she fell in love with the proud lift of his chin.

He'd taken off the tabard and mail, even the tunic underneath, on his first night at Blind Rachel. Erde had not understood the gesture then, or even that it was a gesture, any more than a convenience. But now, tunic, tabard, and mail were all carefully folded away in the bottom of N'Doch's pack. Over his soft leggings and boots, Adolphus Michael Hoffman, Fourth Baron Köthen, wore only the simple garment favored by most of the Tinkers, what they called a T-shirt. Köthen's was loose and black, and it bore the image of a stooping hawk in faded, once-lurid colors. It had been Luther's gift, given freely, for Köthen possessed nothing he would willingly trade, and Luther was the only Tinker big enough to have anything that would fit him. N'Doch, too tall for even Luther's clothing, was hugely jealous of this gift. He said he'd be glad to wear such a shirt if it covered only half his chest. Erde did not think this old and much-worn T-shirt to be a fitting garment for a noble-man, but Baron Köthen would not give it up. He said the hawk suited him well in his new life as a hired mercenary.

But she wished he would don his tunic and tabard again, and help her heart look back, like turning over the hour-glass, to a time when she loved him less. She had not been aware before how love can transform the beloved into an image of matchless perfection. Lately, her longing was such that she could not bear to look at him, to see no love returned in his gaze. Yet looking at him was her greatest pleasure. If anything, he was more beautiful than before.

The constant sun had turned his skin nearly as brown as the Tinkers', and bleached bright streaks of flax into his blond hair. He didn't burn and redden as she did. His hair was shorter now, close-cropped to expose his ears in the Tinker fashion. Ysabel had gotten her clever hands on him, to help him blend, she said, as if this was not just desirable but the only wisdom. But Ysa had failed to convince him to forsake his beard, though all the Tinker men but old Marley went clean-shaven. Baron Köthen said he'd worn a beard since he'd first sprouted one, and wasn't about to give it up now. He did allow Ysa to trim it, until it hugged the contour of his well-formed jaw, a feat of cutting made possible by her remarkable scissors of steel as fine as a sword blade.

He's so changed, mused Erde, watching him covertly while he coolly spun the tale of Margit's rescue as if he had observed it merely from a distance. So changed, in so short a time. As if he was only awaiting the chance. Is this what I intended, when I brought him hither so impulsively? Did I even know what I intended, other than to save his life? Or is it Destiny speaking again, when I'd supposed the choice was mine?

And have I changed as much?

N'Doch, she decided, was exactly the same. Exactly as when she'd met him on the beach in 2013. Except now he had on more clothing. Even in the broiling sun, or perhaps because of it, like the Tinkers, who weren't given to parading about in it half-naked.

Meanwhile, Baron Köthen wiped his palms on his damp T-shirt and made diagrams in the air with his hands. "So I rode in that way, and her father from there, with our vas-

als and armies behind us, and for the sake of a kingdom,
ve were willing to pretend that we liked each other enough
o ally with a madman."

"The hell-priest," supplied N'Doch.

"Ah. You've heard the story."

"Not like you tell it."

"From the wrong side, you mean."

N'Doch returned the most neutral of shrugs.

Köthen tossed his head. "The hell-priest. The central
misjudgment in a series of otherwise reasonable decisions.
. thought he could . . . well, no matter. He didn't, would
never have. When I was introduced to Heinrich's dragon . . .
your pardon, my lady . . . to the dragon Earth in Rose's
barn, I thought, no, this is not my understanding of dragon.
. have met that already, in the eyes of a mad priest who
wields his holy cross as a battle ax!"

"I pray you, speak of him no further!" Erde had that
sense again that the priest was watching her, even through
the veil of the centuries.

"Only to the end of the tale, my lady. And so we made
that devil's bargain, Josef and I, and to seal it, we were
preparing that day to . . ." Köthen's hands floated free a
moment as if unmoored, then sank to his sides. He turned
to her and spread them again. "Rose understood the need,
you must know."

"No! Rose would never have forgiven you!"

"I did not say she would forgive me, nor would I have
asked. I said she understood."

"Understood what?" asked N'Doch.

"The need to burn an innocent woman at the stake."

"Unhh. Not good."

"No, nor am I. I promise you honor always, justice when
I have the power to, and truth where I have knowledge of
t. Goodness I lay no claim to."

"Hey, man. I hear you."

And then they both nodded, satisfied, when Erde thought
they should be ashamed of themselves.

"Besides, she wasn't innocent. She was, is, and will be,
a witch. Like all those women Heinrich's got hidden away."

"It's no excuse!" Erde blurted.

"No, it isn't," Köthen agreed quietly. "And in the end,
we didn't burn her, for milady came to the rescue, with

dragons and King's Knights and mysterious champions, and a lot of other things uncounted on. And perhaps my soul was saved. But that was just a stroke of great good luck, for all too often, what is necessary is not what we'd prefer."

"It wasn't luck, my lord. It was destiny."

"Destiny, is it? Again and always?" His eyes, when he finally fixed them on her, were dark and tired. Perhaps he'd put some memories to rest over the past week, and thanked her little for reviving them. "May I offer you a bit of advice, my lady, for the purposes of accomplishing your, ah . . . Quest?"

"Of course, my lord baron."

"Stop blinding yourself with concern for what isn't or what should be, or even what you'd like it to be. Concentrate on what *is*."

"Good idea," muttered N'Doch.

"Erfurt and all that is past, and we've a job to do in the present. Which is actually the future." Köthen ran a hand through his newly-cropped hair and massaged the back of his neck. "Shall we move on? I feel as though I've spent the afternoon in the confessional!"

He does not believe, Erde realized with a shock, that he will ever see home again.

Köthen clapped a hand to N'Doch's shoulder, turning him, urging him into motion. "Now, tell me, lad. How good are you with that knife of yours?"

The two men moved on through the crowd side by side, instinctively dividing the surveillance between them, left and right, for comparison back at camp. Erde padded after them like their servant or a dog, her fist tight on the hilt of her dagger, hoping to go unnoticed. They stopped at the far end of the square to watch the assembly of the seating, battered lengths of wood and metal that fitted together to form tiers. N'Doch was attempting to explain what a "rock concert" was, when Köthen caught his elbow.

"Dochmann! Over my left shoulder!"

"Looking . . ."

"It's the young woman from the other night. The speaker at the fire."

"Miriam, her name was."

"But we're two days' hard travel from that village!" Erde protested.

"Yup, I see her. Damn! It's her all right!"

"Stay with milady. I'm going after her."

N'Doch snatched him back. "No. Not this time. This is what I'm good at. I was brought up in towns like this. Catch you back at camp."

Before Köthen could stop him, he had eased off through the crowd and melted into it.

Much later, he sprinted out of the darkness to throw himself down breathless at Luther's cook fire.

"Man, that last klick was a tough one!" He wiped his brow on his bare forearm. "These people got watch posted everywhere! There's another Crew, y'know, pulled up down the road."

Luther rose to go back to packing his wagon. "Das Scroon, li' we spected. An' Oolyoot's camped off adda base a da hill."

"So how'd you guys do?"

"Dey agreed. Two waggins frum each Crew. We'll take mine 'n Ysa's. Seems dey need da trade reel bad, too, nah."

"Whew! Gonna be some day tomorrow. Say, I'm dyin'! What's to eat?" N'Doch snatched Köthen's empty plate and filled it from the stewpot. Erde got up to fetch him water from the keg.

"So?" asked the baron.

"The girl? It was her, all right. Real soon after, she hooked up with those two other guys, and they went around town the rest of the day taking people aside real casual-like. I saw a lot of people pretty heavily armed, even a few not too carefully concealed rifles and handguns." He looked to Luther, who had lingered to listen. "That how it is in this town?"

"Dis town, alwiz. But Scroon Crew say dey see a lot moah guns aroun' da villages nah. An' da priests bin ev'reweah, scroungin'."

"The girl, and her companions?" Köthen pursued patiently.

"Oh, yeah. Well, I did fine, till I lost all three of them in an alley. The doors were locked up tight when I tried 'em, but I know they got in one somehow. Maybe they live here, maybe they got connections."

"Hmmm," muttered Köthen. "The scent of rebellion."

N'Doch scoffed. "You've got rebellion on the brain, yer lordship. Whachu say, Luther? You know anything about this?"

"Can't really say, Dockman," the Tinker rumbled, moving off.

But Erde noticed how hard he'd been listening. "She said as much, Miriam did. 'I stand in opposition,' she said. But she meant to this pagan church, not to any lord of the realm."

"The Temple is the lord around here." N'Doch scraped at the remains of his first helping and reached for a second. "Look who we had to go to, to do business. Haven't heard mention of any other form of government."

"A bad idea," said Köthen. "To let the church run things."

"Well, we'll get a chance to see it in action. Guess what else I found out."

"We know! Luther heard it from the woman at the Chapter House. The High Priestess of the dragon worshipers arrives tomorrow with all her retinue."

"Betcha! Major celebration! Folks coming in from all over, not just the Crews. The town's gonna be a madhouse. And with everyone armed to the teeth . . . whew!"

"I hope it won't ruin another trade day."

"I have a feeling," said Köthen with such quiet relish that they both looked at him. "We should be prepared for the worst."

Chapter Thirty-one

The village they stop at the next night is nearly empty, though the streets are clean and the houses scrubbed and patched. The only sign of life is at the Chapter House, where the caravan is welcomed without the usual heavy ceremony by a few overworked and anxious priestesses.

Paia is relieved but curious. "Where have they all gone?"

"Probably down to Phoenix to await your arrival tomorrow," says Luco. "They've planned a huge celebration there in your honor."

She feels so tired today, so strung out. Another night of dreaming. No God to rave at her this time, but the man with the sword was there again, smiling. Paia hasn't had much sleep.

"I can't wait."

Luco laughs. "Come, walk with me, take a look, before it gets dark."

They climb to the brow of the hill overlooking the village to gaze down on their most important destination. The town is many miles away to the southeast, but even from a distance, Paia can see its lights glimmering through the lavender dusk.

"It's big."

"The God's favorite town."

"Really?"

"Where all do his bidding, all live to serve him, and prosperity follows."

"Sarcasm is the God's prerogative, First Son."

"No, I . . . actually, it's true. He's exactly the God they desire. Phoenix is the God's greatest success story."

"Then yours as well, as the God's Right Hand."

Luco shakes out his long hair to let the sweat dry in the breeze. "I'll leave that credit to him." Paia glances up at him, but he is turning away. "Better be heading back. We don't want to miss whatever they've managed to scrape together for dinner."

She reaches suddenly for his sleeve, grabs at the long red folds of his robe. "Luco!"

He stops, turns back. When he sees her face, his blue eyes narrow. "What is it, my priestess?"

Paia isn't sure herself. Something. A feeling. "I . . . don't know."

"You look . . . terrified. There's no need, you know. Phoenix is devoted to the God. It will welcome you with open arms. Besides, you're as well guarded as anyone could be."

"What if it's something you can't guard against?" She glances again at the tightly walled town in the valley below. A moment ago, she was sure she saw it wreathed with flame. "That place scares me. Do we have to go in there tomorrow?"

He drops all pretense of formality. "Paia, Paia, what's this? A premonition? Do you believe in such things?"

She doesn't know whether to say yes or no.

"Look, I know this trip has been hard on you, harder than you're willing to admit. But it has served its purpose, and tomorrow's visit is the most crucial of all. That town supplies a quarter of the Temple income. If you just hang in there for one more night, I'll give you a rest. I promise." He holds out his hand to her. "Now will you come down to dinner?"

Paia throws one last shuddering look over her shoulder, then takes Luco's hand and follows him down the dusty hill like a child.

Chapter Thirty-two

The camp is up before first light, grabbing breakfast, rounding up the mules, hitching the four needed to haul the two wagons, and keeping the others close at hand in case of an emergency.

N'Doch stands with Sedou on a rise in the road into town. The sky is a gray dome above. The valley vanishes away from them into predawn darkness. The wagon circles of the two other Crews are just visible up ahead, one to either side of the road. They, too, will send in a pair of wagons each, coasting in on Blind Rachel's negotiations.

Sedou is more like the dragon than ever this morning. Or, if N'Doch allows himself to remember, more like Sedou before a big rally, particularly once he understood he was a marked man. He's edgy, distracted. He reminds N'Doch twice what to do if Fire shows himself. N'Doch can see the dragon's mind is elsewhere. His own stomach's as uneasy as an ant nest. He wishes he could help but hasn't a clue what would be helpful, or even how to ask.

Köthen walks out to join them when the light turns rosy. "Stoksie is ready to give the signal."

As if by agreement, the three men stand together in silence for a moment, watching the day build. Then they shake hands solemnly and head back toward camp.

Sedou leads the way with Stoksie and Brenda. Köthen, Charlie, and N'Doch follow up the two wagons, Luther's retrofitted delivery van—which must be at least a century old, N'Doch figures, repainted a billion times—and a

canvas-topped flatbed driven by a woman named Beneatha
with Ysabel in the seat beside her. The girl rides up beside
Luther, where the windshield used to be. N'Doch counts
heads. Ten going out. Better be ten of us coming back.

Stoksie hails the other Crews as the wagons draw level
with their camps. Their wagons are ready to roll, so they
wave and pull onto the road behind Blind Rachel. N'Doch
looks them over. They look a little less well-heeled than
his Crew, but otherwise, there's the same lot of recycled
truck bodies and RVs, stripped down, lightened, and fitted
out for mule power, the same determined faces, the same
bristle of weaponry, set back but still in sight.

Charlie points left, then right. "Das Scroon der, 'n das
Oolyoot. Oolyoot from furder sout'. Mebbe we eat wi'
Scroon latah, do sum trade pryvit-like."

"You ever all get together, all the Crews? Have a big
blowout?"

Charlie guffaws, hiding her piebald cheeks behind her
palms. "Betcha. E'ry five yeer. Jeesh! Needa yeer to
recovah!"

"I'd like to see that, all right. bet you'd hear some good
tunes then!"

"Da bes'!"

They pass some traffic heading out of town, mostly older
people and a few kids toting packs or light hand carts.
Maybe they're headed out to work the fields while the day
is cooler, but N'Doch doesn't see much in the way of tools.
They look like they're just . . . leaving town. Then the gates
are ahead of them, and he goes on the alert. But the six
Tinker wagons file through and into town without incident,
and head for the square.

The townspeople seem eager to welcome them. All along
the main drag, rows of goods are arrayed on tables, on
boards balanced between two chairs, laid out on ragged
blankets or just plunked down in the thick dust of the
street. In the market square, guys in purple robes are
sweeping the paving stones. The two-level platform has
been decked out along its sides with drapes of thin red
cloth. A pair of priestess women are fussing with the folds,
chattering excitedly. The bleachers are up and tucked away
at the far end. In the exact center of the square sits a big

flat dish painted a dull gold. Another purple-robed man is pouring liquid into it from a tall red urn.

Luther calls down from the seat of his yellow van. "Yu see dat t'ing? Das weah dey put da sackerfice, y'know? All tied up nise like a prezint."

But N'Doch reserves judgment. He feels too much like he's walking into some kind of fantasy vid.

Along the far side, the local merchants have set up their booths and stands. The Tinkers are directed to park their wagons on the opposite long side. Blind Rachel pulls up in the middle, between Scroon and Oolyoot. The buzz of anticipation blooms into action as everyone leaps down to unload.

With Brenda busy setting up security around the Tinker stalls, Charlie is being extra friendly. She works beside N'Doch, chatting away as if to make up for all the times she hasn't. "Dis howit go, nah. Dey look aroun', we look aroun', but nobuddy duz a deal til afta da sun cross noon."

"Got it." N'Doch's done an inventory of what he's got to trade, and it isn't much. The other water bottle. The clothes on his back. He shrugs. The unpacking is finished. "Think I'll go take a look, then." He collects Köthen and the girl. "Whaddya say we follow Stoksie around, get the hang of things?"

With his permission, they shadow the little man through the crowd, up and down the sides of the square, then up and down the main street, checking out what he passes by with just a glance, what he notes with a nod, what he studies more carefully. A lot of the booths on the town side of the square stock food items, and Stoksie is looking not only to fill Blind Rachel's larder but also to pick up goods for trade in other villages. There are craftspeople in amongst the food stalls, offering some serviceable pottery, a line of tools and utensils that remind N'Doch of his metal shop class back in school, and of course the coveted leather goods the Tinkers have risked coming for, especially the shoes.

"This is the stuff, huh?"

Stoksie fingers a soft brown satchel with many buttoned pockets. "Lookit dis werk, nah. Da bes'! Anabuddy give good trade fer dis."

"Nice, all right." N'Doch admires a handsome leather

vest. He'd be real interested, if he had anything to give for it.

He sees a lot of junk laid out, too. Used stuff, broken stuff, useless stuff, and stuff that might just find another life in the right hands. He can tell how random the acquisition process is. Except for the Tinkers, there's no regular system for product distribution left intact. There's not even much product. But wandering up and down the line of booths, every so often he comes across a sign that things are still being manufactured somewhere in the world. Not very well, or in very great quantity, but enough so that bits and pieces of it somehow find a way to the podunk town of Phoenix. He sees cheap boxer shorts stamped "Made in Tibet." He fingers a series of small pink dolls shrink-wrapped in plastic so brittle it must be as old as he is, and he just knows some fool is going to trade something they shouldn't for them. He sees a flashlight he could well use if there were still batteries to go with it. And he sees a lot of weaponry, whole stalls full of cudgels, knives, crossbows, and old or broken bits of guns. Nothing too impressive, but there's obviously a market for it. Probably folks have cobbled their firearms together out of stuff just like this. He figures the dealer's got the ammo hidden behind the counter. He spots a broad-bladed hunting knife that reminds him of his beloved fish gutter. He picks it up for a closer look, but Stoksie, with eyes in the back of his head, reaches behind him and takes it out of his hands. With a glance at N'Doch, he puts it back on the counter.

N'Doch clucks his tongue. "No touchee the merchandise, eh?"

Stoksie wags his head side to side. "Yu wanna gud blade, I show yu weah."

"Ah, I get it. Okay, sure. Whenever you're ready."

By midmorning, Stoksie seems to have decided what he wants and what he'll give for it. The crowd is thick, and high enough on a combination of religious fervor and greed to make shoving through it a sweaty and unpleasant effort. Köthen's looking irritable, and the girl could clearly use a break. Stoksie leads them back into the shade of Luther's van to dole out water from the big old cooler stashed in a back compartment. The Tinker booths are mobbed with grazing customers, but behind the wagons is an island of sanity.

"Got an hour, leas', 'fore da swap-work start." Stoksie pulls a square of cloth out of his pocket and ties it around his dripping brow pirate-style. "Yu wan' I show yu weah da hi rollahs shop?"

N'Doch is none too eager to be back in that souped-up crowd again. He sees why the Tinkers don't like this town. Even without a monster, it doesn't feel quite sane. "There's high rollers around here? Coulda fooled me."

"Yu green heah, tallfella, aincha. Der's still sum aroun' got moah den dey need, y'know whad I mean?"

The place Stoksie takes them is not another booth on the market square. It's a nondescript house down a quieter side street, with a beefy woman at the door sporting a real functional looking 9-mm automatic. None of the booth security in the square were showing off their heat so boldly. But Stoksie seems to know this one by name, so in they all go.

The inside is shadowed and close, with shades pulled down over the few small windows. N'Doch bites back a whistle of surprise and admiration, for the stuff laid out on these tables is definitely not junk. It's neatly organized by carrying size and firepower, and though none of it looks real new, you could still outfit a small European army here without much trouble. Too bad there's no more small European *countries,* he tells himself. 'Cept maybe the ones on higher ground.

He tries to look nonchalant, sticking close to Stoksie's side. The girl and Köthen don't seem to get it. They just nose into the room curiously and start picking things up in their hands. Worried, N'Doch drifts after them, counting a table of pistols, including a few old revolvers, a table of shotguns, and a long rack of assault rifles. There are bins of ammo clips and boxed cartridges, shelves stocked with grenades and mortar shells. The wanna-be buyers speak in hushed voices in this temple of doom and destruction, and consult lists hidden in their palms. They're being offered tiny cups of what might actually be tea, though the leaves have been recycled a few more times than they ought to. A pale-skinned boy slips one into N'Doch's hand, then moves on to the girl, trailing an aroma of mint. The girl raises the little cup for a cautious sniff, then glances over at N'Doch with a luminous smile. Papa Dja taught her about tea drinking back in 2013. Or, last month, depending how you look at it.

The run-on scatter of his thoughts tells N'Doch the place is weirding him out. He can't imagine why. He's seen the like of it before, back home, especially during government crackdowns. Stoksie points him toward a display of blades, from jackknives to machetes, so he decides to get down to business, maybe actually find himself a knife. The dagger the women gave him is handy, and real aesthetic, but he'd prefer something a little less refined. Stoksie's at the main counter giving serious consideration to a casing reloader, meanwhile trying to explain to the girl just how a bullet works. N'Doch heads for the knives, then sees Köthen picking at a small table in a corner that's piled not so neatly. He slouches over to soak up a bit of the baron's perspective on twenty-first century armaments, or is it twenty-second or -third? He's still not sure, and who could tell from what's laid out in this joint?

"Whacher doin' at the junk pile, Dolph?"

A closer look tells him what's drawn Köthen's interest. It's all repro stuff, replicas of antique guns and hand weapons, like battle-axes and Roman broadswords. Mostly it's cheap plastic, but there's some serious historical work in real wood and metal.

"May look familiar, dude, but it's all fake." N'Doch holds up a funnel-mouthed pistol that looks more lethal to the shooter than to the victim. "They don't really work."

"Why make a weapon that does not work?"

"You're way too logical, my man. People used to collect 'em, for fun."

"I see." Köthen lifts a short, cylindrical object, turns it over in his hand in puzzlement.

"Now that is a serious weapon. That's a light saber."

"A what?"

N'Doch laughs. "Just a kid's toy. Like I said, none of this shit really works."

Köthen sets the cylinder down, then reaches to flip aside a flap of cloth covering the bottom of the pile. It doesn't come easy and there's a rasp of metal as he yanks on it. The ring of true steel is unmistakable.

"Listen to that."

N'Doch helps clear away the plastic dueling pistols and chrome-plated Colt .45s. The fabric underneath is soft and heavy, and looks like someone's used it to wipe the floor of a garage. Köthen feels through its folds for the shape of the object inside. His hand grasps, then stills. N'Doch hears his sharp intake of breath. Then Köthen is hauling on the fabric with both hands and all his strength.

"Whoa! Easy! What's up?" N'Doch scrambles to catch the stuff that's flung off as Köthen drags the whole bundle free of the pile. He has an odd presentiment as the baron stands there with the object cradled in both his hands, staring down at it in disbelief. It's long and narrow, very long, and it looks heavy.

"Is that what I think it is?"

Köthen lays the bundle crosswise on the pile and slowly peels back the wrappings. The inside face of the cloth is unstained, and a deep maroon. Within its rich folds nestles a sword.

Köthen's hands hover over it as if it might disappear if he touches it. Then he flattens the fabric away from the hilt, exposing its intricate design: a winged dragon wound around the trunk of a tree. *"Um Gottes Willen!"*

"Oh, nice," approves N'Doch. "Appropriate, too. Kinda seen better days, though."

"Yes," says Köthen strangely. "It has."

Slowly, as if reluctant, the baron slides his right hand under the hilt and fits his palm to the grip. He stares at it some more. "Surely I am dreaming."

"A perfect fit, eh?"

"Fetch milady."

It's such a strangled kind of murmur that N'Doch finally picks up on there being something more going on here than the dude finally finding a weapon he knows how to use. "Why? What's up?"

Köthen lifts the sword free of its velvet shroud. In the dim light, the long blade glints dully through layers of corrosion and patina. "Fetch her!"

"Okay, okay." N'Doch goes. When he gets back, Köthen has the sword lowered, concealed at his side. There's an odd light in his eyes, but he watches the girl's approach like she might be bringing him news of his own death sentence.

"What is it, my lord?"

Köthen frames a reply, stumbles, falls silent. N'Doch stares at him, amazed. The man's a wreck. Köthen starts again, hoarse and halting. "Milady, I beg you. Tell me if I have entirely taken leave of my senses . . ."

She looks up at him calmly. "Never, my lord."

Köthen takes the sword in both hands just below the crossguard, and holds the hilt up in front of her.

Her response is the same sudden gasp. "Oh! God's Holy Angels! But how . . .? Where . . .?"

Köthen nods once, as if the sentence has been delivered as expected, then enfolds the sword in both arms as if it was a child, and bows his head over it. "What does it mean?"

"I know not, my lord baron."

"Is it all preordained, then? Have we no choice in the matter?"

"Perhaps some do, my lord. I know I do not."

N'Doch shifts impatiently. "Is one of you gonna tell me what the hell's going on?"

"A kind of miracle," the girl sighs.

"It's a sword, not a miracle. C'mon, what's the deal?"

"Not just any sword. Sir Hal's sword."

N'Doch grins at her. "Hey, right. You think I was born yesterday?"

"It's true, N'Doch," she insists earnestly. "You must believe me."

He looks from one to the other, and sees they don't care if he believes it or not. They already know it for a fact. He wonders if the town's undercurrent of hysteria has gotten to them. "C'mon, you guys, be real. There's probably a hundred old swords like that."

Köthen lifts his head. "No, though I, too, would prefer that explanation. But I *know* this weapon, like I know my own hands, every scar, every detail. Ten years I fetched and cleaned and honed this blade, and buckled it on the knight who was my master."

The girl says, "That sword was laid at Lord Earth's feet when Sir Hal first pledged fealty to him."

And then to Sedou, that night in Deep Moor. Damn! The dragon hilt. N'Doch remembers it now, all too well.

He wants to go there with the two of them, really he does, but sometimes the moment gets so heavy, it kicks him smack into rebound. Drowning in momentousness, he swims for the opposite shore.

He laughs. "Well then, I guess we just gotta buy it for you, Dolph, so you can take care of it some more."

Erde knew then what she needed to do. "My lord baron, if you would wait here a moment until we return . . . come, N'Doch, we must speak with Stoksie."

OH, DRAGON, TELL ME . . . IS THIS WHAT IS MEANT TO BE?

THIS IS A GREAT AND MEANINGFUL SIGN. IT MUST NOT BE IGNORED.

DO YOU KNOW WHAT IT MEANS?

PERHAPS THE VERY WEAPON THAT BARON KÖTHEN HAS BE-TRAYED IS PUT INTO HIS HANDS SO HE MIGHT REDEEM HIMSELF BY THE PROPER USE OF IT.

THEN THERE WILL BE FIGHTING.

INEVITABLY.

Erde unpinned the dragon brooch, pressing the carved red stone into the curve of her palm. It was as cold as ice.

AH! THE STONE KNOWS ITS OWN PATH. IT NO LONGER WEL-COMES YOU.

YET I AM SAD TO LET IT GO.

She felt as if the brooch had been with her all her life, though it was barely two months since her beloved nurse Alla had provided her with it and the means for her deliverance from Tor Alte, thus sending her off toward her meeting with Destiny.

N'Doch leaned in to cover up the big jewel glowing in her palm. He was no longer laughing. "You sure about this, girl?"

"Never more sure."

He smiled, but not truly in jest. "I shoulda stole the damn thing when I had the chance."

"You tried. Your own destiny would not allow it."

"Yeah, well . . ."

Stoksie sensed the suppressed urgency waiting behind him and broke off his conversation with the weapons dealer. "Whatsit nah? Sumpin' on yer minds?"

N'Doch dropped one long arm around the small man's shoulder and drew him away from the counter. "Stoksie, my man . . . you think any of these high rollers might be interested in a piece of *real* jewelry?"

She felt naked without it, but by the end of the afternoon, the dragon brooch had given opportunity for the most inspired bargaining of Stoksie's life. Or so he claimed. With it, he managed, without calling too much attention to his intricate manipulations, to provision Blind Rachel's two wagons and one of Scroon's to capacity with food, lamp oil, and trade items, including a small trinket for each of the children. He acquired several new weapons and the ammunition to fit them. For N'Doch, he bought a knife, the leather vest and a coveted T-shirt, for himself a new leather satchel. For Luther, spare wheels for the caravan and several sacks of grain for the mules. For Erde, a woven sun hat and change of comfortable clothing. Boy's clothing, of course. Plus a small kit of items that he swore were of high trade value, to be stowed away in her pack for later use.

Most important, to her if not to the Tinkers, Baron Köthen now walked beside her with Sir Hal's dragon-hilted sword slung across his back. The long leather sheath was made for a heavier, wider weapon, but Köthen declared in still-stunned tones that it was perfectly suitable for the way he'd be wearing it.

"Yu Blin' Rachel Crew nah, fer shur!" Stoksie looked equally stunned by all this sudden good fortune, now that he saw it all actually being loaded into his wagons. "Mebbe we all jus' go home nah, not hafta trade wit' nobuddy we doan like!"

"Dear Stoksie," Erde assured him, "It's only right that we return to you the generosity you've so freely offered us."

"We gib yu a cupla daze. Yu gib us a hafa yeer, mebbe moah."

She noticed how careful the Tinkers were to disguise their astonishing windfall as the results of a normal day's trade, even from Scroon and Oolyoot, who were happily packing away the overflow.

"We godda stik tagedda," said Luther as he opened one

of the grain sacks to give a portion to Blind Rachel's mules.
"But dere's one t'ing we ain't tole 'em yet."

"About Sedou?"

He nodded. When the other Crews' mules caught scent
of it, he sent Charlie over with a canful to keep them quiet.
Though he complained bitterly about the lack of room inside his tight-packed caravan, Erde noticed that he made
sure to leave a good-sized space in the back corner free of
cargo. She asked him why.

He gave her an embarrassed grin. "Well, da day not ovah
yet. Yu nevah know whad else I wanna pick up."

But it was close onto dusk. Surely the Tinkers were finished trading for the day. Tall torches were being lit around
the edge of the square, and Scroon Crew's wagons had
already packed up and headed out, though they were having trouble breaking a path through the milling throng.
From the top of Luther's wagon, Erde could see that the
booths across the square were still busy with customers. As
she helped him fasten the grain sacks to the caravan's roof,
she pointed out a scuffle that broke out around one of
the stalls.

Luther nodded. "Get summa dat nah. S'hot, pebble iz
tired. Dey wan' whad dey wan'. Won' take no fer an ansa."

"Oh, dear . . . look!" Scroon Crew's wagons had made
it to the end of the square, then been turned back at the
intersection by a cluster of robed men and women who
were officiously barring all passage down the main street.
Customers were leaving the stalls, hurrying toward the
hubbub.

"Huh." Luther squinted out over the slate rooftops. A
dust cloud trailed from the direction of the town gates.
Somewhere down the main street, a cry went up. One of
the robed men snatched up a lighted torch, ran through the
crowd to the huge golden bowl in the middle of the square,
and touched the torch to its glimmering surface. A bright
flame shot up from the center, taller than the man was.
"Mus' be her, den. Lookit dem all run aroun'. Da priestess
got heah early."

N'Doch's on his way back from helping Scroon Crew fight their way through the crowd when Köthen grabs his arm.

"Wait."

He sees the wagons halted at the mouth of the square, a flurry of red-and-purple robes, and torches. He and Köthen back against a wall and sit tight to see if Scroon protests the roadblock, and if they'll need any help.

"Must be the princess, knocking at the gate."

"She is a priestess, I believe," Köthen says. "Another heathen witch."

"You got a real problem with that, doncha." N'Doch grins. "Whatever. Helluva fuss to make over some old crone."

The driver of the lead Scroon wagon argues a little with the Chapter House priests and their townie muscle, but meanwhile the other Tinkers hop down to lead the mules aside. Puzzled, N'Doch watches as the wagons willingly split left and right to park right next to the tall torches the priests have lit on either side of the intersection. "Maybe they just want to hang around for a good view of the parade. You hear music or anything?"

Köthen shakes his head. If there is any, it can't be heard over the roar and rumble in the square.

N'Doch is disappointed. He's really been missing his music lately. "A real ceremony oughta have drums at least. Let's head back."

"Let's stay a bit. See what we're up against."

"You're the boss, yer lordship."

They work their way closer to the edge of the crowd. N'Doch's height gives him a useful advantage, for once. He can see clear over the heads of these puny townies, or so he's come to think of them already, in Tinker fashion, after rubbing elbows with too many of them all day in too little space. A few blocks down the dusty main drag, a line of marchers wavers into view through the rising heat and dusk. "Here they come. Soldiers, looks like, with big flashy helmets and . . . hey, get this! Spears!"

"A suitable weapon for infantry."

"Maybe in your day. Won't do much against the firepower we've seen around here. Okay, now there's this big boxy gold thing coming, with four guys lugging it."

The crowd is starting to moan and sway a little, as if a wind has come up. Köthen cranes his neck a little to see. The big sword stiffens his back like a second, crosswise spine. "A sedan chair, Dochmann. I am relieved to discover a few things that I know about the future which you do not."

"Up yours, yer lordship. What's a sedan chair?"

"Most likely, the priestess rides in that chair."

"And those poor suckers gotta carry her? Probably too fat and old to walk on her own. Hey, there's a second one coming up behind it. That one's even bigger."

The soldiers pass by. They're taller, better fed than the townies he's seen, or than any of the Tinkers, and they march in pretty good order, despite their antique weaponry. Köthen studies them with professional interest.

"Some of these men are . . . women!" he exclaims softly.

They are indeed. Tall, strapping women with steely eyes. N'Doch chuckles. "Welcome to that future you know so much about."

When the first sedan chair draws level with him, N'Doch sees that the side curtains have been artfully draped and tied open, so that the occupant is regally framed by graceful folds of rich, gold fabric, made even more picturesque by the lavender dusk and the flickering torchlight. The townies cry out prayers. He's surrounded by a forest of scrawny, reaching arms. Someone here really knows how to stage an entrance. Now he can see inside the chair.

"Hey, that's a guy in there! Big, good-looking dude with too much hair and too much jewelry. Looks like he owns the place."

Köthen tosses him a wolfish glance. "Perhaps he does. Such things are not unheard of, you know."

"Right. Sorry. Forgot who I was talking to."

A bunch of younger guys all dressed alike follow, then another squad of helmeted soldiers, then a pair of women in the same red robes as the women at the Chapter House, only these two are veiled. After them comes the second chair. This one looks like it's really made of solid gold, though N'Doch knows that's impossible, and it has a big red dragon right there on the side, just like the one carved on the brooch. N'Doch wonders where that stone will spend its next millennium.

Up at the entrance to the square, one of Scroon Crew's mules suddenly objects to a particular flare of torchlight, and starts up a loud braying and shying about on his sharp, heavy hooves. The first chair gets hustled past into the square but the second soldier squad ducks sideways in confusion like they've never seen a spooked mule before. Scroon Crew races about trying to calm the mule, though it looks to N'Doch like they're doing just the opposite, and the whole procession staggers to a halt. The bearers of the second chair stop and set it down right in front of Köthen and N'Doch. All around them, the townies fall to their knees, moaning and murmuring.

The gauzy, shimmering curtains are closed. Nothing is visible in the shadowed interior until a tawny, slim hand parts the drapery and the High Priestess herself peers out to see why they've stopped.

The two men share the same reflexive grunt of approval.

The priestess is young and she is beautiful. Really beautiful. More beautiful than any vid star N'Doch can think of, off the top of his head. He wants to whistle aloud, but he's pretty sure it'd be considered inappropriate. She's such a mix, he couldn't begin to guess what her background is, but it looks like she got the very best of all of them. Her eyes are dark, her features delicate but lively, her skin that flawless espresso-and-cream that makes N'Doch wants to put his hands all over her. He nudges Köthen. The baron is transfixed.

N'Doch bends to hiss into his ear. "Hey. Dolph, didn't your mama teach you not to stare?"

As if she feels their gaze, like some kind of magic heat ray, the priestess turns toward them, a slow haughty move like you make when you're showing someone how little you notice them. N'Doch has the word "bitch" all ready on his tongue when the woman's glance slides past him, past Köthen, then flickers back as if surprised, and settles on the baron in what appears to be shock. N'Doch thinks this could be getting dangerous. Everybody within ten klicks is looking at her, while she and the baron stare at each other long past what's polite between strangers. Like, he'd have a big hole lasered through his chest if he stood between them.

He nudges Köthen again. "Whatcha trying to do, get us in trouble?"

Then the logjam clears up ahead, and the four bearers bend, grip, and hoist their golden burden to their shoulders. The procession moves forward again, carrying the High Priestess with it. But her gaze drifts back toward Köthen again, and she gives him a kind of stunned smile that transforms her face from that of a proud, self-contained aristocrat to that of an astonished girl. Then she withdraws behind her curtains, and the chair disappears behind the next infantry squad and a long train of hand-hauled supply wagons.

N'Doch is irritated. Haven't these guys ever heard of mule power? He jogs Köthen's shoulder brusquely. He's pissed at him for attracting all the attention. "C'mon. We're outa here."

Köthen follows willingly this time, as if he's too busy thinking to resist.

N'Doch hugs the facades of the houses fronting the square, where the going's a little easier. The crowd is surging inward toward the center of the square, but coming up against some force or barrier he can't see. "Hey! Watch where you're going, man!" He hauls Köthen out of the path of a loaded hand cart. "So the ice prince has blood in his veins after all."

"Dochmann! I have never seen a more beautiful woman. Have you?"

"Well, she wasn't looking at me, so what does it matter?" N'Doch thinks about how the girl back at the wagon would feel if she'd seen what he's just seen. "And you could wipe that silly grin off your face, y'know."

Köthen laughs, a charged-up, throaty laugh. A townie shoves past him rudely and he doesn't even notice. "You are jealous, friend N'Doch."

He's trying to imagine a way he can reasonably deny this. Through the shifting crowd, a face catches his eye. He stops short.

Köthen is instantly alert. "What?"

"That girl again. The one I was following."

"Alone?"

"Couldn't tell." N'Doch shrugs uneasily and moves on. By the time they're back at the wagons, he's slick with the crowd's close heat and the effort of plowing through it. He sees that during the pack up, the four remaining wagons have been reshuffled into an open square, with the mules all hitched and facing clockwise. Blind Rachel and Oolyoot are clustered inside, in conference. Brenda and Charlie are already perched on the roof of Luther's van, weapons in hand. No one likes the feel of this crowd. N'Doch climbs over the traces of an Oolyoot wagon, and hears Luther sending the girl up into the driver's seat, telling her to stay put with uncharacteristic brusqueness.

"Someone's a little anxious," he comments to the baron. "You are not?"

"Well, yeah, actually I am. But I thought it was just the dragon working on me."

Köthen reaches a hand back to stroke the hilt of the sword brushing his neck. "I feel like a dog before a thunderstorm."

"What say we go sit with the Pit Bull . . . better view from up there."

They scale the outside of the van, using the big steel latches as handholds. Köthen's sword clinks against the insulated metal skin.

"Yo, Brenda!" N'Doch calls out. "Don't shoot, it's only me." As his head clears the top, he finds his nose mere inches from the barrel end of Brenda's new hunting rifle, courtesy of the dragon brooch. He frees up a palm and eases the muzzle aside. "Nice gun, huh?"

Charlie giggles. "Yo, Dockman."

Brenda gives him a sour nod, then offers him a hand to hoist him over the edge. Köthen follows easily on his own. He finds an open spot, unslings and draws his sword, then settles with it across his lap. From a pouch on the sheath, he pulls out oil and a whetstone. N'Doch squints out into the deepening dusk. Torches flare around all sides of the square. Robed men and women are pressing back the mewling crowd, to open up a wide path from the main street and clear the center around the flaming gilt bowl, over the design of the red dragon. A phalanx of them, in red and gold, forms beside the dragon's upraised claw.

"The reception committee," N'Doch observes cheerfully.

Moments later, Sedou climbs up. "Almost as crowded up here as it is down there." He hangs his legs over the outside edge and invites N'Doch to join him. They watch the doings in the square for a while, as the priestess' entourage enters from the main drag and begins a slow ritual circuit around the outside. Then Sedou says, "I've told Stoksie and the others not to be concerned should I suddenly disappear on them."

N'Doch takes a breath. "Disappearing's the easy part. Didja tell 'em what else might happen?"

But Sedou isn't interested in sibling banter. His eyes have a deep-well darkness in them. "I may need a new song, my brother. I may need it soon."

There's that ant nest stirring in his gut again. "Yeah? What sort of song?"

"Not a Sedou song. Not a people song at all."

"Hunh?" N'Doch's shoulders hunch over the keyboard he imagines in his lap. "You want, like, some kind of animal?"

"No." Sedou gets real still for a moment and N'Doch just knows the dragon is struggling to hold her man-shape. Whatever thoughts she's thinking, they're not about being human. "Imagine it, my brother. I need . . . a song of release. Of waves breaking and rivers flowing. Of glaciers melting into the sea. Of the sky giving up its moisture as rain."

"You need a water song," said N'Doch quietly, and suddenly all the ants in his gut are a chill tickling the base of his spine. "I get it. You need *your* song. The others have all been *my* songs."

"Yes." The dragon/man's smile outshines the torches. "And they have served me well in the world of men. But now I must be what I truly am, to the utmost of my powers. And you must help me."

N'Doch coughs. The chill has made it all the way to his throat. "Not sure I'm up to it, bro."

Then Sedou does the thing N'Doch's wanted all along, ever since the song that conjured his brother as a grown man. The thing he can't ask for, because he needs it more than he knows how to say. Sedou leans over, wraps him in the curl of his big arm, and holds him, easy and firm, as if nothing could ever go wrong again.

You're up to it.

Release, damn it, thinks N'Doch, and while trying to

grasp what he means, he does. His hands, his gut, his brain
and finally, his heart, all unclench, as he releases himsel
to the dragon, no longer understanding his reasons for re
sistance. He feels the dragon enter him, almost as a ma
enters a woman. But it's his maleness that she enters, and
her own female nature that he takes inside himself, like
light, like a revelation, like a song. He shudders with it in
his brother's grasp, stunned by the wealth of songs within
him, waiting to be born.

Then he becomes aware of himself again, a grown ma
cradled like a child in another grown man's arms. He imag
ines Köthen behind him, watching this darkly, misappre
hending. He sits up, reaching for autonomy, for a shred o
distance. But he is not the same man he was just moment
ago. He will never be that other man again. He has a
dragon inside of him.

He grasps his brother's shoulder and shakes it lightly
inarticulate with gratitude. "Just let me know. That song'
be there for you."

Down in the market square, the last of the late ligh
seems to have settled over the dragon in the paving stones
The man-sized flame in the golden bowl makes the image
dance as if it was alive. The procession of soldiers and
priests and sedan chairs completes its outer circuit unde
the glow of the torches. The leading squad of infantry doe
a left face right in front of the Tinker wagons, turning in
toward the center and the block of waiting clergy. The
marchers split neatly around them and re-form in an honor
guard behind. The sedan chairs follow and are set dow
side by side on the dragon's breast. All motion swirls to a
halt. Only the dust stirs, and the leaping, crackling torch
flames. Köthen sets down his cleaning rag and slides ove
to watch, sword in hand.

The guy in the first chair steps out onto the pavement
Swathed in red and gold, he is as big as N'Doch ha
guessed, tall and bronze-skinned. His perfect musculature
is revealed to all by an open robe, a glittery open vest and
a magnificently naked chest.

"That dude's seen some hard time in the gym," mut
ters N'Doch.

Köthen sits up a little straighter. "Fighting man."

"Nah. Pumper's muscle, that's all. Look at those show-off duds. Bet he spends most of his day looking in the mirror."

"Trust me on this," says the baron.

The muscle man accepts the many bows of the reception committee, then strides to the second chair, draws back the gold curtain and extends his hand. The High Priestess takes it and steps out of the shadow into the orange-and-lavender flicker of torchlight.

Köthen leans forward.

N'Doch says to Sedou in a stage whisper. "So. Whaddya think of the baron's new girlfriend?"

A sharp crack explodes the silence, then another. A double echo clatters around the walls of the square. N'Doch sees shattered stone puff up right at the priestess' feet.

"Shit! Sniper!" He ducks.

Köthen leaps to his feet, sword at ready, and glares around for the source of the sound.

Another crack.

N'Doch drags Köthen down hard as the others flatten around them and roll off the roof into cover. Köthen struggles to shake him off, but N'Doch hangs tight and yells at him.

"That's gunfire, Dolph! Tryin' to get yourself killed?"

Köthen stops struggling. "Where?"

"Got me. We're sitting ducks here, but so far they ain't shooting at us."

A fourth and fifth shot. N'Doch hears the slugs track above their heads just before the sound ricochet drowns out the direction of fire. Down in the square, everyone's screaming and diving for cover. The big guy in the fancy clothes has already proved Köthen's estimation of him. He's snatched the priestess girl around the waist and dragged her into the thickest part of the crowd. Soon N'Doch sees the golden shimmer of his robe rising like a sail, a billow of distraction, grabbed by one too many eager hands as it floats free. Immediately, there's fighting over it, despite the hail of bullets that follows. Doesn't matter. The big guy's no longer inside it. He and the woman have vanished.

Now the firing is coming from more than one place. What began as panic in the square is devolving into riot and mayhem. At least one priest lies facedown on the paving stones, his blood mixing with the red of the tiled dragon. N'Doch feels the van jerk into motion.

"Dockman!" Charlie pops her head up beside him. "Gichu down nah! Gittin' ouda heah, pronto!"

Köthen's still staring down into the square.

N'Doch grabs his arm. "She's okay! Gotta be. Your fast-thinking fighting man snatched her outa there. Come on!"

Across the square, the trade booths caught unpacked by the procession's early arrival are under attack from sneak thieves and looters. Some of the gunfire's coming from there, as townie security moves in hard, but not all. N'Doch hustles Köthen off the roof of the van, then hangs over the front to peer into the driver's seat. Luther's down with the lead mule, calming him, urging him. The girl's inside, pale and wide-eyed, with the reins in her hands. N'Doch somersaults into the seat beside her.

"Shit's hittin' the fan again, girl! What is it with the two of us?"

He gets the barest ghost of a smile out of her. He doesn't understand. She looks like something terrible is about to happen. He thinks it already has. The van stutters forward as Brenda slides onto the back of the second mule to growl into its ears. In Luther's cobbled-up side mirror, N'Doch sees Charlie vault onto the lead mule of the team behind them, Beneatha's flatbed, now heavy with stacked cargo tied down under the stained canvas top. When that wagon starts to roll, the two Oolyoot wagons turn out of formation to follow.

"Guns." The girl bites her lips. "Where is Baron Köthen?"

"He's fine. Look in your mirror."

Köthen's alongside the van, his sword sheathed across his back again. He's taken up one of the Tinker quarter-staves to fend off looters. Several of the Oolyoot Crew are doing the same. N'Doch counts heads. Shit, Only eight.

"Where's Stoksie and Ysabel?"

"I don't know. Weren't they . . . ?"

"Damn!"

And then the alarm shrills through him, unmistakable as middle C.

The girl stiffens, snatching at the seat with both hands. "Oh, God, oh God! Oh, Holy Mary, mother of God, pray for us now in our hour of need!" The reins snake loose in her lap until she gets a grip on herself and snatches them up again. "He's coming, N'Doch! Oh, dear God, he's coming!"

"I know, I know." He looks around for Sedou. Already the song is rising in his throat.

She's been bored and hot all day, and her premonition has faded.

Only its unusual size has promised to make Phoenix Town interesting. Until two things occur: she sees the man with the sword, and someone starts shooting at her. Her premonition has returned.

I shouldn't have come! I should never have insisted! The God warned me! I should have known better!

Ducking away under Luco's strong arm, Paia forces down her panic in order to concentrate on moving with him as he skillfully dodges and weaves, and not think about the outrage of being shot at. The God has told her that he outlawed the few firearms that were left after the Wars. But now she sees them everywhere in this shoving, panicked, ravening mob. Either the God lied, or the God is not as omniscient as he would like her to think.

And where is he when I really need him!

It's hard, with the crack of gunfire and all the shouting and screaming, to concentrate on her summons. When the first shot spattered marble dust into her eyes, she called out to the God instinctively. Then Luco's defensive maneuver distracted her. Quick, reliable Luco. How could she have ever thought this ex-soldier had gone soft?

He has her tight about the waist, as if he fears losing her to the heave of the mob. She has the odd impression there are strangers racing beside them, in step with their every turn, as if clearing them a path. Where are her chaperones? Where are Luco's strong young men? Suddenly, the wall of a building looms up in front of them.

"This way, my priestess!" Luco ducks sideways along the stones, then into an alley that opens up as if it was exactly where he expected it to be. It is narrow, and choked with terrified villagers fleeing the chaos in the square. Luco jos-

tles through them, hugging the left-hand wall, until one o
the many closed doors that they pass is miraculously oper
Luco hauls her inside, into darkness. The others sh
thought to be their companions are swept by with the mot
Luco kicks the door shut. Sunk in total blackness, she hear
him lock it.

Paia can tell she's in a very small room. Her throat and
lungs constrict. "What if they find us in here? We'll b
trapped! Wouldn't we be safer if we kept moving?"

"We will. First you need a chance to catch your breath."

A soft flare eases her panic as Luco lights an oil lamp
set on a little table in the middle of a low, square room
Shamed by the priest's calm, Paia tries to still the heaving
of her chest. She is not only breathless, she is terrified. Bu
she doesn't want Luco to have to slap sense into her, as h
has a few times in the past. She wants to appear strong and
capable, for once. She has survived assassination attempt
before. Of course, then she'd had the familiar security o
the Citadel to comfort her.

The room she's in now tells Paia almost nothing abou
its usual occupants. Could they really own nothing but the
few dishes and chairs, and the two iron cots lined up along
one wall? She watches Luco as he moves briskly about the
tiny space. She envies his confidence in such a dire circum
stance.

He opens a few cupboards, finds cups and a stonewar
jug. He fills the cups with water from the jug, and hand
one to her. "Drink up, my priestess. I'm not sure whe
we'll have another chance."

Water? How convenient. She eyes him over the rim o
the cup. Does she sense the God's presence somewher
about? She thinks not, and yet, there's just the faintes
echo. "Luco, tell me the truth now. This isn't another on
of your schemes with the God . . .?"

He laughs, but with an edge to it. "No, my priestess.
assure you it is not."

"Well, we should thank these villagers whose hom
we've invaded."

"Easy enough." He opens another cupboard, searche
through the scant piles of clothing there, pulls out hi
choices and tosses them on the table. "You can leave then
your expensive and conspicuous clothing. Put those on."

She gapes at him. Is this the man for whom every Temple garment is a treasure? "Really? Just leave it here? What will my poor chambermaid say?"

Luco's mouth quirks. "She'll survive. If I'm to extract you safely from this tinderbox of a town, you'll have to go incognito."

He's found garments for himself as well. Without even turning his back, he strips out of his golden Temple vest and belted white pants, and slips into darker, looser pants and a long-sleeved T-shirt. He folds the ceremonial glitter precisely and puts it away in the cupboard. "Come, now. We should hurry."

Paia does turn her back. Having many times considered trying to seduce her head priest, now she is shy in front of him. The shirt and pants he has given her are patched here and there, and soft with age, but clean and comfortable. And they conceal her body as completely as her beloved sweats. Paia rather likes them. She steals a look to see if he's watching her change, but only catches him glancing at his empty wrist, a nervous gesture that she recognizes. Her father had it. It's the habit of a man once used to wearing a watch. She has never noticed it in Luco before.

"Ready, my priestess?"

She nods. He gathers up her Temple finery from the floor where she's let it drop, and folds it, regarding her with bemused patience. He stows it away in the cupboard with his own. But instead of the main door, he opens the one narrow closet in the room and holds out his hand. Puzzled, Paia takes it. Luco leans back to blow out the lamp. The void surrounds them once more, but his voice is soft at her ear.

"We must be silent, my priestess. We move between walls and through spaces thought not to exist. We mustn't call attention to our passage."

Finally Paia understands that this room isn't just a happy accident. "How did you know about all this?"

"Has the God not charged me with your safe return, on pain of my life? I'm a careful man, my priestess. I like to plan for any eventuality. Hush, now. Not a sound until I say so."

He leads her through a long and complex darkness. Sometimes the walls are close on either side, sometimes an outstretched hand finds only one. Almost always, the ceiling is right above her head. There are twists and turns too numerous to count, and only occasionally a bit of dim light strays through from the rooms on the other side of the walls. When it does, she hears screams and gunfire. She wonders if the God has heard her summons, or if he's punishing her by ignoring her. She can't shake the sensation that he's nearby somewhere. But even if he is, she can't imagine him manifesting inside these tiny passages.

At last she hears the creak of another door. Luco leads her into another small, dim room, only this one has a curtained window. He goes to it immediately and peers out between the drapes. The screams and shouting are louder here, close to the street, but Paia is sure she hears the rattle of wagon wheels. She joins him at the window, but he does not move aside to let her see out.

"Are those our wagons? Have they come for us?"

"Not our wagons. But they'll do." He turns away from the window and looks down on her, an oddly contemplative expression abstracting his gaze. He surprises her by smoothing a stray lock of hair away from her eyes. A very paternalistic gesture for Son Luco. "Now listen carefully. We are in very grave danger. You must do exactly as I tell you. No questions, no tantrums. You must trust me absolutely. No matter how it may seem, you are safe in my hands."

"Oh, Luco, you needn't frighten me to make me behave. I'm there already. I'll do as you say."

He pats her cheek. "Good girl." He glances through the curtains once more, then grasps her hand firmly and opens the door.

Erde guided the dragon in from his hiding place in the woods just as the shadow of vast wings swept over the square, blotting out the last whisper of dusk. She felt N'Doch's strength beside her, steadying her as if she were a spooked carriage horse. She wanted to tell him about Fire, how she knew and what she saw, but there wasn't time. Fire's passage roiled the hot air, making the torches leap and flare. His shriek shattered the din of the fistfights and shouting and sent even the looters scurrying for their lives. As the great shadow passed, the priests of the Temple looked up from aiding their wounded fellows and fell down on the paving stones in terror and awe.

DRAGON, ARE YOU THERE? I CANNOT SEE YOU.

Earth had never wanted nor been able to hide himself from her before.

I AM. DO NOT ASK WHERE, FOR YOUR OWN SAFETY.

The Tinker wagons moved faster toward the intersection as the terror-stricken mob stampeded into the side streets and alleys, trampling the slower and weaker in their desperation to flee. Luther and Brenda struggled to keep the frightened mules from bolting out of control. Beside Erde, N'Doch was singing. It was a wordless, soaring sort of song, unlike any she'd ever heard him sing. Erde felt the power in it, like the surge of oceans.

The shadow passed again, like the shiver of a dream, with a metallic rattle of wings and another rending cry. The air smelled like ash and molten iron. Erde felt him up there, searching, his inhuman eyes raking the darkened ground. She made her mind go as still as she knew how.

He knows me, just as the hell-priest knows me!

At the mouth of the square, Scroon Crew's wagons blocked the intersection. The mob broke against them like a wave and surged away to either side, scrambling for the lesser exits, or pounding on the doors of the houses along the square, begging for shelter. Others just dropped to the ground where they were and prayed. The wail of fearful believers rose to drown out the shouting. Somehow, somewhere, there was still gunfire. Thumping on the caravan's sides drew Erde's glance to Baron Köthen. His face was alight with grim satisfaction as he wielded his quarterstaff against a pair of men trying to climb up on the wagon. He was glad to be in action at last. They were almost to the intersection.

DRAGON! THE TINKERS ARE LEAVING! WHAT SHOULD I DO?

GO WITH THEM AND BE SAFE. YOU'VE DONE YOUR PART. NOW WE MUST DO OURS.

And don't speak to us! You can't hide yourselves as we can. He'll go after you, and distract us from our task.

As Lady Water's voice faded in Erde's head, the shrieking dragon above swooped down out of the night and settled with a sound of clashing swords in the center of the square. Erde recoiled into the shadow of the caravan's roof. She was sure he would pick her out of the crowd. But she could not keep from easing forward just a bit to stare.

In the jittery light of the torches, Lord Fire's scales glimmered like the fabled treasure hoard of gold and fabulous jewels. He was winged, horned, shred-eared, and clawed. His barbed tail coiled around his muscled haunches like a snake ready to strike. His eyes flamed like blown embers, bright heat in darkness. He curved his plated back, arched his long, sensuous neck, and let a curl of smoke rise from his cavernous nostrils. The very essence of Dragon. He was awesome, magnificent.

And horrific. This was Baron Köthen's understanding of dragon. This was what he'd met in the hell-priest's eyes.

Lord Fire himself.

Erde did not know how this could be, but now she was sure of it.

The wagons slowed and halted as the Tinkers, even the mules, stared at him, astonished. With a deep resounding crescendo, N'Doch completed his song. For a moment, the world was becalmed, as if life itself had paused on its journey to pay homage to this lordly creature, the king of ancient myth, preening himself in the village square.

"I never thought . . ." murmured Erde.

"That he'd be so beautiful?" N'Doch finished for her. "Me neither. He knows it, too. Look at him strut!"

Then the stillness ended. Lord Fire lifted his elegant head and roared. Great booming echoes beat around the building facades and against Erde's eardrums. The priests of the town and a few who had come in with the procession scrambled into a huddle and prostrated themselves before him. The dragon seemed to be waiting. The curve of his neck tightened into an impatient arc. The barb on his tail, as tall as a man, lashed back and forth.

One of the priests, stuttering and stumbling, dragged himself onto his knees and struggled to string together enough words to explain what had just happened before Lord Fire's arrival. "The Great God," he called the dragon, but could get no farther. Another, facedown, tried to help him, then suddenly all of them, men and women, were up on their knees babbling hysterically, begging the "Great God's" forgiveness. Packs of abject worshipers, huddled around the square, added their own chorus of wails and moans.

Fire snaked his head around to stare at the shivering priests. With an angry flare of his enameled wings, he reared up and roared again. Three of the priests collapsed in a faint. The rest threw themselves flat on the blood-stained stones, mumbling incoherently.

Erde sensed a momentous gathering of dragon energies. A decision. The time for confrontation had come.

I CAN TELL YOU WHAT HAS OCCURRED HERE, BROTHER.

Fire dropped to all fours, poised for battle like a cat. N'Doch and Erde shuddered as a new voice invaded their heads: deep, raw, and furious.

WHAT? YOU? HERE?

YES, BROTHER.

Earth's presence was directionless and vast. Even Erde could not tell where he was. Fire glared around the square.

LEAVE ME ALONE! YOU'RE TOO LATE!

NEVER!

WHERE IS SHE? WHERE IS THE PRIESTESS OF MY TEMPLE?

WE KNOW NOT.

YOU HAVE TAKEN HER!

If you'd listen to those humans instead of frightening them . . .

YOU HERE, TOO!

Is this how you greet us after so long?

YOU'VE TAKEN HER!

She flees an assassin.

LIARS! WHERE IS SHE?

WHERE IS OUR SISTER AIR?

HOW SHOULD I KNOW?

Caught in the maelstrom of the dragons' power, Erde still heard the note of petulance in Lord Fire's tone. For some reason, it gave her courage.

WE THINK WE DO.

FIND HER YOURSELF! I AM BUSY.

BUSY TERRORIZING THOSE YOU WERE CREATED TO SERVE. MUST WE REMIND YOU OF YOUR DUTY?

I SERVE THEM AS THEY DESERVE!

The golden dragon rose again, shrieked, and spat a bright stream of fire at the ceremonial dais at the head of the square. The draped red fabric was instantly ash. The dry wooden beams and floorboards exploded into flame with a whoosh like a thousand birds taking flight. Heat washed the Tinker wagons in rhythmic waves.

N'Doch yanked Erde back into the shelter of the caravan's metal walls.

"The sonofabitch even breathes fire! No wonder everything around here's built out of stone!"

She couldn't imagine how he could complete a coherent sentence, with so much raw power coursing through his brain as it was through hers.

"Ev'rybuddy up!" shouted Brenda. The Oolyoots who'd been defending the wagons on foot each grabbed at the side of a wagon to hoist themselves upward. On Beneatha's wagon, Charlie beat out sparks caught in the folds of the canvas. The dragon in the square screamed again. His voice in Erde's head was like knife blades along her nerves.

LEAVE ME ALONE!

BROTHER, WE MUST FOLLOW OUR DESTINY.

THAT DESTINY DOESN'T SUIT ME. I DENY IT!

NO, YOU WILL NOT DENY IT. YOU CANNOT DENY IT.

I AM FIRE! I AM THE LORD OF THIS KINGDOM! YOU CANNOT BEND ME TO YOUR WILL!

We'll see about that . . .

And where there had been one dragon, suddenly there were three, crouched staring at each other in the glare of the burning dais.

Erde heard Luther's yell of exultation and terror and then stopped paying attention to anything but the dragons. She leaned out into the wash of heat, entranced. She'd let the fire consume her entirely, to be witness to so glorious a sight! N'Doch grabbed her, pulling her back. She pushed him away.

"No! No! You must look! Oh, look at them now!"

Earth loomed gigantic in the flickering darkness, as solid and towering as the side of an ancient mountain. His massive head was like a pinnacle of carved stone. His great eyes, like veined agate, glowed with the inner light of righteousness. Erde remembered the confused little dun-colored beast of two months ago, and was proud.

Lady Water stirred and rocked at her point of the triangle, a sea vision in blue and green and lavender, rising from the Deep. Her luminous crest and frills eddied around her like a dancer's sibilant veils. Her sleek head was the shifting center of a swirl of rainbow phosphorescence. Her actual shape was no longer possible to determine.

Silhouetted against a leaping wall of flame, Fire screeched and lashed his tail. In answer, the paving stones rippled. The ground shook. The stones of the houses shivered and rattled. Lightning flashed, and the heated air of the square rose in hissing columns of steam as water fell out of nowhere to douse the flames. Fire searched about for something else to put to the torch. His glare fell on the priests groveling at his feet.

N'Doch said, "Uh-oh. Time to go."

Baron Köthen jogged up from behind to shake Luther out of his dragon daze and slap the flanks of the mule he was mounted on. The stalled caravan lurched forward. Köthen swung up into the driver's seat, shoved Erde over, and grabbed the reins. "The battle is joined! Would we could stay to witness it!"

"They told us to leave!" Erde regretted it as much as he. She feared leaving them, yet knew she must bow to their dragon wisdom. "They say we'll only get in the way."

Köthen nodded. "They fight a different sort of battle. And the Tinkers have need of us."

Scroon Crew had lit the side lanterns on their lead wagon. With all their walkers piled on in a confusion of clinging bodies, they pulled ahead out of the intersection just as Blind Rachel reached them. But for a few scurrying villagers, the main street lay empty and shrouded in darkness. Another lightning flash. Scroon's mules leaped forward and set a breakneck pace. Bending low over the lead mule's neck, Luther urged his own team after them.

Erde's head cleared as she withdrew from the dragon contact. But she kept glancing back. She was disturbed by Lord Fire's denial of his destiny. Not only because it was outrageous and unforgivable, but because he spoke as if he knew very well what that destiny was. An exact understanding of this still eluded his siblings.

As the wagons clattered out of the square, she gripped the edge of the caravan and leaned out for a last backward look, in time to see Fire rear up again and launch himself at Earth, spewing a stream of white heat aimed straight at the big dragon's heart. But he only melted stone. In a blink, Earth was not there, but behind him instead. As Fire landed from his leap, the ground bucked viciously beneath him. His huge wings beat furiously as he tumbled off-balance. Shrieking his outrage, he whirled on Water, not with flame but to tear at her with his claws. Water danced an hovered, just out of his reach.

Brother Fire, where is our sister Air?

Fire lunged, snagging an edge of Water's crest with one scimitar claw. N'Doch was singing his song again, first under his breath, then out loud, a fervent paean of anguish and prayer.

No! We shall not make this town a battleground!

As Fire lunged again, Water danced away and, as suddenly as a sound, glistening wings were born out of the rainbow hues of her frills, many-folded wings like the tails of exotic fishes. N'Doch fell back against the seat, eyes closed. A ragged gasp of relief shook his entire body.

"We did it!"

And then the blue dragon sang, a lilting, whistling taunt that drew Fire snarling in pursuit as she soared away into the darkness. The rain stopped. The ground stilled. Erde looked for Earth. The square was empty.

Paia smells smoke. She pulls on Luco's hand as he eases head and shoulders around the cracked-open door. "We shouldn't go out there! We should stay here and wait for the God to come get us."

Luco peers out. "What a mess. Worse than I . . . we're going to have to make a run for it." He draws his head back. "Let him what?"

"Come and get us."

"He'd have to know where we are."

"He does. Or he should." She shouldn't share this secret,

but the First Son is working so hard to protect her and it's the only help she has to offer. "I summoned him."

"That won't work here. We're out of locator range."

"I have . . . a different kind."

His brow creases faintly. "Are they somewhere other than on your clothing?"

"Yes. They . . . that is, it . . . is in me. I am the locator."

"I don't understand."

"I don't either, but you know that I always know when he's calling me, and that I can't ever resist his summons . . ."

Luco nods, slowly.

"Oh, Luco, don't ever tell him I told you. He'd be humiliated."

"Because . . .?"

"Because it's the same for him. He hears me, and he *has* to come when I call him."

The priest's handsome face goes slack, and Paia worries that she's miscalculated. Perhaps Luco's devotion to the God is not only about gaining power within the Temple. Perhaps it is also about belief, and now she has shaken the foundations of his faith, by implying that the God is not entirely omnipotent.

"How could I not have known this?"

"I only learned it myself very recently."

"And he knows where you're . . . summoning him from?"

Paia nods faintly. She has never seen the priest look so at a loss.

He closes the door behind him and leans against it heavily. "When did you summon him?"

"When the shooting started."

"But . . . he isn't here."

"No. Not yet." This is the part Luco will really hate. It makes the God sound too much like an ordinary . . . person. "He's probably punishing me. He hates it when I summon him. But he always comes eventually. Of course, the longer he resists, the angrier he is when he arrives." Paia pushes dust around with the soft toe of the shoes Luco had given her to replace her gold temple sandals. "But how could he be angry when our lives are at stake? He should be . . . Luco? What is it?"

He's pressed his palms to his eyes with a soft moan. He

holds them there for the length of a breath. "He'll lay the town to waste!"

"What? No, he . . ."

He pushes abruptly away from the door. "Oh, what have I . . . I can't ask the . . . no, we must . . . they can . . . Damn! That's the end of it, then!" He reaches the wall, rebounds with both hands, and strides back toward her. Outside, the rattling of cart wheels nears. He grips her elbow, guides her toward the door. "This is what we'll do. Once we get out of town, you will call him again, as urgently as you can, to draw him away while the townsfolk get to cover. If anyone's to survive this, we've got to hurry!"

Paia resists. "He won't . . .!"

"He will!"

"He wouldn't just kill innocent people!"

Luco grabs her by both shoulders and shakes her. "The hell he wouldn't!" Then he collects himself and says more gently. "He will. Believe me. We must do what we can to keep down the death toll."

The death toll? She stares at him.

"Paia, listen to me! I have relatives and friends in this town! So do . . ." He stops, monitoring the sounds outside. "They're here. Let's go."

Paia has no relatives and friends in any town. "All right," she says faintly.

Luco opens the door again, drawing her into the opening. She hears the sound of glass breaking nearby and shrinks into the shelter of his arm. Night has fallen while they've been in hiding. The reek of burning thickens the air. The dark street seethes with fleeting shadows, people running, ducking into doorways. But the wagon clattering toward them has lanterns swinging from the driver's perch, like a promise of rescue. Luco hustles her out of the house as the wagon thunders past. There are others behind it. Some of the shadows swoop down on them, cluster, and move alongside. Luco is talking, hoarse and insistent. "We have to warn them! All of them! Even his own!" Paia hears a man's voice answer, and then a woman's, but not the words they're saying. Fear seems to have numbed her senses. She is focused too desperately on keeping upright. Luco is dragging her directly into the path of the oncoming wagons.

But the wagons slow. A man leaps off the lead mule, struggling to halt it. A shadow scuttles past Paia and yanks open a door in the rear of the wagon. Luco scoops her up and bundles her inside, then springs in behind her, reaching one hand to hoist the shadow in after them.

"Go!" the shadow hisses through the open door.

The door is slammed shut from the outside, sinking the inside into total darkness. The wagon surges forward. Paia is thrown against a wall. She reaches blindly for a steady hold. She finds only smooth metal, other people and rough, lumpy, shifting surfaces. Bags of onions? Cabbages? The wagon rocks harder as it picks up speed. Paia is pressed against sweating bodies and stinking vegetables. Luco and the shadow man whisper urgently in the darkness. The man's odd accent blends with the din of the wagon. Paia can make no sense of it.

Abruptly, her courage shatters. She is terrified and uncomfortable, and angry with the God for not showing up when her life is truly in danger. She is used to being taken care of, not abused and ignored. "Luco!"

He hushes her and returns to his muttered conversation. "What?" she hears him exclaim. "Others? When?"

"Luco, please! I can't bear . . .!"

"Keep still!" he hisses. "We have the gates to get through!"

"But it's so . . ."

He swears quietly but obscenely, shocking her into silence. She feels him moving about, struggling with something invisible in the confining darkness. "Here, I want you to hide under this, in case they search the van!"

"If dey ev'n bodda ta stop us," murmurs the shadow man.

"Can't take the chance." Before Paia can protest, Luco has thrown a piece of canvas over her and pressed her to the jouncing floor. "Just breathe easy and keep still!"

The canvas is heavy and she fears suffocating in its folds. Unable to shift it off of her, Paia struggles for a bit. She thinks Luco may be holding the edges down. But she has heard in his voice the same sharp alarm that spun her own senses into a blur. This time it wakes her to vague reason.

Besides, it's cool and damp beneath the soft fabric. There's a clean, medicinal smell that Paia finds oddly comforting. The wagon's rocking eases. They must be slowing down for the gates. She hears the barking of sentries and the driver's muffled reply. Paia goes still, as Luco has warned her to, and waits for the back doors to be yanked open, waits to be hauled out and exposed to her would-be assassins. Instead, she is overcome by drowsiness.

She knows she should be more startled by the brief crackle of gunfire, the shouting, and the wagon's sudden forward jolt. But by then she is more inclined to let sleep take her wherever it will.

Chapter Thirty-three

Once Luther gets his hands back on the reins, the old van cruises right along, faster than these messed-up roads are good for. N'Doch is holding on for dear life. He's also holding Luther's pistol, a big old gun with a kick like one of these breakneck mules, that might go off in his lap any second, 'cept it might not be loaded. Luther's put it to good use at the gates. The barrel's still warm.

He'd fantasized maybe they'd zip through the walls unchallenged, with the surly guards occupied with the chaos elsewhere. No such luck. The rattle of Scroon's wagons raised a couple of armed men out of nowhere. Scroon took the challenge, and dealt with it swiftly. Then Luther followed with the mop-up detail. N'doch saw at least three shadowed heaps facedown in the dust as they clattered past, and he didn't have to lift a finger, except to grab the gun as it got tossed into his lap when Luther piled back into the cab and snatched the reins back from Köthen.

The baron's still wearing his grimace of disapproval, like this kind of killing's too easy for his tastes. But N'Doch is ready to be grateful. He's had enough fracas for one day. And he's worried about the blue dragon. She's told them not to check in via the dragon internet, but he hopes if he just sort of hangs his mind open, he'll pick up a signal. No dice. Just like a woman, he muses. No sooner does he declare his undying devotion than she up and disappears on him.

The girl's in the same boat, anyhow, and without the

dragons, they may be headed for a language problem again. But here's the surprise. The German's right there in his head, even without Water's help. He's picked it up. Pretty cool. Dragon osmosis.

It's crowded in the cab and he's feeling bruised and battered, being tossed against Luther and Köthen on one side, the girl on the other, and a hard wall of trade goods behind him. He heard new passengers board when they slowed just before the gates. He leans around Köthen.

"Was that Stoksie and Ysa we picked up, back at the gates?"

Luther nods, but oddly. N'Doch's pretty sure something's up, more than he's telling. Like something's been up all day, maybe even since they were invited along on this expedition. Usually it pays to be suspicious, and N'Doch feels like what he hasn't been paying is good enough attention.

From the direction they turn after slamming through the gates, he surmises they're not heading back toward camp. It's dark as pitch out on the road and Luther's not volunteering any information. He only breaks his intent driver's silence once, to ask about the dragons.

"Wich one wuz da Pilgrim?"

N'Doch is impressed that he's figured out that much. "The blue one."

Luther nods. "I taut mebbe da odda one wuz yer man heah." He grins at Köthen. "Till he's dere shakin' me outa my daze!"

"I'll tell him you thought so." And he laughs, thinking that's probably what Köthen would like, not to have a dragon, but to be one.

Luther goes back to his reckless driving. The road is not as empty as N'Doch would have supposed. Fairly often, they rumble past the shadows of fleeing villagers, alone or with family and a cart piled high with household goods. When the road forks, Luther veers left. Instinct tells N'Doch they're headed not up or down the valley but straight for the surrounding hills. The ride is getting rougher, and the mules are laboring. They're starting to climb. He guesses the plan is to go as far as the mules can manage, then maybe take cover in the boulders on the southern slope. But he's not sure what they're still running from, now that they're clear of the mess in town. He wonders if it was only Stoksie and Ysabel they picked up back there on Main Street. Maybe they had something with them, some interesting contraband. Maybe the Tinkers run a black market alongside their legal barter. Having watched how Stoksie worked one little piece of jewelry into a half year's living for forty, N'Doch wouldn't be surprised.

The van's really rocking now. N'Doch keeps thinking Luther has got to slow down soon if he wants to have a van left instead of a pile of broken truck parts. But Scroon's wagons up ahead are pushing it just as hard. He can hear them more than see them, expects every minute to find them crashed along the roadside. Köthen has figured out the van's side mirrors. He's keeping an eye on the road behind them. If N'Doch leans forward, he risks being thrown onto the backs of the mules, but since they've turned, he can see past Köthen to the flare of torches and burning trade stalls in the town square, and the backlit columns of steam still rising from the doused flames. There's no pursuit, least not so's you'd notice, but the Tinkers sure don't seem to think they're out of the woods yet.

Suddenly the rocks rise up in front of them like an ocean wave. A solid wall, blacker than black. N'Doch ducks back hard as Luther drags the mules into a turn. He feels the outside wheels leave the ground. He can't fathom that they'll make it. The girl grips his wrist and bites back a little scream.

The wagon tips back, settles, and the rocks swallow them whole.

Miraculously, space opens up before them. Luther braces his legs and hauls back until the mules slow to a panting trot. He drops the reins on his knees and palms sweat out of his eyes with both hands.

"We ovah da bordah nah," he exclaims softly, but N'Doch hears more worry than relief.

The echo of Oolyoot's wagons in the rear is thrown into reverb as somehow, something massive seals the opening behind them. N'Doch feels the pressure change in his ears and swears a bit until his heart stops running away with him. He's sure the girl has left nail marks in his wrist. Just saying "wow" starts feeling inadequate. Finally, he gets a few actual words out.

"A tunnel! Man! Where'd all this come from?"

"Oh, reel ole place, dis," Luther mumbles between wipes. "Frum da baddle daze."

From the "bad old days" or the "battle days"? N'Doch is not sure. Either sounds interesting enough to occupy his thoughts for the length of time it takes to catch his breath. He sees the soft light of Scroon's lanterns tossed up on an arched ceiling just a Tinker's height above the van. The tunnel is two, maybe three wagons wide and looks to have been blasted out of solid rock. What's weirdest is how smooth the floor is. It's too dark to tell, but he's willing to bet it's been paved.

"So when did . . ." he begins, but Luther waves him silent.

"Latah, Dockman. Der's big t'ings happinin'. I showyu sum'un give bettah ansas den me."

"Sure, man, you got it." N'Doch wishes the Tinkers had let him in on *all* of their plan, but he decides to see if being patient is part of his new persona. He checks on the girl. She's heard Luther's request for silence, but she's got her shoulders all hunched up, like it ain't easy for her either. Köthen's sitting still and quiet, just taking it all in stride, like he can't wait to see what other bizarre adventure awaits him around the corner.

And then they roll out of the small tunnel into a much bigger one. N'Doch can tell by the echo timing of the wagon rattle and the swallowing up of Scroon's reflected light that the ceiling just got a whole lot higher. They trot along in blackness for a while. The mules must know the route 'cause he's sure nobody else can see where they're going. Then there's a ghosting of light up ahead, and a new sound, a low-register moaning all around him, both huge and quiet. As the wagons approach, the light resolves into scattered point sources that vanish and reappear at regular intervals. As N'Doch's eyes adjust, he sees more distinct shapes, sharper edges. Pillars, then, of some kind. Rows of them, leading off to either side. The space is even vaster than he thought, because the lights are lanterns, the brightest nearby as the wagons move in among them, the fainter ones at least a soccer field's length away. Then the wagons slow to a crawl and there are tables and chairs and boxes and other wagons, and people getting up and crowding toward them.

It's an encampment. A huge one. N'Doch glances up, wondering if he'll see the faint ruddiness of the night sky. But the darkness overhead is profound. The big quiet noise has to be the wash of air through this gigantic cavern. He purses his mouth in a silent whistle. Hell of a ventilation system. He can see he's about to learn a whole lot more about these Tinker folk and their hidden resources. But it's more than that he's feeling. The whole place is resonant, like being inside a big bass woofer. Resonant in his head, in the place where the dragon usually lives.

N'Doch nudges the girl. "Does it feel weird to you in here?"

She nods mutely.

"What is it, do you think?"

She shakes her head. Her eyes are wide, but more with anticipation and awe than with fear. She's been so scared in her short life that she's way beyond fear by now.

They're nearly there, wherever "there" is. Soft greetings float up around the Scroon wagons, head-counting, status-checking. The Scroon riders drop off even before their wagons roll to a stop, stumbling into glad embraces and back-pounding. Shadows surge up around Luther's van. N'Doch recognizes the murmur of Blind Rachel voices long before he can pull out a face from the gloom. People gripping hands and shoulders. Hugs of relief. No shouts or loud laughter. Everyone's keeping their volume down, but they're here, all those left behind in the gray morning. The rest of Scroon Crew, too, he guesses, and Oolyoot and who knows what else. He's amazed that so many people can make so little noise.

"Made it thru!"

"So fah!"

"Whadda run! Shuda seen us!"

N'Doch nudges Luther. "Why are we whispering?"

The reply is a gentle warning. "Da Monsta has reel gud eers."

The six wagons pull up in a line. Lanterns bob alongside. N'Doch spots Ysabel climbing down from Oolyoot's lead wagon. All's needed now is Stoksie to make a full ten.

Luther tosses down the reins like a man glad to have a long day's work finally over and done with. "Ev'rybuddy out."

Chapter Thirty-four

N'Doch nods Köthen off the side, then jumps down after him. He's not sure what to do next in this milling of relief and greetings and bobbing lanterns. Just standing there, he gets his own hugs and pats from Blind Rachel Crew, and that makes him feel good, like he's a part of their family, now he's risked his life for them. He senses a general drift toward the back of the wagons. Time to unload. These Tinkers don't waste a minute when it comes to counting their loot. But he's forgotten about Luther's extra cargo.

All the Crews, plus a lot of other folks who look more like farmers and villagers, are gathering at the rear of Luther's van. Dark, eager faces full of upspoken questions. Someone's up on the roof of the van hanging lanterns from the corners. Luther comes around from the side and eases them back a bit so he can unlatch the door and swing it wide. Stoksie is waiting just inside. Even in the near dark, N'Doch knows him by his slow, stiff moves as he clambers down, waving back the hands held out to help. But there's another guy behind him, a stranger.

Well, no, he isn't. N'Doch recognizes him the minute he steps into the lantern light, mainly because he'd be impossible to disguise unless you cut his legs down and threw dirt on him. It's the big, good-looking dude who snatched the pretty priestess out of the line of fire, only he's shucked his gold duds for dark sweats and jeans. Except for his flowing red-gold hair, he looks more like a power-built linebacker than the overdressed fancy man he'd seemed like before. N'Doch tries to imagine Stoksie taking him prisoner, even with help. He wonders what's been done with the priestess. He doesn't think the Tinkers would harm her, but she is the Temple's main rep, after all, as Luther said back in town, "da Monsta's t'rall."

As the light reveals the linebacker's face, the milling crowd stills, in a collective intake of breath. Then a sound like a billion bird wings swells in the gloom, a wave of muffled applause that goes on and on, until the big dude lifts a hand in acknowledgment, like he's used to this kind of welcome. The soft eager patter dies into echoes. The crowd waits. N'Doch is totally confused. He was sure this guy was as much the enemy as the priestess.

The linebacker smiles. He looks weary and relieved. "We've done it, friends. We're committed. It's good to be home."

The patter swells again, louder, as if the listeners just cannot contain their joy, and the guy holds up both hands to quiet them. He is easy in front of the crowd. His smile is wide and winning. He knows how to look at the people like he loves them. "Phase One went off without a hitch. We've taken the first big step on our journey out from under the thumb of the Beast!" More applause. He quiets them again. "But there's more! For those of you who haven't heard it already from the Crews, we have . . . astonishing news!"

N'Doch feels Köthen slide up beside him.

"Wie gehts, Dochmann?" The baron has adapted N'Doch's Tinker nickname to rhyme with his own.

"Damned if I know." N'Doch settles in to translate as best he can, now that the linebacker's got the crowd hanging on his every word and move.

"Help has arrived!" the big man announces. "Help . . . like we could only have dreamed of!" He looks down into one of the faces most intent on his own. "Luther! Tell them what you saw!"

Someone shoves an old metal crate up beside the van. Stoksie and Brenda urge Luther up on it. His head down, his back stooped, he begins as usual like a reluctant public speaker, but N'Doch knows he will give himself to the telling of the tale soon enough. Once he does, his back straightens and his rough voice gains strength and rhythm, carrying into the darkness without increasing volume. His big active hands go to work, and the whole sequence of events in the square comes to life, the terror and chaos of the mob, the smoke and fire, lighting up the dark town, the arrival of "da Monsta." The rapt, amazed faces around him prove the success of his eloquence. Even the linebacker is enthralled. N'Doch thinks he's being polite until he remembers the guy was busy rescuing the priestess when the shit hit the fan. Likely all he knows is what Stoksie told him in the van.

Luther builds the tale skillfully. The wonder of new dragons, the fiery confrontation. Finally his hands fly up, flickering in the lantern light, and seem to vanish. "An' dey'r gone, jus' like dat!"

A predictable commotion follows, restrained by hissed reminders to keep the noise down. Everyone has a question, or an opinion about what this miracle might mean.

"Gone? Gone weah?"

"Help at last!"

"How we know dey's help?"

"Any challenge to the Beast is help to us!"

"Who says they won't just turn on us?"

The linebacker's hands are in the air, pleading for quiet. "We don't! We don't know anything! But listen! We nearly had a disaster. The Beast showed up unexpectedly, and then a miracle happened. These new creatures drew him off, kept him from laying waste to the town! Countless lives were saved. Where did they come from? We don't know. For now we lay low and find out all we can. Blind Rachel has . . ." He pauses, looks to Stoksie.

"New frens," Stoksie offers enigmatically.

"New friends! With new information. And of course . . . we will consult the Librarian." He pauses again, as if to let some big idea sink in, and apparently it does. The listeners nod sagely, and murmur their awe and agreement. "Meanwhile . . ." He tips his head toward the interior of the van. "We have our hostage."

More excited pattering, and this time, from behind the ranks of the Tinker crews, a darker mutter of anticipatory glee. N'Doch cranes his neck to see who's back there hungry for blood, but past the first few rows, the crowd is lost in darkness.

"What?" Köthen demands.

N'Doch can't locate the word for "hostage" in his dragon-built data banks, but the baron seems to get the idea. He gives new attention to the dude up on the wagon, who's honed in on the nasty undercurrent from the rear. A hint of sternness stiffens his easy manner, the iron fist within the velvet glove.

"Hey, now . . . we'll have none of that. Remember, the only valuable hostage is a live one. And we need her cooperation. So keep it down." He ducks back into the van.

"It will be *her*," Köthen says quietly.

"Yeah, sure looks like it." How long, N'Doch wonders, has the handsome linebacker been leading a double life?

The voices at the back take advantage of the wait to say a few things about their preference for immediate revenge over long-term hostage maintenance. Luther climbs back up on his box and suggests they repeat their remarks when "the preacher" can hear them. This silences some, but not all.

"Betcha!" A stocky woman elbows her way to the front, and immediately, a phalanx of support forms behind her. "I'll sure tell 'im!"

Even if her face and body language weren't so weighted with ancient rage, this woman would still look like she's seen major trauma. N'Doch thinks of a statue he saw once in a park, after a big shootout—the fine marble, all chipped and broken. Then the linebacker steps back into the light carrying a limp lump of old clothing, swaddled up in dirty canvas. A delicate sleeping face is just visible among the folds.

Köthen shifts, easing his sword sling onto one shoulder, then down to his side. N'Doch agrees. This crowd, or at least a part of it, could turn ugly at any minute. A glance about tells him that he and the baron have been quietly percolated up to the front rank beside Luther and Stoksie, with the girl and Brenda and the rest of Blind Rachel ranged behind them. Maybe this is where the hired muscle was really supposed to come in handy.

Luther says to the linebacker, "Dere's sum heah gotta diffrint idear 'bout t'ings."

The linebacker stands tall on the tailgate. The lanterns burnish his hair and chiseled profile with a kind of halo. N'Doch is envious. The guy sure knows how to find his light.

"Let them speak up, then." He waits, the hostage cradled in his arms. The broken-faced woman glares but says nothing. The linebacker nods, and from over by Oolyoot's wagons, two strapping guys still partly swathed in red and gold come forward to help lift the hostage down.

But the moment she leaves the linebacker's arms, the crowd destabilizes, surging forward to press around the two aides and their burden, snatching back the concealing canvas, grabbing for a closer look. The aides twist and turn to get away, but they're surrounded and the mob's temperature is rising fast. N'Doch hears the now familiar rasp of steel being drawn. Köthen shoves forward at the same time that the linebacker leaps down from the van, shouting for everyone to back off. The skirmish is quick, and it leaves two men with blood seeping between fingers hastily clamped to a forearm or bicep. Sword at the ready, Köthen plants himself firmly in the space he's opened up around the aides and the hostage. The crowd backs off in muttering surprise. The wounded and some of the naysayers are hustled off into the dark nether reaches of the cavern. But the stocky, broken-faced woman holds her ground as the linebacker steps forward.

She glares at him. "Why shuld we risk ouah lives fer dat reptile's whore? An' yers, too, mebbe, fer all I know."

Gasps all around, but the linebacker regards her patiently, like he's heard all this before. "She's nobody's whore, Sel. Not mine, not his. Let's get that straight."

"She ain't done nuttin fer us!" shouts a voice from the back.

"Keep it down, Paddy. She's his victim as much as we are."

Derisive laughter rises out of the gloom.

"You don't believe me? Then you go do the kind of time in that place that I have! Go on! I dare you!" The linebacker stands a head taller than the rest of the crowd, and his blue eyes compel with the light of conviction. N'Doch can see why Luther calls him "preacher."

"This woman has been the Beast's prisoner inside the

Citadel! She knows nothing about what he does out in the villages. She has no power other than the Beast's devotion to her. Besides, it's not what she's done for us before that matters. It's what she's going to do for us now!" He takes a step forward and leans over the broken-faced woman, so that she has to crook her neck hard to keep looking him in the eye. "We've been over this a thousand times, Sel."

"An' yu ain't neva listened onct!"

More laughter, but thinner this time.

"I've listened. We've all listened. And most of us think this is the way to go."

"The right way!" someone murmurs.

" 'Bout da only way," Luther seconds.

"Do we blow this opportunity just to exact petty revenge? Waste the luck of a miracle we never expected? New and powerful allies, like a sign from the One herself?" The linebacker spreads his arms in protest, but it feels more like an embrace. N'Doch feels himself getting snagged by the dude's crowd appeal. Is he priest or politician? "Is that what you want? To throw away all our months of . . ."

"Years!" chimes in Luther.

"Yes, years! Of planning and readiness? Look what we can do when we work together! Pulled it off without a hitch, without a life lost! We'll only get this chance once, Sel. The power of a miracle . . . on our side!"

The woman spits on the worn rock at the linebacker's feet. "Da reptile'll jes get isself anudda doll baby."

"I don't think so. But we'll just have to take that chance."

N'Doch glances over at the girl, listening hard at Stoksie's side. Another coin has just dropped and he wonders if she figures it the way he does. The pretty priestess is Fire's dragon guide. Got to be.

The aide holding the priestess shifts his burden and whispers something to the other one, who steps respectfully around Köthen and his gleaming blade. "I think she's coming around."

"Already? Okay." The linebacker turns. His gaze finally takes in Köthen and his sword. "Who's this, Luther? One of your . . . new friends?"

Luther clears his throat. "Yah. Dat's, um, dat's Doff. A fren frum Urop."

"Europe?" He cocks his head dubiously.

"He wouldn't be lying. And he doesn't speak English, but I'll speak for him." N'Doch takes a step into the light. This dude's the first since Hal at Deep Moor who's tall enough to look him in the eye, but N'Doch's interested to see that his cool's finally been ruffled. *Do I look that strange?* He beckons the girl out from behind Luther. "There's one more. Might as well meet us all at once."

Stoksie murmurs, "All da viziters I tole yu 'bout, Leif. 'Cept one."

"Um . . . ?" says the aide nervously.

"Right. Coming. Luther, Stoksie, explain later. Bring your friends along. We'll take her down. Don't want her knowing about all this right off." The linebacker steps up to Köthen's warding blade, then holds out his hand. "I'm Leif Cauldwell. Thanks for the help, whoever you are."

They share a brief measuring stare, then Köthen puts up the sword and takes the offered hand. *"Schon gut."*

Cauldwell laughs softly. "I cannot wait to hear your story."

N'Doch thinks: and I can't wait to hear yours. The big man moves past him to take the priestess from the skittish aide. Blind Rachel opens up a protected path through their midst. Luther unhooks a lantern from the van and leads the way. Cauldwell and the aides follow. Stoksie, taking up the rear, turns back briefly. "Lady, Dockman, Doff—yu come wit', na."

It's more like an order than an invitation, but N'Doch is glad for it. He guesses Köthen ain't gonna let this priestess woman out of his sights, now he's got her back in 'em again. As they follow Stoksie, N'Doch sees anticipation flicker in the baron's eyes before he can hide it.

Luther leads them through more crowds, past other wagons and darkened campsites, rumpled bedrolls and cold meals hastily set aside, to a concrete wall with what looks like a big door in it. A dim light burns steadily above the doorframe. N'Doch squints at it. An *electric* light. Luther presses his palm to a glassy plate alongside. The plate pops open like a lid. Luther flips it back. Inside are two rows of little buttons. Luther taps out a hurried sequence, a red idiot light switches to green, and a deep hum starts up somewhere down in the depths of the rock.

N'Doch swallows the exclamation of recognition that leaps to his lips. He's thinking, *it can't be,* but sure enough, the hum stops and a crack of light appears along the floor. The big door lifts horizontally to reveal an evenly lit, square silver room. Luther and Cauldwell head right in. Stoksie and the aides wait outside, beckoning to N'Doch and his companions, herding away any others. Köthen scowls at the too-bright, too even light, but he follows N'Doch and the girl as the door starts to close and Stoksie scoots in behind them.

"Damn!" whispers N'Doch. "An elevator!" He's near delirious to be bathed in glorious artificial light again. He slides a hand along the textured metal shell. It's cool, hard, and so familiar. He checks for the control panel. There isn't one visible. He's willing to bet that Luther's neat palm print maneuver would reveal one if needed, but apparently this car's on automatic. The door seals soundlessly as it touches the floor. The elevator sinks, with almost no sensation of motion.

N'Doch says, "Luther, my man, you're just full of little surprises."

Chapter Thirty-five

As the floor of the bright square room fell gently out from under her, Erde suffered a flash of childhood memory, of falling once when she was five into the deep end of the mill pond. It wasn't just the sensation of sinking slowly into the unknown. There was also this strange, increasing pressure on her eardrums, in her lungs, inside her head.

Not painful, only . . . disorienting. Erde glanced around to see if anyone else seemed to notice it.

N'Doch was looking her way. She searched his round ebony face for helpful clues. Perhaps her own face showed more distress than she felt, for he winked at her and smiled encouragingly.

Part of the oddness, she knew, was being apart from the dragons, inwardly as well as outwardly. She recognized the disappointing dulling of her senses—sight, smell, and especially sound—and the loneliness of being once again remanded to the confines of her own narrow skull.

And yet . . . being entirely within herself once again made her feel peculiarly *collected*. Strong, and clear-minded. Grown up.

She had listened closely to the confrontation in the cavern. The dragons had planted all the necessary language in her head, but the day's sequence of events had left her reeling with smoke and violence and revelation. The mystic reunion with Sir Hal's dragon-hilted sword. Lord Fire denying his destiny. Her own Earth, and Lady Water, coming into the fullness of their powers. And all the human events as well.

But it wasn't necessary, Erde decided, to understand all the complex ramifications of those events, of the relationship between the town and the Tinkers, or the Tinkers and Lord Fire's Temple, or even the Temple and the general populace. Or of the arrival of the man Leif Cauldwell. Erde would await the dragons' reading of him. She thought of him as a sort of beautiful giant. If she were a sculptor, she would use him to model an archangel. Not fierce Michael, with the sword. Gabriel, rather, the Messenger.

All that really mattered was knowing how any of this bore on the dragons and the furthering of their Quest.

They had found Lord Fire and confronted him. As Baron Köthen had said, the battle was joined. Erde knew she should be filled with foreboding. Instead, she was exultant with purpose. Oh, the strength of purpose that swelled within her as the white room sank into unknown depths! It had been ripening, like a secret child in her womb, all along, while she was distracted with concern for the dragon's growth and welfare. She felt as if nothing could dismay her now, not a day of confusion and bloodshed, not the piercing eye of the hell-priest, not even the hopelessness of her love for the man standing next to her.

She wondered if N'Doch felt the same.

It was not a question to be asked out loud, not in present company. And it was complicated. She wasn't quite sure how to put it to him. So she turned it over in her mind, forming and re-forming the question, then glanced up to find him still staring at her. Only he wasn't smiling now. He looked both amazed and horrified.

Stop thinking so loud, his voice growled in her mind. *The answer is yes!*

Omigod! She knew she must not gape at him, and draw the others' notice. *What . . . ?*

A rueful chuckle tickled a corner of her mind. *Guess it finally got quiet enough in our heads for us to hear what else is going on.*

Do you . . . mind?

No. Not really. She feels his surprise. *Seems sorta . . . right. Long as I know there's places you can't go and things you can't know.*

Erde turned away to hide her smile from the casual on-looker. *N'Doch! Your thoughts are even more musical than your speech!*

Oh, yeah?

Won't they be pleased!

The dragons? You mean, 'cause we finally learned some-thing on our own?

But we didn't! They taught us. We just weren't aware of it at the time.

I suppose.

But it wasn't quite like talking with the dragons. This entire communication had been instantaneous, contained in the few seconds it took Stoksie across from her to raise his hand and scratch his head. Erde had always assumed that the dragons slowed down their thoughts to suit the more sluggish pace of human minds. What if it was the other way around?

She considered how the tiny rapid heartbeat of a bird in hand made one's own human pulse seem inexorable and slow. Was it so with tiny humans and their dragons?

Hey, girl . . . Erde . . . lemme ask you something. I got a thought here.

She looked his way. He was studying the limp bundle in the archangel's arms. *The priestess? What about her?*

Fire's dragon guide, I'm betting. Whadda you think?

Oh. Oh, my. Well . . . perhaps so.

When she wakes up, maybe we should ask her.

Like . . . this?

N'Doch laughed, and Luther glanced over curiously. N'Doch shook his head. "Nothin', man, nothin'. Just a thought."

But in her head, he said, *Well, yeah! If she answers, we'll know we're right.*

Chapter Thirty-six

Paia stirs. How curious. What has happened to her ability to tell dream from reality, or waking from sleep? Too much of that unaccustomed dreaming. She thought she'd waked cradled in Luco's arms, not a terrible place to be. Now she feels a subtle floating sensation that calls up memories of the Citadel's elevators. Either she's still dreaming or . . . she drifts away, then back, suddenly awash with relief and an explanation. Luco has brought her home, through some miraculously secret back entrance!

But her head is clearing, and logic intervenes. The Citadel is four hard days' travel away. Even at the speed of those mad cart animals, such a distance could not be accomplished . . . unless they've been traveling in one big circle since they left the Citadel. But Luco said his locator was out of range. She must be dreaming. Where else could there be a working elevator? Paia ponders this muzzily as the cab continues to drop.

Further proof of the dream: she can't seem to move or talk. Still wrapped in this tenacious drowsiness. It smoothes out any impulse to exert brain or muscle. She's paralyzed with lassitude. Well, no worry. The God will show up soon, as he does in all of her dreams. So what if he'll be furious.

Over the background hum of the elevator comes a soft babble of voices. In her dream, even though the words sound unfamiliar, Paia seems to understand them. One man is trying to explain to another man what an elevator is. She summons the effort to open her eyes. The first face she sees tells her she's dreaming for sure. It's the man with the sword, the man from her dreams, who stood in the crowd and stared at her as if he owned her. Now she begins to question that sighting. The rocking sedan chair, the soporific heat . . . had she dozed off, and dreamed in daylight? But here he is again. He's still staring at her. She should be insulted by his boldness, then and now. Instead, Paia welcomes it. She's never seen a more beautiful man.

There are others in this dream, as well: a tall skinny youth who looks like he's of pure African blood. Paia recalls colleagues of her father's who resembled him. Perhaps this dream figment is the embodiment of her survivor's guilt. She has suffered it since childhood, since the floods and epidemics that wiped out most of the African continent.

The next figment is a younger boy, no, it's a girl dressed as a boy. A pretty girl, but with little sense of herself. Perhaps she is the beautiful man's child, though they look nothing alike except for the lightness of their complexions. For some reason, Paia thinks of the chambermaid, and what her inventive hands could do with this girl, with her dark curly hair and her impossibly pale skin. Then there are two older men as well, smaller, darker than herself but clearly of local stock, except for their strange accents and their very independent manner. Why would she be dreaming these people? No matter. This dream has a mind of its own.

She is about to sneak another look at the man with the sword when the elevator breathes to a stop and the door lifts. A current of blessedly cool air swirls in and around her as she rests in Luco's strong arms. Paia hears the quiet sigh of climate control, and has another seizure of being sure she's back at the Citadel. Even dreaming, she's glad of the long sleeves and the long soft pants she's wearing. It's cold down here.

The light outside the door is dimmer than inside. The elevator seems to pour light like a liquid into the darkened corridor. When Paia's dream characters step out, the door closes behind them and there is just enough light in the corridor to see the way, as if half the recessed ceiling fixtures are burned out and the rest set to low power. But it's enough light to see all the books, piles and piles of them, real books as well as the electronic kind. Not carefully shelved and catalogued like her father's, but scattered about, right out in the open. Where are the servants, to clean the place up? There are stacks of papers and rows of storage cabinets lining the hallway left and right. They narrow it to a single lane or sometimes none, where a pile has been pushed aside into the path or simply tumbled down like a paper landslide.

The taller of the older men leads them through the mess. They pass intersections with other disordered, obstructed corridors, and many half-open doors that reveal dimly lit rooms stocked with more books, more shelving, and storage racks.

"It's a library," Paia says finally, and in the dream, everyone turns and looks at her. She has startled them. "It's even bigger than my father's."

Luco stops, shifting her in his arms. "You're awake."

"I am?" Paia realizes he's right. She's not even sure when the transition happened between the dream and reality. "I'm not dreaming? I thought I was dreaming."

Luco sets her down gently. "Can you walk?"

She gets her balance, but her eyes will not focus. "Where am I?"

He supports her elbow, urging her forward. "Wait."

Some of the drowsiness returns and it's all she can do to walk. "I didn't know," she mumbles, "how exhausted I was."

"Of course not," Luco murmurs. "We're almost there, and then you can rest. Just like I promised."

Chapter Thirty-seven

N'Doch doesn't mention how he sees the drug, whatever it was, working its way out of the priestess' limbs. Either it was a real clever one or she's completely drug innocent. She doesn't seem to know she's been doped. He wonders if the Tinkers are hip to it. They must be. This whole weird day has all the marks of a carefully planned event. He's picked up a little of the why or what for, so he decides to let the rest of it ride for now. There's a lot that's gotta smell just as fishy about him and Köthen and the girl, but the Tinkers have gone with their instincts, kept the questions to a minimum. N'Doch figures he owes them the same.

But, damn, it's a pisser not to be able to ask what the hell this place is, so high tech and still in working order. Is there a whole hidden infrastructure nobody's told him about, or just this one functioning artifact? Whatever, it's a major relief. The cooled air caresses him like a woman's hands. Now if he can just find a shower, or even a bath. There's got to be running water down here somewhere. The priestess probably has the library part right, but a library for what, buried so deep in the ground like this? A seriously hardened burrow for some big-deal government installation? It can't be a multinat hideout. The bizmen would never let it get into this much of a mess.

The odd resonance of the cavern upstairs has faded with the descent into the depths. Just the ghost of an echo as they dropped down the shaft. Now, it's dead as a doornail.

Hey, girl. I feel like my brain has on earplugs.
I feel the same, N'Doch.
You know what an epicenter is?
No.
I think it's just where we're headed.

Hard to remember that this is how he was all the time, before a certain blue dragon. As he pads after Stoksie, dutifully mum, he wonders for the billionth time how the dragons are doing. The girl hugs his side where the pathway allows, or dogs his heels where it doesn't. Köthen sticks close behind, once again taking up the rear.

Finally, Luther turns into one of the many identical doors. They all file into a long, high-ceilinged room, ringed by a railed gallery. More shelves and data storage line the walls on both levels, but the center of this room is dominated by a big conference table and a collection of tattered sofas and armchairs, gathered in pools of light from dark-shaded lamps on the side tables scattered among them. The overheads are either dead or switched off. A good choice, N'Doch decides. This room looks cozy and welcoming compared to the chill corridors outside.

There are people at work at the big table, bent over papers and printouts, and others huddled in conference in some of the seating areas. They all leap up when Cauldwell comes into the room and greet him with eager relief. Someone rushes off for water. Another hurriedly clears papers and clothing from the largest of the sofas. The others crowd around.

"Set her down here, why doncha?"

"Thanks." Cauldwell eases the priestess into the corner of the couch. He shakes a few hands in welcome. "Couple of you stick by the door, okay? We had a little show of resistance upstairs."

"Serious?"

"Could be, down the road."

"Anyone hurt?"

"Not so far." Cups and a pitcher of water appear beside him. The woman who's brought it pours and sets a filled cup in Cauldwell's outstretched hand. He drains it himself, then lets her refill it. He smoothes hair from the priestess' face and molds her hands around the cup. "Paia? You awake enough to hold on to this?"

The priestess nods quickly, like she's afraid he might steal the cup away. She gulps down the water and holds the cup out for more.

"Paia." Köthen's murmur speaks entire volumes, at least to N'Doch. He prays the girl hasn't heard it. Who ever would have guessed this hard nut could crack so fast?

Cauldwell stands back as the priestess inhales a second cup. The woman with the water sets down the pitcher and stands back with him. He curls an arm around her and draws her into his side. She's a lot shorter than he is. She can nestle right under his shoulder. It looks like they haven't seen each other for a while. He bends his head to nuzzle her dark hair. "So far, so good."

The woman nods. She has an alert, intelligent face and bold eyes that flick searchingly across the faces of the new arrivals. N'Doch finds himself smiling at her.

The priestess empties her cup, then looks around dazedly as if trying to decide what to focus on. She sees Cauldwell and the woman arm in arm, and her eyes go round with surprise. "Luco . . . what . . . ?"

The woman inclines her head in an ironic little bow. "My priestess . . ."

"You . . . but . . ."

Cauldwell comes to her rescue. "Paia, I'd like you to meet Constanze. My wife."

His wife? But it's the chambermaid! The chambermaid! With her chin up and smiling, looking not at all downtrodden. And she's talking! But . . . his wife? How could she be Luco's wife? The priests of the Temple are not allowed to marry.

Paia sets down the little ceramic cup very carefully. "I . . . don't understand." And that is an understatement. Maybe she is still dreaming, no matter if he's said she's not. Tears well up, hot tears of fright and confusion and humiliation. What is this sudden weakness? Paia hates tears she cannot control. "Luco, please. I'm very . . . not very well."

"I know. We had a rough trip. You were . . . exhausted. I gave you a little something to help you sleep."

"You . . . ah. I see." But she doesn't, really. A mere sleeping potion can hardly explain away the chasm yawning within her, the vast howling emptiness. Where is he? Why does the God not come for her? Hasn't he punished her enough? "I feel like I've . . . gone deaf. Where are we? Are we still in danger? Who are all these people? What's going on?"

Luco crouches in front of her. "Ah, Paia. I hardly know where to start. But let me try . . ." He grasps her hands as if he has waited all his life to tell her this news. Paia sees none of his usual hooded caution. His expression is open, intent with purpose. She searches for something known in him, finds only his familiar, perfect face. "First, you must forgive us for our deceptions over the years. There was no other way."

"Deceptions?" Her brain is shrouded in fog. Does he mean concealing his romance with the chambermaid? Comprehension will not come, except that she's suddenly very worried for them both. "Then don't tell me now, for your own sakes. If you tell me, the God will know it, too. All of it."

"It doesn't matter now what he knows or doesn't know."

"Well, Leif, it might," the chambermaid says.

"As long as she's down here, he can't hear anything."

The chambermaid's voice is low for a woman. What did she call him? A private name among themselves? Paia reaches out an astonished hand, remembering the last time she'd seen her. "All that terrible . . . You escaped! Oh, I'm so glad. Did you get out on the wagons? I feared . . . I didn't know . . . !" She can't make any thought come out right, for fear of the one she wishes not to voice, that she hasn't thought of the chambermaid at all since just after the shooting began. How could she be so heartless? "Your name is Constanza?"

"Constanze."

"How lovely. Why didn't I know that?"

"Did you ever ask?"

The chambermaid's smile is much kinder than her words, but Paia's tears brim over hopelessly. She can't imagine what's opened up this bottomless well of emotion. If the

God were here, she would be yelling at him. She buries her face in her hands. "I didn't! I didn't! I'm so sorry! I don't mean to be a bad mistress! You must all hate me so much!"

Erde hoped N'Doch was wrong about this weepy woman being Lord Fire's dragon guide, but as she held back in the gloom and watched the beautiful priestess lure the entire room, even the women, into focusing on her own problems, it did make a certain sorry sense, given the nature of Lord Fire himself. She had both his selfishness and his glow. Even the electric lanterns seemed to burn brighter in her aura. No wonder Lord Fire was so out of control. His guide had not been paying him proper attention.

Here we are, she complained to N'Doch, *worried to distraction about the dragons, half deaf and half blind without them. Do we indulge ourselves with such mewling and moaning?*

He returned her a kind of mental shrug, and Erde reminded herself that N'Doch had also begun hopelessly, but he had learned. No reason why this Paia couldn't learn just as well. It would be a different situation, of course. N'Doch had had a sensible dragon to teach him. With Lord Fire as her dragon, Paia would need all the help she could get.

Erde knew she should be more charitable. But the situation was desperate. Their dragons were off battling each other; who knew where or what was happening to them.

The three of us should be putting our heads together, figuring out a way to help!.

Can't ask her to do that till she figures out which end is up.

Erde subsided. He was right. She must contain herself. Besides, she feared her intemperance was being fanned for other reasons, by a thing she was trying to ignore: Baron Köthen's odd behavior. He seemed to have appointed himself the priestess' protector, despite the very capable-looking men standing guard at the door. It was true she was very beautiful, but the baron would not stop looking at her. It hurt. It made Erde irritable. She hadn't brought

him all this way to look at women. She'd brought him here
to work!

But she could not let herself be distracted by personal
issues. Not now, when the dragons might be fighting for
their lives. Now she must hold fast to her new resolution
and strength of purpose. But oh, how strange, how very
strange, that all the people she found to believe in—first
Rainer, then Hal, now Baron Köthen—seemed each to be
drawn away from her by some private destiny or purpose.
Stranger still that N'Doch, of all people, should become the
stable anchor she could rely on. Perhaps because, as dragon
guides, they shared a common destiny. She supposed this
meant that Paia shared it, too. Erde hovered in N'Doch's
shadow and pondered this possibility, while the big handsome priest who was not a priest struggled to explain himself to the weeping priestess.

"A people's consensus, Luco? You've been conspiring
against him! You and the . . . and Constanze!"

"And others, Paia. Many others. This is no palace coup
we're about. Our real strength is not inside the Citadel."

"But . . . how long? For how long?"

"Since I understood he wasn't going to make things better. That's been rather a long time."

"But he *did* make things better!"

"Better for himself."

"Better for you, too. Better for all of us!"

"Better for a very select few. That's how he's bought our
service. Actually, he doesn't *want* things to improve. As
long as conditions are bad, the Faithful will continue to
pray to him for help, which he will promise but not
deliver."

"He put things in order again!"

"So I thought. So it seemed."

Luco lets go of her hands and settles to the floor cross-
legged, confident and informal, a posture Paia has never
seen him in. How could so simple a thing be so
disorienting?

"Then you put the notes in my studio."

"Constanze."

"And the old monitor?"

"My office staff has always been privy to my true purpose. We hoped to help you see what he really is . . ."

"I know what he is! Better than you!"

Luco's blue eyes go somber. "You still believe that, after all you've seen?"

There's the chasm again. He's dragging her up to its edge, insisting she look downward. This collision of emotions is crushing the very breath from her lungs. "What about the landscape?"

"What landscape?"

"You know, the painting. Never mind." Paia instinctively deflects his curiosity with a wave. House was right. Two sources of tampering. Then who is the other? Paia hugs herself, shivering now in the unaccustomed air-conditioning. She feels like her blood has stopped flowing. "Ah, Luco. And I always thought it was *my* job you wanted."

He is incredulous. "I don't want anybody's job! Do you take me for a fool? Replace one tyrant with another? What would be the point of that? Besides, I can't do what he can. He's a miracle, a myth come to life. He's a *dragon*. He has merely to fly overhead to evoke the most primal terrors and the deepest devotion. He gets people to labor and obey as no human has been able to do for centuries, which is one reason we're in the state we're in."

"You see, Luco! You do love him, just as I must!"

"NO!" But even he knows his denial has been too quick and too hot. "Once, I might have. And I risked my life for his sake, for the miracle of his . . . magic. But what has he done with his supernatural gifts? Turned them to the perpetuation of his own pleasures. It's an unconscionable waste! A crime! Of the worst order!"

Paia wants this all to be over, wants to wake up, to be back in her uncomplicated bed at the Citadel, with only the safe dullness of her Temple duties to trouble her. She tries to imagine what the God would say to his rebel priest. How would he explain himself? She knows the answer. He wouldn't.

"We had to do something," Luco continues. "The dry up gets worse and worse. The scant resources of a hundred suffering villages are being squandered on needless luxury to feather the tyrant's nest!"

Paia cannot deny it. She's seen it now for herself, trekking across desiccated fields, through dust-blown farmsteads and villages. She's seen the desperation in the townspeople's eyes. No wonder Luco agreed so easily to back her plan for the Visitation. A further chance to open her eyes to the realities. Perhaps he even planted the notion himself.

Paia feels the chasm yawning.

The tyrant. Erde thought of the hell-priest, and the war at home, being fought for such similar reasons. But there were many kinds of tyranny. She understood Leif Cauldwell's righteous outrage, and that he must explain to the priestess why he'd brought her here. But she didn't think his full frontal assault was helping matters. Couldn't he see he was asking Paia to deny her dragon? It was like watching a wall crumble beneath the blows of a battering ram. The priestess was collapsing slowly into herself, her eyes gone listless, her vital glow dimmed.

Baron Köthen scowled, held back from open protest, she thought, only by N'Doch's hand and simultaneous translation. Erde almost thought to protest herself. If Paia, as Lord Fire's guide, was to regain any influence over him, she would need to have things explained to her in the proper terms by people who understood the true nature of the connection.

"He's a one-sided god," Cauldwell continued relentlessly. "He only takes. I tried persuasion, early on. Nearly got myself incinerated. And he thwarts all my covert attempts to steer the Temple toward a more civic-minded policy. But we can't fight him. We don't have the weapons that would bring him down. The only solution is to convince him that it's in his best interests to show responsibility to the people who've served him so loyally!"

The priestess sniffed, wiped her eyes. "How are you going to do that?"

"I'm not. You are."

She stared at him. "What?"

"You are. Paia, you have the power. He will not hurt you. You know that."

"No."

For a dizzying moment, Erde thought the priestess had spoken in her mind, but perhaps it was because the pain was so eloquent in Paia's eyes. Entire volumes of terror and confusion and frustrated love. Erde guessed that she'd actually tried to do her duty to her dragon lord, but he'd rejected her service.

Luther and Stoksie moved off to a darker corner of the room to mutter among themselves, but Erde almost stepped forward again. Couldn't the rebel priest see that his priestess was on the verge of hysteria? She wasn't strong enough for this. She wasn't yet aware of her Duty. She needed comforting, not more things to think about.

Cauldwell's wife also saw the crisis coming. She went to sit at the priestess' side, patting her, whispering soothing nonsense. But Paia batted the woman's hands away, both arms pinwheeling, her sobs rising uncontrollably until it seemed that she might choke, unable to catch her breath.

Then an amazing thing happened.

Baron Köthen, who'd been standing behind her protectively, leaned over the back of the big, soft seat and laid his hand on her shoulder. Quietly, firmly, he hushed her, as if she was a child.

Paia froze, shuddered, hiccuped a few times, and stopped crying.

"Good." Köthen settled himself on the arm beside her. "Now, speak to the man, *Liebchen*. Your life is in his hands."

Of course, he spoke in his own German, so the priestess couldn't understand him. But his tone of voice served well enough. She wiped her eyes without even looking at him and sat up straighter, while the whole room stared in astonishment.

Cauldwell sat back, bemused. "Well, that's better."

"Um . . ." N'Doch began, "He said . . ."

"I know what he said. Haven't had much use for my diplomatic German in a while but . . ."

"You really oughta back off a bit."

Cauldwell blinked at him.

N'Doch shrugged. "Just an idea."

"I . . . all right." Cauldwell rose, stood uneasily for a moment, his arms crossed. "But you see, the point is, he's got it wrong. Our lives are in *her* hands. That's what's at stake here."

"Well, that ain't all of it."

Cauldwell looked around, taking in Köthen's calm stare, the Tinkers' silence, Erde's own disapproving frown. "Luther? What am I missing here?"

"Just that you oughta back off," N'Doch repeated. "Give her a chance to get her bearings, y'know?"

"We don't have time to wait ourselves through one of her tantrums!"

"It isn't a tantrum." Erde was shocked by the hoarse sound of her own voice.

"Luther . . . ?"

"Yu ought lissen to 'em, Leif. Dere's t'ings dey know."

Cauldwell rubbed his brow in disbelief, then appealed directly to the priestess, his big hands spread. "Look. Paia. I wish we had time to get you up to speed on all this gradually, but we don't. We've committed ourselves to a rather desperate course of action. We need your help and we need it now!"

Constanze stroked the priestess' hand as if she were a frightened kitten. "We need to be able to tell the others you're willing, or it'll be hard to keep you safe from Sel Minor's faction. Their view right now is a short one, focused entirely on revenge."

It looked for a moment like Paia might break down again. A half-glance up at Köthen stopped her. She seemed surprised to find him still there. She gathered herself, sniffing. "What kind of help? What could I possibly do?"

"Convince him to change his ways. You're the only one he'll listen to. The only one he must listen to."

"He'll come after you! All of you!"

"He'll try."

"He'll find you!"

"He hasn't so far."

"And of course, we'll have you as a hostage," said Constanze.

"What?" The priestess looked at Cauldwell. "Hostage?"

He nodded, somewhat apologetically.

"Luco! How could you?"

Constanze ticked items off on her fingers entirely without apology. "And we've cut off food and goods shipments to the Citadel, and evacuated our people from the towns and farms as best we can."

"Life's going to get real hard at the Citadel, Paia. You're better off here with us."

The priestess lidded her eyes, folded her hands in her lap, and took a deep, shuddering, and hopeless breath. "I always knew you feared the God, Luco, but I thought you loved him, too. Or, at least, believed in him."

"What's to believe in?" Constanze demanded. "What does he offer but the end of the world? There's a better way, Paia."

"Amen!" breathed Luther, from out of the shadows.

"There's One who offers hope instead of despair."

"She walks in light," someone murmured.

"Ah." The priestess glanced up. "You talk of helping the people, but I see what this really is. Just another heresy. I'm surprised at you, Luco, having put down so many of them yourself."

Heresy. The word alone gave Erde a chill, but Cauldwell only sighed. "Not just another, Paia. The Beast is not the only force of nature abroad in the End of Days." He settled himself again in front of her and held out his hand. "By the way, may I introduce myself properly? My name is Leif Cauldwell. Your father was my uncle, Paia. We're cousins."

She looked at him dumbfounded. "Cousins?"

There was a sudden commotion in the corridor.

Cauldwell paused, listening toward the door, as the guards moved swiftly out into the hall. "Mick? What's up?"

"Visitors," said one of them.

Erde feared the angry damaged woman from upstairs had armed herself and her cohorts. But it sounded more like children, a lot of them. And it was! A wild pack of children, spilling, bursting into the room, squealing and laughing, racing around the adults as if in the middle of a mad game of tag, most of them younger than Mari and Senda. Erde's hands were grabbed, her arms pulled. She felt like an ancient grown-up among them. Where did they all come from?

"Gotta come! Gotta come!" they chanted. "He wants yu come now!"

A blonde little girl threw herself at Cauldwell's knees. His impatient frown vanished. He bent, scooped her up, and swung her in the air. "Young one! Hello! What is it?"

"Gotta come now, Da! Gotta come now!"

"He wants to see me?"

She shook her head. "He wanna see dem!"

"Who, them?" Cauldwell pouted comically. "What about me?"

The resemblance between them was unmistakable. Erde saw the priestess watching, her wonder entirely transparent. Not only was her supposed priest married, he had children as well. Or one child, at least. A perfect, healthy one. And Erde was beginning to understand how rare that was in this devastated future.

The child giggled and laid her small hand on Cauldwell's cheek. "Das okay, Da. Yu kin come, too."

"Who does he want to see?"

Immediately, a child fastened itself to Erde's arm. N'Doch and Baron Köthen were similarly claimed, and the two Tinkers. A young boy, perhaps the oldest, presented himself bashfully before the priestess. His thin, dark limbs seemed to move each in a different direction. He stuck out his hand like he'd just gotten it and wasn't sure how it worked. "He say, yu gotta come special."

Cauldwell seemed surprised at last. "How could he have known . . . ?"

"Ain' a lot he doan know," remarked Luther.

Cauldwell nodded, then snugged the little girl high on one hip. "Well, off with us, then, young one. We've been summoned."

The priestess let the young boy pull her to her feet, but it was Baron Köthen's arm she sought blindly, for support. The other children had regrouped by the doorway, waiting none too quietly. "Hurry hurry hurry! He wants yu to come now!"

Summoned. This word was a final key, fitting into a lock in Erde's ears. They had indeed been summoned, and now she could hear it, inside, in the dragon's place. But it wasn't the dragon. It wasn't words, or even images. More like an articulate breeze. It distracted her from the sight of another woman on Baron Köthen's arm.

N'Doch! Do you hear it?

He shook his head like a dog. *I hear it. Comin' in loud 'n clear.*

So he's back in the crowded corridors again, with kids hauling on his arms, and a big dragon buzz in his head, only there's no dragon, or at least, if there is, she's not talking to him. And he's not sure what got into him, making him stand up like that for the priestess. N'Doch thinks things are starting to get weird, even by his definition.

Soon the clutter's so thick in the passage that just walking has to be skillfully negotiated. Then there's a door ahead of them, circular and armored like a vault but standing wide open. N'Doch guesses it would take several hours and some good strong men to shift away all the piles and nondescript electronics shoved against it. He hopes it doesn't ever have to be closed in an emergency. The joint looks a little derelict, but through the opening he sees console lights and screen glow. Someone's up and working.

The kids get real quiet at the door, like they've turned of the noise faucet. Even the Tinkers hesitate, Luther especially. Though he goes in ahead of Stoksie, he moves with the same faintly awed respect that Sedou brought out in him. Is it for all the high tech inside, or for the person running it?

Whadda ya think girl?

There is great power in here.

N'Doch cracks a nervous grin. He can feel it in his bone marrow. *And it ain't just electrical!*

The big room is even dimmer and colder than the corridors. Part of it is divided into low-walled cubicles, empty workstations with desks and small banks of monitors. But the far wall is curved, one huge wraparound screen or series of screens, with a big curved console at the center point of the arc. Someone is working there, and the kids halt a short distance away and wait silently to be noticed. Köthen lets the priestess move ahead of him. She kind of floats into the room with her kid escort beside her. Cauldwell's girl-baby squirms in his arms. He sets her down, and she races off to rejoin the pack.

The guy at the console is muttering to himself. N'Doch is pretty sure it's a guy because of the hulking width of his shoulders, but its hard to see much detail. He's mostly a dark, rounded silhouette against the bright blue screen. N'Doch reads the image as a map of some kind, or aerial view, with three colored blips tracking across it. A fourth blinks faintly in a lower corner. Surveillance of some sort, he guesses, and pretty advanced at that.

The priestess woman steps away from her kid escort, still a bit wobbly on her feet, and drifts toward the screen. "What is . . . ?"

"Missus!" The kid catches her, hauls her back. She tries to shake him off, still weak and vague with the aftermath of the drug and the emotional pounding she's taken. N'Doch can see she's not used to being manhandled, at least not without her permission. But her regal air cuts no ice with this determined kid, and it looks like another scuffle might erupt.

N'Doch catches Köthen's arm halfway to his sword hilt. "Easy, man. He ain't gonna hurt her."

Then the guy at the console rises. He strips off what looks like some kind of VR headset, unwinds himself from various cables and cords. He's heavyset and seriously round-shouldered. He walks with a shambling gait as if he's carrying around a little too much weight for his years. As he moves out of silhouette into the light, N'Doch notices first how the bright blue of his loose jumpsuit matches the screen, then how hairy he is. He's got a wild head of salt-and-pepper, a full mustache, and a bushy, silver-streaked beard. His brows are so long, they veil his eyes. At first he doesn't seem to notice them. He tosses a piece of paper down, picks up another. Every surface within reach of him and his console are layered with books and disks and print-out. He searches through a stack of crackling leather-bound tomes, doesn't find what he's after. Then suddenly, he glances up. He seems astonished to find new people in the room, or any people at all. Yet, within one quick sweep of this guy's dark and piercing gaze, N'Doch feels he's been surveyed, identified, analyzed, and understood. But not, somehow, dismissed. Instead, he feels welcomed.

N'Doch! I know him!

The girl moves toward the guy as if in a daze. Sure enough, the guy opens his stubby arms to her and she walks right into them, before N'Doch can stop her.

"Gerrasch!"

Erde had given up asking how the inexplicable could come to be. It simply did. It wasn't Gerrasch, and yet it was. Less like an overgrown pond animal, more like a man, yet still Gerrasch in his essence, as well as in the connection she felt with him, had always felt, from the first time they met. At least one particular cascade of events had somehow come full circle. She didn't need to know what he was doing there. It just seemed right that he was, and that she should let him enfold her in a smothering hug. His warm woodland smell was exactly the same.

"Long! Long! Relieved. Finally. Four now." His voice was still a raspy bass. He held her away from him to eye her solemnly. "Grown!"

Erde knew a laugh would violate the gravity of the moment. One sneaked out anyhow. "Oh, Gerrasch, you saw me only a few weeks ago!"

"No. You saw. Me, centuries. Waiting. Get it?"

It made her spine tingle to think about it, but she thought she did. She took his soft pink-palmed hand and drew him toward the others. "Gerrasch, this is . . . ."

"Yes." Gerrasch made directly for N'Doch and held out his other hand. "Brother. Songs of welcome. Work now. Quickly."

N'Doch said, "Huh?"

Luther watched all this with happy astonishment. "Dis heah da fren' yu bin lookin fer?"

"No, but . . ." N'Doch began.

"An old and cherished friend just the same," Erde finished for him.

N'Doch laughed. "You, too?"

"What?"

"Modern English? Not even dragon English, all of a sudden?"

Goodness. He was right. She did sound better. *Modern.* A resident of both past and present. Gazing into Gerrasch's knowing face, Erde understood there would be no language she could not speak right then, right there. She nodded at the vast blue brightness, and the strange table lit with what looked like a hundred tiny candles. "Gerrasch, what is all this?"

"Library. Librarian, me."

"Epicenter," said N'Doch.

Gerrasch beamed at him.

"What's an . . ."

He took her hand. "Wait. Four. Then talk." He guided them through the solemn ranks of children and amazed Tinkers, toward the heathen priestess. Paia seemed even more confused than she had in the other room, as if the blue-lit strangeness of this one had unmoored her further. No wonder she recoiled when Gerrasch shambled up and without preamble, reached for her hand.

"No! Don't touch me!"

Leif Cauldwell stepped forward. "I'm sorry, G. She's not in the best of form. This is the Librarian, Paia."

"Don't let him touch me!"

"He won't hurt you. He's a good and wise man. If he wants to talk to you, it's for a very good reason."

Luther added, "Da Liberian isa proffet, lady. A holy oracul. He speak fur da One who come."

Speaks for the One . . .

"He does?" Four, he'd said. Erde's eyes clenched shut with comprehension and gratitude. *N'Doch, do you hear? Do you know what that means?*

I can guess . . .

He must be!

She was sure of it. Prophet or oracle the Tinkers might think him, and he might even be, but Gerrasch was also Lady Air's guide in the world of men. She was so sure, she didn't give it further question. Would he have answers to the mysteries and unknowns that had plagued the Quest from its beginnings? *Oh, if only the dragons were here!* The fourth dragon guide! Their number was complete.

But Gerrasch was rather large and strange looking, and the poor weepy priestess, who knew nothing of her Duty or her Destiny, saw his friendly overture as a threat.

"Keep him away from me!" she shrieked, backing into Baron Köthen's arms

Since waking up, Paia's felt like she's trapped inside someone else's skin. Someone she doesn't like very much, but can't seem to shake. Who is this frantic, sobbing woman who's suddenly terrified of everything, who's lost her dignity, who can only think of screaming for the God to come and rescue her? She's not even a woman. She's the protected little girl whose world was turned upside down once before, who never had to learn to live with change and instability, because the God came and made the world right again. The God saved her then. He could save her now. She has only to call him.

But she cannot. This strange creature will not let her. Something he's doing is blocking her summons. Her head is filled with static. She knows he's the God's enemy, one of them, at least. Yet he smiles at her so sweetly, as if he is overjoyed to see her, relieved even, as if now that she's there, his life can move onward. But Paia looks down and sees the chasm yawning between them. She would have to cross it to take the creature's offered hand. Why should she, though he entreats it so gently and fervently? Who is he, but the God's enemy? She owes him nothing. Nothing! Yet, she is tempted.

No! A part of Paia sees the panic seize her and admits it isn't logical. But the reflex runs riot in her head, screaming about duty. Her duty must be to the God! She must not be tempted! She fumbles inside her layered clothing for the thing she has concealed there. Her grip is oddly weak, but it's a small thing, easy to grasp. She jerks it out and points it at the enemy.

The enemy smiles again and spreads his hands, as if inviting her. She sees that his palms are soft and pink, so vulnerable. But there is a danger in him, terrible danger, if she could only comprehend what it is. She struggles to think, the gun shaking in her outstretched fist. The girl dressed as a boy steps in front of the awful creature. Paia hears Son Luco swear, actual heresy and filth. But he should understand her confusion. He also has become someone else. He has become her cousin. Even so, he moves abruptly to stop her, so Paia turns the gun on him instead.

"Paia, be sensible. There's a hundred villagers upstairs thirsting for your blood. Even if you murder us all, where are you going to go?"

"The God will save me! He'll come in a glory of light and he'll . . ."

"I don't think so," says Luco. "If he hasn't done it already . . ."

"Don't look for it," the tall African agrees. "He's kinda busy right now."

He grins at her in the most presumptuous, irritating way and dances a few steps to one side, so Paia shifts her glare and the muzzle of her little gun toward him.

"What do you know about the God?"

"You'd be surprised, lady."

Then someone's beside her, calmly lifting the gun from her hand, the man with the sword, to whom, in her mind, she has already given herself. She stares at him, right into his eyes for the first time. They are as dark as she remembers from the dreams. If the God cannot save her, she will let this man do it. He smiles back, his devotion already unconditional. "Tch, tch, *Liebchen*."

"Smooth move, Dolph." The African takes the gun and sticks it into his waistband. "What the hell did you give her, preacher man?"

Luco lets out a breath.

Now the sword man takes Paia's hand. He's leading her toward the enemy, but she cannot resist him. His eyes hold such promises.

The God's enemy has linked hands with the girl and the African. Now he takes Paia's hands and places one in each of theirs. When the tall African grips her hand, Paia hears faint, poignant music and the sighing of oceans. The young girl's touch brings perfumes of meadows and pine boughs. Hungrily, Paia's senses shake off their fog and drowse, to embrace these scents and sounds. They are unfamiliar yet longed for. She has known them all her life. A dry, clearing wind blows through her head. She has never felt more alive.

The African has lost his snarky grin. His eyes are anxious. The three of them stand awkwardly, joined by hands in an arc, until the strange creature takes the others' free hands in his own and completes the circle.

Then Paia learns what the real danger is.

Chapter Thirty-eight

. . . $\mathbf{A}$nd it's like being jacked in to each other's brains. Freaky. Not like his silent converse with the girl. Virtual reality. Much worse than the old dragon internet. Dragons, it turns out, know how to respect your privacy. But at least now he doesn't have to ask who this hairy guy is. It's there for the knowing. Like all the files are open. All the histories, the personal stories, the varied roads taken by each of them to this place of . . . *convergence*. A meeting that it looks like everything in creation has been trying to prevent, yet one that could never have been avoided.

. . . all of this, surging like music through his head. Close to but not completely overwhelming. He's amazed his brain is big enough. It scrolls past like program code: the lineage of the three, himself, Paia, the girl, down through the millennia, their engendering preordained. And of Gerrasch, the focal link, an eternal nexus, a lump of leaf mold and clay inspired by dragon energies, set to evolve and learn until that programmed event when, half man, half beast, he met the girl along a dark lakeshore . . .

. . . a system, a fail-safe, maintained by myth and mysticism, nurtured by kinship, functioning on automatic. But . . .

. . . what is it for?

. . . The danger is in the revelation. The chasm is not emptiness, but infinite possibility. She reels under the weight of it. Layer after layer of her ignorance peeling back like drying bark, sloughed like an obsolete snakeskin, until she knows the truth of how much she didn't know, how much he kept from her, all that her father preserved in his precious library, all that the House Computer tried (too late!) to prepare her for. Not one dragon, omniscient and omnipotent, but four who are neither, and a great and sacred Duty for which she is, so far, a failure. As a dragon guide, she is, so far, a failure. None of this, once learned, amazes her. It all seems . . . right.

. . . and yet, the awful choice that lies before her! The God is her . . . god. How can she betray him? She struggles to explain it. He appeared at a time of confusion and loss! His promises of security, his opulent visions lent vital strength, got things going again! She believed him for so long. What makes her believe three strangers now?

. . . but they are not strangers, not anymore. She's learned their lives. She's lived them in an instant. She's walked with their dragons and cannot imagine them the enemy. She's grown up with N'Doch as bush child (ah, lost Africa!), as street urchin, as master sneak thief, dodging smooth and cynical through the disease and drought and corruption of a century that knew no better than to gun down its best and its brightest, his brother among them.

. . . and she's come of age with Erde, in terror and bloodshed, hounded by another dragon-inspired golem. She tells them that the God, too, time travels. The pieces fall together. The mad priest in white is Lord Fire's creation, no doubt of it. But why, they ask? For what purpose? She does not know. If she did, they would know it, too.

. . . and then the Librarian, the one who frightened her, so halting in his human speech, so eloquent in this . . . joining. Both source and resource, a vibrant stream of sensual data—image, scent, sound—rich with drama and knowledge and portent. His console links the world's surviving com-nets, the sensors, the archives, even her own House Computer, yet he has kept himself invisible to them.

. . . she has longed desperately for both comprehension and friends. These three are not what she would have chosen for herself, yet they bring a sort of comprehension, and the joining of minds is a wonder. There's so much they understand that no one ever has, about living with the God . . .

. . . the past and her clinging to it have been a restraint, she sees that now, a burden she can willingly set down, so that others more pressing may take its place.

. . . ah, the relief! A joyful release into the now! Past, present, future are one continuum. Didn't the dragon try to tell her this, long ago? There's no sense of *then* in the new now, no pain at having left her past so far behind. Only a clarification of purpose, brought on by this union of minds. Four far-flung dragon guides at last united by the fourth's miraculous gift, that Paia and N'Doch have words for—"virtual reality," "synergetic," "psi"—but which the Librarian tries to explain as something, well . . . electrical. The machines are his eyes and ears on the world, but he doesn't run them. They run themselves. He only "feels" them, as she feels the surge of collective power his psi gift brings to the circle. All they lack now are their dragons, and a reason why . . .

. . . Wait. So long. Despair.

SEE: a gray curl of woodsmoke coiling up through firelight. Beady eyes in the darkness.

SMELL: burning pitch, damp earth, the pungency of drying herbs.

HEAR: the quiet lap of water against the reeds.

FEEL: a chill of waiting . . . waiting . . . waiting.

. . . visions stir up the darkness. Dreams. Inarticulate. Speak it without words. Oracle. Wait . . .

. . . and waiting is learning.

SEE: a snow-scattered farmstead, steep dark hills with a bristle of trees. A large man with a rough black beard and an armload of books.

SMELL: damp cattle, rooting pigs, hay, and manure.

HEAR: the rhythm of the ax, the shuffing of the oxen steaming in the paddock.

FEEL: ice in the wind. Waiting. Still waiting.

. . . the visions brand him as a madman, yet he will not deny them. Loneliness. Confusion. But instinct becomes knowledge, and the library grows.

SEE: fluorescent light, a nest of cables, shelves stuffed with equipment. A wild-haired man at a keyboard, before a constellation of screens.

SMELL: the tang of hot metal, the cold coffee on the console.

HEAR: the whine of accessing memory, faint rock n' roll.

FEEL: disbelief, outrage, despair.

. . . one after the other, the screens show disaster: war, famine, plague, death. He taps a key. Overlay of horsemen, red, black, white, and pale. He slaps at the power switch. The screens darken. He buries his face in his hands.

. . . a time passes. Then . . . he sits up, alert. He has heard something at last. Still, none of it makes sense. He can feel her, not see her. Guess at her, not know her. He interprets as best he can.

. . . Four and three. Missing the One. Visions. She speaks. Work. Work. The time nears. Quickly . . .

In the circle of hands, consciousness melds but the self is not lost. There is no confrontation, no accusation, no recrimination. Perhaps those will come in time, that a Duty has been neglected, that a man loves and is loved by another . . .

But not now. For now, only acceptance of what is, a vast and spontaneous learning across cultures and centuries, and the planning of what is to be done, as much as can be without a full understanding of the task at hand.

And still Paia asks, how can I betray him?

The Librarian breaks the circuit. A gentle parting of hands, the trailing of now familiar fingers across all-known palms. The four stand with their heads bowed, eager to reclaim autonomy, reluctant to give up the bond.

Erde shows them the next step, entirely by accident.

N'Doch!

She calls. And all of them answer. The connection holds.

It is not the total intimacy of the meld, but that is . . . just as well. The melding is turned inward, toward the mirror of self. There is no outer awareness. The connection is . . . more like never having to raise your voice.

Their eyes meet. They smile, bashful now. A bit self-conscious.

N'Doch says: *Hey! Now wasn't that something else?*

So what do we do now?

We must find the Lady Air. She will know. She saved me, I'm sure of it, when the hell-priest came after me.

She. The One. Imprisoned.

Yeah, but where?

Lord Fire is sure to know.

He won't tell them willingly. He'll resist, with everything in his power! Oh, how can I betray him? How can I?

No betrayal. Greater cause.

How can I know that? How can I know?

Feel how strong we are! If we call out to Lady Air together, she is sure to hear us!

Cannot. Jamming. Zone of silence. Only protection.

Just a thought but, like, all this nature stuff in the data banks? That can't just be coincidence, right?

Chapter Thirty-nine

There is no signal agreed to, yet, in unison, the four turn away from each other, directing consciousness outward into the darkened room in a show of independence.

Erde would have guessed that they'd stood in their circle for hours, but every eye is still on them, surprise still lingering. Luther is still on his knees. It's been but an instant. She catches Stoksie's inquiring look, then Luther's. She glances down, away, uncertain.

Some explanation will be required . . .

N'Doch laughs aloud, a small explosion of release. *Hey, girl! You wanna try it?*

Gerrasch unsettles the moment further by producing several complete sentences. "The circle is closed. Struggle alone no longer. The work begins."

And still they are waiting. Standing about quietly, their eyes full of questions. The vast and quiet sighing of the air is the loudest sound. Something unexpected has occurred. Something perhaps momentous. Erde realizes they are waiting to be told what to do.

As it happens, she has a plan. One, she thinks, that fits the gravity of the situation. And yes, it is risky.

Give us a second to recover, huh? Before you spring it on 'em?

But we should tell them . . . explain . . .

Yeah, yeah.

The four agree that N'Doch should tell their story. All of it. The children bring cold water and plates of dried apple, and settle down around him. It takes him slightly longer than an instant.

"I coulda sung it to you faster," he grins when he's finished.

Stoksie and Luther nod intently, mulling over all they've heard. Many of the children have dozed off, curled into balls like little animals. The rest crouch among the empty desks, playing quiet games with whatever comes to hand. Köthen, having heard it all before, has eased carefully among the teetering book stacks for a close-up study of the Librarian's console. He leans over it but does not touch.

Only the rebel leader is uneasy. The guy is no ranting rabble-rouser. He's planned his rebellion carefully. N'Doch thinks he'd be well in his rights to feel put out by this sudden left turn of events. "Huh," he says. "Huh."

Paia laughs, a rueful silvery sound that makes Köthen glance up from his detailed scrutiny. Astonishment still lurks in the corners of her eyes, but the tension and terror are gone. "Oh, Luco! I mean, *Cousin* Leif. The proverbial monkey wrench! We've disrupted your plan, haven't we!"

He shrugs, though it's more of a grimace. If it bothers him not being the center of attention in his own stronghold, he's concealing it well, even if he is wound a bit more tightly than he'd like to admit. "I'm always ready to hear a better one."

N'Doch says, since everyone's playing at being so casual here, "And we'll get to that. But there's a few things I'd like to point out first."

He's always had great faith in coincidence, but his faith is being sorely tried. The Librarian's oblique response in the meld suggested he doesn't consider anything a coincidenced. It's all one big pattern to him, or maybe an endless stream of program code.

For instance, N'Doch has just learned that this facility was originally a top secret center for climatological research. Coincidence? He puts his back to the big blue screen and lays it all out, as much for himself as for the others: the Library's heavy focus on a combination of myth and earth sciences, the local belief in a messiah who will regreen the planet; four dragons named after the elements of Nature.

"Dragons don't just show up for no good reason!" He sees Erde beaming at him. He agrees. He's on a roll, even without the blue dragon to coax him along. He jabs a thumb at the readout of disaster that the Librarian's brought up on the big screen. Temperature levels, weather patterns, erosion where there's land left, salinity where there's water. "All the data his network can access—satellite instruments, ground sensors, archives, and data banks, no matter that they're all half-broke and winding down—all of them are screaming that ole Mother Earth has just about had it."

"We know all this," Leif Cauldwell interjects. "That's why we . . ."

"You know it, but you don't know what to do about it. It's too far gone, right? That's why a magical fix looks like the only solution. Well, we think that's what we're here for. Why else would we have all ended up at this particular time, this particular place?"

He has to laugh. It's like some moldy old vid, but it's probably true. They really are here to save the world. Or at least, give it a damn good try.

The girl agrees, but of course, she would.

"And now you're gonna ask me how. And I'll say we gotta leave that to the dragons."

The Tinkers are still nodding, like they're ready to get right on the problem whenever he says so. They've accepted the idea that their awaited messiah is a dragon with surprising equanimity, even, N'Doch thinks, with relief. They're not of a seriously mystical bent. They're more interested in actual help. And what better weapon to combat a dragon than another dragon, or in this case, three more dragons?

Nor do they seem bothered by the notion of visitors from another time.

"Whadevah," is Stoksie's response to N'Doch's cautious explanation.

Luther says, "Can't wait ta heah all da detales."

They do not believe you, Erde says in his head.

N'Doch knows better. He's sure they're the most pragmatic and flexible folks he's ever had the privilege of dealing with. Leif Cauldwell, however, is still an unknown. N'Doch waits for the rebel leader to be full of ideas and suggestions. He just seems like the type.

But Cauldwell raises an eyebrow and fidgets silently, waiting to see where it's all going to lead. The source of his spiritual doctrine is the Librarian, after all, and N'Doch is speaking with the Librarian's full support. Cauldwell may be the rebels' spokesman and leader, but Gerrasch is their oracle and prophet. It took the arrival of the planet's endgame to produce a population that would finally listen to him. And Cauldwell listened, reshaping the prophet's bizarre visions into a kind of liberation theology that the frightened farmers and villagers, and at least some of the Tinkers, could accept. Thus Air, shanghaied by Fire, became the discorporate One who Comes, the Imprisoned Messiah. No mention of dragons. N'Doch suspects Cauldwell's own belief. He knows a politician when he sees one. And right now, it's good politics to hear the prophet—or his surrogate—out.

The Librarian, meanwhile, doesn't think in terms of messiahs. He thinks in hardly any recognizable terms at all. N'Doch recalls some self-appointed egghead lecturing him once about hypertext. He didn't bother much with it at the time, but now he's glad he listened long enough to pick up the basic concept. Hypertext is a handy metaphor for the Librarian's thought structure. Keeping it in mind helps N'Doch decipher what the dude is getting at.

"Okay, so what do we know about Air, a.k.a., the Imprisoned Messiah?" He looks to see if this gentle sacrilege bothers his audience, but it's clear he's already preaching to the converted. "Let's start with the fact that someone, some*thing,* has been sending the Librarian 'visions' for centuries."

"Centuries," murmurs Luther reverently.

"And that all those aeons he put in of tireless research and analysis suggested an ageless and mystical source. Eventually, he tells us, the visions narrowed the definition for him: a dragon named Air. By now, he's convinced that Fire kidnapped Air and stashed her somewhere because of something she knows about the reason the dragons were awakened in the first place." N'Doch privately refers to this as The Big Mystery, though he's about to rename it The Big Fix. "Air can't talk to him from her undiscovered prison, but recently, the visions have been coming in via this old semifunctional communications network. How 'bout that? A cyberdragon!"

Cauldwell asks softly, "How can she be accessing the Net?"

"Good question."

Erde objects. "Do you ask how Lord Earth can transport, or Lady Water transform?"

"You bet. All the time. Don't you?" N'Doch grins at her, just to let her know he's never gonna stop teasing her at least a little. But she's learned to take it. She smiles and shakes her head.

"What does the . . . ah, what does Fire do?" Paia asks.

"Misbehaves."

"No. Please." Her lovely face clouds, and N'Doch is instantly miserable. "If each of the four has a special gift, what is his?"

Cauldwell has a ready answer. "He's a leader of men, Paia. That's a gift like any other. It's not only fear that makes so many follow him. Add but an ounce of compassion and the Beast could well be a god."

Erde frowns at him. "A miracle, yes. But not God."

"God? Singular?" Cauldwell peers at her curiously, then seems to think better of it and subsides into a tense crouch against the console. Silently, N'Doch congratulates him on his good sense and restraint. He's glad his little lecture has finally evolved into dialogue, but this is no time to get the girl going on about religion.

"So he's waiting and waiting, then suddenly he gets the sense something's about to happen. Right?"

Gerrasch nods. Because he cannot predict when the visions will come on him, or in what form, he has put himself on perpetual round-the-clock duty, for a generation or more, buried in this dark hole like a giant mole in the earth.

"You, like, sleep at the console?" N'Doch pulls up a chair from one of the desks and kicks back. "Man . . . that's dedication."

"Da kids help, y'know," explains Luther. "Dey make

shur he's eatin', and if a vishun come by, up deah onda wall, well den, dey wakim up."

"The visions never come when he's napping," Leif puts in sternly.

"And they come, like, actually on screen?"

"Not then," explains the Librarian. "Now. Yes."

"Too cool! Dragon vid."

Luther is almost purring. "It wuz da One ledyu ta make yer move, Leif."

But if the visions are random in their occurrence, their subject matter is not. Mostly they focus on the dire condition of the planet, which is, of course, what's encouraged Luther, as well as Leif and his rebels, to believe that when the One who Comes arrives, she'll know exactly what's wrong with the world and how to fix it. N'Doch can only hope they're right. He's run pretty short of ideas himself.

He decides it's time to head the conversation where it needs to go. Time's awasting. He can feel it in his gut. He waves Köthen closer so he can translate, then sets Erde up and gives her the floor. When she's done explaining her plan, most everybody's still nodding.

Except Leif Cauldwell. He's dead against it.

"Drop the cordon? No. No way. I can't allow it!"

The meld was exhausting, mentally and physically. Erde's sense of time and place is entirely in flux, with the present more present than ever and her own past beginning to seem like a tale someone else has told her. But this is the least of her worries.

The discussion has hit a snag. Leif Cauldwell is backed up against a desk, declaiming like the ex-military man that he is. Her plan has vaulted him out of his wait-and-see calm. His big hands clench and unclench fitfully. She catches his anguished glance at the small girl asleep against a partition. He doesn't understand. "How can you even ask it? You'd expose our stronghold? Risk the lives of six hundred people? Of all our children? Our only chance of success rests on there being some place the Beast cannot get to! Or even know about! If he flushes us now, we'll take heavy casualties and be forced into a ground war we're not equipped to fight!"

"But this might work. And it might work now. No drawn-out guerrilla struggle." N'Doch is trying to sound rational and empathetic while he wolfs down pieces of apple.

They are all exhausted, Erde realizes, as exhausted as I am. We need rest and sustenance and there is no time for either. We must get out of this muffling cave and back in contact with the dragons!

"He'll be down on top of us in a minute!" barks Cauldwell.

"Maybe not. We'll never know 'less we try."

"Easy for you! These aren't your people!"

"It's my world, least it was. You're not exactly seeing the Big Picture."

Luther hovers, a dark silhouette against the blue screen. "Leif, we bin talkin' 'bout how we gonna free da One fer ten yeer nah. If dis bring us closa to da ansa . . ."

"We might as well open the doors and invite him in! Luther, we haven't survived this long by being reckless!"

"Lotta dem down in camp wuld wanna try it, probby," Stoksie offers. "It ain't all yer call, na."

A brave thing, Erde thinks, for a little man to say to a giant. But though Cauldwell's jaw tightens, he listens. He is bigger and louder, but this is, she realizes with interest, a debate among equals.

"Okay, it's not all my call. But I have to deal with the military consequences, and—damn it—someone's got to be the voice of reason here! Paia says he always knows where she is. So no matter how briefly the Librarian's jamming signal is down, the Beast could still hear her, and if he does . . ."

"He will hear our summons as well." Erde savors the feel of this very "modern" language on her tongue. She can at last give voice to her impatience, but she doesn't want this earnestly misled man thinking that time or space have anything to do with these matters, now that she's been freed of them herself.

"But if he's occupied with battling Earth and Water," Paia points out, "how could he come right away?"

"Right." N'Doch swallows his apple. "So we should have time to try to contact Air. Now there's four of us, we might actually get results."

"And we can let the other dragons know we've found Gerrasch."

"And maybe just lend a hand, y'know? Right now, they're fighting this war all by their lonesome!"

"And we must do it quickly!"

Cauldwell looks assaulted. He whirls on the Librarian, who is listening quietly. "You agree with all this? Should we take this insane risk? Is it worth it?"

"Big chance. Yes."

Erde notes how this reply could easily be read two ways.

"Da only chance, mebbe," says Luther.

"Your embargo's a risk, too," adds N'Doch. "Who knows how long his people can hold out?"

"I know! I know every ounce of grain in the Citadel!"

"He's got wings! He can reprovision! You could end up starving yourselves in your precious hole in the ground!"

The rebel leader drops into a chair, his eyes wild. "If! If! This is madness!"

The Librarian gets up slowly, comes over to lay a wide soft palm on Cauldwell's head. It seems to calm him a little. "Come. Each one. A lesson."

He gathers them around his big console, then directs their eyes to the wall screen while he fiddles at his touch pad. Paia knows the blue of that screen so very well. Was it here the message on the monitor originated? It's as good an explanation as any right now.

"Mattias!" the odd creature calls. "You tell!" His voice is rough. He's unused to speaking aloud. And he moves like a man feeling his way through a fog. Paia cannot imagine how she could have thought him dangerous.

The oldest boy, the one who'd guided Paia into the room, lopes forward from the shadowed group of desks where the children have retreated. Paia chides herself to remind them of the God's repopulation program, one vote in his favor, at least. She's sorry there have been so few children around at the Citadel, but for the occasional festival. They're so bizarre and funny, so sure they're being grown-up, as she no doubt was when she was their age. Like this Mattias, who rests one skinny arm atop the console and clears his throat importantly, waiting to be taken seriously.

The Librarian taps at his pad. In the center of the screen, overlaying the blue tracking diagram, appears a map. It's an old map, the hand-drawn sort with antique Latin lettering and little drawings of castles and cathedrals where the towns are. The contours are unrecognizable, except to Baron Köthen, whose name Paia has finally absorbed even if she has not quite come to grips with his point of origin. He has seen such documents in his lifetime, and says as much, while N'Doch translates.

However, the boy Mattias has been asked to "tell," and he intends to do it himself. He puts on his best false-adult Standard English. "This is a map of Ancient Europe, centering on the German duchies of the tenth century." He glances over his shoulder, kidlike again, and catches his audience's eye. "He show us dis alla time, doan know why. He say, we gotta know dese tings."

"Mattias!"

"Yessir."

The map zooms outward. The German duchies are now a tiny glow in a larger landscape traced by fanciful coastlines and dotted with puffy-cheeked wind gods. A good deal of it is blank parchment, labeled *Oceanus* or *Mare Exterius,* or simply, *Terra Incognita.*

"A tenth century European map of the world. The second century mathematician and geographer Ptolemy did a whole lot better."

Paia suffers a brief memory quake, an upsurging of ancient history studies. The House Computer liked this map, too. She's sure it's the very same. Somewhere on it is the legend: *And here there be dragons.*

Before she can look for it, the image cross-fades to a crisp and colorful, mechanically produced map dated 1900.

"Another oldie," says Mattias. "Now, watch carefully. He'll do the overlays in ten-year increments."

Sure enough, the map begins to evolve. National boundaries appear and vanish, often to reappear two or three increments later. Names change. Empires dissolve and re-form in altered configurations.

But one element of the change is gradual and consistent. N'Doch spots it first. "Okay, everybody—check out the coastlines . . ."

The years click by in the label window in the lower right corner: 1990—2000—2010.

"There! That's me! 2013. That's my time. Can you freeze the frame? See? The water's rising already."

2020—2050—2080. The inexorable creep of blue, swallowing up the green and yellow and brown. The Netherlands. Belgium. Northern France. The Mediterranean flows unimpeded into the Persian Gulf. The Amazon and the Congo are inland seas. A whole lot of India, vanished. All gone to water.

2120—2150—2180. Entire island chains have disappeared. The contour of North America is blunted by the loss of the eastern and Gulf coasts. There is no sign of Florida.

Leif has his brow pressed tight against his fists. "I know, I know . . . but the risk! The risk!"

Luther says, "If da One can't makit heah ta help us, it woan mattah if da kids grow up or not."

2200—2210. The clock edges up to 2213 and freezes. There is so little green left, N'Doch has to search for it. 2213. No further.

"That's it?" asks N'Doch. "That's where we are now?"

There's not much more yellow and brown than there is green. The entire world is being sucked back into the oceans.

"2213. I was sure it woulda been further. To get so bad, y'know?" He sits back, looks at Cauldwell. "That make any difference in your thinking?"

"Makes me think how precious our lives are. Not to be thrown away on grand gestures and guesswork!"

N'Doch leans forward again. "But what if that's all we have?"

"Yu tellit yerself, Leif. How da One'll show us da way."
Luther eyes the disconsolate rebel leader in quiet challenge.
"Wheah's ya fait'?"

Paia has thought she would resist them, that she must
resist them, out of duty to Fire, her dragon. A clear and
present duty, even when redefined by what she knows now
about the nature of their connection.

Instead, she cedes the floor to Luco—or Leif Cauldwell,
as she must now learn to call him, her cousin Leif—as he
resists their plan for entirely different reasons. For the
cause of sanity. For "his people," who she used to think
were her people, or the God's. And for the lovely sleeping
child he's picked up to cradle in his arms.

But just as he's bottoming out in an agony of guilt and
indecision, they both get a kind of answer. The whole room
shudders gently, and then again. Paia sways, reaches out to
catch her balance, and finds Baron Köthen's waiting arm.
She sees he is relieved to have something to do. She smiles
at him gratefully as he realigns the sword sheathed across
his back so that the hilt does not point at her eyes. She'd
almost forgotten he was there. She's gratified that he hasn't
forgotten her.

"Quake?" mutters N'Doch. "You get those here?"

"No." The Librarian taps at his console and the tracking
map reappears on the wall screen. The moving colored
blips have converged somewhere over what Paia now realizes to be the practically endless ocean. The room tilts
again, even more faintly.

Leif hugs his daughter closer. "Has he found us
already?"

"Sir, that is Lord Earth," Erde insists primly. "Keeping
him away,"

The Librarian points at the blips. "Long way battle.
Echo just."

"N'Doch leans in. "Wow. The fight? Can you get any
visual?"

The Librarian searches for a working sensor at the indicated location, a buoy, a satellite, anything. The screen splits into four, then sixteen images, a lot of them static, the rest showing open water and empty sky.

"Shud be deah somweah, ri'?" worries Stoksie.

"Look!" Mattias cries. "There!"

He points at a screen. The Librarian quickly enlarges it, but all that's visible is a faint smoke trail.

N'Doch mutters, "Hope we ain't looking at no crash n' burn there."

Erde grabs his arm. "We have to try to reach her! We have to do it now! Oh, what if they're . . ."

Abruptly, the big imagine breaks up in static, plunging the room into near darkness. Only the pinpoint lights on the console offer any sense of direction. The children cry out, a chorus of awed expectation, as if this were planned solely for their entertainment. Sure enough, the screen flashes to life again.

Paia gasps, a half second before Erde does the same. "There it is!"

It's the landscape, *her* landscape, the pristine first version. It fills the entire wall with soothing green and breathless blue and tinkling silver. It's more like a wall blown away to the outside than a picture on a screen. Now she knows what the place is. She's been there in the meld, and it looks as actual now as it did then. The meandering river makes soft music. The breeze in the branches ruffles her hair and tickles her nose with pine scent and flowers.

"Oh, Deep Moor!" the girl exclaims. "Oh, Gerrasch! Where did you find such a painting? It's so . . ."

"A photo, girl," N'Doch says. "But it's . . . wow, it's really . . . real!"

When they take a step forward, Paia moves with them. She recalls what the God said: the painting is a portal. Is it a portal here as well? It certainly looks like they could walk right into the tall grasses stirring gently where the wall meets the floor. There's a path there, narrow and curving, just wide enough for single file. It leads down a soft slope toward the riverbank, and the luscious shade of broad-leafed trees.

Behind her, the children exude a collective sigh. Paia takes another step forward, but a firm hand holds her back.

"Warte! Das ist nur eine Täuschung!"

An illusion, he says, her lover to be, her new protector. His antique language is in her head since the meld. He eases her back against him without force or presumption. How remarkable that, having exchanged at most three words, they already have an understanding, that satisfaction postponed due to circumstances will be all the sweeter. N'Doch has reached to snatch Erde back as well, just as the image starts to break up. Paia fears it's the quake returning, but it's the image evolving, exactly as the painting did. Clouds move up along the verdant profile of the mountains, the sky darkens, the glowing vista dims. The river hardens to solid white. When snow starts to fall, Paia shivers, though she has never seen real snow before. She is thankful for the heat of the baron's body. His breath is steady at her ear. She senses him taking possession, final and absolute, and in her head, she gives herself utterly. He will never desert her or do her harm. She is as sure of him as she is of anything since waking up to find that nothing in her world is what it seemed to be.

But the comfort he offers cannot dispel the very real chill that rises in her gut as the idyllic valley is smothered in ice and snow, then racked by howling gales that whirl the flakes into a blinding whiteness. The winds drive the drifts before them in a scourge of icy needles that scour the forests and fields until the frozen land is exposed and barren. Then comes the melt, and with it, rain, in sheets and torrents, shredding the last leaf, shearing off branches, tearing the bare trees up by the roots. The little river swells to an angry flood choked with mud and boulders. The valley sinks beneath it.

Paia hears weeping, feels the ache in her chest as if it were her own. But it's Erde, huddled like the child she really is, against tall N'Doch's side.

"Is it happening now?" she sobs. "Is it happening now?"

"Now's a relative thing, girl," soothes N'Doch.

"Then what does it mean?"

Poor girl. She's had to grow up so fast. Paia understands how awful that can be. Impulsively, she moves up beside them, away from the security of the baron's aura, compelled by the kinship of the meld to offer comfort as they watch the valley flood, melt, then dry up under the sudden, searing heat of a sun as relentless as the one outside. The trees shrink and wilt, or burst into spontaneous flame. The river thins, then vanishes. The grass shrivels. As the color bleaches away, from green to brown to beige, Erde buries her face in N'Doch's arm, shuddering.

"No, please, Gerrasch, no more! Make it stop! Make it go away!"

"Cannot." The Librarian's hoarse voice startles them. He's there behind them, his stooped shoulders tight with pain and knowledge. "Cannot. Not me. The One speaks."

"She walks in light," someone murmurs in the darkness behind. Paia hears a sound she knows well, the rustle of awed worshipers falling to their knees.

The girl lifts her eyes, stares again at the screen. "Oh . . . ?"

Paia says, "I saw it, too . . . my painting . . ."

"Yes. You, too. Wake-up call."

"But why does she show us Deep Moor?" Erde asks.

The Librarian's stubby arms lift and sink back helplessly. He has only the vision to offer, not its explanation.

"Damn!" N'Doch mutters. "I hate to think of it looking just like it does around here."

"It used to be green and fertile around here, too," Cauldwell reminds him. "Once upon a time."

Baron Köthen speaks up unexpectedly, a low-voiced question, almost a growl.

"Tough one, Dolph," says N'Doch.

From his crouch on the floor, Leif Cauldwell chuckles. It's as bitter a sound as Paia has ever heard from this man she thought she knew as well as any. "No, it's not," he says.

"Whatsit?" asks Luther.

N'Doch translates. "He wants to know . . . who has destroyed the earth, God or Man?"

"Das easy," Stoksie mutters.

"Well, tell him," says Cauldwell. "It's no theological conundrum. It's not like we don't know."

N'Doch shrugs. "We did it, Dolph. A long time after yours. God had nothing to do with it."

The baron sucks his teeth pensively, as if someone's just told him that half his army has deserted. A disaster, yes, but not, in his mind, a cause for despair. "Then we should do what is necessary to fix it. Is this not what you've been suggesting?"

N'Doch grins to hide the sudden grip of fear on his gut. "Put up or shut up, huh? I guess that makes it unanimous, but for . . . well, whadda you say now, preacher man?"

Leif Cauldwell moans softly. "May the One help me. Do it."

Chapter Forty

The elevator ride to the top of the mountain takes longer than Paia's memory of the trip to the heights of the Citadel. Bathed in the flat white light, both alien and familiar, she wonders if her father knew of this facility, perhaps had dealings with its builders, perhaps even rode in this very car. After the collapse of order, the House Comp has told her, contact with the outside became dangerous, even between former friends and allies, especially if you had something they lacked, like power or good water.

Her father is very much on Paia's mind, as if the memory of him might help her face the terrible choice that awaits her on the mountaintop. Her head has cleared of Leif's soporific, though there's a dull pounding between her temples, hangover from the drug, maybe, or simple exhaustion. She's hoped that settling her brain might help settle her decision. She feels a lot more like the self she recognizes, but her head aches and her dilemma remains: *how can I betray him?*

She'd snatched a moment with Leif in the communications room, while the possible backlash from Erde's plan was being hurriedly prepared for. He was in motion, distracted, giving orders. His people flowed around them, moving weaponry and children and supplies. Still, they talked, in snatches, as if both of them needed the exchange in order to move onward. They talked about the past, about her father, about his death. Paia realized that her father had broken his nephew's heart.

"He lost hope. He . . . gave up! He'd never done that! Ever! I was . . . desperate, furious. Maybe I was getting back at him for dying when I joined up with the Beast. By the time I came to my senses, well . . ." Leif grabbed the arm of a man hurrying past. "Marcus! Send someone down the tunnels to check the seals!"

She should be angry with him for drugging her, for kidnapping her, for setting all this in motion. But how could she blame him for wanting to fix things? He still cared so much. Paia studied his handsome face, so familiar, trying to place it in her childhood. "You were one of his aides then? How could I not have known you?"

He grinned at her crookedly. "I was around sometimes. Mostly I was out in the field. Shuttling from meeting to meeting. We were the ones they sent out, the young ones who didn't have families. They'd always invite him, but after a while, they knew the best they were going to get was me. Then it got hard to get from meeting to meeting. I never made it home in between. I was stuck in a bunker in South Africa when the word came that he was . . . that he'd passed away."

Leif stared at the stack of books he'd picked up absently, then shrugged and put it down. He glanced at Constanze in mute appeal as she edged past with two children in tow. She paused, leaned her head against his arm for a fraction, then moved on. Leif cleared his throat. "The com-net was badly shredded by then. The news itself was a month old. It took me seven months to get back here. By then, it was too late . . . *he* had arrived." He looked away, signaling to a woman across the room to hurry. "If I'd been there, Paia! If only I'd been there, I could've kept the Old Man alive, I know I could have! Could've kept him from sinking into despair. Together, we could've fought the Beast off somehow!"

"You don't know that," Paia soothed automatically.

The Beast. The God. The Dragon. But no longer the only dragon. One of four. The black sheep of the family.

As if she had spoken out loud, Leif waved Luther over. "You go on up there with them. I know you want to. But keep an eye on this one." He shook Paia's shoulder, not ungently. "If he shows, she'll run back to him in an instant. She won't have any choice."

And then he'd marshaled his own aides, gathered up the rest of the children, and gone down to the big cavern to be with "his people" for whatever might occur. Unlike her father, Leif Cauldwell had not given up. Except on the God.

She won't have any choice.

Paia wonders. It may be wrong, but she misses him, his edgy magnificence, his energy, even his sharp tongue and cruel wit. Will he come for her this time? A surge of ambivalence and guilt presses Paia back against the cool metal side of the elevator. She has her own darkness to make peace with. If all the tales are true, she has been abetting a monster.

Monster.

She has called him that herself, to his perfect, golden face. But wrapped in her cocoon of safety and privilege, she meant it in an entirely personal way. She never thought to extrapolate his endless capacity for emotional cruelty into a notion of how he might behave out in the world. She just didn't think.

Now she can do nothing but think, as her head pounds and the elevator continues its silent ascent.

Paia lets her aching head loll back against the metal wall. Baron Köthen watches her from across the cab, keeping a cool public distance but fooling no one. He looks concerned, as if he senses she is not entirely recovered. Paia knows their sudden and inexplicable attachment is causing Erde a lot of anguish. Paia is sorry for it, but it's like asking the sun not to shine. Did she not dream him even before he arrived? Nothing to be done, except adopt a certain decorum in the girl's presence. Because Paia is so sure of him, she has no impatience, only deep, stirring tremors of anticipation. She smiles at him wanly, as if she has known him forever, this beautiful stranger from another millennium. A quiet light blooms in his eyes. Paia's glad she's given up asking the world to make sense.

But as the elevator rises, the throbbing in her head worsens. It feels less like pain now than noise, like a great bass yowl that her ears can't hear. Perhaps it's the lift mechanism in need of oil. But Paia cannot make sense of it as machine noise. It sounds somehow more . . . organic. She is about to ask N'Doch if he hears it when the elevator hisses to a stop and the doors yawn open.

For a moment, no one moves. They are at the end of a short, sheltering tunnel that leads out into a blast of heat. Past the opening, just visible in the gray dawn, is a broad, exposed shelf of wind-scoured rock. An old heliport, from the looks of it, which, when it was functional, was intended to blend in to the mountaintop. To the east, the sky is brightening. The full heat of day will rise with the sun and pour down on them like molten lead. Paia is sorry to leave the cool of the elevator cab. She's sorry to be here at all, to be in such danger and causing such pain, and yet there seems a certain rightness about it. As if it really is, all of it, even the miracle of Baron Köthen, part of some Great Inevitability, this Duty Erde speaks of with such conviction. If it is, then Paia can tear herself apart about betraying the God, and still there'll be no stopping Destiny's forward momentum.

She finds this soothing. She wonders if Leif's drug really has flushed itself from her system, or if gentle traces of it linger to soothe her toward this oddly tranquil state of mind. Or is it the sturdy blond man in the black T-shirt, who calms her with a nod? His acceptance of danger as an expected part of life shows in the set of his jaw, and shames her into searching out her own bravery. Her headache eases faintly. Paia returns the baron's nod. She is ready.

N'Doch and the girl move ahead down the tunnel, with the local man they call Luther. Köthen follows. Paia falls in behind. But the Librarian is reluctant to venture out into the open at all. He lingers in the doorway, then takes a few halting steps into the dim gray light of the tunnel and stalls, shifting his ponderous weight from one foot to the other, uttering his slow monosyllables, like the moans of an anxious bear.

Erde looks back. *Oh, Gerrasch, I forgot! You haven't been outside for ever so long, have you!*

Paia waves her onward. *Please. Let me try.*

She recalls her own panic of not yet a week ago, when she left the Temple grounds. She turns back, though she is tingling with her own sort of dread, and hooks her hand around the Librarian's soft elbow.

"Come now, don't be frightened! A big thing like you . . ."

"Noise," says the Librarian.

Paia starts. "Yes! Can you hear it, too?"

"The Intemperate One. He searches but cannot find." Another complete sentence. He touches one pink finger to Paia's temple, and the noise recedes until it is no longer painful. Then he lets her urge him down the tunnel to where Köthen waits, his mouth quirked with approval. Together, they venture out from under the rock overhang and across the shattered tarmac.

The old landing pad is a circular area still oddly smooth and clear of the brittle weeds and scrub that have taken over everywhere else. Paia guides the Librarian to the edge of the circle, where the others have stopped. She feels Köthen's palm, gentle against the small of her back. She wants to lean into it, and into him, but he murmurs something about having a look around. N'Doch rubs one foot along the unscarred surface of the pad.

"You still got copters landing here?"

"Not fera long time," says Luther.

"It's just . . . it looks so clean an' all . . ."

"Yes. It does." The girl Erde lifts her pale face toward the light swelling in the east. Paia detects a glint of tears tracking her cheeks. But her back is straight and purposeful as she turns aside to walk the perimeter of the landing pad with slow and measured step. "A magic circle."

N'Doch laughs, but nervously. He looks around. "You'd think there'd be, like, maintenance equipment around, or something . . ."

To Paia, schooled so long in the God's calendar of ritual, the circle is a heavy omen. She hopes it's a good one. Magic or not, its formal geometry lends credence and dignity to what they are about to attempt. Baron Köthen, she notes, instinctively respects the aura of ceremony that clings to this open ledge. In his alert, restless pacing about, he does not set foot past the circle's curve. And Luther steps out of it as soon as the Four are assembled inside.

N'Doch dusts his hands together. "Well, let's get on with it."

Paia admires his bravado. "You're very no-nonsense."

"That so?" He ruffles Erde's curly dark hair. "This one thinks I'm all fulla nonsense. Doncha, girl?"

Erde has a brave little smile that lights up her face as she flashes it, briefly, gratefully. Paia wishes she had bravado enough of her own to put a sisterly arm around the girl and dry those tears, but it's too hard, knowing she is the almost certain cause of them.

"Yup," says N'Doch, filling the void. "Once you're into something with these dragons, there ain't no getting out of it. I've learned that much. Best to just get it over with, whatever it is."

The Librarian is also walking the perimeter, hands shoved in the pockets of his blue jumpsuit, humming pensively to himself. He finishes up in the center and stands there flat-footed, his nose in the air like an animal, searching the hot dawn breeze.

The mountain shivers, as it had in the Library, the echo of some distant and continuing catastrophe. The swell of light on the eastern horizon reveals a tortured profile of roiling cloud.

"Time," the Librarian intones. He beckons the others to him. His soft pawlike palms cradle a tiny remote keypad.

N'Doch glances behind him. "Luther? Dolph? Be cool, eh?" He repeats it in German, and Paia wonders if he really thinks Baron Köthen could be any more alert than he already is.

"Sorge dich nicht, Dochmann." He's drawn the antique weapon he wears slung across his back. It glimmers icily in the dawn glow. *"Ich gebe dir Rückendeckung."* His eyes meet Paia's, serious and reassuring.

N'Doch grips Erde's thin shoulder with one hand and Paia's with the other. "Go for it."

The Librarian taps out a sequence on the keypad, then shoves it in a pocket. As the mountain shudders again beneath them, he reaches for the two women's hands.

Chapter Forty-one

. . . He can tell the difference right off, like he was in a soundproof room before and now some-one's blasted down the walls. Like maybe if he concen-trated, he could hear every sound being made at this very moment all over the world. He could hear them all simulta-neously and still know each one for what it is. What a symphony they would make!

. . . then he sees, as if standing right in front of him, his grandfather Djawara's knowing face. So wise, so steady, so unperturbed by knowledge. No wonder the girl first thought he was her "mage." He's smiling, but there's a warning in his eyes.

. . . *What do you know, Papa Dja? Papa? Tell me . . . !*

. . . She senses the dragon as an accelerating vastness but cannot truly connect with him. She sees flashes of light, blurs of motion. An ivory claw. He is not, she decides, quite in this world. He is not thinking in her direction, in her time, or even in her scale. The battle still rages, somewhere far away . . .

. . . yet an image reaches her, from . . . where? A well-loved face, every wrinkle familiar, floating in a swirl of mist.

Alla, her old nursemaid and tutor, dead these three months . . .

. . . *Alla? Alla!*

. . . Alla smiles, and is gone . . .

. . . He is after the blue one, the rage howling in his blood. The smaller dragon sets the pace, but she is like sound through water, deflected, diffuse, omnipresent. The other, appearing out of nowhere, slams him off-balance each time he tries to rest. Paia tastes his fury and frustration like bile in her own throat. They dance and feint. They will not confront him. He trumpets that his strength is greater. Like two crows harrying an eagle, their only hope is to exhaust him. They lead him ever farther from the inhabited lands, to keep their battle from damaging the humans. He does not care about the humans. Soon he begins to suspect some other strategy, and decides he must have one of his own . . .

. . . but this is odd. As she watches, or seems in her mind to watch, the vision shrinks until it is a moving image framed by darkness, as on a screen. Words scroll rapidly across the bottom. She has missed the start of them . . .

. . . *and who will be the guide's guide in this ruined world, if not me?* . . .

. . . *House? Is that you? House?* . . .

. . . LISTEN! LISTEN! LISTEN! . . .

Yes! Something new in the meld. Not a voice, no, not at all, but each of them has heard it before, in what they thought were their dreams. Or in waking moments of drifting inattention, daydreams, a stirring of the subconscious. Or so they thought.

That articulate breath of wind, that sighing gust so rich

with meaning. That motion of atmosphere that is more formed than wind, yet less than a voice, a word. That presence at the corner of an eye, just out of view.

N'Doch N'Djai hears it as the universal harmony.

Erde von Alte sees it as the colors of the spectrum.

Paia Alexii Cauldwell feels it as the entire range of emotion, human and beyond.

The Librarian absorbs it, collates it, interprets it. He offers what he can of the nature of the new presence: huge, discorporate, a being of vast intellect as yet unfocused, of shape as yet undetermined. More potential than actual. But the potential takes their breath away.

Ah! The magnificence! A power beyond imagining!

AIR! AIR! AIR!

Toobigtooloudtoovasttoomuch! The specter of overload. The Four draw back as if burned. In that instant, a debriefing:

Clever dude, Fire. He trapped her, like a genie in a bottle, before she'd come into her powers.

But where? Where?

Nowhere.

So we gotta go nowhere to find her?

No place that we know of, he means.

No **where.**

Can she be a bit more specific?

Listen! Listen! Listen!

She is there. Air. His dragon. He is made whole for the briefest of instants. A taste of totality. His centuries of waiting are . . . and then she is gone.

Ah, the ache! Ah, the loss! And yet, the gain . . .

SEE: nothing.

HEAR: nothing.

SMELL: nothing.

FEEL: the outward expansion of consciousness toward infinity.

What he would say for her if he could but find the words,

the all-too-human words? He wouldn't say, he would show.
Image, sound, scent, touch, taste: a tidal surge of sensation
and dream and memory, washing over, around. She has
seen all. She has seen what you see. She remembers it for
you. A green valley bathed in the golden mist of a summer
evening, resonant with bee hum. The crisp sparkle of snow
on a sunlit windowsill at Tor Alte. A symphony of birds
and salt water cascading along an African shore. The sweet
cacophony of Blind Rachel plunging cool and crystalline
from a pine-scented height.

Treasure it! Hold it in the now! Do not let it pass into
memory! Is it not all that is right and good? Is it not the
truest miracle? Can it be that, instead, we choose nothing-
ness and death?

Ah, the ache! The loss! There is no gain . . .

Paia feels the message as remembered grief, her mother's
death, her father's decline and fall. Yet she understands
how the mutable painting has prepared her to receive this
message in a larger sense. Inside her now, no lazy, clichéd
notion, no old denial like she heard so often as a child:
hey, it wasn't me who wrecked the planet!

Instead, a profound, abiding rage that her birthright has
been taken from her, and from all the other dwellers on
the Earth. Only through another's memories will she hear
the salt roar of the African surf, or taste the pure snowmelt
of a German mountain stream. All she can know firsthand
is heat and barren rock and devastation.

What can be done? What must I do?

The blue screen swims again behind her eyelids.

White letters read: *DENY HIM.*

No word, no voice. A sudden avalanche of emotion. A
shock wave of rage and negation shakes the Four until their
bones rattle. They see shredded wings, a flash of scales and
smoke and blood. The contact is shattered. They are flung
apart, flying, gasping, falling, slammed down hard on the

weathered tarmac, overwhelmed, tumbled, scattered like rag dolls around the perimeter of the circle.

Without the multiple voices of the meld to fill her mind and her attention, Paia knows the exact moment when he arrives.

Chapter Forty-two

Suspended in air, he sees the ground coming up hard. He tucks and rolls, gets the wind knocked out of him but keeps his head. He comes up gasping and coughing but conscious.

And in a haze of fury. Thrashing to regain his stance. Fists nose level and clenched. Ready to strike out with nails and fangs.

His lips pulls back so tight it hurts. His jaw attempts a snarl too big for his human mouth. His hands spasm with the effort of unsheathing claws he doesn't have.

N'Doch!

Her voice is a hand snatching him back from the edge of a cliff. N'Doch reels and steadies. The haze clears. Wait. Not his. This is some other's senseless rage that swept over him like a wave and sucked him into its undertow before he knew what was what. He feels nauseous and violated. Raped.

"N'Doch! Help Luther!"

Audible words this time, even more centering. He can see again. A flash of motion draws his eye: the girl racing toward Köthen up in the surrounding rocks where he stands at the ready, staring up at the sky.

Another voice, gasping. "Dockman! Ovah heah! Now, man!"

A shadow passes over. N'Doch doesn't need to ask. He hears the ear-splitting screech. He searches around wildly.

Luther is half the circle's arc away, tugging on the crumpled form of the Librarian and not getting anywhere.

"Into the circle, my lord! Quickly!" The girl's yelling at Köthen, but N'Doch gets the idea. He staggers toward Luther.

"Wrong way! Luther! Wrong way!" The Tinker is trying to drag the Librarian into the elevator tunnel. A trap, a disaster in the making. "Luther! Into the circle!" It seems like forever until he reaches them. He grabs one of the Librarian's stocky legs and hauls for all he's worth. The shadow slides past them again, lower this time. N'Doch doesn't look up. He knows what he'll see. Half the screeching is in his own dragon-racked brain. He fights Luther briefly for control over the body, but the Librarian is coming to now, starting up his own struggle to regain the protection of the circle. Man, but the guy is slow!

On its third pass, the circling shadow darkens the entire mountaintop. The scream is like a detonation. It rakes N'Doch's nerve endings, leaving him trembling and weak. A line of flame erupts behind them, targeting them as directly as a lit fuse. Luther gives up his disagreement at last and together they hoist the Librarian by his armpits and drag him stumbling over the perimeter.

The bright heat splashes upward and sideways behind them as if it has hit a solid wall. N'Doch hears the girl's alarm call winging out across the dragon com-net. There's no reply. She's grabbed Köthen by his sword arm and won't let go. He's running with her toward the circle, trying to free up his weapon and shield her with his body at the same time. A sear of heat explodes in front of them. The girl squeals and ducks away blindly. Köthen snatches her up and plunges straight through the flames and across the perimeter. N'Doch races to meet them, tearing off his T-shirt. Köthen's hair is smoldering. He drops the girl at N'Doch's feet. Her long linen shirt has caught. Little fiery tongues rise up her back. N'Doch leaves Köthen to deal with his own conflagration and blankets the girl with his shirt, rolling her around on the tarmac until he's sure he's put her out.

"Where are they?" she gasps, when he lets her up. "What has he done to them?"

"Easy, girl." It's all he can think of to say as the

screeching overhead rises deafeningly, then morphs into inhuman laughter inside their heads.

Her back is tender. She knows she's been burned but
not badly enough to worry. The loose light layers of her
linens took most of the damage. The dragon will soothe it
as soon as he returns. When he returns . . .

She has pushed her panic aside for the immediate emergency. Now dread assails her anew. She grabs N'Doch's
arm. "Where are they? Isn't the barrier down? Why don't
they answer? Why don't they come!"

"Don't know, but it looks like we're gonna have to deal
with this one on our own . . ."

Erde follows his horrified gaze, past the priestess woman
who stands as still as marble in the middle of the circle, to
the vast shining beast wheeling at eye level just past the
outer ledges of the mountainside.

". . . 'cause here he comes."

The golden dragon rises, a swift muscular ascent. The
first red light of the morning sun glints off his gilt scales.
Reflected shards as hot as flame sear Erde's cheeks and
eyes. He hovers a moment, high overhead. His great wings
cock back for his stoop. He screams again, and then he is
plunging toward them, in a dead fall like a rock kicked off
a precipice, dropping until Erde is sure he means to dash
himself against the mountaintop just to be able to kill them
all in the process.

But moments before the inevitable collision, the dragon
begins to glow—red, orange, yellow, white, like molten iron
in the forge. At the instant of impact, there is no sound,
no concussion. The dragon is a white-hot halo too bright
to look at. Then the brightness winks out and out of this
crucible is born . . . a man.

Even as she stares in wonder, Erde's first thought is for
Hal, avid collector of dragon lore. She's sure Lord Fire's
spectacular translation would astound even that good
knight's fertile and learned imagination. For, unlike Lady
Water's exact replications from N'Doch's memory, very lit-

tle is truly human about Fire's man-form. He is huge, ten or twelve feet tall, and shining gold all over, from the writhing mass of his long hair to the sharp-clawed toes of his unshod feet. Here, then, is the fierce angel of the sword, the Archangel Michael, from the chapel at Tor Alte: inhumanly beautiful, ruthless, and cold. But this face has the yellow, slitted eyes of a reptile and a surprisingly sensuous mouth. And the Beast is boldly naked, but for a billowing cloth-of-gold cloak. It swirls around him as if alive and makes him seem twice his already monstrous size, but conceals no part of his scaled and glittering anatomy. Erde expects to see horns and a tail, for surely he is the Devil incarnate. But he has left those behind in his transformation. She would look away if she dared, *should* look away in all maiden modesty, but in truth, she can't take her eyes off him. Nor can anyone else. He is riveting, magnificent, terrifying. It's what Leif Cauldwell meant about the Beast compelling men to follow him. Foolish men, who mistake beauty for truth, and believe all his lies and promises.

But where are they? Where are the others?

Fire towers above them, turning his perfect profile to catch the sunrise just so. He fixes his gaze like a snake on his prey, savoring their awe, then slowly advances in long graceful strides. The humans gather in a protective arc around the priestess. Köthen has his sword ready, but even he seems to realize how little use it will be against such a monster. The Librarian has his mysterious little device in hand again and is muttering over it like an alchemist.

"Will it hold him?" N'Doch asks.

The Librarian looks unsure, or maybe he still suffers from the shock of being slammed about. He mutters and fiddles some more. Silently, Erde prays.

But Lord Fire halts at the edge of the circle. He doesn't even try to enter it, just draws himself up with a gloating and superior smile. His slitted stare settles on Paia as if she is standing there alone. Erde sees she is trembling, but with rage and indignation as well as fear. Baron Köthen plants himself firmly behind her. Erde sees them as a single image, a pair, a joining, and grapples suddenly with a fuller notion of why Destiny bade her bring him here. A small moan escapes her. Quickly, she stifles it. If it is necessary, she must accept it.

"Our enemies are vanquished, my priestess." The golden giant's voice insinuates a razor's edge behind its languid, silken tones.

"No!" Erde reaches for the others in panic. *Is it true? Has he caught them?*

"Burned right out of the sky! My sister went up like a tinderbox!"

"Liar!" N'Doch bellows.

"New friends, my priestess? Tell me, rather, you are their prisoner."

Paia's mouth quivers, but nothing comes out. She puts her hand to her throat as if amazed to find it there at all.

Erde thrusts herself forward, a step past the priestess, then two. Baron Köthen reaches out to hold her back. She shakes him off and advances. He does not come after her. He has his own Duty. She knows that now. She walks as close to the invisible wall as she dares and stares up at the golden giant.

"My lord Fire!"

Fire glances briefly downward, a mere deigning to take notice. "Children! They send children against me!"

"My lord Fire, what have you done to them? How dare you threaten your siblings or seek to divert them from their holy Duty! A Duty that you share, my lord!"

"Oh, please!" He levels a scimitar nail at Erde's nose. "How dare you meddle in matters you don't understand? Lecture me, will you? Your ignorance and folly are equaled only by the gracelessness of your rhetoric!"

He looks to Paia again. His glowing eyes mock. "Come, come, my priestess. Who are all these riffraff? Surely such company cannot interest you, when you could have mine instead!" He turns to pace along the outside of the circle, smooth and agile as a stalking cat, and Paia turns with him. His living cloak swirls around him, concealing, then revealing him anew, all of him. He is not shrieking now. His voice is tuned to its most intimate pitch, yet each of them hears its inviting, sensuous tones as if he is standing next to them. "Surely you have not grown tired of your sacred duties to me? Remember how I said I was thinking on ways to bring us closer?"

He is using the power of his summons to compel her. Paia knows this. Even so, she is drawn by its inexorable gravity, like the pull of tides. She knows also what he is promising this time. He has never appeared to her naked before, and his beauty and magnetism stir her more than ever.

She won't have any choice.

But matters are different now. Paia has lost a different kind of innocence. What the God has done is unforgivable. She must prove that she does have a choice.

She wrings the paralysis from her throat, the reflex submission and the weakling excusing of his arrogance and cruelty. She steps forward as Erde has. "I am no prisoner, my lord. These are my friends, my . . . cousins in Duty."

"Duty!" With Fire's bark of contempt, a small gout of flame spatters heat against the Librarian's invisible barrier.

Paia shudders. He's never been able to manifest anything real while in man-form. Perhaps the flames are an illusion, but Paia feels a difference in him. His customary languor is now but the thinnest of veneers.

The God laughs. He knows he's frightened her. He grins nastily as he stalks slowly around the perimeter. "Your duty is to me! Dare they tell you otherwise, these new friends? You should choose your friends more wisely, my priestess . . ." He waves a hand lazily. ". . . as it seems I should better choose my lieutenants. Where is the traitorous priest, by the way? I thought sure to find him among you."

"If you don't know, so much the better for him."

"A brave speech from a silly woman!" Fire arcs his head back so that his hair stands up in writing coils. "No matter. He'll not stay hidden from me for long, my dear disloyal son, my precious Luco to whom I trusted the secrets of my Temple. Ah, he will rue the day, my gallant soldier who's lost the stomach for battle, for what must be done. For what WILL be done! There are none left to stand against me now!" He lets his brass voice ring across the open ledge, echo in the boulder piles, then calms his rant to dulcet tones of seduction. "But you and I, beloved, when I have found the priest and riven him limb from limb, we will forget all this foolishness. Come, take me in my forgiving mood, before I lose the impulse."

Paia sees Erde glance back at her wide-eyed, both incredulous and comprehending. Behind her, the Librarian growls, deep in his throat.

The God has arrived full circle, due south in the landing pad's compass rose. He settles himself there and slowly extends one arm, palm out. Tiny pinpoint explosions dance where his curved and glided nail intersects the barrier. His viper hair gentles into curling locks of burnished gold, his claws to well-formed fingers. His eyes plead and promise. "Come home to me, beloved."

He can stir her mind and her body from a distance. He is practiced at seduction without contact. He can slip behind Paia's eyes with the memory of his dragon tongue coiling upward around her thigh.

Paia's breath quickens. The God's call thrills in her mind and commands the beat of her heart. She sees the walls of the Citadel loom up around her, the musky darkness of the God's sanctuary. She takes a step forward, lost in her own rising heat, going willingly to meet him, to take him into her at last.

Sudden motion at her side, and then . . . a man in front of her, blocking the way. Paia tries to step around him. He moves to meet her. She ducks the other way. He is quicker than she could ever be. He closes on her gently. With a cry, Paia shoves at him, arms fully extended, but it's like shoving at a wall. There are others, in a circle around them. The God is calling. She dodges again. She is frantic with need. The man blocks her, then backs off. Abruptly, silently, a sword appears in his hand. The long blade flashes dully as he levels it at her, his other arm outstretched for balance. He steps lightly. He is being very careful. The sword's tip hovers at her throat. If she feints left or right, the blade's keen edge prevents her. Confused, distracted, the God's call dimmed by this unexpected threat, Paia freezes.

The man lifts the sword until the flat of it rests beneath her chin. It's the uncanny chill of the steel that gets her attention, so sharp it almost burns. That, and the hard, clear look on him that says he will absolutely kill her now rather than give her up to the Beast. He could do it, a quick, short stroke, before anyone—even the God—could stop him.

Paia believes this just long enough for the thought to sober her up. The man presses the sword upward, forcing her glazed and troubled eyes to meet his. She sees there the same male promises that the God has offered, but something else, more shared and lasting.

"*Liebste,*" he says gravely. "*Benimm dich.*"

His voice reminds her who he is. The Citadel walls thin and vanish like morning fog. Fire roars his outrage and claws at the barrier. Sparks shoot high and scatter.

Baron Köthen lowers his blade, but his gaze holds Paia as firmly as the God's ever could. He sheathes the sword, then steps quickly forward to cradle her chin between his hands. She expects he will be rough with her, but instead, he kisses her with an ardent sweetness that brings tears to her eyes, of relief, of gratitude, of surrender. She lets him wrap her in his arms, hoping the feel of him against her can drown out the sound of the God screaming.

N'Doch thinks he finally understands what Erde's been going on about when she talks about Destiny. He grabs her as she turns away from the circle, from the spectacle of her dream-lord so impassioned, and lets her press her face into his side.

"Easy, girl," he murmurs.

"It must be," she intones hoarsely. "It must be!"

"Listen!" The Librarian's nose is testing the air. N'Doch doubts he could hear anything over Fire's furious ranting.

Erde jerks away from him, her anguish tossed aside. She points in two directions simultaneously. "Look! Oh, look!"

N'Doch's glad whoop echoes across the circle.

"It's a trick. An illusion!" bellows the golden giant.

"No, my lord Fire! It is not! Your vanquished enemies have returned!"

N'Doch appreciates bravado as much as the next man, so he feels himself seized by a shameless fit of admiration for Fire's sleight of hand, thrown up like dust in desperation, in hopes of luring Paia back to him before the others returned. N'Doch has seen such performances before, even been guilty of a few of them himself. He's interested to learn that this dragon is not all screech and brawn. There's a lot of bluff in him, too.

He tries to see surprise in Fire's lizard eyes as the vast, stony bulk of Earth appears on the rock ledge at the eastern compass point. There is none, and Fire knows to look exactly to the west to find the changeable spot of wings and glare that is the blue dragon perched on an overhanging ledge. What N'Doch would swear that he sees instead in the giant's glance is a shadow of exhaustion and despair.

What is he hiding? Something big. N'Doch is sure of it.

The returned dragons do not fly at Fire in immediate attack. They salute the Librarian with solemn respect, and receive and return the fervent silent welcomes of their guides. But they ward off all questions after asserting that both are well and whole. They hunker down on the periphery of the ledge to regard their black-sheep brother impassively. A peculiar stillness falls over the landing pad. Fire stares back at them with the appearance of arrogant nonchalance, but N'Doch reads the effort he's putting into it. It comes to him that most of the dragons' warring will not be physical.

The lovers relax their desperate hold. The humans drift together into their loose unconscious circle to wonder, and wait. The Librarian gazes at Earth and Water with longing.

Finally Water stirs, flaring a rainbow of gossamer. N'Doch drinks in her difference. He's gonna have to get to know her all over again.

We know where she is now, brother.

Where?

WHERE?

HUSH!

Fire seems buoyed by Water's challenge. He has made her speak first. "The least of victories, honored opponent! It's a clever device, you must admit. Without her help, you lack the very power required to release her. Without her, you cannot defeat me."

The how is only a matter of time. And we wish not your defeat, but your strength on our side. Will you continue this wrongheaded resistance?

Fire holds his man-form as if relishing the distinction it affords him, and the excuse to indulge in the spoken word.

"A matter of time? Time is what I am trying to win for us, sister. Soon enough, none of your meddling will matter." He lowers his gaze to the priestess sheltering in the curve of Köthen's arms. "You claim I've forsaken my 'holy duty'? Look on this mawkish spectacle before you, and consider the perfidy of these weak-willed creatures. Consider them in all your wisdom, then tell me for what reason they deserve our service . . . or our sacrifice!"

He levels his gleaming nail as if it could spout fire and annihilate the lovers on the spot. "This woman was sworn to me through the thousand generations of her blood."

AND YOU ABUSED THAT PRIVILEGE! A PLEDGE MUST WORK BOTH WAYS.

"I acted as I saw fit and necessary, given the extremes of the times! But see how she holds to that ancient vow! She'll not even do me the honor of denying me to my face!"

N'Doch thinks, *Oh, be careful what you wish for.*

Erde scolds him for giving the giant the slightest share of his sympathy.

And sure enough, Paia stares solemnly into Köthen's eyes, then gently disengages herself from his embrace. She turns and takes a few unsteady steps toward her accuser. "My lord Fire, I have been loyal to you past all reason. Do not blame me now if reason reasserts itself."

The gilded nail curls into a claw aimed at Köthen's neck. "You call that a reason?"

"Reason of the soul, my lord."

"The soul?" His voice is soft, incredulous. "Oh, no, beloved. So wrong. So very wrong. The body perhaps, but not the soul. Your soul belongs to me. To me! If you have been restless in my care, then I must, I *will,* work harder to satisfy. And look how much I will sacrifice to content you: you may keep your concubine. Come with me now and you're welcome to him, as the Suitor we've been searching for, for so long as he amuses you. A pretty thing, I admit, but just a man, after all. The interest will pall." He leans forward, and Paia's body shifts in his direction like a reed in water. N'Doch is amazed to see actual hope soften the giant's glare. His hand is out again. He is almost singing to her. "Come, my lovely priestess! Come, my most beautiful beloved! They cannot stop you. It's ah . . . against the rules."

Paia sways, toward Fire, away from him. N'Doch is surprised when Köthen backs up a step to give her room. He knows something N'Doch isn't sure of yet, until Paia reaches out within the circle.

Is my cousin right about this? Can the bond between this dragon and myself compel him to change his ways?

WE HOPE IT WILL BE SO.

You are our only hope of winning him to our cause.

IT WILL NOT BE EASY.

No.

Will you try it?

It seems I must.

Way to go!

When Paia moves forward this time, her step is firmer. "How poorly you perceive the truth, my lord, when it's not in your own interests." She advances slowly, in almost ceremonial step. "You speak of honor. Tell me, where is yours? Have you forgotten it? Mislaid it? Or simply put it aside? When you find it again, I will keep that pledge laid on me by my ancestors. Until then, my lord Fire . . ." She stops a mere pace from the barrier. The golden giant looms over her as she draws herself into her formal Temple stance: head up, arms out, palms at right angles. "I do deny thee."

"NO! YOU WILL NOT DENY ME!"

Fire lashes out, smashing his clawed fist against the barrier. Sparks explode through it, catching in Paia's clothes and hair, driving her backward. The barrier itself seems to catch flame. N'Doch has seconds to wonder if the fire is real, and how could a force field or whatever it is be burning, before he feels the heat and hears the roar above his head.

"YOU WILL NOT DENY ME!"

"Kill it! Kill it!" N'Doch shouts frantically to the Librarian, who's already tapping at his remote. He grabs Erde, drags her behind him. They're all about to be suffocated and broiled alive.

Then the barrier is down, a hissing release of air, and suddenly water is falling around them, sheets of it, cool and quenching, then a rising curtain of steam and a bronzy mountain of scales and claws is between them and the raging giant. N'Doch swears Earth gets bigger every time he sees him. He shoves Luther and the Librarian into the dragon's protective shadow. Water, newly winged, hovers above. Erde follows, calling to Köthen and Paia to hurry.

For Paia has stopped, long paces away, to gaze back through the smoke and mist at her errant dragon.

"YOU WILL NOT DENY ME!" shrieks Fire. He is a whirl of flame and smoke and motion. He spits magma with every word, but he keeps his distance. "Listen well, my reckless kin! You can hold me at bay, but you cannot defeat me! Without the Fourth, you are nothing! NOTHING!"

He stalks them around the perimeter, as if the barrier is still in place. Water hovers, hissing showers of mist at him in warning. He ignores her. He pulls up opposite N'Doch.

"You boy. You have . . . a favorite grandparent. And a mother, as I recall." He points at Erde. "And this presumptuous child has a circle of women she cherishes. Do you not, brat?" He laughs at Erde's stricken look. "Did you truly believe you are strangers to me? Even the puny man-thing there has a friend he would die for. We all can play at the hostage game!"

Then Fire swivels his heated glare toward the dark and huddled figure of the Librarian. "And you! So quiet there. Still hoping to hide from me? You've hidden very well, all these years. Too well. But for you, my plan would have gone undetected. This requires proper recompense . . . one day soon."

He gestures, an abrupt arc that scatters a bright rain of embers hard into the staring human faces. Earth roars, a sound like continents shifting, and rises hugely to his feet.

Suddenly dwarfed, Fire holds his ground. "Will I continue my resistance? To the end of Time! And what do I promise you? War, with no quarter! War here, and war wherever your puny humans call home! I will harry and destroy, up and down the centuries, until not a soul known and loved by any of you is left alive!"

With a blinding concussion of light and air. Fire leaps and is sky-borne, a dragon again. His gilt-and-enamel wings beat the new-made mud into a cloud of grit and dust.

AND WHEN I WIN, MARK MY WORDS, YOU ALL WILL THANK ME FOR IT! IF THE WORLD MUST END, IT WILL END ON MY TERMS!

He circles once, dark and vast against the rising sun, and is gone.